≽YOU'VE GOT MAIL≼
The PERILS
of
PIGEON
POST

↣YOU'VE GOT MAIL↢
The PERILS
of
PIGN
POST

③

WRITTEN BY
Blackegg

COVER ILLUSTRATION BY
Leila

INTERIOR ILLUSTRATIONS BY
Ninemoon

TRANSLATED BY
alexsh, Tywon Wynne

Seven Seas

Seven Seas Entertainment

You've Got Mail: The Perils of Pigeon Post - Fei Ge Jiao You Xu Jin Shen (Novel) Vol. 3

Published originally under the title of 《飛鴿交友須謹慎》
Author© 黑蛋白 (Blackegg)
Illustrations granted under license granted by I Yao Co. Ltd.
Cover Illustrations by Leila
Interior illustrations by Ninemoon
English edition rights under license granted by 愛呦文創有限公司 (I Yao Co. Ltd.)
English edition copyright © 2025 Seven Seas Entertainment, Inc.
Arranged through JS Agency Co., Ltd.
All rights reserved

Seven Seas press and purchase enquiries can be sent
to Marketing Manager Lauren Hill at press@gomanga.com.
Information regarding the distribution and purchase of digital editions is available
from Digital Manager Kristine Johnson at digital@gomanga.com.

Follow Seven Seas Entertainment online at
sevenseasentertainment.com.

TRANSLATION: alexsh, Tywon Wynne
ADAPTATION: Abigail Clark
COVER DESIGN: G. A. Slight
INTERIOR DESIGN: Clay Gardner
INTERIOR LAYOUT: Karis Page
COPY EDITOR: Ami Leh
PROOFREADER: Imogen Vale, Nino Cipri
EDITOR: Hardleigh Hewmann
PREPRESS TECHNICIAN: Salvador Chan Jr., April Malig, Jules Valera
MANAGING EDITOR: Alyssa Scavetta
EDITOR-IN-CHIEF: Julie Davis
PUBLISHER: Lianne Sentar
VICE PRESIDENT: Adam Arnold
PRESIDENT: Jason DeAngelis

ISBN: 979-8-89160-590-9
Printed in Canada
First Printing: March 2025
10 9 8 7 6 5 4 3 2 1

CONTENTS

CHAPTER 1

THE UNSETTLING FEELINGS AS ONE DRAWS CLOSER TO HOME

"If the general also holds true and deep affection for you, would you be willing to continue your relationship with him?"

Wu Xingzi had not expected this question. His mouth fell open, but he was unable to make a sound. Dumbfounded, he stared at Rancui, then closed his mouth and licked his dry lips. Smiling wryly, he said, "Rancui-gongzi, that relationship is already over."

"Life is unpredictable. There's always the possibility of rekindling an old flame."

"No matter how important Haiwang is, he still belongs to someone else." Wu Xingzi bowed his head and chuckled, but to Rancui, it felt like he was silently weeping.

"What if he doesn't belong to anyone? Would you want him then?"

A shudder ran through Wu Xingzi's thin body. His breathing turned faint, and he did not respond for a long time.

Rancui sighed deeply in his mind. What did he still not understand?

CHAOS UNFOLDED in the general's estate, where Guan Shanjin had vomited three liters of blood.

Meanwhile, Wu Xingzi was finally feeling at ease.

He'd been on his way to the capital for some time already, and now he felt cheerful enough to open the curtains of the carriage and look around.

Rancui had originally said they would be leaving together, but at the last second, he said he wouldn't be able to leave until two days after Wu Xingzi did. It wouldn't be difficult for him to catch up with Wu Xingzi and the girls on horseback, so they'd arranged to meet in a little town called Lishui in four days' time.

Wu Xingzi had taken this very path quite a few times before, and the scenery was mostly the same. However—perhaps because his mood was different—everything seemed so much brighter than before. The rays of the sun sparkled like gold, scattering light across the grass, the gravel, the trees, and the brook.

Osmanthus leaned out the window, pointing at the brilliant colors dancing in the wind. "Wow, jiejie, look at the field of flowers over there! What flowers are those?"

"Hmm..." Mint knew about as much as Osmanthus did, so she didn't recognize the flowers either. After all, they rarely saw such delicate and pretty things in Horse-Face City.

"Those look like irises," Wu Xingzi answered, turning to look at them.

Hearing that, the two girls looked at Wu Xingzi with worshipful eyes. They listened to him gently explain, "*Shennong's Herbal Classic* says the iris is bitter in taste and mild in effect. It mainly treats gu poisoning, demonic incursion, and various toxins. It breaks embolisms and conglomerations, removes water, and precipitates the Three Worms.[1] Irises naturally grow in mountains and valleys. In a place like this with no mountains or valleys, someone must have planted them intentionally."

---

1 In Daoism, the Three Worms (三虫) are entities that live inside the body and cause diseases.

"Master, you know everything!" Mint's eyes shone so brightly, she seemed ready to venerate Wu Xingzi as a god.

"It's only something I remembered reading when I was younger," Wu Xingzi said with a light smile. Inside his bag were a few books that his father had left behind, and one of them was *Shennong's Herbal Classic*. There was only one elderly physician back in their small town, so his father had always dealt with the family's minor pains and ailments himself.

Hei-er drove the carriage steadily. Inside, Wu Xingzi and the two girls only felt a slight swaying, and it was not uncomfortable at all. It was now March, and the spring weather was perfect. Warm weather arrived earlier in the south, and the gentle breeze carried with it the fresh scent of leaves and foliage, pleasantly warming their skin. Drowsiness soon descended upon them; Wu Xingzi closed his eyes and fell asleep.

Osmanthus carefully covered him with a cloak. She exchanged a look with her sister, and the joy on her fair little face swiftly faded. The girls were somewhat apprehensive. Although they had not run into any trouble when leaving—their departure was unbelievably successful, in fact—when they thought about what would happen when the general finally found them, chills ran down their spines. The two of them were unable to keep themselves from shuddering.

So as not to wake Wu Xingzi up, Mint and Osmanthus climbed out of the carriage and sat next to Hei-er. They asked in hushed voices, "Commander Hei, how long can we hide from the general?"

Hei-er turned to calm the two girls down. "There's no need to worry. When it's time for the general to find us, he'll find us." He was unsure himself—Rancui and Man Yue were the ones who'd orchestrated the entire thing. He was merely a puppet who listened to instructions and followed orders. His main duty was to protect Wu Xingzi from danger.

The girls' little faces twisted even further at his answer, as if they had just swallowed the bitterest medicine.

"I hope the general won't be too angry with Master," was all Mint could say.

They'd witnessed the blood-soaked general cut through his enemies. He was still very handsome, like a beautiful jade statue. However, he had the aura of a demon climbing out of hell. Just one glance made them tremble with fear, afraid he would devour their very souls.

"Don't be afraid," Hei-er said. No matter what happened, there would still be Man Yue to protect them.

Four days later, Wu Xingzi and his party met Rancui in the town they had agreed upon. Under Rancui's advice, they stopped temporarily to browse the bird and flower market. This market was held in Lishui for ten bustling days once every three years, and it featured strange and rare flowers and exotic species of birds. It was possibly the most famous event on the southern border. No wonder Rancui had chosen this specific town—he probably wanted to help cheer Wu Xingzi up.

When Wu Xingzi made the decision to leave, he pushed everything about Horse-Face City to the back of his mind. He would miss some aspects of it, but he did not feel the slightest bit of regret. Even though the memory of Guan Shanjin was vividly present in his heart, he never thought about what might have happened if he stayed.

Sometimes when Wu Xingzi slept at night, he would have the mistaken impression that he was in a warm and familiar embrace, and startle awake from his dream, unconsciously reaching out next to him.

Shivering from the cold sheets, he would toss and turn for the entire night before he managed to finally doze off again.

He figured this would pass sooner or later. After all, he had left Horse-Face City days ago, and Guan Shanjin must have already brought Mr. Lu along with him to the capital, right? Was there a possibility that they would bump into each other along the way? Wu Xingzi felt a little worried.

Rancui was observant, and adept at handling people with warmth and grace. He noticed Wu Xingzi's apprehension and did not hurry them along on their journey. Although Lishui was a small place, it had many famous scenic spots to explore; they stayed until the market event was over and all the tourists had left before Wu Xingzi eventually realized that he had stayed in Lishui for over a week. After spending all that time strolling through the town and seeing all its sights, his longing for Guan Shanjin decreased considerably.

When they resumed their journey, it was nearly the end of March.

The timing was now a little awkward, so they quickly packed up all their belongings, continuing on their way to the capital. They would likely arrive in about two or three months. Rancui gave Wu Xingzi a few editions of *The Pengornisseur* to peruse and encouraged him to make more friends.

Wu Xingzi was more than happy to do so. The capital's edition of *The Pengornisseur* was truly impressive! All the great men listed within had outstanding family backgrounds, educations, and careers!

Keenly aware of Wu Xingzi's preferences, Rancui hid his smile behind his hand. "Don't worry, Mr. Wu. I've gone through this edition of *The Pengornisseur* myself—every man is exceptional and the pengornises are mighty. Send all the letters you want. No matter where we are, I'll be able to forward the replies to further your reputation as the pengornis curator."

Whatever a "pengornis curator" was aside, Rancui seeing right through him like this was mortifying. Wu Xingzi's blush instantly spread all the way to his neck. For the next few days, he dared not read *The Pengornisseur* carefully at all, afraid that if he looked at all the portraits of handsome men, all he'd be able to think of were their mighty pengornises.

But the penises were not that troubling in the grand scheme of things; it was the imminent arrival of Qingming that worried him.

Wu Xingzi took paying respects to his ancestors very seriously. After all, he was the sole remaining descendant of both his paternal and maternal lines. When it came to occasions like Qingming, he could not miss a single one; if he didn't pay his respects, his ancestors would surely give him a resounding earful in his dreams.

Qingcheng County was on the way to the capital, so it wouldn't be burdensome to stop by and sweep the family graves. It was just that... Withering, Wu Xingzi huddled into a corner of the carriage.

He still remembered how Guan Shanjin had promised to accompany him back to Qingcheng County for Qingming. Before the day could arrive, Wu Xingzi had fled. Still, Wu Xingzi's roots remained in Qingcheng County, and he believed that Guan Shanjin would not deliberately seek him out. Now that Guan Shanjin had finally captured his evasive first love, why would he still need its shadow?

For some reason, though, Wu Xingzi felt a little guilty. The night before he left, Guan Shanjin had made such lofty promises to him. Even if those promises were not sincere, would Guan Shanjin be angry with Wu Xingzi for embarrassing him like this? The general might even be waiting in Qingcheng County for him to return and pay his respects to his ancestors... And he certainly wouldn't wait in vain, because Wu Xingzi would never forget about his ancestors, wherever he ended up running off to.

Wu Xingzi was anxious. He tried to discuss the matter with Rancui a few times, but he always found himself swallowing the words back down. This dragged on and on; before he managed to say anything, they'd already reached the outskirts of Qingcheng County.

"Mr. Wu," Rancui spoke up, "it'll be Qingming in a few days. Do you plan on returning home to sweep your ancestors' graves?"

Not expecting this question, Wu Xingzi froze, then nodded vigorously. "Yes, yes, yes! Ah, I've been wanting to discuss that with you!"

"Discuss?" Rancui tilted his head, then laughed. "Are you afraid that Guan Shanjin will be waiting for you in Qingcheng County?"

He had hit the nail on the head. Wu Xingzi scratched the back of his neck, looking around furtively to confirm that the two girls weren't in the carriage. He could hear their clear voices outside traveling through the curtains—they seemed to have seen something interesting and were insisting that Hei-er explain it to them.

"I've made a fool of myself." Wu Xingzi hung his head, ashamed. "And I know that I'm overthinking things. Haiwang has Mr. Lu now. He must be enjoying his romantic triumph right now, so how could he have the time to spend on someone like me? But..."

Guan Shanjin had said he would care for Wu Xingzi's grave when he died. Wu Xingzi felt a pang in his heart, and he rubbed at his aching chest.

"You're not overthinking. We've all seen what the Great General of the Southern Garrison is like," said Rancui sardonically. He snorted, glaring at the curtains.

"The general always dotes on the people he likes. We have indeed all seen it for ourselves," came Hei-er's deep, placid voice from beyond the curtain.

Despite knowing nothing good could come from being caught by the general, Hei-er still could not allow Rancui's insults against Guan Shanjin.

"*Hmph!*" Rancui spat, then replaced his sneer with a smile when he looked at Wu Xingzi. "How about this—we'll go two days after Qingming, and you can pay your respects at night. Unless that would make you frightened, Mr. Wu?"

"No." Wu Xingzi shook his head. He felt a little apologetic, toward Rancui, Hei-er, Mint and Osmanthus, and to his ancestors. However, it seemed like this was the safest plan. If he were to return to Qingcheng County in broad daylight, who knew what sort of predicament would befall him?

Having formulated a plan, Rancui calculated the time. He asked Hei-er to make a slight detour to nearby Xingyi Village for a short trip. Xingyi produced tung oil, which meant tung trees abounded there. Now that it was spring, the trees were in full bloom. The tung flowers' petals were a snowy white, their stamens a light red, and their centers a soft yellow. The flowers grew in clusters, and from a distance the trees looked as if they were covered in snow. Plenty of poets and writers would make a special trip to Xingyi simply to admire the tung flowers.

Qingcheng County was not far from Xingyi, but it would still take three days to reach it by ox cart. With a horse, it would only take about a day and a half. Wu Xingzi had heard about Xingyi's springtime "snow," but never had the chance to see it before. Hearing Rancui's plan, he couldn't help but perk up a bit, and the unease he'd felt before began to dissipate.

Xingyi Village was indeed a lovely place, and the tung flowers were a feast for the eyes. Carrying a bamboo basket filled with snacks, Rancui led Wu Xingzi into the mountain.

Hei-er trusted Rancui implicitly; he did not feel the need to follow them. He instructed Mint and Osmanthus to take care of Wu Xingzi, and then he turned and disappeared.

Rancui snorted coldly as he watched him go. Mild disapproval and anger marred his beautiful face for a moment, but he quickly wiped the expression away. He was familiar with the route, so he brought Wu Xingzi and the girls around the mountain. They spent the entire day there. When the sun started to set, they returned to the inn. But Hei-er had not yet returned.

"Hmph, I should have sewn that man's mouth shut," Rancui sneered. It was clear he knew where Hei-er had gone. Seeing the ugly expression on his face, Mint and Osmanthus dared not ask Rancui anything; instead, they dragged Wu Xingzi back to his room to wash up.

Hei-er was gone for nearly four days. When he returned, he looked a lot paler, probably from exhaustion. As soon as he saw Hei-er, Rancui rushed forward to strike him. Although he was tired, Hei-er was still alert enough to dodge Rancui's hand—but Rancui was merely feinting; he ended up kicking the back of Hei-er's knee. The tall, sturdy man swayed and nearly fell.

"What an exceptional dog you are—so loyal," Rancui spat, still smiling beautifully. He reached out and grabbed Hei-er's chin, his eyes narrowing. "If you spoil my plans, don't blame me if I get vicious."

"You're jumping to conclusions." Hei-er was so tired that his footsteps dragged. He no longer had the energy to handle the cunning manager of the Peng Society. Calmly, he removed Rancui's hand and walked over to Wu Xingzi—who had been scared silly.

"Master, I've checked it out," Hei-er said. "The general has been in Qingcheng County for the past few days, and it seems like he'll be staying there for at least a couple more weeks. He has people guarding the cemetery at night, I think...it's going to be challenging for us to go back."

"He has far too much time on his hands." Rancui pursed his lips. He picked up a peanut from the kung pao chicken and popped it into his mouth.

"Take a seat first, Hei-er. Have you eaten?" Wu Xingzi hurriedly invited Hei-er to sit, and Mint and Osmanthus nimbly placed another bowl and set of chopsticks on the table.

"Many thanks, Master." Hei-er picked up his bowl and started eating. Whatever they did next, Rancui would be the one making the decisions, and he did not plan on saying anything else.

The meal progressed rather cheerfully. After all, it was hard for Wu Xingzi to think about difficult matters while eating. He usually finished his meal before he contemplated anything.

Rancui looked at Wu Xingzi, then at Hei-er. The corner of his lips quirked up. No one knew what he was planning.

After the meal, Wu Xingzi walked a few laps around the courtyard to aid his digestion. They were currently staying in one of the properties owned by the Peng Society in Xingyi: a small, exquisite compound. The meticulously maintained courtyard featured a small patch of tung trees, their white blossoms gently falling and covering the ground in a layer of snowy petals.

Rancui had originally wanted to accompany Wu Xingzi on his walk—it was the perfect opportunity to sow discord. It would be ideal if Wu Xingzi completely gave up all affection for Guan Shanjin. However, Hei-er had stepped forward to stop him, shaking his head with a hostile expression and exuding a somewhat threatening aura. Hei-er knew that Rancui did not like Guan Shanjin, and he was not naïve enough to believe that this little fox wouldn't take the chance to breed contempt.

Fine, let him stop me! Rancui snorted to himself, sulking. Pulling his hand back, he gave Hei-er a fake smile. "Tell me, what are Man Yue's plans?"

"Man Yue?" Hei-er frowned. He was not surprised that Rancui knew he had met with Man Yue, but he was astonished that Rancui knew Man Yue wanted to send him a message.

Rancui sneered. "You went to see him. He must have a message he wants to pass on to me. That man looks like a mooncake filled with bean paste, but he only seems sweet. When you bite into that mooncake, you end up with a mouthful of knives."

"He does have a message for you..." Hei-er sighed. What had Man Yue said about Rancui? The manager was like a water lily—rising from the mud unsullied, but pitch-black at the core. In Hei-er's opinion, neither man was easy to deal with.

"Man Yue says he hopes you will honor your agreement, and how the general treats Mr. Wu has nothing to do with you at all. He also hopes that you'll consider how delicate your neck is. If you go too far, you'd best be prepared."

This was a reminder—and an undisguised threat. Rancui's face darkened as he glared at Hei-er in silence.

"I know you don't like the general, but he truly has affection for Mr. Wu." Hei-er's heart softened when he saw Rancui huffing with anger. "Why are you taking on Mr. Wu's matters as if they're your own?"

"Hmph! Because I want to," spat Rancui. He thought about the ten years he'd spent striving to make the best matches among members of the Peng Society. Meeting a heart-stealing bastard like Guan Shanjin, how could he not be angry? What kind of scumbag went around toying with others when he already had someone else in his heart?

Rancui knew that he was ultimately powerless, though, which was the most frustrating aspect of all. The most he could do was vex Guan Shanjin a little—he wouldn't truly be able to protect Wu Xingzi.

Hei-er sighed to himself.

Over on the other side of the courtyard, Wu Xingzi was unaware of the surging tension between Rancui and Hei-er. Instead, he was worrying about Guan Shanjin staying on guard in Qingcheng County, a deep frown on his face. He had no idea what to do. He paced one loop after another, over and over again, until his clothes were soaked in sweat.

"Is Mr. Lu in Qingcheng County as well?" Wu Xingzi asked. The sudden question caught Hei-er by surprise, and it took him a moment before he hurriedly nodded.

"Yes, Mr. Lu is also in Qingcheng County, accompanying the general... Mr. Wu, don't read into it too much. The general still cares for you the most." Guan Shanjin was only using the pretext of bringing Mr. Lu on a sightseeing tour to prevent any slip-ups. Unfortunately, this was something Hei-er could not disclose; he could only stew over it in anxious silence.

"Is that so..." Wu Xingzi sighed, wiping his forehead with his sleeve as he sat down on a wooden bench. He murmured, almost to himself, "It's been hard on Mr. Lu."

Rancui lazily fanned himself with a silk kesi fan, deciding to let his vicious tongue run rampant despite Man Yue's warning. "What's so hard for him? He's the general's beloved. Everyone knows that the men of the Protector General's bloodline are dedicated to their one true love. No one is fighting with him for the general's affections anymore."

"That's true." Wu Xingzi nodded, convinced. He seemed to not think any more deeply about why Guan Shanjin was trying to intercept him in Qingcheng County. Rancui was a little surprised—Wu Xingzi even had the time to worry over Lu Zezhi.

Anyone could see how Wu Xingzi felt toward Guan Shanjin, but Rancui's eyes were very sharp—not only could he see that Wu Xingzi liked Guan Shanjin, but he also noticed that Wu Xingzi had placed Guan Shanjin in the most important position in his heart. Under all the right circumstances, Wu Xingzi would remember Guan Shanjin forever—he'd even be willing to die for him.

When a person found out that the object of his affection was willing to do something so extreme for him, even expressing a determination to once again keep him by his side... Who would not be moved? Who would not dream of a future where the two were meant for each other?

He should at least believe that he held a rather weighty position in the other man's heart. Even if Wu Xingzi was a go-with-the-flow sort of person who never took anything seriously, he should not be completely unmoved. In fact, he should be secretly pleased.

However, the only thing Wu Xingzi was concerned about was tidying his ancestors' graves. He was anxious and upset, worried that he would not be able to fulfill his filial duties. No matter what Guan Shanjin did, it was not as important to him as Qingming. It was fine if the general had feelings for him, and it was also fine if he did not. Wu Xingzi was completely unbothered.

Unable to repress his curiosity, Rancui hesitated for a moment, then put on a concerned expression. "Mr. Wu, don't you think the general still holds affection for you?" he asked.

"Do I think he still holds affection for me?" Wu Xingzi blinked— and, to Rancui's further surprise, laughed. "Naturally. But it will pass."

Rancui realized that he might not understand Wu Xingzi as well as he thought. "What do you mean by that?" he asked as he gracefully sat down next to Wu Xingzi. He pulled open the brocade purse tied to his waist and revealed a stash of melon seeds, inviting Wu Xingzi to eat some.

Wu Xingzi looked a little distressed. *Does he want to have a casual chit-chat?* He grabbed a handful of the seeds, and after eating a few, he could not bear Rancui's curious gaze any longer. He figured they were friends now, and it was fine for friends to confide in each other.

He wasn't sure where to start, though. "It's embarrassing to say this... I don't have much talent, but I've worked in the magistrate's office for over twenty years." He absentmindedly straightened his back and ate a few more melon seeds. "Qingcheng County is a small place, but conflict and misdeeds occur there just like anywhere else. Human beings are like that."

Wu Xingzi sighed. He finished all the melon seeds in his hand, trying to decide how he should continue. He had always buried his personal feelings deep within his heart, never sharing them with anyone. For him to share such secrets now... He really did not know what to say.

Rancui was in no hurry. Seeing that Wu Xingzi had finished his melon seeds, he passed him another handful, then turned his head and raised his delicate chin at Hei-er. "Brew some tea."

Hei-er glanced at him apathetically, then instructed Mint and Osmanthus to prepare some tea and other refreshments.

Rancui clicked his tongue. "You would make a good manager." He flicked the shells of the melon seeds at Hei-er. Frowning, Hei-er caught the shells and placed them one by one on the railing. Rancui pursed his lips and ignored the commander, turning back and silently eating seeds with Wu Xingzi.

"The Mao family lives in the southern part of Qingcheng County," Wu Xingzi said, his voice gentle and pleasant, flowing like warm water. "Master Mao was a merchant—he was considered one of the richest people in the county. He was successful and handsome, but also polite and modest. He was a good son and brother. He took great care of everything, and whoever spoke of him had nothing but praise to give.

"Master Mao and his wife were a match made in heaven. They grew up together as neighbors, and Madam Mao married him before she even came of age. At the time of their marriage, the Mao family had yet to make their fortune. Their family wealth was truly built up together by the both of them.

"I'd met Madam Mao before. We are close in age, about four or five years apart—I used to call her 'jiejie' when we were children. Master Mao was very good to his wife. He invited my father to teach her how to read. My father would go to their house every few days and bring me along."

Wu Xingzi seemed to have fallen back in time. The distress on his face faded away, replaced by the joy of reminiscence.

By now, the two girls had brought over the tea and snacks. Rancui deftly poured out a cup for Wu Xingzi, and stopped eating melon seeds so as not to disrupt Wu Xingzi's recollections. There was clearly no happy ending to this story, or else the magistrate's office would not have been involved.

Sure enough, Wu Xingzi continued, "Later on, Madam Mao took over the accounts for Master Mao. Master Mao trusted his wife more than anyone else. Whether it was housework or their shop's finances, Madam Mao managed all of it herself. Unfortunately... Madam Mao never bore a child. She tried many medications and sought out many famous doctors, but it was all fruitless."

As the saying went, there were three ways to be unfilial, and to have no heir was the worst of all. Wu Xingzi had not finished the story, but the others could roughly guess what had happened: Master Mao probably took a concubine. He might have even taken more than one. Madam Mao must have been pained, but as a woman, what could she say? She could only blame her own womb for being barren.

The concubines later gave birth to Master Mao's children, and this only made Madam Mao's position more awkward.

"Madam Mao never resented Master Mao for it, and Master Mao still respected her greatly. After all, they had been together since they were young, and they had a different relationship from anyone else's. However..." Wu Xingzi sighed, but never finished that sentence. "After that, Master and Madam Mao separated, peacefully parting ways. A separation request must be notarized by the magistrate's office before it is considered official. We also need to ensure that the request has been personally signed by both the husband and the wife, and no coercion is involved. If we find that both parties have agreed to it, then the separation will be approved."

As the adviser working in the magistrate's office, Wu Xingzi was the one who'd handled this matter. His face turned sorrowful; even though this had transpired many years ago, it still greatly saddened him.

"Master Rancui, the one thing that should never grow old in this world is affection. Once affection ages, it can only come to a sorrowful end. Haiwang feels more anger toward me right now than longing. He already has Mr. Lu, who was someone he wanted but could not have. Even if he's unsatisfied right now, it won't last long." Wu Xingzi smiled at Rancui, his gentle voice drifting out into the night. It was like warm water, but it left the others speechless.

Rancui had great confidence in his ability to read people. However, he was not as adept at reading Wu Xingzi. Rancui seemed to have completely misjudged this seemingly shy, ordinary, and carefree man. He sought neither fame nor fortune, and although he was the sort to have enduring feelings, he always acted with the proper decorum—so proper that he even seemed a little cold sometimes.

As an adviser, Wu Xingzi had seen too much of life—both its joys and its sorrows. He understood the ruthlessness of the world all too well. He had seen too much, and yet he still could preserve his own sense of self; this unique form of naivety was sharper than a blade.

When he said he was leaving, he really meant it. Rancui had been worried over nothing.

Wu Xingzi would not turn back, since he knew he could no longer control his love for Guan Shanjin. He had truly fallen for the general. Thus, Wu Xingzi would make a clean break, swiftly and decisively cutting the connection between the two of them. He would not give himself even a moment to miss Guan Shanjin.

If Wu Xingzi was not truly in love with Guan Shanjin, he might have returned to him by now, or he might not even have left in the first place. Guan Shanjin was the Lanling Prince of pengornises! If he passed on this penis, would he be able to find another one like it? Alas, he had to fall in love...

"I didn't realize this when I was young, and I fell for a perfume sachet. It was an affection only worth a few coins, but those coins were enough to last me quite some time." Wu Xingzi started chewing the melon seeds again. He was quiet as he ate them, sucking on the seeds to soften them before peeling them. He slowly piled up the shells in a neat arrangement. "Ah, I'm just worried about how I'm going to sweep my ancestors' graves. I can't wait around for half a month like this. I'm afraid that my parents will end up berating me in my dreams."

"Hmm..." Rancui fanned himself and narrowed his eyes at Hei-er, who stood there silently with his head bowed. "I have an idea, but I don't know if Commander Hei will be able to help us."

"Do tell, Manager."

"Go tell Man Yue that there's someone following behind us who might pose a threat to Mr. Wu. As for what happens afterward, Man Yue will know what to do." Rancui gave a charming smile, fanning away the fireflies that had begun to appear. "Don't worry, Mr. Wu. I estimate it'll be four or five days at most before you can go home—two or three days if things move quickly."

After spending only four hours in Xingyi, without even a good night's rest, Hei-er once again had to make his weary way back to Qingcheng County. Before he left, Rancui promised to set off for Qingcheng County with Wu Xingzi and the two maids tomorrow, so as not to make further traveling time for Hei-er.

"I still hope to be able to bring Mr. Wu back to the capital around mid-June." Rancui covered his smile, his beguiling brows suggesting he was up to no good.

Hei-er looked at him in silence. He didn't need to ask to know that Rancui was up to something.

"Is something happening in mid-June?" Wu Xingzi asked.

"Something interesting. I'm sure you'll enjoy it." Rancui tapped on his lip, putting on an enigmatic façade. He turned and hurried Hei-er. "Why are you still here? Scram! I don't want to bump into Guan Shanjin in the outskirts of Qingcheng County."

With Rancui provoking him like this, Hei-er could no longer maintain his calm demeanor in front of Wu Xingzi. "Don't order me around. You're not my master."

"Why? Do I have to perform an entire formal ceremony to make a request of you? Hush! There's no way I'll ever want a bastard like you!

A bone is a good enough reward for you." Rancui pulled out a jade counting rod from somewhere on his person and tossed it at Hei-er.

Hei-er reached out and caught the counting rod. Other than glaring at Rancui, there was nothing else he could do. He gloomily turned and left.

With Hei-er gone, Rancui found an excuse to send Mint and Osmanthus away. When he turned to look at Wu Xingzi, his ever-present smile faded. "Mr. Wu, I need to ask you a question. Please don't take offense."

"Huh? Ah, Rancui-gongzi, please don't be so formal. Just go ahead and ask!" Wu Xingzi jolted up, straightening his back. His hands clenched uneasily on his knees, and he seemed to be frightened by Rancui's unusual facial expression.

"If the general also holds true and deep affection for you, would you be willing to continue your relationship with him?"

Wu Xingzi had not expected this question. His mouth fell open, but he was unable to make a sound. He stared a while, then closed his mouth and licked his dry lips. Smiling wryly, he said, "Rancui-gongzi, that relationship is already over."

"Life is unpredictable, Mr. Wu. There's always the possibility of rekindling an old flame." Rancui picked up his teacup and took a sip. He continued, speaking sincerely for once: "Mr. Wu, I'm sure you're aware that I do not care for the general. No matter how I look at it, I feel that he's unworthy of you. If I'm good at anything, it's reading people, and that man is too harsh and too cold. It isn't an exaggeration to say he is completely heartless. You're so unlike him. But…have you never thought of finding someone to spend the rest of your life with? Not everyone is like that perfume sachet, only worth a few coins. At the very least, Guan Shanjin is worth a few thousand taels."

Wu Xingzi bowed his head and chuckled. "No matter Guan Shanjin's value, he still belongs to someone else." His expression was impossible to make out in the dark of evening, but Rancui had the feeling he was silently weeping.

"What if he doesn't belong to anyone? Would you want him then?"

A shudder ran through Wu Xingzi's thin body. His breathing turned faint, and he did not respond for a long time.

Rancui sighed deeply. What did he still not understand?

Man Yue rubbed his stinging eyes in the dim light, carefully reading the information he had received from the capital.

It had been a dozen or so days since he'd gotten a good night's sleep. He always put on weight like a balloon whenever he was busy. This time around, he gained over ten pounds at first, but then he'd started losing it. His trousers were very loose now—he could fit his entire fist into the waistband.

If he thought about this optimistically, it wasn't bad to lose weight in and of itself; he'd just be a crescent moon instead of a full one. On the other hand, the baseline of his health had been affected, and he was afraid that he would need to spend some time recovering.

It was all Guan Shanjin's fault.

That mental breakdown had been incredibly poorly timed. Couldn't he have waited until just a little later to lose his sanity? He just had to collapse at a very critical moment!

The general's internal injuries were more extensive than they'd thought. After resting for many days, Guan Shanjin finally managed to recover a fair amount, but he did not want to behave. The moment he woke up, he hurried to chase after Wu Xingzi. He even refused to take a carriage out of fear he wouldn't be able to catch up, and rode a horse himself. Moving as fast as he could, he searched through

Qingcheng County, Goose City, and the outskirts of both. Then he vomited blood again and collapsed. With no choice but to stop and recuperate, he stayed in Qingcheng County.

The second instance of blood-vomiting really shook up Man Yue. He really thought Guan Shanjin might not make it.

He and Guan Shanjin had been childhood friends; they were all but inseparable. Although Man Yue was younger, and so he had arrived at the northwest battleground a few years after his friend did, he gladly took the position of adjutant to Guan Shanjin, assisting him as leader of the Guan family army. Man Yue could pound his chest and proclaim with full confidence that no one else understood the general better than he did.

Man Yue had never expected to assess a situation so incorrectly. He had lain a savage trap for Guan Shanjin, but in doing so he'd trapped himself as well.

Wu Xingzi had managed to flee without leaving a single clue; Guan Shanjin was unable to find a trace of him despite personally leading his men in the search. How could Guan Shanjin not know that Man Yue had a hand in this matter? But in the past dozen or so days, Guan Shanjin had not asked Man Yue a single question. There had been no change in his attitude toward him, and he still liked to pinch Man Yue's tender, fleshy chin. He even complained, "Man Yue, did you lose weight? I don't want to see a crescent moon instead of our full moon."

Man Yue spat at him.

Guan Shanjin's attitude gave Man Yue mixed emotions. For once, he didn't know what his leader was thinking; he could only carefully help him through his worries and come up with plans.

Guan Shanjin had badly injured himself this time. His entire body was sickly and pale from damaged circulation and lack of proper rest.

It was fortunate that Guan Shanjin had a very strong baseline of health, or they would have prepared a coffin for him already. Touched by the fragility of illness, his godlike looks were even more enchanting. A casual glance from him could set a fire within someone and leave them in a daze.

Man Yue could not help but sigh again, staring up into the sky. Tidying up the letters in his hand and tucking them into his clothes, he planned on heading to the kitchen to brew Guan Shanjin's medicine.

Man Yue heard a few light knocks at his window. His forehead creased as he hurriedly opened the shutters. Hei-er, who had only left three days ago, now appeared in front of him again.

"Why are you here?" Man Yue asked, quickly letting him in. Guan Shanjin's room was only two windows away, and he didn't want the general to catch Hei-er, then subsequently Wu Xingzi.

Hei-er's lips were white from fatigue. He was travel-stained, and a simple shake of his head scattered dust and sand everywhere. Without answering, he walked over to the table, grabbed the teapot, and drained it directly from the spout. At last he caught a breath, collapsing onto the seat next to the table and brushing off the layer of dust sticking to his clothes.

"Rancui says someone is following us," Hei-er said, his tone flat. He did not have the energy to even consider his words.

"Oh?" Man Yue sat down next to him. Carefully studying Hei-er, he revealed a mocking smile. "Who's following you?"

"It might be someone with evil intentions toward Mr. Wu." Hei-er shook his head like a dog and sent dust flying, making Man Yue wrinkle his nose and back away a little.

"And?" Man Yue leveled Hei-er with a look. He knew what Rancui meant, but he was frustrated and was looking for someone to take it out on.

Hei-er turned to look at Man Yue, annoyance on his face. However, he was used to following Man Yue's orders. "He said that you'd know what to do," he quietly replied. He mumbled to himself a little, then added, "Mr. Wu wants to clean up his ancestors' graves."

"I know." Man Yue snorted and waved Hei-er away. "All right, you should get going. Don't expose yourself. If the general catches you now, he'll flay you alive."

At the mention of the general, Hei-er looked even more serious. "How has the general been recovering? If he were to give chase again, will he...?"

Man Yue shook his head. "It won't come to that." Guan Shanjin's internal injuries were very serious, but they were caused by his own inner turmoil; he would be fine if he took his medicine and rested well.

"Should I reveal some of this to Mr. Wu?" Hei-er asked. He dared not visit Guan Shanjin. He still had a mission, and he could not allow anything to go wrong now. However, how could he not blame himself after hearing more about the situation from Man Yue? Even if the goal of all this was to give Guan Shanjin and Wu Xingzi a push, the price being paid was rather dear.

Furthermore, once they returned to the capital, the general would have to deal with another battle among officials. It was very possible that Guan Shanjin would not have the chance to recuperate properly.

If Wu Xingzi found out that Guan Shanjin had lost control of his sanity, vomited three liters of blood, and searched for him at the expense of his own health...would his heart soften? Would he be willing to return? It would at least prevent that crafty little fox Rancui from causing any further complications.

But to Hei-er's surprise, Man Yue shook his head.

"He does need to know, but now is not the right time."

"What do you mean?" Hei-er's brows knitted deeply. If he hadn't known very well how loyal Man Yue was to Guan Shanjin, he would have suspected that he was trying to manipulate the situation to Guan Shanjin's disadvantage.

Man Yue rubbed his face, exhausted. "Let me ask you this: how does Mr. Wu currently feel about the general?"

Hei-er pondered this for a moment, recalling what Wu Xingzi had said about Master and Madam Mao. "His feelings for him must be quite deep." He was not as perceptive as Rancui, but he could understand Wu Xingzi's feelings.

His answer piqued Man Yue's curiosity. He had not expected Hei-er to be able to tell. "How so?" Man Yue asked.

Hei-er told Man Yue the story of Madam Mao. After that, Man Yue's round cheeks seemed to wilt a little, and his shoulders hunched over as well. "Ah, things are going to be difficult..."

"Difficult?"

"You're right—Mr. Wu has developed very deep feelings for the General." Man Yue wanted to pour some tea for himself, but when he lifted up the pot it was completely empty. He sighed heavily. "That's why things are going to be difficult! Mr. Wu realized his own feelings a long time ago—why do you think he told you that story? He is much more stubborn than I thought."

"He thinks that the general likes Mr. Lu, so he was unwilling to stay. But if we let Mr. Wu understand that he's the most important person in the general's heart, do you think he might be willing to come back?" Hei-er asked. He didn't understand why Man Yue and Rancui were twisting everything like this. In his mind, it was better to just lay everything out in the open than speculate over it in secret. Feelings were hard to predict, and a careless mistake could cost them everything. This was not war—why endure such suffering?

"Before the wedding, laying things out in the open might have worked," said Man Yue. "Hei-er, let me put it another way... It's true that once Mr. Wu finds out that the general vomited blood and is severely injured, he will come back immediately. However, what will he think? Will he think that the general has fallen in love with him, or will he think that the general does not cherish the heart that has been given to him? Don't forget, Mr. Wu has always believed that the general's beloved is Lu Zezhi." Man Yue slammed his fist on the table, his smooth, plump face turning dark. "He's only just torn apart the Yue family for Lu Zezhi and snatched him away from the wedding hall. The Great General of the Southern Garrison fell for his childhood teacher and flew into a rage over that beauty—this story has spread beyond Horse-Face City. Even people in the capital have heard it. Right now, if you were to tell Mr. Wu that because he left without saying goodbye, the general lost control of both his qi and his sanity... Ah, never mind about Mr. Wu—would *you* believe it?"

Faced with this question, Hei-er opened his mouth, but he was unable to provide an answer. When Man Yue put it that way... Of course he would not believe it. How could he? Philanderers were everywhere in this world, but they were often also the most heartless sorts of people, just like that Master Mao...

Although Hei-er could understand the logic behind not telling Wu Xingzi, he still could not feel at ease. His eyebrows creased tightly. "What should we do about Manager Rancui, then? He keeps goading Mr. Wu, and he wants to return to the capital before mid-June."

"You don't have to worry about him," Man Yue said with a wave of his hand. "Wu Xingzi is the sort of man who holds onto his affection for a very long time. The man in his heart is our general, and any other cocks are only like passing clouds. Rancui understands this as well."

Hei-er was not reassured at all. He decided he'd watch them closely to prevent any sudden situations from cropping up. With that in mind, he did not plan on staying any longer. Nimbly, he opened the window and exited, melting into the night in the blink of an eye.

Man Yue stared at the darkness outside the window, sighing faintly. He still had to brew the general's medicine.

But when he opened his door, he was startled to see who was standing outside.

"General?" He pressed his hand to his chest, putting on an exaggerated expression of shock; his chubby face even turned pale.

"Mm." Guan Shanjin acknowledged him, a hint of something that looked like a smile curling around his lips. With no change in his expression, he surveyed Man Yue's room.

He was not alone. In his arms was Mr. Lu, and Guan Shanjin was lazily playing with his slender, marble-like fingers.

"Why aren't you resting in your room?" Man Yue noticed the reddening of Mr. Lu's lips, and the few red marks on his fingertips. Guan Shanjin was truly giving this performance his all. Even Man Yue was ready to believe that Lu Zezhi was being showered in affection.

"I'm accompanying Teacher for a stroll." A faint smile appeared on Guan Shanjin's face. He looked rather spry, but his complexion was still terrifyingly pale.

"Oh." Man Yue nodded with an understanding look. He was deliberately bringing Mr. Lu all over the place, trying to catch everyone's attention, and he was unhappy, so his actions were even less restrained. Man Yue was beginning to feel sorry for Lu Zezhi.

However, to Lu Zezhi's ears, this conversation had a completely different meaning. The man's elegant face tinted red as he shyly lowered his head. He pulled his hand out from Guan Shanjin's palm and hid it in his sleeve.

Lu Zezhi knew that Qingcheng County was Wu Xingzi's hometown. For the past few days, he had been quite vexed. If the old fellow wanted to leave, let him leave! Why did Guan Shanjin have to search for him so earnestly? However, without the support of the Yue family, and with news of his relationship with Guan Shanjin spreading everywhere, staying close to Guan Shanjin was the only option he had.

Probably because he saw Lu Zezhi's unease, Guan Shanjin doted on him even more, not mentioning Wu Xingzi a single time. When Mr. Lu thought about it, the reason they were in Qingcheng County was only because Guan Shanjin could not take the indignity. After all, how could that ugly old thing have the gall to run away without saying a word? It was a slap in Guan Shanjin's face!

"General, why don't you return to your room to rest? I'll brew your medicine and bring it over," Man Yue said, heading down the stairs.

"The medicine can wait. There's something I need to say to you." Guan Shanjin stopped Man Yue. He looked down, coaxing Lu Zezhi, "Teacher, return to your room and wash up, all right? I've made a special request for the chef from Restaurant of Songs in Goose City to come cook for us. We'll have dinner together later, all right?"

"All right." Lu Zezhi nodded obediently, suppressing the vague unease welling up within him. He returned to his room as Guan Shanjin watched.

Once the eyesore was gone, Man Yue dispensed with formalities and glared at Guan Shanjin. "If you have something to say, it can be said later. You need to take your medicine."

"I can take it later. Let's go into your room first." Guan Shanjin dragged Man Yue away. After closing the door quietly, he turned to look at his vice general. "Who was in your room just now?"

"You know I won't answer that question," Man Yue said with a raised brow.

Guan Shanjin smiled. His steps were a little weak. He sat down by the table and inhaled deeply, his voice somewhat hoarse. "Get me a cup of tea."

The teapot in Man Yue's room had already been completely emptied by Hei-er. Frowning, he opened his door and whistled. A bodyguard came over, and Man Yue quietly instructed him to brew the medicine as well as a pot of tea.

When he turned back again, he saw Guan Shanjin's profile as he stared out of the window. His jade-like skin glowed softly in the candlelight. The lines of his features were soft and exquisite, as though they had been carefully carved by an artist. However, no matter how handsome his appearance was, it could not cover the look of defeat between his brows. Lu Zezhi was truly too negligent—something was obviously wrong with Guan Shanjin, but he shut his eyes to it. Compared to how attentive he'd been six years ago, now he was practically blind.

"What did Hei-er say?" Guan Shanjin got straight to the point. He was severely injured, but it was only his circulation that was affected, not his brain. He lived only two windows away—how could he not have known what was happening in Man Yue's room? Hei-er's skills were far below his own. Guan Shanjin had already noticed him when he visited three days ago. The only reason he hadn't mentioned it was that he wanted Man Yue to admit it to him.

Man Yue understood what he meant. "Do you want the truth, or would you prefer a lie?"

Guan Shanjin laughed. Shaking his head, he said, "Let's hear both, hmm?"

"Sure. The truth is, Hei-er passed on a message that someone's watching Mr. Wu." Man Yue was not afraid Guan Shanjin would cause him any grief. It was not easy to gain Guan Shanjin's trust, but once a person had it, it was not easily lost—especially a person like Man Yue, who had gone through life and death with him.

Guan Shanjin's shoulders tensed, his voice becoming even more hoarse. "And who told Hei-er this?"

Man Yue pressed his lips together. "Rancui."

This answer made Guan Shanjin relax. "Is that so..." Coughing lightly, he then asked, "What about the lie?"

"No one came looking for me." Man Yue shrugged, giving Guan Shanjin a good-natured smile. "Hei-er wouldn't dare show his face here. He took off with Mr. Wu. He's afraid you'll skin him alive for that."

"Nonsense." Guan Shanjin chuckled lightly, reaching out and pinching Man Yue's chin. "How much does Hei-er know?"

Man Yue sighed. "As much as he needs to."

Guan Shanjin nodded.

Not too long later, there was a knock at the door. The bodyguard was back with a teapot, quietly telling Man Yue that the medicine was brewing.

"Bring it up once it's done."

Man Yue poured himself and Guan Shanjin a cup of tea each. Guan Shanjin lifted his cup with a trembling hand, spilling a few drops. Despite his worries, Man Yue did not say a word.

The silence did not last long. After wetting his throat, Guan Shanjin spoke. "What are your plans?"

Man Yue paused. He looked at Guan Shanjin, his mouth still full of tea. After a few moments, he swallowed. "Would you be willing to hear me if I told you?"

"Tell me."

Man Yue considered for a while, then heaved a sigh. "We have to leave Qingcheng County for the capital immediately."

"Oh?"

"General, the longer we stay in Qingcheng County, the more danger we'll pose to Mr. Wu. We've finally managed to push Lu Zezhi out into the open—didn't we do that to ensure Mr. Wu's safety? Yan Wenxin is no fool. If we'd just stayed a few days, we could've said that we were simply looking into his background, but we've already been here for over a week. It's hard to say if he will find out about Mr. Wu." Man Yue looked very stern, but his words made perfect sense, jabbing right into Guan Shanjin's weak spot.

Guan Shanjin stopped fidgeting with his teacup and frowned. He maintained his silence for a while longer. "You're right," he said at last, glumly. "I became obsessed..." Now that their plan was at this stage, he could not let their previous efforts go to waste.

"Shall we leave tomorrow, then?" Man Yue probed.

"Mm. Give the command." Guan Shanjin carefully placed the teacup back onto the table. His complexion seemed to pale even further; his greenish veins starkly stood out under his skin, spreading like fissures.

"Yes, sir." Man Yue cupped his hands together in a bow. Just as he was about to open the door and call for the guards, a question that sounded like a faint sigh suddenly came from behind him:

"Why, Man Yue?"

Why?

Man Yue's plump face stiffened, but very quickly returned to normal. As though he did not hear Guan Shanjin's question, he opened the door, summoning the guards to give them their orders.

Almost the very moment Guan Shanjin and his companions left the boundary of Qingcheng County, Wu Xingzi and the others, who had come across Hei-er a few hours ago, arrived.

Finally back in his hometown, Wu Xingzi could relax. Although the world outside was vast, it could never compare to the bottom of the familiar well he called home.

Wu Xingzi's little house was not enough to accommodate so many of them, and there were the two girls to consider as well. Rancui decided to book two rooms at Qingcheng County's only inn. Impeccably considerate, he left with the others for the inn so that Wu Xingzi would be able to rest quietly in his house.

The tiny house was very clean. Not just the table, chairs, and the bed, but the floor was clean, too—not a speck of dirt could be seen. The table and chairs had been wiped until they shone; it seemed that someone had gone to the trouble of tidying everything up.

There was no need to guess who the culprit was. Wu Xingzi stood at his door, hesitating for a moment before he carefully stepped into his house.

He pushed the window open. The slight breeze swirled into the room, carrying with it the scent of earth and grass. A note left on the table fluttered lightly in the breeze. Wu Xingzi glanced at the note a few times, feeling rather glum. He knew who had left the note behind, but he did not have the courage to read it.

Instead, he pottered around his house, both inside and out. Taking out his blanket from the trunk, he shook it out and laid it on the bed. It smelled clean and warm, with no trace of dampness or mildew from being stored for too long. It had been sunned outdoors and meticulously packed away, so that when he came back to stay, there was no need for him to waste any time sunning the blanket himself.

Guan Shanjin had always been a very thoughtful person. When they were together, even during the moments when Wu Xingzi had been ignored, the general had never let him suffer the tiniest bit. Hugging the thin blanket, Wu Xingzi sat on the bed in a trance. The only image in his head was Guan Shanjin's smiling face.

Some time later, he sighed and put the blanket down. Clutching his little money pouch, he readied himself to go out and purchase some offerings for his ancestors. It was still early, and the timing was perfect for tomb-sweeping.

Qingcheng County's marketplace consisted of just one short street. The inn, the magistrate's office, and various other buildings were all located here. It was just past noon, and many of the stalls selling vegetables and meat had already packed up. However, there were still some stalls selling snacks; Wu Xingzi could see Ansheng's tofu stall in the distance. The handsome young fellow still had a bright, sunny smile on his face as he talked to a man sitting at his stall. After looking closely, Wu Xingzi saw that the man was Constable Zhang. His relationship with Ansheng was still going strong. Their actions were reserved, yet filled with tenderness.

Wu Xingzi had no plans to disturb them, but the street was only so big. Ansheng immediately caught sight of Wu Xingzi the moment he lifted his head. A delighted smile lit up Ansheng's face, and he called out with great friendliness, "Xingzi-ge! I haven't seen you in ages!"

The tips of Wu Xingzi's ears turned red. He felt a little uneasy, but he still made his way forward. "Hello Ansheng, Constable Zhang."

"Adviser Wu..." After Constable Zhang greeted Wu Xingzi, he remembered that Wu Xingzi was no longer the magistrate's adviser. He didn't know how to react, so he buried his head down and silently ate his tofu pudding.

Being called "Adviser Wu" also made Wu Xingzi cringe a little. Who was the current adviser in the magistrate's office, he wondered...

"Xingzi-ge, have you eaten?" Ansheng asked, standing up to fetch a bowl of tofu. The moment he lifted the lid, the fragrance of the tofu filled the air, accompanied by the aroma of stir-fried pork and shallots. Wu Xingzi's stomach gurgled. Blushing, he forcefully pressed down on his belly, swallowing down the refusal on the tip of his tongue.

It had been ages since he'd eaten Ansheng's tofu!

Smiling, Ansheng glanced at him and deftly prepared a huge bowl. He knew how much Wu Xingzi could eat, so he poured the mix of minced pork, mushrooms, and shrimp over the tofu in the biggest bowl he had.

The snow-white tofu was covered in a thick brown sauce, tinged with red and black. Crispy pieces of fried shallot floated on top, smelling extremely appetizing. Ansheng finished it with a dash of fresh coriander; Wu Xingzi's stomach grumbled even louder in delight.

"Hurry up and try it!" Ansheng said, urging Wu Xingzi to a seat. "See if my skills have improved even more." He placed the huge bowl in front of the older man and sat down across from him, watching him with bright eyes.

Wu Xingzi knew Ansheng well. He didn't know how to act at first because he hadn't seen him in so long, but he quickly settled in. Not paying Ansheng's gaze any mind, he dug into this dish he had not tried in a long time.

It had to be said that Ansheng was a skilled cook. In the months since Wu Xingzi last ate Ansheng's tofu, it seemed to have become even tastier. Wu Xingzi almost wished he could swallow his tongue down together with the food.

Constable Zhang had already emptied his bowl. After he'd washed it, he went back to Ansheng and wrapped an arm around his shoulders, leaning over to whisper into his ear. Ansheng listened carefully, then gave a small, joyful laugh, nodding and agreeing to whatever it was he'd said.

Although Wu Xingzi was eating heartily, he couldn't help sneaking looks at the couple. He remembered that it was all thanks to these two that he'd joined the Peng Society. Seeing that their feelings for each other hadn't wavered, he felt extremely gratified.

"All right, hurry up and go! I'm reminiscing with Xingzi-ge over here." Ansheng pushed Constable Zhang's shoulder, his lips brushing past his firm chin. His bright eyes curved up like crescents with his smile.

"Mm." Constable Zhang nodded. Although Qingcheng County had always been peaceful and crime was rare, the constable still had to make his usual patrols. He could sneak in a break here and there, but he could not slack off. He glanced over at Wu Xingzi and awkwardly invited him to eat more before leaving.

Wu Xingzi never stood on ceremony when it came to food. The huge bowl of tofu pudding disappeared in no time at all. He exhaled in satisfaction and wiped his mouth with one hand, rubbing his belly with the other. He clearly had not eaten his fill yet.

Ansheng understood him very well. Worried that Wu Xingzi would get tired of just tofu pudding on its own, he stood up and went over to the neighboring stalls. Soon he returned with a big bowl of noodle soup, four hand pies filled with chives, and two scallion pancakes. He knew Wu Xingzi often ate these in the past.

Qingcheng County was a tiny place with a small population. When it came to food, this was pretty much as fancy as it got. However, the dishes were hearty, the prices were cheap, and there was more than enough to fill one's belly.

When he learned Wu Xingzi was back for tomb-sweeping, Ansheng was a little surprised, but he immediately asked the uncle next door to help buy some candles, incense, and other offerings for him to use.

"Oh right, did you come back alone?" Ansheng asked, looking up and down the street. Confirming that there were no unfamiliar faces, he could not suppress his curiosity.

"No, I came with some friends." Wu Xingzi had already cleared out the noodles, and was now sipping the soup. Finally remembering Rancui and the others, he started to become restless.

Rancui would not let himself suffer, but Mint, Osmanthus, and Hei-er would not go out to eat without him. At this time, all of them must be hungry, and Wu Xingzi could not bear to let the two girls endure too much hunger.

"Xingzi-ge..." Ansheng lowered his voice. "How are things between you and that otherworldly man?"

Wu Xingzi's hand shook, nearly dropping his bowl.

"Ah, w-we're fine..." He recalled that Guan Shanjin had been in Qingcheng County just a few days ago, and Qingcheng County only had the one inn—where had the general's large entourage stayed? Ansheng must have seen something.

"That's good." Ansheng nodded. Not pointing out the distress on Wu Xingzi's face, he deftly changed the topic. "How long will you be staying this time? Would you like to come by my place tomorrow for food and drinks?"

Wu Xingzi was a little hesitant. "Ah, I'm leaving after the tomb-sweeping..."

They'd initially planned to go to the capital to evade Guan Shanjin's pursuit, but Wu Xingzi had to return home to pay his respects during Qingming. This drew Guan Shanjin to Qingcheng County. Although Rancui hadn't said anything, Wu Xingzi knew that Guan Shanjin's departure from Qingcheng County meant that he would not appear again for a while—perhaps even for the rest of his life. Wu Xingzi saw no need to go to the capital anymore. It was safer to stay here, since he might end up accidentally bumping into Guan Shanjin there.

He had finally returned to his hometown, after all. He wanted to remain here quietly for the rest of his days. Although he no longer had a job at the magistrate's office, perhaps he could become a teacher like his father, do some farming in his spare time, and earn back his stash of money so he could increase his treasure trove of pengornis pictures.

Ansheng watched as Wu Xingzi's expression morphed from embarrassment and unease to a joyful smile. He was truly curious about what was going through his head. "What are you smiling about, Xingzi-ge?"

"My hoard of pengornises... Uhh..." Wu Xingzi realized he'd made a mistake the moment he opened his mouth. Thinking about it had made him so happy that the words just came out. Instantly, his face turned red. "I-it's nothing, don't mind me. I'm just thinking about how to earn a living in the future."

"Do you not want to return to being the county adviser?" Ansheng asked.

"Return?" Wu Xingzi blinked. He had been gone for the better part of a year—did the magistrate's office still not have a new adviser?

"Ah, yes." Ansheng nodded as he shot a look in the direction of the magistrate's office. "Fu-ge said that Auntie Li wanted to push her second son to become the adviser at first. After all, there are not many in our county who can read. Everyone who went to school has either left here or has a better job. The position of adviser cannot be left empty forever, right?"

"Li Desheng?" Wu Xingzi took a breath in surprise. He knew of Auntie Li's second son, a man ten years younger than he. Wu Xingzi's father had even taught Li Desheng; as a child, he'd been cute as well as clever. He picked up everything very quickly, but unfortunately, he did not like to study. After attending a month of classes, he kept skipping school to play and scavenge for bird eggs.

It was true that Li Desheng was one of the few literate people in Qingcheng County. However, he could only read—he couldn't write. It was unlikely he could handle the other responsibilities of the job, either.

"Of course, things didn't go Auntie Li's way," Ansheng said. "Everyone knows what Li Desheng is like. He thinks he's above everyone else just because he can read—he doesn't even tend to the crops properly. He never passed, despite participating in the examinations for years. Auntie Li is probably the only person who thinks he's worth anything."

Ansheng was a very polite man, so it was rare to hear him disparage someone like this. Wu Xingzi scratched his nose, chuckling obligingly. He was unsure how to respond. He'd had no idea that Li Desheng wanted to be a scholar. But if he couldn't even write an essay, how was he going to participate in the imperial examinations? Wu Xingzi sighed inwardly, starting to sympathize with Auntie Li.

"Fu-ge says an adviser is not a must in the magistrate's office," Ansheng added. "After you left, the county magistrate did not look for a replacement—he could muddle through by himself. However, most people think it would be nice to have you come back to the magistrate's office. After all, the magistrate is replaced every six years, and no one understands Qingcheng County better than you."

Ansheng watched Wu Xingzi closely as he spoke. His gaze made Wu Xingzi a little shy. Bowing his head, Wu Xingzi tore the scallion pancakes into pieces and ate them; he was in no hurry to reply. Contrary to his outwardly unaffected expression, he felt quite flustered.

He thought that after being whisked away by Guan Shanjin for so many months, his halcyon days as county adviser were long gone. However, Qingcheng County seemed to be frozen in time, as if he had never even left. These familiar people were all waiting in the same places for him, and he could return to his old life at any time. He could taste familiar food, see familiar people, and smell familiar scents.

Wu Xingzi almost wanted to open his mouth and tell Ansheng that he was staying, that he'd return to his position as adviser and continue to take care of the little house that his parents had left him. He would grow chives, nutmeg, and other plants in the little plots at the back of his house. When it was farming season, he would go over to Auntie Liu's place and help her family, as well as help his fellow villagers resolve their various issues...

But it was only almost.

Wu Xingzi's stomach was full. He reminisced a little with Ansheng, and the uncle from the stall next door returned with some incense, candles, and other offerings for tomb-sweeping. Wu Xingzi thanked them both profusely, receiving an affectionate smile in return and a welcome for his thanks.

In the end, he did not agree to stay.

CHAPTER 2

THE PENG SOCIETY GATHERING

"Vice General Man, rest assured that my relationship with the general has always been casual. The reason I actually want to go to the capital is the Peng Society gathering..."

Man Yue looked directly at Wu Xingzi, unable to speak a word of what he had been planning to say. He had finally heard for himself how passionate Wu Xingzi was about making friends through the pigeon post. He began to pity Guan Shanjin.

"Vice General Man, do you plan on attending the gathering as well?"

This question truly floored Man Yue. He put on an enigmatic smile, neither confirming nor denying it.

ANSHENG MIGHT HAVE noticed Wu Xingzi's inner conflict, but he did not insist on an answer from him. Seeing Wu Xingzi was nearly done eating, Ansheng looked at the sky, then hurried him to the tomb-sweeping. If he didn't leave now, it would be hard to make his way there and back before the sun set.

Wu Xingzi was touched. After arranging to come tomorrow to have another bowl of tofu pudding, he took the offerings with him and left.

Wu Xingzi had been planning to go to the inn to meet Rancui and the rest of his group. However, now he changed his mind. He stopped a neighbor he knew on the street and asked him to help pass on a message to them, then headed toward the graves alone.

Last time he was here, Guan Shanjin had accompanied him on this path. This time around, he wanted to walk it alone, just like he always had. But when he reached his ancestors' tomb, Wu Xingzi froze.

It had already been swept. The mound was bare, with no weeds or grass covering it, and the tombstone was clean and shiny. The person who did this had clearly spent much more effort than Wu Xingzi would, if he had done it himself.

He reflexively looked around him. Qingming had been over for a few days already, so no one should be coming to this valley. A breeze rustled through the trees nearby, the branches and leaves swaying slightly; he could vaguely hear birds calling over by the mountains.

Wu Xingzi sighed again without realizing it. He stood there in a daze for quite some time before he finally arranged his offerings in front of the grave. Lighting three sticks of incense, he began to pray to his ancestors.

During New Year, he'd even asked his ancestors to bless him with plenty of pengornises every year. His ancestors must have been furious at him! It had only been a few months since then, but his pengornis affair had ended. In the past, he'd nearly been drowning in cock, but now, he would most likely face a drought instead. One really should not take success for granted!

"Father, Mother, all my ancestors—I'll be making a trip to the capital. Please keep me safe. Even if I no longer have the Prince of Lanling, a Han Zigao is fine. To see such a fair, handsome man, gentle and considerate... It would not work to stay with only one pengornis my whole life. Now that I finally have a chance to leave the bottom of my well, it will be good to expand my horizons." After murmuring on for a bit, Wu Xingzi clamped his mouth shut, the blush on his face spreading to the tips of his ears. He must be a fool to make such a request to his ancestors! His parents would likely give him a spanking in his dreams tonight.

But then when he considered it for a moment, didn't most people request their ancestors to bless their marriages? Requesting some cock wasn't going *too* far, right? Wu Xingzi felt a little conflicted. The incense in his hands had burned up almost completely by the time he quickly bowed and completed the rest of the ceremony.

As he burned the joss papers, steady footsteps slowly drew closer. Wu Xingzi was not scared at all. He guessed it would be Hei-er looking for him, and he looked over with a smile.

His face froze.

In front of him was someone Wu Xingzi had never expected. His hands paused in midair, and he only returned to his senses when the flames from the burning paper licked at him. Tossing the entire stack of joss paper into the fire without thinking, Wu Xingzi stood up, patting away the ashes on his clothes.

The newcomer was Man Yue.

"Vice General Man?"

Wu Xingzi had not interacted with Man Yue much. They'd only met a few times, and barely ever spoken to each other. To tell the truth, Wu Xingzi always felt a little nervous about the vice general. Man Yue looked so very harmless, with his honest smile and round, plump body. He had a good temperament. Everyone who met him felt at ease, and they would unconsciously draw closer to him. However, Wu Xingzi was a little fearful of the chubby fellow.

"Mr. Wu." As usual, Man Yue had a smile on his face. He nodded, walking toward the grave with no hesitation as he watched the flames slowly grow again after the huge pile of joss papers nearly smothered them.

Wu Xingzi followed his line of sight, biting his lip a few times yet still not saying a word. He had pretty much never spoken to Man Yue in private before, and now that he had an idea of why he was here, Wu Xingzi's palms grew clammy with sweat.

Man Yue didn't leave him in the lurch for too long. With a broad, honest smile, he said, "Do you have any time to spare for a chat, Mr. Wu?"

Wu Xingzi blinked. He first shook his head fiercely, then nodded vigorously. "I have the time. Have you eaten yet, Vice General Man?"

"I ate a little." Man Yue looked up at the sky. The sun was making its way toward the horizon, and it would set in a couple of hours. "However, I'm in a hurry to return to the capital. I'm afraid that I won't have the opportunity to share a meal with you, Mr. Wu."

"Ah, I see..." Wu Xingzi nodded. He hesitated for a moment. "Would Vice General Man like to visit my humble home for something to drink, then?"

This time, Man Yue did not refuse. "I'll have to trouble you then, Mr. Wu." With a surprising deftness for such a round man, he bent down and tidied up all the offerings, placing them in the basket and holding it in his hand before gesturing at Wu Xingzi to go ahead. "I'll walk with you."

"Thank you. You're too courteous..." Wu Xingzi cupped his hands together. He wanted to take the basket of offerings, but, with agile movements, Man Yue prevented him from doing so several times. Although nothing was said, Wu Xingzi could see a decisiveness in Man Yue's chubby, smiling face that did not allow for any refusal. He was Guan Shanjin's right-hand man, after all; he naturally carried himself in an imposing manner that made it difficult to defy him. Wu Xingzi rubbed his nose and made no further attempts.

The walk home took an hour. During their journey, Man Yue did not speak a single word. This silence flustered Wu Xingzi, and he did not even realize that he had started to walk with his arms and legs swinging in unison. When he finally pushed the door to his house open, he exhaled forcefully, and did not feel so lost anymore.

"Please come in, Vice General Man. It's just a small place, so there's not much I can offer. I hope you don't mind." Wu Xingzi could now finally take the basket from Man Yue. His entire being felt relieved. After placing the basket on the table, he wiped the chair with his sleeve, warmly inviting Man Yue to take a seat. "I haven't been back in a very long time, and I don't have any tea leaves prepared. However, there is hot water—could you please make do with that?"

"Don't go to all that trouble, Mr. Wu. I just want to talk to you for a little while. Please, take a seat as well." Man Yue stopped Wu Xingzi from rushing around. His broad, plump hands somehow managed to push Wu Xingzi lightly onto a chair without startling him or making him stumble.

Wu Xingzi was a little stunned as he sat facing Man Yue. The vice general was sitting up very properly, giving off a rather noble air. He lowered his head halfway, as if arranging his thoughts, and it took him a few moments before he spoke. "May I know what you have in mind for the future, Mr. Wu?"

What I have in mind? Wu Xingzi gazed at Man Yue. His mouth fell open, but he did not know what to say. He did not understand what Man Yue meant.

Perhaps realizing how lost Wu Xingzi was, Man Yue smiled in a soothing manner. "Do you plan on remaining in Qingcheng County, or will you be traveling to the capital?" he clarified.

"I...I plan on going to the capital, just to take a look," Wu Xingzi replied, his head sagging.

"Is that so?" Man Yue sighed before he continued. "You must be puzzled about what my plans are. I appeared rather suddenly in Qingcheng County."

"Yes." Wu Xingzi shot Man Yue a swift glance, his expression somewhat embarrassed. Man Yue had seen right through him. However, he truly could not understand Man Yue's intentions whatsoever.

"If I have to put it into words, I'm here for the general," Man Yue said frankly.

Wu Xingzi's thin shoulders jerked violently, nearly burying his head into his chest.

"The general does not know that I've come to see you, Mr. Wu," Man Yue said. "There are simply some things I'd like to speak to you about."

So Guan Shanjin didn't know... Wu Xingzi could not tell if he felt relieved or disappointed. He wrung at his clothes and wiped away the sweat that had gathered on his palms. He lifted his head, giving Man Yue a faint smile. "Please go ahead, Vice General Man."

Man Yue studied Wu Xingzi for a moment. "Mr. Wu, you must have heard about the general and Mr. Lu from Manager Rancui, yes?"

Although it was a question, he sounded very certain.

Wu Xingzi shifted uneasily in his seat. Drinking half a cup of warm water in a single mouthful, he feebly acknowledged Man Yue's question.

"What do you think about it, Mr. Wu?"

What did he think about it? Wu Xingzi's brows knitted slightly as he looked at Man Yue, feeling extremely perplexed. This man was Guan Shanjin's confidant—why had he come all this way to ask him about this?

However, after he thought through it carefully, Wu Xingzi understood. Man Yue was a highly trusted confidant of Guan Shanjin, so he naturally would come up with plans for him. Now that Guan Shanjin had finally confessed and exchanged vows of devotion with his beloved after such a long time, Man Yue would definitely not want to disturb them.

Wu Xingzi understood his position in all of this. He quickly adjusted his expression and spoke solemnly to Man Yue. "Don't worry, Vice General Man. I am not a tactless person. I understand that Haiwang...er, the general and Mr. Lu are happy with each other, and I will never come between them. If you do not have faith in my promise, then...then I won't go to the capital."

Despite his complete and utter sincerity, Wu Xingzi still felt a slight squeeze around his heart; he even felt a little breathless. He rubbed at his chest instinctively. When his eyes met Man Yue's, he nervously dropped his hand, moving it behind his back.

Mixed emotions stirred within Man Yue. He had always been an intelligent man. Although he didn't dare claim to be a master hiding in the shadows, he felt like he wasn't *un*like one. Who could have imagined that Wu Xingzi could give him such a slap in the face? A person's heart truly was a mystery. Somehow, Man Yue understood how Guan Shanjin had fallen for this old fellow.

Anyone with a clear set of eyes could see Wu Xingzi's feelings for Guan Shanjin. Man Yue also had Hei-er's close observations of the adviser to factor in, making him all the more confident in Wu Xingzi's heart. However, he never expected that this old fellow could promise to withdraw from the relationship so decisively, as if he had never had feelings for Guan Shanjin at all.

Man Yue had no choice but to adjust his approach. "I'm afraid you've misunderstood me, Mr. Wu. I am not trying to persuade you to stay in Qingcheng County, but the opposite. I earnestly wish to see you in the capital."

"Why is that?" Stunned, Wu Xingzi blinked rapidly at Man Yue. Was this a test? He blushed faintly, his embarrassment becoming even more obvious. Man Yue could clearly tell he had feelings for Guan Shanjin; he must be deliberately testing him.

With this in mind, Wu Xingzi responded even more seriously, "Vice General Man, I understand that you're still worried. However, I can't make the general fall for me—a melon forced off its vine is not as sweet. There were never any promises between the general and me, and our relationship has always been casual. We have merely returned to our proper paths. The reason I actually want to go to the capital is the Peng Society gathering..." Wu Xingzi scratched his nose in embarrassment. "There are so many talented and handsome men in the capital, so imagine the number of pengornises... I mean, the number of Peng Society members! After all, I'm just an ordinary man."

Man Yue looked directly at Wu Xingzi, unable to speak a word he had been planning to say. He had finally heard for himself how passionate Wu Xingzi was about pengornises. He began to pity Guan Shanjin for having vomited so much blood for nothing. He had nearly lost his life, yet all his beloved could think about was other cocks.

"You... You've not considered meeting the general in the capital?" Man Yue asked, unwilling to give up.

Yes, but only secretly. He didn't dare tell anyone, especially not Man Yue. The smile on the vice general's face had already faded away, and his expression clouded over. Man Yue's serene gaze directed at Wu Xingzi disconcerted him, making him squirm in his seat.

"Mr. Wu, I'll be honest—I didn't come here because of the general. That was just an excuse," Man Yue lied, his expression perfectly composed. He had given the matter a great deal of thought before deciding to come and see what Wu Xingzi's feelings were. He had not expected to make such a big mess of things. If Wu Xingzi decided against going to the capital because of him, Man Yue would truly no longer be able to show his face to Guan Shanjin.

From what he understood of Wu Xingzi, his flight to the capital had been simply to avoid Guan Shanjin's pursuit. However, since Guan Shanjin had retreated, there was no longer a need for Wu Xingzi to go to the capital—especially since the position of county adviser was still unfilled. He had imagined that Wu Xingzi probably planned to stay here in Qingcheng County.

He had never expected that Wu Xingzi would still plan on visiting the capital. He was completely disregarding the script they had written for him! Man Yue furtively wiped away the sweat beading on his forehead.

He's not here because of Guan Shanjin? Wu Xingzi looked confused. He didn't understand where Man Yue was coming from. It flustered him more than facing Rancui!

"I see. May I know what you wish to talk to me about, Vice General Man?"

"I'd just like to remind you that a man's heart is difficult to guess, Mr. Wu, and what you see may not be the truth." Man Yue deeply regretted his decision to come and see Wu Xingzi. This old fellow might have seemed honest and simple, but he had quite the independent streak. "The Peng Society gathering may leave you disappointed. After all, a pengornis and its owner may not be well matched."

"That's true..." Wu Xingzi nodded along. He wasn't wrong—the pengornis illustrations often did not match the portraits of their owners. Some men looked fair, slender, and clean, but their cocks were curved and dark; some men were tall and muscular, but had delicate, demure dicks. Men whose members looked as mouthwatering as the rest of them—men like Guan Shanjin   were a rare sight indeed.

Despite this, Wu Xingzi was still very interested in attending the Peng Society's gathering. He finally understood the reason Man Yue had come looking for him.

"Vice General Man, do you plan on attending the gathering as well?"

This question truly floored Man Yue. He put on an enigmatic smile, neither confirming nor denying it.

"So, you came to me because of the Peng Society gathering?" Now that he had an idea, Wu Xingzi felt a lot more at ease, and he revealed a friendly smile. "Don't worry, the meeting is administered by Manager Rancui. It'll just be like sailing on a large vessel—safe and reliable. If there's anything you're worried about, why don't you tell me? I can help you pass it along to the manager."

Man Yue finally understood why Guan Shanjin was always losing when it came to Wu Xingzi. He himself couldn't figure out how he'd managed to dig himself into this hole.

Nevertheless, he still beamed and cupped his hands together. "Thank you, Mr. Wu. We'll see each other at the gathering."

"Yes, yes. I'll see you there." Wu Xingzi cupped his hands in response. He thought for a moment, then added in concern, "What sort of man do you like, Vice General Man? Perhaps I can ask Manager Rancui to keep an eye out for you."

As face after handsome face appeared in his head, Man Yue pursed his lips. "I'm not particular."

"Hmph. How articulate, Vice General Man." A gentle yet sarcastic voice floated through the window. Man Yue cocked a brow and looked over to see a gorgeous face.

"Manager Rancui." Man Yue cupped his hands toward him in greeting. He'd already heard his footsteps before he spoke, but he chose not to expose him. After all, what he'd planned on discussing with Wu Xingzi had already gone out of the window, so he wasn't worried about Rancui's eavesdropping.

Leaning lazily against the window, the beautiful man narrowed his eyes enchantingly at him. "I had no idea that Vice General Man was so interested in the Peng Society gathering. I thought once you returned to the capital, you and the general might both die from court matters."

"I'm afraid I'll have to disappoint you, Manager Rancui." Man Yue smiled his customary honest smile; it was truly an eyesore for Rancui.

Rancui did not insist on pushing the issue. Instead, he waved his hand and went with the flow of the conversation. "Of course, the Peng Society welcomes your attendance, Vice General Man. I'll also try my best to invite the gentlemen you have been in contact with—I'll make you feel right at home."

This little fox! Man Yue spat internally, but he did not reveal his emotions. Putting on an appropriate expression of anticipation and bashfulness, he cupped his hands together, thanking him.

Now that Rancui was here, Man Yue did not plan on staying any longer. After their little verbal sparring match, Man Yue bade the two men farewell.

Once Man Yue was a long distance away, Rancui casually informed Wu Xingzi, "I heard that the general's inner energy had fluctuated badly—apparently, he vomited three liters of blood. Is that true?"

Wu Xingzi froze. Choking on the water in his mouth, he coughed violently, tears welling up in his eyes. Finally, he managed to catch his breath. "Haiwang vomited blood? Is he all right? Has he recuperated? Why would he suddenly vomit blood?" he asked anxiously.

"Did Vice General Man not tell you?" asked Rancui, clicking his tongue. Leaving the window, he walked through the door and sat down across from Wu Xingzi. He still looked rather lackadaisical, but there was a trace of seriousness around his brows. "If you're concerned about him, shall we gather some information once we're in the capital?"

Wu Xingzi hurriedly nodded. He paced a few circles in his house, his expression changing several times. Seeming to have come to a decision, he gritted his teeth and looked at Rancui. "Why don't we leave tomorrow morning?"

"Why don't we?" Rancui poured himself a cup of water, answering with a smile. His charming eyes caught sight of Wu Xingzi exhaling in relief before growing anxious again, and he sighed silently.

A cool, subtle scent wafted through the air. Wu Xingzi twitched his nose slightly in his sleep. Blearily opening his drowsy eyes, he peered out through the bed curtains.

The moonlight outside was the color of water, cascading into the room along with the cold. Wu Xingzi shivered, pushing himself up slowly. Just as he was about to pull the canopy open to go close the window, somebody caught his wrist.

It was a hand that looked carved from nephrite jade. The fingers were perfectly sculpted, and the structure of the hand was impeccable. A few calluses from wielding weapons were faintly visible; the skin felt coarse despite how smooth it looked.

Even though it was only a hand, Wu Xingzi recognized whose it was.

A shudder ran through him as he fully awoke. Trembling, his eyes followed along the hand and up the arm. Inch by inch, his eyes traveled the strong and muscular arm shadowed by the night until

he caught sight of the face that he had been dreaming of all this time. Wu Xingzi inhaled sharply.

"H-Haiwang..."

"Hmm?" A slight smile appeared on the general's face like a flower blooming in spring. Wu Xingzi's heart skipped a beat.

Gulping, Wu Xingzi blinked rapidly, afraid that he was still dreaming. An old saying came to mind: What you think during the day, you dream of at night. Ever since he'd arrived in the capital a few days ago, all he could think of was Guan Shanjin. He was even going to have to avoid the man at the Peng Society gathering. It would make sense to dream of him at night.

"Y-you... How did you...?" Wu Xingzi's head teemed with questions. However, when the words came to his mouth, he was unable to say anything. He sat there staring foolishly at Guan Shanjin, not even daring to touch him.

Guan Shanjin was a lot more straightforward. He leaned toward Wu Xingzi, soundlessly gathering the older man into his embrace and patting his thin back in comfort. "I've missed you."

Wu Xingzi had been well taken care of lately. He had filled out a little—his sharp chin rounded out, and his shoulder blades that used to jut out severely no longer protruded as much. As Guan Shanjin hugged him, he even felt a little softer.

Guan Shanjin picked up Wu Xingzi's hand, placing it by his lips. He licked at each pink, tender fingertip one by one, finally placing the tip of the pinky finger into his mouth. His soft, flexible tongue curled around the digit, taking Wu Xingzi's breath away.

"Don't, Haiwang... Don't be like this..." His face blushing a bright red, Wu Xingzi wanted to free his hand from Guan Shanjin's mouth. However, Guan Shanjin would not allow him to get his way. The arm wrapped around his thin waist tightened further, pulling him flush against Guan Shanjin's chest. Guan Shanjin lightly smacked the area where his torso and buttocks met a couple of times with his palm, quickly getting the older man to stop squirming. He curled into Guan Shanjin's arms and dared not move anymore.

"I've missed you," Guan Shanjin repeated. His straight, white teeth nibbled lightly on the knuckle of Wu Xingzi's little finger, sending tingles throughout Wu Xingzi's body and making him bashful. He bowed his head and didn't reply, trying to distract Guan Shanjin by nuzzling his cheek against his shoulder.

He had missed him too.

Guan Shanjin clearly had no intention of waiting for Wu Xingzi's response. He released his little finger—red from him sucking on it—and nibbled his way up Wu Xingzi's palm and wrist. After leaving a few reddish marks on his wrist, he lightly pressed the man in his arms down onto the bed. His dark, clouded eyes locked onto Wu Xingzi as they slowly turned bloodshot.

Uncomfortable under his stare, Wu Xingzi tried to sit up. It had been so long since they had last seen each other, and there were many things he wanted to say to Guan Shanjin. However, slipping into his bed in the middle of the night like this, the general obviously did not plan to spend any time chatting.

After pushing Wu Xingzi down, Guan Shanjin swiftly stripped Wu Xingzi out of his clothes. As the old fellow cried out in surprise, the general lowered his head toward his prick.

"Ah, Haiwang, you..." Wu Xingzi hurriedly reached out, about to push the younger man away. But Guan Shanjin had already enveloped Wu Xingzi's cock into his warm, wet mouth, slowly sucking on him.

"*Oh*..." Wu Xingzi's hips jerked, his entire body turning into jelly. Tears pricked his eyes, his blush spreading from his face to his entire body.

He could no longer recall exactly how long it had been since he and Guan Shanjin had slept with each other. At first, Wu Xingzi had only had a tryst in mind, but it soon became a persistent entanglement with the Lanling Prince of penises. The sex was relentless, day and night, and his body was now utterly familiar with the act.

The general's mouth was hot and soft, and Wu Xingzi felt as though he was submerged in boiling water. Soon enough, he was moaning in pleasure. Guan Shanjin wrapped his lips around Wu Xingzi's cock, massaging it with his slightly rough tongue as he went. When he reached the base, Wu Xingzi found that the head of his cock was now somewhere even tighter and hotter, and the convulsions there clenched down on him. The feeling made Wu Xingzi tremble. His legs flailed as he gripped the thin blanket, soft moans spilling from his throat.

Guan Shanjin's tongue now slid back up, saliva combining with the fluid leaking from the tip of Wu Xingzi's cock. Sucking sounds filled the air as the tip of his tongue reached the head, twirling around the tip of Wu Xingzi's prick before lapping right at the top and digging into the slit.

"H-Haiwang, ah, ahh... Slow down, slow down..." Wu Xingzi lay there feebly, his body jolting. He tried to push away Guan Shanjin's insistent mouth with a trembling hand; however, the general raised his alluring eyes and gave him a smile, making Wu Xingzi collapse weakly. Sprawled on the bed, Wu Xingzi panted so hard that his eyes teared up. His cock shivered from the nonstop stimulation. He was leaking precum continuously, but Guan Shanjin swallowed it all down immediately, not leaving a single drop behind. But it wasn't enough for him. He wrapped his lips around the head and sucked harshly.

"Ahh!" Wu Xingzi shrieked, his round little toes curling up and digging into the bed. His feet kicked out a few times as a small spurt

of fluid erupted from his cock. If Guan Shanjin hadn't squeezed the base of his dick just in time, Wu Xingzi would have come all over himself.

Still, the sensation was not pleasant. He was about to reach his peak, yet he was held back from it so forcefully; tingles ran through his body and permeated his soul. The heat inside of him had nowhere to escape, left to simmer within his limbs. It felt as though even his fingernails were screaming with lust. He writhed on the bed, mewling his pleas for Guan Shanjin to release him.

Guan Shanjin laughed softly, sucking at his cock. "My dirty darling, we've only just started. You can't hold on any longer?"

His teeth scraped lightly against Wu Xingzi's sensitive cock. Wu Xingzi jerked, his hand fumbling about on his smooth, pale belly.

Guan Shanjin refused to let him go, gently and carefully sucking on Wu Xingzi's little pengornis. Periodically, he would lap at it with his tongue, drilling into the small slit at the top. Guan Shanjin's tongue pressed quite forcefully, and when he backed off, the little hole would gape open slightly, exposing soft, tender skin and fluids. It made Guan Shanjin want to nibble on it.

Lavished with such wanton affections, the head of Wu Xingzi's cock swelled up, as red as an overripe peach. A deep thrill ran through Wu Xingzi's body with each spurt of precum, making him twitch continuously on the bed. However, Guan Shanjin's grip at the base of his shaft did not relent, and there was no way he could come. Layer upon layer of pleasure built up until Wu Xingzi hiccupped with sobs, his face covered in tears.

It was as if he stood on the edge of a mountain with an abyss stretching below him on either side. There was only room enough for one foot to just barely support him, and each time he swayed, he was pulled back. He didn't know how to escape from this place.

Guan Shanjin was still servicing him. However, this time, he no longer licked at him, just sucked his cock relentlessly. Wu Xingzi couldn't even cry out. He was swept away in convulsions, his eyes rolling back slightly as he stared at the ceiling.

Guan Shanjin knew exactly how to suck Wu Xingzi's cock. Although it was not that big, it was still the size of an average man's dick. When he swallowed it all the way down to the root, the head would shallowly enter his throat. It was not to the point that Guan Shanjin felt uncomfortable, but he still felt something when he swallowed; the muscles there twitched and pressed down tightly on Wu Xingzi's leaking, sensitive head.

After sucking a couple of times, Guan Shanjin brought up his hot, rough palm to play with Wu Xingzi's balls, and he would repeat this cycle of sucking and fondling. Wu Xingzi felt his soul was about to escape his body, his hips jerking nonstop. Crying hoarsely, he begged Guan Shanjin to let him come. However, the general refused, switching between just sucking the head and swallowing Wu Xingzi's entire cock into his mouth. The old man shuddered so much that he almost bucked the general off of him. Guan Shanjin casually placed a hand on his tender belly, pressing him onto the bed and not allowing him to move. Wu Xingzi could only kick his fair, slender legs out in response.

"Haiwang... Haiwang..." Wu Xingzi gasped for air, constantly pleading as he cried out Guan Shanjin's name. Finally, the general let out a quiet laugh, releasing his grip on the base of Wu Xingzi's cock and sucking harshly on the head.

"*Ahh—!*" Wu Xingzi clutched at the thin blanket, his slim waist tensing up as he kicked out wildly. Thick, white cum finally burst from his cock into Guan Shanjin's mouth. The general choked slightly, his charming eyes misting over a little. His throat bobbed as he swallowed everything Wu Xingzi gave him.

The old quail stared blankly at the smile curling around Guan Shanjin's face; his red lips were shiny from Wu Xingzi's fluids. Wu Xingzi had yet to recover from the intense pleasure that had crashed into him, and his body still twitched and jerked. Tears slipped down from the corners of his eyes and landed on the soft pillow beneath his head.

Guan Shanjin swallowed a few more times before slowly leaning in. He opened his mouth slightly. "Take a look—did I swallow it all down?" he teased.

Wu Xingzi's jaw fell open, but no words came out. He obligingly peered into Guan Shanjin's mouth. His pink tongue contrasted against white teeth, and his lips were full and soft, still wet from sucking cock. Guan Shanjin was so handsome that even his mouth was beautiful. Although Wu Xingzi could not see clearly in the middle of night, it was still alluring enough to melt his heart.

Furthermore, this mouth had just sucked on his pengornis, refusing to let go... Wu Xingzi came back to his senses with a jerk, hurriedly averting his eyes.

"How is it?" Guan Shanjin refused to back down, drawing even closer. The scent of white sandalwood and orange blossom tinged the air Wu Xingzi breathed. He had only just managed to clear his head, but it turned muddled once again.

Seeming very satisfied with the state he'd left Wu Xingzi in, Guan Shanjin chuckled quietly. He pressed his lips against Wu Xingzi's, kissing him with all his might, taking his bottom lip between his teeth and nipping it. He gave Wu Xingzi's upper lip the same treatment before finally licking his lips apart, forcing his tongue inside. He twined his tongue with Wu Xingzi's timid one in a fiery kiss that was both deep and hungry. Unable to withstand it, Wu Xingzi pushed Guan Shanjin's shoulder, only for his wrist to be caught and held down. The kiss only turned more violent; it was as if Guan Shanjin wanted to swallow Wu Xingzi whole.

Once the kiss ended, Wu Xingzi panted, his breathing as deep and harsh as a bellows. The saliva he was unable to swallow trickled from the corner of his mouth, forming a thin thread between Guan Shanjin's lips and his. Smiling faintly, the general licked it away with his pink tongue.

"My dirty boy," Guan Shanjin said. The general seemed to love addressing him this way in bed, and the lilt in the words scratched at Wu Xingzi's heart. "Have you missed me? Hmm?"

After each question, Guan Shanjin kissed him, causing a blush to spread through Wu Xingzi. Even his hole started to twitch a little. He tried to turn his head, only for Guan Shanjin to hold onto it and initiate another deep kiss. Wu Xingzi felt his tongue ache from the force of it.

"I missed you..." He had missed the general quite a bit, and after this tireless provocation, Wu Xingzi's thoughts spilled quickly. He shyly reached up and clasped his arms around Guan Shanjin's neck, his lips brushing past the general's perfectly formed ear. "So did my hole."

Guan Shanjin's pupils constricted at the blatant invitation. He no longer held himself back.

Wu Xingzi was thin and fair. When the moon shone through the canopy onto his body, it looked as if his smooth, pale skin glowed. Desire slowly spread through his body, bringing a pink flush with it.

Wu Xingzi shivered, his mouth going completely dry. He tried his best to swallow, the tip of his tongue still aching. Guan Shanjin had used too much force when he kissed him, and Wu Xingzi felt like he was bleeding.

The general slowly removed his clothes, the snow-white inner robe sliding off his broad shoulders to reveal powerful muscles. They were not excessive, but perfectly showcased his fitness. Wu Xingzi gulped, so enchanted by the aura of masculinity in front of him that he could barely breathe. Greedily and somewhat foolishly, his eyes followed the sculpted lines of muscle—from Guan Shanjin's wide shoulders to his narrow waist, from his abdomen to his... *Oh!* What a magnificent specimen this was before him!

It was not clear if it was deliberate or unintentional, but Guan Shanjin's trousers were not fully removed. He had only tugged them down halfway, perfectly revealing his slightly curved, hefty, pleasingly veiny, and rather savage-looking Lanling Prince of a pengornis.

Wu Xingzi's entire body itched—his fingers, his throat, his hole. The channel within him tingled so badly that he desperately craved for something to fill it and soothe the ache.

Guan Shanjin looked at him with a defiant gaze that held an animalistic savagery. His broad palm gripped Wu Xingzi's slender ankle, then caressed the sole of his foot.

Wu Xingzi was not a child, nor was he a pampered young master. The soles of his feet were rough and coarse, the skin a little thick. Although his toes were round, they had a few calluses. His feet made it obvious that he'd spent a life in poverty, and he felt rather ashamed to be caressed like this.

"Ah, don't play with them," he protested softly, wanting to pull away. Guan Shanjin seemed to have many tricks up his sleeve tonight, refusing to go straight to the main event. Wu Xingzi felt rather impatient. His hole twitched slightly, and he could vaguely feel it getting wet.

However, it seemed as though Guan Shanjin liked his feet very much. He massaged the sole firmly, before sliding his hand up to stroke the calluses. Finally, he pressed a kiss to the instep, making Wu Xingzi blush a bright red. What did Guan Shanjin want? Why was he suddenly playing with Wu Xingzi's feet?

"Haiwang..."

"Hmm?" Guan Shanjin raised a brow, smiling as he caught Wu Xingzi's other foot and pressed the two soles together. "You owe me this—it's been too long."

"Ahh..." Wu Xingzi trembled, turning his head away.

The next moment, Wu Xingzi understood what exactly Guan Shanjin wanted him to do. The general held the soles of Wu Xingzi's feet around his cock and began to move them up and down.

"Come on, use a little strength and conquer it, all right?" Guan Shanjin let go with a chuckle, staring at Wu Xingzi.

The cock between his soles was thick and scalding hot, the vein on it pulsing slightly. Wu Xingzi could not describe how he felt, except that it was pleasant. His whole body blushed red, his eyes shining as he stared at Guan Shanjin. Gritting his teeth, he carefully rubbed his feet against Guan Shanjin's dick.

This was his first time engaging in such an act. His movements were clumsy and slow, his toes nudging against the head of Guan Shanjin's cock with each stroke. In no time, the tip was leaking sticky fluid; it felt as though flames burned under his feet, like ants biting his soles. It ignited the desire in his heart.

Guan Shanjin seemed to be enjoying it as well. His eyes were half lidded, his thick, long eyelashes casting shadows upon his face. His breaths became heavier, and he was no longer satisfied with Wu Xingzi's cautious movements. He grabbed Wu Xingzi's feet and controlled the rhythm himself.

"Ah... Mm... Ahh... H-Haiwang, slow down a little... Slow down," Wu Xingzi begged. He was only using his feet to grind against

Guan Shanjin's cock, but for some reason, he felt as though the shaft was piercing right through him.

Squelching sounds resounded through the entire room. It felt as though steam was pouring from Wu Xingzi's ears. Unable to withstand the heat, he tried to pull his legs back. This time, Guan Shanjin went along with his wishes, releasing his feet. Once Wu Xingzi moved his feet away from the source of heat, the fluids on them cooled down very quickly. Wu Xingzi curled his toes uneasily, tingles spreading up his calves to his naughty little hole, which leaked continuously; a huge wet spot stained the mattress.

The old quail was so mortified that the tips of his ears turned a dark red. He dared not even glance at Guan Shanjin, only using his feet to stroke the man's thighs.

"You filthy old thing," Guan Shanjin teased him. Grasping Wu Xingzi's plump buttocks, he pulled the older man onto his crotch. His stiff, hard cock rubbed against the outside of Wu Xingzi's wet hole. Without waiting for the old fellow to urge him on, he pushed his way into Wu Xingzi in a single breath, aided by the juices flowing out of him.

"Ah... *Ah!*" Wu Xingzi cried out in pain. He had not been penetrated in several months, and his hole was as tight as it had ever been. Having such a long, thick cock buried inside him to the hilt made him shudder.

Guan Shanjin had shed all the tenderness from before, and he fucked into Wu Xingzi brutally, his balls loudly smacking against Wu Xingzi's perineum with every thrust. A rough thumb stroked the edge of his stretched hole. Occasionally, Guan Shanjin would even pinch the flesh there, making Wu Xingzi cry out and twist his hips. He tried to escape, only to be held down and forcefully fucked further.

The night had just started, and the general was already torturing him. Guan Shanjin seemed to think that Wu Xingzi's panting breaths were too loud; he held his waist with one hand and covered his nose and mouth with the other. Guan Shanjin fucked him loudly and furiously, and it wasn't long before the old quail began to feel faint. His body trembled nonstop, and he feebly grabbed at the hand on his face.

"Look at how hungry you are, sucking on me so tightly..." Guan Shanjin continued to restrict Wu Xingzi's breathing. Fluids gushed from Wu Xingzi's slick, wet channel like a river, and he began to convulse from the general's brutal pounding.

No matter how Wu Xingzi tried to appease him, Guan Shanjin still fucked him savagely. The huge head of his cock perfectly reached the deepest part of Wu Xingzi every time, causing the blood in his body to rush there. It was both painful and pleasurable; with his eyes and nose leaking tears and snot, Wu Xingzi was fucked in and out of unconsciousness. Guan Shanjin's hand still firmly covered his mouth and nose, and it felt like he was going to be fucked to death.

When spasms once again shook Wu Xingzi's body, his eyes rolling back in orgasm, Guan Shanjin finally released his hand.

Wu Xingzi's head tilted back and his mouth gaped open. His tongue lolled out of his mouth halfway as he stared at the top of the bed with wild eyes. He was unable to utter a sound, his thin back tensed up like a tightly strung bow; after this stiffness persisted for a moment, he finally released a hoarse whimper. Juices spilled from his hole and his cock spurted, spattering his belly with filth. His legs flailed a few times on the bed before he collapsed, twitching continuously.

"That's all you can take?" Guan Shanjin smiled as he looked at Wu Xingzi. Beads of sweat had formed on his forehead, and a few strands of his black hair clung to his neck. Against the moonlight, he looked as enchanting as a demon. "Shall I make sure you won't be able to forget me for the rest of your life?"

He whispered this directly into Wu Xingzi's ear. The old quail was surprised to find himself still able to hear him so clearly.

Guan Shanjin did not need to hear a reply. He lightly tapped at Wu Xingzi's belly with a finger and softly laughed. "Here, this time I'll fuck you all the way to here. Would you like that?"

This spot was beyond the depths of Wu Xingzi's channel. Before he even had the time to calm down, he already knew what Guan Shanjin had in mind for him. He could not decide if he felt fear or great anticipation as he cried and shook his head in shyness and fright.

But Guan Shanjin's appetite had already been stimulated. How could he let go of the older man so easily? He held onto Wu Xingzi's twitching waist, entering him with a *squelch*.

Wu Xingzi mewled softly, a cry that curled its way into Guan Shanjin's heart. His alluring eyes darkened, and his actions became even more ruthless. It was as though he wanted to impale himself right through Wu Xingzi, so he could keep him within his grasp, instead of letting him run off for another few months.

Guan Shanjin's long, thick cock had its way with Wu Xingzi's tight, slick hole, every trembling inch of his ass stretched open. Fucked into shuddering, Wu Xingzi felt like a soft sleeve just for Guan Shanjin's pleasure.

Aiming right where Wu Xingzi was sensitive, Guan Shanjin jerked his hips a few times, pushing himself even deeper. A faint bulge jutted up under the skin of Wu Xingzi's belly as Guan Shanjin pounded furiously inside.

Wu Xingzi cried piteously. Touching his belly, he could feel how much force Guan Shanjin exerted as the head of his cock pushed in.

The juices leaking from his hole spilled all over the two of them. The damp spot on the blanket was wet enough to be wrung out, yet Guan Shanjin had no intention of letting Wu Xingzi go.

"It's too deep... Please, please..." Wu Xingzi shuddered as he begged for mercy. He was about to be pierced through.

Cum spurted from Wu Xingzi's cock once again. This time, it was as thin as water, a pathetically small amount. The slit at the tip of his cock gaped open, trembling slightly.

The fluids from their joining had foamed up from the friction, but the general still held him down, fucking him as he pleased. Only when he made Wu Xingzi piss himself again did he abruptly pull out and flip Wu Xingzi over before thrusting back inside.

Wu Xingzi could not even cry out now. His tongue hung out of his mouth, his face slack. The endless ecstasy left his mind completely blank. He reached another climax when he could clearly feel Guan Shanjin's cock thrusting into his belly, trembling everywhere and letting out a shriek.

Wu Xingzi had lost count of the number of times Guan Shanjin fucked him that night. He fainted and woke up several times; in the end, he could no longer tell whether he was dreaming. Guan Shanjin held him down on the bed, filling him with enough cum to bulge his stomach out as if he was pregnant. His face a bright red, he lay weakly in bed, shivering. Guan Shanjin cradled his head, kissing him until he could not breathe. This time, when he fainted again, he did not wake...

"Ahh!" Wu Xingzi jerked up from the bed. Since he'd slept on the edge of the bed, he ended up tumbling to the ground. Landing on the floor, his head started spinning, and half his body went numb

from the impact. He hissed in pain and rubbed his eyes, looking blankly at the unfamiliar room.

Wu Xingzi could detect a faint scent. When he recognized what it was, all the blood rushed to his face.

Looking around him, he finally realized that this was Rancui's property in the capital, and Rancui had lent it to him as lodging. He had only been sleeping in this room for around a week, and he had yet to get used to it—he did not recognize it immediately.

"I..." Of course, after recognizing his surroundings, what was most urgent was the wet sensation clinging to his lower body. Supporting his old waist that ached from the fall, Wu Xingzi slowly stood up and stumbled back onto the bed. Hiding beneath the blankets, he took off his pants.

He was alone in the room. The familiar scent of white sandalwood and orange blossom was nonexistent; only his own scent, gentle yet bleak, could be detected.

What had happened last night was only a wet dream...

Wu Xingzi covered his face, thinking about dying right then and there. He was forty years old! Even when he was a teenager, he hadn't had wet dreams. This one had been so indescribably intense. He was only in the same city as Guan Shanjin—was he unable to let go of the man, even in his dreams?

Ah... Wu Xingzi, Wu Xingzi, he scolded himself. He saw that the sky outside had already brightened. Mint and Osmanthus would soon carry in a basin of water for him to freshen up. If he didn't quickly get rid of the evidence, and put some new pants on, having the dream wouldn't be the only thing he'd be embarrassed about.

He sneakily balled up his dirty trousers. Although he didn't want to give up this pair of pants, it would be difficult to secretly wash them in such an unfamiliar place. It would be much easier to just throw them away.

He tucked the pants firmly into one corner of his trunk. As he did not have many clothes, the trunk was not full; he was not afraid of getting the clean clothes dirty. Next, he took out clean undergarments and trousers. Wu Xingzi finally breathed a sigh of relief.

He could hear the girls greeting him from outside the room. He quickly dressed himself before hurrying over to open the doors for them to come in.

In Mint's hands was a basin of water, and Osmanthus carried a box of food. They greeted Wu Xingzi with smiling eyes, then deftly arranged the things they'd brought on the table.

After she put the basin down, Mint's little nose twitched. "Hmm?" She seemed to have smelled something, her little face a picture of puzzlement. Wu Xingzi's heart pounded anxiously, the tips of his ears turning red.

Due to the dream, he had woken up a little late. After dealing with his semen-stained trousers, he'd had no time to open the windows to get rid of any smell. A vague scent of photinia lingered in the bedroom.[2]

"Jiejie, what's wrong?" Osmanthus asked, opening the box of food. The aroma of plain porridge and other dishes quickly filled the air, and that distinctive smell soon faded away.

Mint's nose twitched again before she shook her head. "It's nothing. I probably just imagined it." After all, the blooming season for photinia had been over for a while now, and there weren't even any in the garden. Where would the smell have come from?

Wu Xingzi had nearly been scared to death. Rubbing his chest,

---

2   Specifically *Photinia serratifonia*, or Taiwanese photinia. *This tree's flowers are known for their semen-like smell.*

he forced himself to calm down. The next time he had a wet dream, he would make sure to open the windows as soon as he woke up.

The two girls didn't notice him acting a little oddly. "Master," they said brightly, "the Peng Society's gathering is today."

Their eyes lit up as they mentioned it—they were unable to conceal their curiosity.

It had been over a month since they arrived in the capital. Summer had come, but having lived their entire lives in the south, the girls had no issue acclimatizing to the northern summer. Their spirits were even higher, in fact, and they would drag Wu Xingzi all over the capital every day. Without realizing it, they had already explored many of the scenic spots in the city.

Wu Xingzi had also taken the opportunity to make more friends through the pigeon post, adding to the collection of pengornis pictures in his rattan case.

It had to be said that the capital was truly a remarkable place that produced many talented people. More importantly, the capital had a much larger population, making it easy to communicate through the pigeon post. The Peng Society was not very hidden in the city, and the size of its office was twice that of the Goose City branch.

Wu Xingzi's ranking of cocks in his collection—which was previously immovable—had experienced a number of changes in just one short month. Even Guan Shanjin's position as the Lanling Prince was in jeopardy. Before he went to bad last night, Wu Xingzi had held onto the illustration of Guan Shanjin's pengornis, comparing it side by side to another drawing he had received a couple of days ago. In the end, the victor was decided based on familiarity points.

If Guan Shanjin's pengornis was the Prince of Lanling—magnificent, gorgeous, and awe-inspiring—the new drawing was Murong Chong, another famous pretty face.

Its girth and length could not lose to Guan Shanjin's, and its overall appearance was a little more refined. Wu Xingzi was unsure if Rancui had given the artist instructions, but this pengornis picture was painted in color. The skin was as fair as a budding flower, while the cockhead was slightly darker, heavy, and full, like a ripe plum. The hole at the tip gaped a little, allowing a peek within. Devastatingly beautiful, it seemed as though a careless bite could leave it bleeding.

The vein running down the shaft was not as robust as Guan Shanjin's. It was less savage, but there was danger lurking behind it, like a needle wrapped in cotton. As he looked at the illustration, Wu Xingzi's mouth went dry, and he gulped down half the contents of his teapot to soothe his thirst.

His wet dream clearly had something to do with these two penis pictures! Before he had fallen asleep, he'd been wondering if Guan Shanjin would tear up this drawing of the Murong Chong of pengornises like he had the others...

As such thoughts drifted through his head, Wu Xingzi buried his face in his porridge, ignoring the side dishes. When his stomach was half full, he turned to the girls. "You young ladies shouldn't attend the gathering. I'll ask Hei-er to accompany me."

"We can't go?" Mint's lips curved downward, the cheer disappearing from her face.

Wu Xingzi shook his head. "It's improper for you to be there. The attendees are all men—there's no reason for girls to go."

"We want to look at beauties, too." Osmanthus pouted, looking at her sister and nodding firmly. "Master, don't worry, my sister and I will be good. I promise we won't make any trouble."

A few days ago, Manager Rancui said that the gathering of the Peng Society only took place once every two years, and it was by invitation only. The guests were all either noble and illustrious men, or great, honorable beauties. Their family backgrounds were all spotless, and their talents were remarkable. Ten years ago, they had even invited the ninth prince, who was known to be Great Xia's most beautiful man. The gathering that year was held at Linfeng Mansion, by the Guting River. It was said that half the capital had gathered outside in the hopes of catching a glimpse of the charming prince!

"I know that you're well-behaved girls, but..." Wu Xingzi faltered.

He knew the girls were curious, but a Peng Society gathering was, after all, not an ordinary gathering. It was an occasion to allow men looking for partners to get to know each other. Wu Xingzi could not help but feel that it would be very awkward to have two young girls there.

Seeing that he had no intention of giving in, Mint's and Osmanthus's shoulders drooped. They both hung their heads pitifully.

"Master, we understand. We won't be stubborn about it."

Wu Xingzi breathed a sigh of relief, but felt sorry at the same time. He took out a few copper coins from his pouch and handed them to Mint. "Didn't you want to try the sugar sculptures? Rancui said that news of the Peng Society gathering has spread through the entire city. This time, the gathering will be held at the Lianxiang Residence, and there's a fair outside. Why don't you go buy some sugar sculptures as a treat, and we'll meet back up when the gathering ends?"

As soon as he mentioned the sugar sculptures, the gloom over the girls' heads vanished, and their little faces filled with delight.

"Then, Master, you have to make sure you take a really good look at everyone this time," Mint advised Wu Xingzi like a wise adult as she tucked the copper coins into her little purse. "Manager Rancui says that the young masters he invited this time are not only out-standing in appearance and background, but they also..."

"They also...?" When Wu Xingzi saw how amused the girl looked, laughing like the cat who got the cream, he couldn't keep himself from ruffling Mint's hair.

Mint and Osmanthus exchanged a smile, lowering their voices and speaking at the same time: "Their pengornises have been carefully selected."

Pengornises... Wu Xingzi froze, his face blushing red. With a trembling voice, he asked, "Wh-wh-what... What are you saying? Y-you're little g-girls... D-don't...!" He sighed.

"It's what the manager said himself." Seeing Wu Xingzi's face flush a dark red, Osmanthus hurriedly wet a handkerchief to wipe his face.

Wu Xingzi didn't know what to say to the girls. He could only take the handkerchief and wipe his face vigorously, only stopping to take a breath when he'd nearly rubbed his skin raw.

Knowing that they had gone too far with teasing Wu Xingzi, Mint and Osmanthus stuck out their tongues. Obedient once more, they made no further mention of the Peng Society gathering and turned to help Wu Xingzi pick out his clothes. However, before they could open his trunk, Wu Xingzi stopped them. With evasive eyes, he chased the girls out of the bedroom, then collapsed weakly onto a chair, his back covered in cold sweat.

He finally managed to calm himself down, then made a clean sweep of the food on the table. He ate four bowls of rice porridge and emptied all the plates of food. Mixing the side dishes into the porridge, he finished everything. His appetite was as huge as ever, and he ate until his belly plumped up. With a hand supporting his back, he walked around the table to aid his digestion.

Their pengornises have been specially selected. Mint's clear voice echoed in his head. Wu Xingzi felt both bashful and abashed; he was also worried that the two girls had been led astray by Rancui.

He then remembered that the gathering would take place in four hours—and wondered if the Murong Chong of pengornises would be there. Bai-gongzi, who played the qin, might be there, too. During this month in the capital, when walking on the streets, Wu Xingzi had heard people discussing Bai-gongzi's skills. It made Wu Xingzi yearn to hear him play.

Wu Xingzi couldn't tell if what he felt was anticipation or excitement. Although Wu Xingzi had yet to digest his breakfast, he picked up a snack from the table and started eating again. He had always been thin, never putting on weight despite the immense amount he ate. Even when Wu Xingzi's stomach bulged from food, he still looked very slender. Pulling on a loose and elegant Confucian robe, he even looked like a delicate, fragile scholar.

Knitting his brows slightly, Hei-er stared at Wu Xingzi's belly for a moment, then handed him a red-tinted pill. "Master, this medication aids digestion—would you like to take it? The manager has invited the top chef in the capital to cook for the Peng Society gathering, and I don't want you to upset your stomach."

Hei-er's words were very direct. Wu Xingzi scratched his cheek and quietly thanked Hei-er before swallowing the pill. The pill had a refreshing taste to it and melted in his mouth; his stomach immediately settled.

Hei-er was meticulously considerate. Seeing that Wu Xingzi was still a little uncomfortable from overeating, he did not prepare a horse or carriage; instead, they walked to the Lianxiang Residence.

The journey was not far: It was about half an hour away. The summer sun was scorching hot, but it was completely unlike the humid, thick heat of the south. Sweating a little left them feeling revitalized rather than clammy, and Wu Xingzi was now in the mood to think about this spectacular Peng Society event.

A crowd had already begun to gather about a hundred steps away from the Lianxiang Residence. Wu Xingzi stared blankly at the fair in front of him, unable to resist rubbing at his eyes with his fists.

The Lianxiang Residence was a famous site in the capital. The courtyard was designed in the manner of the classical gardens of Jiangnan, with bridges, streams, and winding paths. Every inch was delicately beautiful, decorated with a smattering of ornaments. Serenity seemed to rest in all corners of the garden, but there was also a bamboo-like sturdiness to it.

The main sight in the Lianxiang Residence was a man-made lake. A winding path connected a few pavilions in the lake, but people mostly traveled through the lake on bamboo rafts. Lotus flowers and water chestnuts grew thickly in the water; in the summer sun, a lush layer of leaves covered the surface. The lotus stems extended gracefully above the water, holding up their flowers, white with a tinge of pink.

Wu Xingzi and Hei-er had to squeeze through the crowd to reach the door. The gathering had already begun.

An employee of the Peng Society stood guard at the door—Wu Xingzi had met him before. The moment he saw Wu Xingzi, he welcomed him warmly. "Mr. Wu, the manager has been waiting for you! Please follow me inside."

"Thank you, thank you." Wu Xingzi hurriedly cupped his hands. He was about to follow the employee, but he somehow managed to bump into a man who was waiting for an employee to confirm his identity. "Ahh... Good sir, please excuse me!"

"It's nothing—no need to worry." The man's voice was soft and gentle; it felt like a mellow wine or a warm spring breeze. Wu Xingzi's ears inexplicably reddened, and he hastily covered them before he turned to look at the man.

The man wore dark blue Confucian-style robes. He was tall and muscular, but rather than being intimidating, he carried a sort of elegant refinement. He was not outstandingly handsome, but his gentle and friendly looks were pleasing to the eye. He had his head turned to study Wu Xingzi. His black eyes were like warm water, perfectly restrained.

This face... Wu Xingzi lightly pressed upon his chest.

"M-Murong Chong?" The name burst from his lips. Wu Xingzi clamped his hands over his mouth, so embarrassed that he wished the ground would open up and swallow him.

This was the owner of the Murong Chong of pengornises! Ah, why couldn't he keep his mouth shut?

The man looked confused. "Good sir, did you mistake me for someone?" he replied politely. "I'm Ping. Ping Yifan."

Ping Yifan? He's the complete opposite of his name![3] *Not ordinary at all...* Wu Xingzi was unable to stop the picture of Ping Yifan's penis from appearing in his mind. *Oh no! Guan Shanjin's top position is in danger!*

The street beyond the wall was a stark contrast to the interior of Lianxiang Residence. Outside, a hubbub of voices buzzed.

The men and women of Great Xia were not traditionalists. As long as they called upon friends with a maidservant to accompany them, most daughters of ordinary families could stroll the streets as they wished. Although the girls of the capital were slightly more reserved, many of them were still young and passionate. When fairs and festivals were celebrated, the rooms of restaurants and tea houses would fill with young, blossoming girls. Upon seeing young

---

3 *Pingfan* (平凡) *means "ordinary."*

men on the streets or in a room of another restaurant across the way, they would toss some snacks, flowers, and other trinkets, exchanging flirtations from a distance before going their separate ways.

Now that there were so many magnificent men gathered at the Lianxiang Residence, the bazaar outside attracted large crowds of curious young ladies as well, all trying their best to peek inside the gates. Hearing that Bai-gongzi had accepted the invitation to the gathering this time, they were all determined to linger outside the venue to listen to him play the qin! In comparison to the bustling activity outside, the Lianxiang Residence itself felt serene. Not many invitees were in attendance; there were only about twenty participants in all. Besides the talented Bai-gongzi, a few scholars of literary fame were present.

The fragrance of lotus flowers drifted on the breeze, and the pleasing sounds of a flute floated through the air. Wu Xingzi hadn't taken a single sip of wine, yet he was already intoxicated.

The pavilion where Rancui sat was rather remote, but its location was the perfect vantage point to see everything the Lianxiang Residence had to offer. When Wu Xingzi stepped inside the pavilion, the banquet had already started. The first dish had been served and eaten, and the participants drank as they waited for the second dish to arrive.

"Mr. Wu," Rancui said. He was dressed in a long white robe with an outer robe of gauzy green material. He sat with his legs crossed casually on a cushion, his face slightly flushed. He looked like the spirit of a lotus flower, elegantly enchanting yet also reserved.

"Rancui." Wu Xingzi cupped his hands together and sat down across the low table. The attendant next to them immediately served up the first dish: a bowl of clear, golden soup. Delicate lotus petals decorated the bottom of the bowl. A couple of exquisite, snowy dumplings floated on top of the soup; they seemed to be made of sticky rice. They were plump and white with a faint pink sheen, and Wu Xingzi was almost unable to bear eating them.

"These are dumplings filled with lotus root paste. Please try them, Mr. Wu," Rancui said warmly to Wu Xingzi, but his sly eyes darted over to the silent Hei-er, who stood in one corner of the pavilion. Rancui frowned disdainfully. "Commander Hei, you should take a seat as well. It's rather nauseating to have you standing around like that."

Hei-er glanced at Rancui, his expression tinged with a vague sort of surrender, but he did not say anything. He sat down at the farthest table, holding up his cup to toast Rancui.

Rancui drank but did not pay Hei-er any more attention. Instead, he turned to chat with Wu Xingzi, persuading him to eat more. The chef he had invited today was from the capital's most famous restaurant, and the dishes not only looked exquisite, but tasted divine as well.

Wu Xingzi didn't have to be told twice to dig in. On occasions like this, he did feel very out of place—like an ugly duckling stumbling into a lake of swans. It was quite enough for him to look at all these beautiful men from afar. He had no intention of getting to know them or talking with them; he just buried his head in the food.

However, after five dishes had been served and everyone drank five glasses of wine each, the restrained atmosphere had dissipated a fair amount. Men who chose to attend this gathering were here to look for a partner with whom they could spend the rest of their lives, after all. And no matter how refined, reserved, and reticent men could be, they were still men, with men's innate nature to conquer and boast; they could not resist the desire to put themselves out there.

Rancui saw it was nearly time. Throughout the meal, most of the men had already made their observations. They themselves were aware of who was interested in whom. It was time to let their trembling peacock feathers flare out and show off.

Very quickly, one of the men picked up his chopsticks. Rapping on the rim of his glass, he suddenly burst into song. He sang a tune describing the scenery of a desert. His voice was pleasant, and the melody evoked the feeling of vastness and freedom. This man must be a rather unbridled, reckless sort. As Wu Xingzi watched him sing, he completely forgot to chew the morsel of food in his mouth.

Smiling, Rancui glanced over at Wu Xingzi. He leaned in close and whispered, "This is a subordinate of the ninth prince. He was stationed in the west for a period of time, but he injured a tendon in his hand and had no choice but to return to the capital. His pengornis is ranked seventh on your list."

The seventh? A drawing appeared clearly in Wu Xingzi's mind. This cock was not especially thick or long. Whether it was his old list or the new one, it ranked about in the middle, mainly due to its pleasant shape. It was straight and upright, the shaft slightly tapering toward the head in a way that made it look somewhat like a spear.

Without thinking, Wu Xingzi wrapped his arms around his middle, his face blushing red.

"Lord Meng is a frank and forthright person. Don't be fooled by his refined and scholarly looks—he was born with extraordinary strength. Back in the west, his skills with the snake-headed spear were truly something to behold. He can be considered a Zhang Fei among the pengornises."

Zhang Fei? When Wu Xingzi recalled Lord Zhang from the stories of the Three Kingdoms, he could not help but smile.[4] The moment he smiled, a pair of soft, gentle eyes fixed onto him from a distance not too far away. A trace of gloom and bloodlust flashed past those eyes.

Wu Xingzi did not notice it, but Hei-er, who had been busy eating, lifted his head sharply. He met that gaze that made no attempt to hide itself, and his stern face froze for a moment.

The owner of those eyes ignored him. Instead, he stared at the flushed Wu Xingzi as he whispered with Rancui, as though he could not rest if he didn't devour him.

Hei-er became a little anxious. He turned his head and looked at Wu Xingzi, whose eyes shone brightly. He hadn't even touched the newly served dishes. Hei-er hesitated, wondering if he should give Wu Xingzi a warning. Then, a scorching gaze was directed straight at him, almost burning holes through his head. Hei-er's heart jolted, and he decided to keep his head down and continue eating.

As a subordinate, he had no right to meddle in the affairs of his masters.

---

4   Zhang Fei is a major figure in *Romance of the Three Kingdoms*, in which he is also depicted as using a snake-headed spear.

CHAPTER 3

A Self-Defeating Plan

Wu Xingzi could not explain why he was so attracted to Ping Yifan.
As though noticing his gaze, Ping Yifan slowly lifted his head.
Very quickly, his eyes met Wu Xingzi's. He blinked, looking a
little startled; then his lips curled up into a faint, warm smile.
Wu Xingzi rubbed his chest unconsciously. His heart pounded
as if it was ready to burst its way out.

AFTER MENG-GONGZI'S PERFORMANCE, a series of other men put their talents on display. One by one, Rancui introduced them to Wu Xingzi, matching each man to his ranking on Wu Xingzi's list of pengornises. Whether featured in the old list or the new one, every one of their cocks had occupied Wu Xingzi's thoughts at some point this past month.

Just as the atmosphere was growing more lively, the twang of a qin sounded out, like a melody from heaven or dewdrops at dawn. The sound clutched at everyone's hearts as it made its way through the crowd, silence spreading through the gathering. The men's eyes darted around, seeking the source of the music; they did not even dare to breathe too loudly.

Wu Xingzi's gaze flickered across various different spots before finally landing on the pavilion furthest from him. The pavilions in the Lianxiang Residence were all built from bamboo, which made them pleasantly cool in the summer. The color of the bamboo cheered viewers' hearts and refreshed their minds. Some of the pavilions had their blinds half lowered and some let the breeze blow through, but since they were all bamboo pavilions, they all looked quite similar.

Still, the pavilion where the sound of the qin could be heard stood out clearly.

It was the same sort of bamboo pavilion, and the same half lowered blinds. However, since it was situated further from the other pavilions, the lotus flowers and water chestnuts surrounded it more thickly. From afar, it seemed to float on the lotus pads. There was no practical difference in its construction from the other pavilions, but there was a sort of ethereal air to it—perhaps due to the man playing the qin within.

Wu Xingzi hadn't had anything to drink, but he felt intoxicated nonetheless. His whole body relaxed, and he felt as if he was floating through the clouds.

The man in the pavilion must have been Bai-gongzi. His head was half tilted down, and a wisp of his hair clung to his fair, smooth cheek and fluttered in the wind. He played the qin with extreme focus, as though nothing else existed in the world. His turquoise robe made him look even more delicate; even an immortal from the heavens could not compare!

"This piece was written by Bai-gongzi himself. I hear that it's called *The Tree to Heaven*," Rancui said softly, then fell silent. He sipped on his wine, not looking in any particular direction.

The Tree to Heaven... As Wu Xingzi reveled in the music, it felt like the song itself was sinking its hooks into his heart. The melody grew more and more otherworldly, and the feeling in his heart solidified into pain. It felt as though he was looking at something that was once within his reach drifting farther and farther away from him.

Of course he was aware that it had never belonged to him; this was the reason why he had let go of it. However, although his mind had let go, his heart could not give it up. He had no way of reaching out to pull it back, and he could only stand right there, all alone, watching that person walk farther and farther away...

This bridge between heaven and earth was not easily traversed.

As the music became so faint it was about to recede into silence, the audience in the Lianxiang Residence all held their breaths, leaning forward unconsciously. They strained to listen, afraid to miss even a single note, only for the music to sharpen abruptly, like the northern wind slicing through the air. The music cut into them aggressively and came to a sudden end.

For a long moment, no one made a sound. As though possessed, they stared at Bai-gongzi as he lifted his hands from the qin.

In the past, Bai-gongzi's music had always been refined and elegant, like a spring breeze dancing through the air. This was the first time it had made the hearts of his listeners ache. The song's ending caused the audience to recall Fuxi's fall from the tree. He was finally about to achieve his aim of ascending to the heavens, only to tumble back to earth.

Bai-gongzi didn't seem to notice the effects of his music. He took a handkerchief from an attendant to wipe his hands, then picked up his cup and made a toast in all directions before slinging the contents down his throat. Perhaps because he had drunk in too much of a hurry, a couple of drops of wine overflowed from the corners of his mouth, sliding down his long, slender neck before they faded into the bobbing knot of his throat.

In an instant, the mouths of the men in the Lianxiang Residence went dry. As though they were trying to conceal something, they all turned away, eating and drinking instead.

As for Wu Xingzi, he seemed to have turned a blind eye to Bai-gongzi's amorous display. The delighted blush on his face had vanished, and he pressed tightly against the left side of his chest, lost in thought.

Seeing him like this, Rancui sighed silently and poured a cup of wine for Wu Xingzi. "Mr. Wu, have a drink."

"Ah... Many thanks." Wu Xingzi still hadn't snapped out of his daze. He slowly sipped from the cup, taking a long time to finish the wine.

With how distracted Wu Xingzi looked, both Rancui and Hei-er knew exactly who he was thinking about, but they couldn't say anything. If this had been the past, Rancui might have taken the opportunity to make a biting remark about Guan Shanjin, but now... He shot a look at a nearby pavilion. Inside it was a man who looked gentle and ordinary, and who had been staring at Wu Xingzi right from the start.

"Bah! What a fool," Rancui spat. He summoned an assistant and quietly gave him an instruction.

The assistant nodded, then turned and ran off. Shortly afterward, he came back with a long bamboo case. He headed toward the pavilion where Ping Yifan was seated, where he handed the box over.

Ping Yifan frowned at first, directing a cold, sharp gaze at Rancui before opening the lid. A tinge of anxiety appeared on his face, and it took him a few seconds to regain his calm and gentle appearance as he took a flute out of the case.

Soon, the melodious sounds of the flute filled the Lianxiang Residence. It was clear and bright, skillfully rising and falling, brushing away the gloom left behind by *The Tree to Heaven*.

Wu Xingzi came out of his trance. When he saw who it was playing the flute, a flush suffused his face. His eyes were starry, and his hand continuously shoved food into his mouth, as though he was devouring Ping Yifan along with his meal.

Ah, he's worthy of the top position on my list!

If Ping Yifan's appearance had to be described, it was just like his name: ordinary. Compared to the carefully curated attendees of this Peng Society gathering, he was rather forgettable. This did not mean that he was ugly; his facial features were as gentle as a spring breeze, with perfectly composed angles that could have been smoothed out by water. One glance at him gave Wu Xingzi a pleasant and comfortable impression. Altogether, none of his features stood out; they were like water that could not be brought to a boil.

Wu Xingzi sat in a daze as Ping Yifan played the flute, his marble-like hands fair and smooth. His fingers were slim and perfectly proportionate, painting a beautiful contrast against the green bamboo flute.

The gentle melody dancing through the Lianxiang Residence sounded like delicate spring rain, unobtrusively pattering into the hearts of the audience. It evoked the aroma of lotus flowers and the sight of dew dripping off bamboo stalks.

Eating the food made by the top chef in the capital, listening to the refreshing melody of the flute, and seeing the number one man in his pengornis rankings right in front of him—life truly didn't get better than this.

When the melody ended, Wu Xingzi couldn't resist applauding, and the light shining brightly in his eyes made Hei-er silently lament.

Hearing his applause, Ping Yifan smiled timidly and gave a slight nod. He seemed to be pondering if he should come up and speak to him. Wu Xingzi was nervous as well. He was not that naïve—he knew what could happen when two men at a Peng Society gathering found each other pleasing.

Wu Xingzi had originally thought that he was only here in the capacity of a guest, someone sitting by the sidelines. After all, this was the capital, where talented men and scholars abounded. Not only was the capital's edition of *The Pengornisseur* thicker than other cities', but every man within its pages was outstanding. When he thought about it, men from ordinary backgrounds would probably prefer not to be published in the capital's *Pengornisseur*—it was better to be a big fish in a small pond rather than a small fish in the vast ocean, after all.

Wu Xingzi himself had not appeared within the pages of the capital's edition. His interest was not in finding a partner, but in receiving pengornis pictures. If not for Rancui's warm invitation, he might not even have attended today's gathering at all. The fair going on outside the wall was much more his speed.

But one could never predict what the future held, and everything was left up to fate! Amid this forest of beauties, a man like Ping Yifan had appeared... Wu Xingzi bowed his head, taking a few more bites of his food. His ears were tinted a light red. He wondered if he should make a move, or if he should wait for Ping Yifan to give him a signal. Perhaps Ping Yifan was also attending the gathering as just a humble guest.

As soon as he had the thought, Wu Xingzi shrank back and buried himself in his food. He didn't have much tolerance for alcohol; he had sipped tea instead of wine for the past five courses, but the cup of wine Rancui had given him to dispel his gloomy thoughts was enough to make him a little tipsy. He wanted to indulge himself a little, but he was missing that last little bit of determination and courage.

However, before Ping Yifan had even taken a step, Bai-gongzi stopped by instead.

Bai-gongzi's name was Bai Shaochang, and his courtesy name was Qiuxiao. He lived on Qingzhu Lane, and his father had been Great Xia's most talented qin player. He learned the art of the qin from his father, and eventually, pupil surpassed teacher. Bai-gongzi was now the top qin musician in the capital. He was handsome as well, perfectly encapsulating the type of man that Wu Xingzi admired—as ethereally beautiful as a jade statue. Even Mr. Lu would seem like an ugly duckling next to Bai-gongzi.

Following behind Bai-gongzi was a serving boy carrying a qin. He looked to be around thirteen or fourteen years of age, but he already had a rather tall stature. He looked quite likable, with a round face and bright almond-shaped eyes. As he peered about playfully, he gave a friendly grin whenever he met anyone's gaze, making their hearts soften. With this boy around, Bai-gongzi's unworldly and aloof personality was not as intimidating, and people would not be as guarded with him.

"My greetings to the manager," Bai-gongzi said. It was as though he did not see Wu Xingzi or Hei-er at all, only acknowledging Rancui.

"Greetings to you, Bai-gongzi." Rancui returned the sentiment, then turned apologetically to Wu Xingzi. "Mr. Wu, there's something I have to discuss with Bai-gongzi. Why don't you walk around and take a look at the grounds?"

"There's no need to go to such trouble, Manager. The things I have to mention are not important; you don't have to ask your friend to withdraw." Bai-gongzi was very open—or perhaps he just didn't care. After his servant arranged a cushion for him, he lifted his robes slightly and took a seat, crossing his legs.

Rancui didn't bother with further propriety. He shifted the few dishes in front of him over to Wu Xingzi and bade him eat, before pouring out cups of tea for both himself and Bai-gongzi. "Go ahead, Bai-gongzi. This is a Bailu green tea from Panyun Mountain—please try it."

"Thank you, Manager." With half-lowered eyelids, Bai-gongzi picked up the cup and took a sip. His brows twitched slightly in what looked like surprise, but his expression gentled considerably, which brightened his face.

Sitting by the side, Wu Xingzi stole some glances at this beautiful man. He had felt that Bai-gongzi was very good-looking when he'd first seen his portrait back in Horse-Face City, and he had yearned to hear his music someday. Getting the chance to fulfill his wishes today like this felt like his ancestors must be bestowing their blessings upon him.

However, the longer Wu Xingzi stared at Bai-gongzi, the more uneasy Hei-er became. He looked up periodically, glancing in Ping Yifan's direction. As for Ping Yifan, he completely ignored Hei-er, holding up his wine cup as he enjoyed the food and drink.

After a moment of silence, Bai-gongzi finally spoke quietly. "Manager, you must have heard the news. I've found the man who is right for me."

"Congratulations, Bai-gongzi." Rancui neither denied nor confirmed his statement, smiling as he toasted him with a cup of tea instead of wine. "Here's to a happy life with your partner."

"Thank you for the well-wishes." Bai-gongzi put down his tea and cupped his hands together. His fair, flawless skin revealed a slight blush, momentarily energizing his ethereal, fairy-like face.

"Is your partner featured in *The Pengornisseur*?" Rancui asked. He didn't seem to be implying anything by the question, but Bai-gongzi froze slightly, revealing a bit of distress as he shook his head.

"No, he's not." Bai-gongzi shot a probing glance at Rancui, but he couldn't see through Rancui's expression. He stroked his teacup, his tone a little hesitant. "Did the news not reach your ears?"

The Peng Society was very well-informed, especially when it came to the matters of its members. The only people in the capital who knew what had happened to Bai-gongzi recently were his handful of close friends, but even so, the Peng Society ought to have already found out. If anything, it was a little inappropriate for them to invite him to this gathering.

This was why he'd deliberately sought Rancui out to speak to him. After all, his heart now belonged to another, and he should no longer remain an active member of the Peng Society. However, due to his partner's unique status, Bai-gongzi had to hide his relationship from his family, and so he still had to look the part of a Peng Society member. The letters from his partner had been disguised as letters from other pen pals, and Bai Shaochang felt very sorry that Peng Society members were still sending him letters without knowing he was taken. Now he had no choice but to grit his teeth, coming forward to confess in the hope that Rancui could do him a favor.

Rancui smiled, not giving a response. Instead, he filled both their teacups again.

After waiting a few beats, Bai Shaochang realized that Rancui had no intention of replying, and he had no choice but to continue. "The man I've met is not in the Peng Society. I know that the Peng Society has its rules, and people with partners should step away from *The Pengornisseur*."

"You're very understanding, Bai-gongzi." Rancui nodded, a smile curling around his lips as his lids lowered. Bai Shaochang was a little frightened.

"I know that this is a big favor, and it doesn't comply with the Peng Society's rules, but..." Bai Shaochang gritted his teeth, glancing toward Wu Xingzi. Wu Xingzi had just happened to shove an egg into his mouth at that moment, and he met Bai-gongzi's eyes with bulging cheeks. A moment later, he curled up into himself, retreating.

Whether he left or stayed, it would be awkward. Wu Xingzi was unable to extricate himself from this sticky situation. Although he had only withdrawn a slight distance, though, at least Bai-gongzi's voice was no longer that distinct.

Wu Xingzi wondered silently what sort of strapping man was worthy of Bai-gongzi. Who could be wonderful enough to match him? However, a moment later his thoughts drifted to Ping Yifan, who sat nearby.

Ping Yifan was drinking alone. His flute recital just now had not attracted many people's appreciation or curiosity. After all, this gathering boasted an abundance of outstanding people. Although Ping Yifan played the flute very well, he could not be classified as a brilliant musician to such sophisticated ears. To these men, he seemed rather unimaginative. Furthermore, he had played after Bai-gongzi's *The Tree to Heaven*, and his song was unable to cause any ripples in comparison.

Ping Yifan was also rather dull in appearance. His temperament was carefree, but very unremarkable. Naturally, he was quickly forgotten by the various noble attendees. If one did not have an excellent family background, they should at least have talent—and if not talented, they should at least have a face of unsurpassable beauty.

Both Ping Yifan and Wu Xingzi met none of these criteria. Because of this, even though the gathering was very lively, there was a quiet atmosphere around them both.

Wu Xingzi could not explain why he was so drawn to Ping Yifan. Just last night, he had dreamt about Guan Shanjin, and the two had been so intimate in his dream. His semen-stained pants still hid in one corner of his luggage—he really needed to find an opportunity to throw them away.

As though noticing Wu Xingzi's gaze, Ping Yifan slowly lifted his head. Very quickly, his eyes met Wu Xingzi's. He blinked, looking a little startled; then his lips curled up into a faint, warm smile. Wu Xingzi rubbed his chest unconsciously. His heart pounded as if it was ready to burst out of his chest.

Ping Yifan glanced at Rancui and Bai-gongzi, his eyes finally falling upon Hei-er. The towering man trembled slightly without Wu Xingzi noticing. He put down the chopsticks in his hand, his tanned face seeming to turn even darker.

After a moment of hesitation, Hei-er stood up and called out to Wu Xingzi. "Master."

Wu Xingzi bit his chopsticks. He had just shoved a chunk of braised pork into his mouth, and his cheeks puffed out like a chipmunk stealing food. He looked at Hei-er blankly.

"It's a rare opportunity to visit the Lianxiang Residence," Hei-er said. "Wouldn't you like to explore the grounds?" There was no need to explore, really; the scenery of the Lianxiang Residence could be seen completely from within this bamboo pavilion. If they moved away from the pond, there was nothing to see. This was why, after a great amount of thought, Rancui had selected this place—the hidden corners were very convenient for men who had caught each other's eye.

Wu Xingzi hurriedly swallowed the braised pork in his mouth, nodding away. "I should, I should... Rancui..."

Bai-gongzi had left at some point. Rancui sipped from a cup. It seemed like he had drunk a little too much—his cheeks blushed peony-red as he eyed Hei-er with a vague smile on his face. "Of course it's good that Mr. Wu wants to walk around, but there's no need for you to accompany him, Commander Hei," he said. "Will you join me for a drink?"

"Manager, please excuse me. I'm an uncivilized man, and I'm afraid I may cause offense if I get drunk." Hei-er had to stick close to Wu Xingzi to protect him, so he refused Rancui.

"I'm not afraid of you offending me." Rancui gave a low chuckle, lifting his hand and waving it at Hei-er. His wide sleeves slid down, revealing a well-proportioned, slender arm. Under the summer sun, it was smooth and clean, making one feel warm.

Rancui was a little drunk, Wu Xingzi noticed. Although he had some employees with him, they were busy running about, and they probably had no time to look after their boss. Wu Xingzi didn't want Hei-er's watchful eye on him when he spoke with Ping Yifan, so after weighing his options, he apologetically spoke to Hei-er. "Why don't you just stay with Rancui?" he asked, a little unnaturally. "The Lianxiang Residence is only so big, and everyone here is from the Peng Society. Nothing bad will happen."

Hei-er was about to say something, but then his neck and shoulders abruptly stiffened. Although the movement was fleeting, Wu Xingzi still noticed that something was wrong. Just as he was about to ask, Hei-er spoke up. "As you wish, I'll have a few drinks with the manager. Master...don't stray too far from the lotus pond."

"Yes, yes." Wu Xingzi's head bobbed a few times. He merely wanted to go over to Ping Yifan's pavilion and speak to him. After all, this was only their first meeting—he could not do anything unseemly!

Watching Wu Xingzi gaze joyfully at Ping Yifan, Hei-er sighed gloomily. He turned his head and took the wine cup from

Rancui's hand, tossing its contents back before saying, "Don't drink any more, you're still sick."

"Oh? You're actually showing me some concern?" Rancui snorted a laugh, turning to lean against the railing. Seeing Wu Xingzi so happy, like a flower about to bloom, made his chest feel stifled. "Hmph. Let's see how you explain this to Mr. Wu."

To ensure privacy, the bamboo pavilions were situated quite a distance apart. They appeared to be close to each other, but the paths that led to each one were cleverly made, twisting and winding around. Although the paths were not sheltered, the trees provided shade. With a cool breeze carrying the fragrance of the lotus flowers, the journey was not uncomfortable in the least.

Three other men stood in the same pavilion as Ping Yifan, and Rancui had introduced them to Wu Xingzi earlier. They were scholars from poor and humble families. Riches and power led the way in the capital, but these men were neither condescending nor servile, and had become officials based on their own abilities. The fact that they'd managed to make a name for themselves in the capital showed how capable they were.

Coincidentally, these three men had lingered on Wu Xingzi's pengornis rankings for a few days. He had no idea how Rancui was so clearly aware of it—he felt a swell of embarrassment rush up within him.

The closer he got to the pavilion, the harder Wu Xingzi's heart pounded. He was, after all, a shy and reserved person. Whether it was Yan Wenxin in the past, Ansheng later on, or even Guan Shanjin, he had never been one to take initiative. He only dared to admire them in silence. He couldn't say how he managed to muster up the courage this time.

There were still other men in the pavilion, so he was unsure what to say without seeming impolite. He twisted his fingers around his sleeves as his knees knocked together, his forehead covered in sweat. He hesitated, wondering if he should enter.

He did not expect the three men to be so observant. Seeing that he had finally taken a step into the pavilion, they swiftly cupped their hands together and greeted him before finding an excuse to leave. Perhaps some other men had caught their eye?

Wu Xingzi released a breath of relief, and a smile appeared on his face as well. With somewhat floaty steps, he walked over to Ping Yifan and bowed deeply in front of him. "Hello, Ping-gongzi."

"Greetings." Ping Yifan hurriedly stood up and bowed back, looking a little confused.

This was not surprising, considering he had only met Wu Xingzi once. He didn't even know his name. He must have been trying to recall the drawings in *The Pengornisseur* in the hope of matching Wu Xingzi with one of the entries.

However, Wu Xingzi was not featured within the pages of *The Pengornisseur* at all. Ever since Guan Shanjin had left his mark on him, his images and background had been falsified in all editions of *The Pengornisseur* other than the issues Wu Xingzi personally held. This gave him an easier time amassing his collection of pengornis drawings.

At first, Rancui had refused to allow him to break the rules. However, the strength of someone's arm was never stronger than that of their thigh. Although both Rancui's boss and his boss's partner were very powerful, they were still unable to go toe-to-toe with Guan Shanjin, who had the might of the army behind him. Furthermore, Rancui's boss had no reason to miss an opportunity for Guan Shanjin to owe him a favor—the only one left against this decision was Rancui, who was quickly defeated.

Wu Xingzi knew nothing of this matter. He knew that he did not appear in the capital's edition of *The Pengornisseur*, but he assumed he was still included in the southern border's issue. After all, he would be returning home one day, so he had nothing against keeping his entry there.

"Ping-gongzi, I'm not in the capital's edition of *The Pengornisseur*," he explained. "It's only because of the manager's invitation that I am able to attend this grand occasion."

Ping Yifan understood. He nodded, revealing a warm and friendly smile. "I see. Then I won't waste any further time on pleasantries. May I know your name?"

"My family name is Wu. I'm Wu Xingzi. I come from Qingcheng County, and I'm forty years old. In the past, I was the adviser in my local magistrate's office, and I'll be returning to Qingcheng County to work as an adviser in the future. I live alone—there are no elderly or young ones in my family. Although I have no properties to my name, I have a good resting place settled already. It is truly a great location, and it's quite comfortable—even for two people." Wu Xingzi told Ping Yifan all about himself. He looked sober and shy, but in reality, the alcohol from the cup of wine he drank had just kicked in.

Wu Xingzi himself did not realize that he liked Ping Yifan this much. It was just like that time he had seen Yan Wenxin standing among the peach trees—his heart flew to him without hesitation, and there was no way he could stop it. All he could think about was the man in front of him. Guan Shanjin had long been shoved into a corner, collecting dust.

"A resting place?" Ping Yifan froze, a shadow appearing in the depths of his gentle eyes. "From what you are saying, Adviser Wu... Do you like me?" His reply was rather tactful. After all, Wu Xingzi had basically asked Ping Yifan if he would like to share the same grave.

"Like" wasn't even strong enough to describe what he was feeling! No one would object if he described this as a deeply rooted love. Who would believe that this was the first time Wu Xingzi and Ping Yifan had met? They hadn't exchanged more than a handful of sentences!

"Yes, I like you..." Wu Xingzi stared foolishly at Ping Yifan's face and nodded. If he was a little more sober, he would probably be deathly embarrassed by his own boldness, and he wouldn't dare face Ping Yifan for months.

"Why do you like me? We've only shared a chance meeting, and we've barely spoken. Such passion, I..." Before Ping Yifan could finish his rejection, Wu Xingzi lurched a couple of steps forward. Their breaths mingled together in the air. When he smelled the alcoholic fragrance emanating from Wu Xingzi, Ping Yifan's tongue turned clumsy. Wu Xingzi came even closer, twitching the tip of his nose as he sniffed Ping Yifan.

It was the same familiar mix of white sandalwood and orange blossom, cold and elegant. "You smell really good."

Unease spread across Ping Yifan's face. He wanted to withdraw, but was afraid of hurting Wu Xingzi's feelings. After that moment of hesitation, he could see Wu Xingzi was about to tuck himself into his arms, and Ping Yifan had no choice but to hold his hands out and stop him.

"Hmm?" Wu Xingzi blinked, discovering he could not get any closer to Ping Yifan. He first moved his hands, then his legs. He looked at his freely moving limbs, troubled. Why was he unable to get closer?

As he observed Wu Xingzi's clumsy actions, Ping Yifan's heart softened. "Are you drunk?"

Ping Yifan helped Wu Xingzi down onto the cushions, and guided Wu Xingzi's head onto his shoulder. Ping Yifan's fingers twitched for a while, clenching into a fist that rested on his own knee. "I only had one cup. It doesn't count," Wu Xingzi said. Surrounded by that familiar scent, he was delighted. He inhaled deeply, holding his breath before carefully exhaling. Then, he took another big sniff.

Wu Xingzi did not seem drunk, but his behavior wasn't quite normal either. His eyes fell upon the wine cup on the table. His head hurt. He massaged his temples with his thumbs.

Only good wine would be served at this gathering. The aged wine from Songlaochun was mild and gentle, its fragrance sharp and enchanting. It was smooth to drink, and was not very strong. However, it was more than enough for a lightweight like Wu Xingzi.

Every angle of Ping Yifan delighted Wu Xingzi. Leaning on his shoulder for only a moment, he started to become restless once again. The thin, clumsy old fellow shifted about, thinking he was being very subtle as he wormed his way from his cushion into Ping Yifan's arms. His foolish face nuzzled into the other man's broad chest, his broad nose flattening against it. Such an unattractive image made Ping Yifan chuckle at first, but his breezy smile quickly faded. He bent his head, staring icily at the half-lidded, satisfied man in his arms.

He pinched Wu Xingzi's squashed nose, then pinched that smiling face of his. Wu Xingzi let him do whatever he wanted. Not only did he not struggle, he even slid his arms around Ping Yifan, tightly hugging his trim waist and refusing to let go.

Even ivy wrapped around a tree wouldn't cling as tightly as Wu Xingzi did. Ping Yifan didn't have the heart to push the man away. He sulked gloomily, but it was impossible to tell what he was thinking. Wu Xingzi, on the other hand, found a comfortable spot in Ping Yifan's arms, and fell asleep.

Hearing the old fellow's steady breathing, Ping Yifan harshly pinched his cheek again, only letting go when the skin reddened between his fingers. Frowning, he struggled for a little while, but still ended up tucking the man into his embrace. He shifted him into a position that that didn't squash his face; it wasn't comfortable to sleep with a crushed nose.

The three men who had left the pavilion returned, and one of them spoke to Ping Yifan. "Master, are you bringing Mr. Wu back?"

"Back where?"

The drunk man in his arms felt warm and toasty, emitting heat like a little burner. Soon, Ping Yifan was sweaty, and sweat beaded on Wu Xingzi's nose as well. He was obviously too warm, but he kept trying to burrow further into Ping Yifan's embrace.

Clicking his tongue lightly, Ping Yifan took out a handkerchief and carefully wiped Wu Xingzi's sweat away. The three subordinates had never seen Ping Yifan so painstakingly gentle.

They exchanged looks. One of them finally braced himself before asking, "Umm... Do you plan on bringing Mr. Wu back to the estate, Master?"

"No." Ping Yifan didn't even have to think about it. Looking at the clueless man in his arms, he felt annoyed, but he could not bear to abandon him here. "Tell Rancui I'm sending Wu Xingzi back right now. And that Wu Xingzi shouldn't drink wine in the future."

"Yes, sir." The men immediately left to follow his instructions.

Wu Xingzi was sound asleep, smacking his lips as though he was eating some delicacy. Ping Yifan endured it, clenching his fist. He did not take the opportunity to steal a kiss, instead carefully picking the man up and leaving the Lianxiang Residence.

Exiting via the back door, they did not bump into the crowd from the fair. None of the young ladies watching the commotion disturbed an ordinary-looking man like Ping Yifan, especially when he was carrying another man in his arms—although a few of them clustered together, glancing at them and whispering to each other with reddened faces. Peals of goosebump-inducing laughter occasionally rang out from their group.

In the carriage, Ping Yifan wiped away more sweat from Wu Xingzi's face. He had originally intended to remove Wu Xingzi's outer robe to cool him down. However, Wu Xingzi was still clinging to him tightly, and he found himself unable to separate from him. The entire time, Wu Xingzi kept trying to press himself even closer to Ping Yifan. Ping Yifan had no other option but to keep holding him. Every now and then, he would pat him, afraid that the old fellow would have a nightmare that would affect his sleep, or that he might have a hangover when he woke up.

When they arrived at Rancui's mansion, Hei-er was already waiting at the door. Once he saw Ping Yifan pull the carriage's curtain open, he immediately strode forward to accept Wu Xingzi.

Ping Yifan avoided Hei-er's hand, raising his chin instead. "No need for that. Please lead the way, Commander Hei."

Hei-er didn't know what to do with himself. He sighed privately, then led the man inside accordingly.

Once he'd set Wu Xingzi down, Ping Yifan decided to make his exit. Before he left, he quietly instructed Hei-er, "Tell Wu Xingzi that I'll visit him two days from now. If he really wants to be friends, we can go for an outing then."

"Don't worry, sir. I'll pass the message on to Mr. Wu." Hei-er cupped his hands together. However, Ping Yifan's mood did not seem to improve. Snorting coldly, he left after lowering the carriage's curtain.

Only when the carriage could no longer be seen did Hei-er lift his head up, wiping away the cold sweat gathering on his forehead.

"What's with that reaction? Look at you. Does Ping Yifan eat people?" A pair of snow-white arms clung onto Hei-er's neck, and he felt warm breath against his ear. The smell of alcohol and lotus flowers wafted past. His ear flushed red immediately.

"You know what's going on," Hei-er said. Acquiescent, Hei-er pulled Rancui's arms down from his neck, tucking the man into his arms.

Rancui huffed. "You ass-kisser! You'll swallow anything your master gives you, no matter how pleasant or how rotten. You aren't afraid it'll upset your stomach at all." Irritated, he smacked the firm arm around his waist. He added coldly, "Let go. Clinging to me like this—what will people think?"

"I'll take you back to your room. You're drunk." Hei-er sighed. So much for this Peng Society gathering—it was more like a trap disguised as a banquet.

"I'd know if I were drunk!" Rancui sneered. His face was peony-red from the alcohol, and his typical aloofness had fled the scene some time ago. He looked like a seductive demon who could suck the vital energy out of anyone. A lift of his lids was enough to hook a man's heart from his chest.

"All right, you're not drunk," Hei-er humored him. "But you've drunk a fair bit—do you want to go back to your room to rest?"

"No! The gathering has yet to conclude. I have to go back and hold down the fort." Rancui shook his head. He truly wasn't drunk. If he hadn't been so worried about Wu Xingzi, he would not have left the Lianxiang Residence with Hei-er.

"Would you like to have a bowl of sobering soup before you return?" Hei-er asked. Rancui's drunken state was magnificently enticing, and Hei-er wasn't eager to let him go back.

"Get the kitchen to prepare the soup and send a bowl over to me."

Rancui glanced at him, a vague smile curling around his lips as he wrapped an arm around Hei er's neck. "I'll have to trouble you to take me back to the Lianxiang Residence, Commander Hei."

Hei-er had carried him here using his qinggong abilities. He had to employ the same technique to carry him back.

He really was completely helpless against Rancui. Sighing, he lifted the man up in his arms before leaping up onto the roof.

As Guan Shanjin's vice general, Man Yue was so busy that he barely had time to breathe. He'd managed at long last to come back to the capital to submit his reports, but he still had no time to return to his own home—instead he had to stay in his old room back in the Protector General's estate.

Today, he had the rare opportunity to steal a few hours for a breather. Man Yue opened every window in his room. The plants in the yard were lush and green, with clusters of bushes and low trees that made for a refreshing and comforting sight. Although the summer sun was scorching hot, a cool breeze blew in the afternoon, accompanied by the buzzing of the cicadas.

With some iced fruit wine next to him, he flipped through a few pages of a book he had read months ago as he chewed on a stick of spicy jerky. He dove into the story of a top scholar battling a princess, which finally culminated in a child being born.

The scene he was currently reading involved the top scholar pointing right at the princess's nose to reproach her:

They all said that the princess was virtuous and kindhearted, never speaking a word of evil or probing at anyone's secrets. Who would have known that all the lovely things said about you were mere rumors? Although you are a woman, you carried yourself like a seven-foot-tall man! Now that I've seen everything for myself, I have no choice but to suspect that these were all lies spread by you yourself! Such a young girl, yet deplorable to the bone! How could I, Top Scholar, marry a vicious woman like you?!

Man Yue shook with laughter. The top scholar in this book was actually named Top Scholar!

How would the princess respond to the arrogant and overbearing Top Scholar? Man Yue wiped his tears of mirth away and drank a mouthful of his fruit wine before picking up another piece of spicy jerky to chew on. He flipped to the next page eagerly...

Bang! The door to his room burst open. Man Yue nearly fell off his seat in shock, only to see his door bounce closed from slamming into the wall. It was then kicked open again. A hinge came loose with a crack and the door just hung there, swinging limply.

Man Yue tossed away the jerky in his hand, leaping up and watching as Guan Shanjin ripped off the mask that gave him an ordinary appearance. The devilishly handsome face underneath was furious. Before Man Yue could open his mouth, the general lifted his leg and flattened the table in front of him.

"Uhh, that's..." Although Man Yue was staying in the Protector General's compound, he'd paid for all the furniture in the room himself. It wasn't that the Protector General was stingy, but Man Yue just preferred furnishing his own place of residence.

This table Guan Shanjin had destroyed was made of top-quality rosewood, warm and smooth to the touch. He'd used it very carefully over the years; even when he was not in the capital, he would assign people to take care of it. Man Yue's heart now dripped with blood.

"He invited someone to share his grave!" Guan Shanjin exclaimed, throwing the mask to the ground. With a threatening look in his eyes, he lifted his foot to stomp on the mask. Fortunately, he managed to hold himself back, using the tip of his foot to flick the mask into Man Yue's hand instead. Like an injured beast circling an enclosed space, he paced with such heavy footsteps that he almost shattered the stone slabs under him.

"Mr. Wu?" Catching the mask, Man Yue hurriedly stowed it in a box. This mask had cost quite a bit of money. It was difficult to find the maker of such masks; after constructing it, the maker disappeared to parts unknown. Man Yue had to keep a close eye on it for the sake of future meetings, or he might have to face Guan Shanjin's wrath.

"Who else could it be?" Guan Shanjin glared daggers at Man Yue. "He's been treasuring that grave of his. All he thinks about is resting there in peace. He even saved up to buy a Liuzhou coffin for that cherished plot of land! Why did he not invite *me* to share the burial spot? Forget a Liuzhou coffin—I can pluck the stars from the sky and bury them with him!"

"Didn't you two just meet for the first time?" Man Yue was astonished. He was well aware of the sort of person Wu Xingzi was: timid and shy. Even when he saw something he liked, he wouldn't dare reach out to it. Why this sudden change in character?

"Hmph! The moment he saw Ping Yifan, it was like an ant looking at sugar! His greedy eyes were practically glued to that man. Did he think no one saw his intentions? What's so great about Ping Yifan, huh?" As Guan Shanjin spoke, he kicked the fallen rosewood table in fury, completely shattering it.

Man Yue's heart clenched. He was truly afraid of Guan Shanjin taking out his anger on his furniture. Every time the general got angry, he destroyed things. How could he be so wasteful?

"*You* were the one who specifically ordered the creation of Ping Yifan's appearance. It's not a surprise that Mr. Wu likes it." As Man Yue spoke, he herded Guan Shanjin into a chair and pushed a jug of fruit wine into his hand, hoping it would abate his anger.

Unfortunately, he underestimated the fury that Wu Xingzi had set ablaze in Guan Shanjin. Guan Shanjin lifted the jug to his mouth and gulped down the entire thing. He tossed the empty jug back at Man Yue, saying darkly, "This old fellow didn't dare to like me, but liked a face that was only halfway similar to mine. This means that if I were just a little uglier, he would feel more at ease! Such an ugly thing—how dare he get together with another hideous man? Isn't he afraid of hurting the eyes of passersby? Fuck him!" It was clear how angry he was; Guan Shanjin didn't often curse.

"What did Ping Yifan do?" asked Man Yue. "Mr. Wu is a timid old quail. No matter how much he likes someone, he would never take the initiative to offer himself up like this. Even if he had the bravery of a hundred men, he would never have the courage to invite Ping Yifan to be buried with him, right? Did you flirt with him?"

"Hmph. Ping Yifan only played one piece on the flute. Dry and monotonous, completely void of spirit. Only an uncultured oaf like him would enjoy it," the general said maliciously, pursing his lips.

There was no way to reason with a furiously jealous man. Ping Yifan was merely a character played by Guan Shanjin, but because Wu Xingzi showed some interest, Guan Shanjin bitterly insulted him the moment he removed the mask. Wasn't he just cursing himself?

"Mr. Wu has always enjoyed listening to music. And you are truly very good-looking when you play the flute. Isn't it normal for him to like you?" Man Yue had no choice but to flatter his superior, despite knowing very well that nothing he said would help.

As expected, Guan Shanjin glared at him in anger. "The one playing the flute wasn't me, it was Ping Yifan! Wu Xingzi doesn't want me, he wants Ping Yifan! If he stares at Ping Yifan like that again, I'll find a way to dig his eyes out!"

Then do it! Man Yue roared internally. No matter how harsh and vicious Guan Shanjin was now, the moment he saw Wu Xingzi, he would become a paper tiger. What use was it to keep glaring at Man Yue? He should just go glare at the old quail he kept ranting about!

However, it had to be said that Guan Shanjin really understood Wu Xingzi—perhaps even better than Wu Xingzi understood himself.

Ping Yifan had talent, but he was not outstanding. His appearance was friendly, but ordinary and dull. His temperament was gentle but as placid and mild as still water. More importantly, every single characteristic was essentially a faded version of Guan Shanjin. Wu Xingzi thought that he liked Ping Yifan, but the truth was that he still desired the general. Subconsciously, he was attracted to this washed-out version of Guan Shanjin, and had fallen for him instantly.

Everything had happened according to Guan Shanjin's expectations, starting with the pengornis drawing. Man Yue didn't even want to recall that painful day. Guan Shanjin had barged into Man Yue's room with his own cock illustration, instructing him to draw another copy from it. However, he had to "apply a little makeup, and adorn it in red." Man Yue had been stunned. Why was Guan Shanjin using this phrase to describe his dick? It sounded so absurd! Furthermore, Man Yue did *not* want to know what Guan Shanjin's pengornis looked like! Alas, his poor eyes...

After he finally managed to produce a passable dick picture, Guan Shanjin then requested he add color too... *What color—pink?!* Man Yue felt extremely suffocated. He gave up and decided to paint it the color of plum blossoms in March. He didn't think that Guan Shanjin would be so satisfied! The general then submitted both the illustration and Ping Yifan's portrait to Rancui, and only then did he have the opportunity to attend the Peng Society's gathering.

Guan Shanjin had been defeated by his own plan!

"If you don't like that Mr. Wu likes Ping Yifan, then don't let Ping Yifan appear again. Mr. Wu is not a persistent man, and he will quickly forget this sudden bout of affection. He'll return to his varied and colorful collection of penis drawings."

Man Yue took the opportunity to stop a servant walking by and instructed him to bring more fruit wine. Who knew how long Guan Shanjin would be angry? It was the perfect time to drink away their sorrows.

"I've arranged to meet up with him two days from now for a hike," Guan Shanjin said gloomily, after a short pause.

Man Yue really wanted to kneel down to him. "Oh, my general! Brother! The weather is so hot now—why are you taking a hike? Your skin is thick and rough, so you're not afraid of the sun, but that's not the case for Mr. Wu!"

Guan Shanjin glared fiercely at Man Yue. "Oh? You sure know how to take care of someone, don't you?"

This was truly unwarranted anger. Man Yue hurriedly shook his head, spreading his arms wide, palms open. "The only person I've ever cared about is you! Think about it—if Mr. Wu feels uncomfortable and falls ill from the heat, whose heart will be the one aching? In any case, it wouldn't be mine. My heart will ache for the man whose heart is aching for him."

Guan Shanjin was speechless. He reached out, pinching Man Yue's fat, soft chin. "How glib."

Man Yue secretly breathed a sigh of relief. It was over now. Adjusting his face back to a normal expression, he tried to persuade the general. "Haiwang-gege, I know that you can't let go of Mr. Wu, and you want to continue pampering him and doting on him using Ping Yifan's identity. However, if Mr. Wu really ends up falling for Ping Yifan, how will you explain it?"

How will I explain it? This was the exact thing Guan Shanjin was frustrated about. He had thought that at most, he'd become pen pals with Wu Xingzi as Ping Yifan. According to Wu Xingzi's character, he would not fall for another man in such a short period of time. Even if Ping Yifan was full of fantastic qualities, Guan Shanjin should at least still occupy some space in Wu Xingzi's heart, right?

He had been proven entirely wrong.

Wu Xingzi had a steel backbone wrapped in softness. Once he made up his mind, he would follow through with it fully. He would never do things halfway, neither faltering nor hesitating once he made a decision. If he said that he wanted to get over Guan Shanjin, he was really going to do it.

Even if he still could not let go of his feelings for now—he accidentally had a wet dream that revealed his lingering feelings—he was still very firm in his decision, and he would not be easily shaken. At a moment like this, how could he not fall for someone like Ping Yifan? This man had everything he appreciated, but he was so very placid. It was as if the heavens had crafted the perfect man for him! Bolstered by alcohol, Wu Xingzi had mustered up his courage to seek out the man's affection.

Guan Shanjin understood Wu Xingzi's preferences, but he never understood his thoughts. He deserved to be trapped in this pit of his own making.

Of course Man Yue saw everything clearly, but what could he say? It was already unheard of for Guan Shanjin to do so much for a relationship, but employing the wrong method would only result in his being left empty-handed. He wanted to persuade Guan Shanjin to stop, but when the words were at the tip of his tongue, he ended up swallowing them down.

Guan Shanjin had to personally taste the bitter fruit of his own making. After all, the one who wanted a wife was General Guan, not Man Yue. Where was the justice if he was the one doing all the scheming?

He decided to change the topic. "Right, there's quite a number of people keeping an eye on your marriage." They had not returned to the capital for the sake of love affairs, after all—there were still many tasks they had to complete first.

"He took the bait?" Guan Shanjin snorted, tapping his toes on the floor. "I heard Bai Shaochang play *The Tree to Heaven* today at the gathering. What a pity for his loyal and devoted heart."

"I received a letter from him, too. He's inviting you to a private qin recital." Man Yue walked over to his table and rifled through the papers on it. Finding the invitation, he handed it to Guan Shanjin.

It was made from top-quality Chengxin Tang paper, dense and smooth. The handwriting was bold and unyielding, evoking a pleasant, refreshing feeling.

"He put a lot of thought into this," Guan Shanjin chuckled, tucking the invitation into his clothes. "And how could I disappoint Bai-gongzi? Say, doesn't Teacher like listening to him play the qin as well?"

"If you say he likes it, then he will like it," Man Yue responded with a heartless laugh.

"Well said." Guan Shanjin's lips curled up coldly, his eyes narrowing in thought.

At the outskirts of the capital, there stood a Taoist temple called Chongxu Temple. The royals of the Great Xia dynasty followed both Buddhism and Taoism, and many of their customs, temples, and rituals featured a mixture of both religions. However, Chongxu Temple was strictly a Taoist temple—a rare sight in Great Xia. It was home to many believers and trusted implicitly by the royals, though, so the temple was responsible for the annual ceremony of the emperor's sacrifice to the heavens.

Chongxu Temple was located in Qingyun Peak, about half a day's journey from the capital proper. Qingyun Peak was not dangerous or insurmountable; its terrain was gentle, and the scenery along the way was beautiful. It featured rugged mountains, towering rocks, and fields of blooming flowers. The scenery was so varied, it was impossible to take it all in. After the gradual incline of the mountain, the height rose steeply near Chongxu Temple. One needed to climb nine hundred and ninety-nine stone steps to reach the gates of the temple.

Of course, the royals and noble ladies were not expected to climb nearly one thousand stairs. There was a private path at the back of the mountain suitable for horses and carriages that led directly to Chongxu Temple.

Ping Yifan had invited Wu Xingzi for a hike on Qingyun Peak, and they could reach Chongxu Temple around lunchtime for a vegetarian meal.

It wasn't that Ping Yifan was cheap and wanted to mooch a free meal from the temple. Chongxu Temple was famous for its vegetarian dishes, and although they were all very plain and made without any fancy cooking techniques, just one vegetarian dumpling left a lasting impression on countless temple attendees. During the first and fifteenth days of the month, when adherents to Buddhism would eat vegetarian meals, many women from noble families liked to request their family go up to Chongxu Temple and bring their dumplings home. They never got tired of them. The Taoist priests of the temple normally had classes to attend, so the vegetarian dishes usually could only be consumed in Chongxu Temple. They only had food available for purchase on the first and the fifteenth of the month, so people always scrambled for a taste.

Wu Xingzi was not very interested in the famous view. His entire focus was on the man next to him.

The moment he woke up in the early morning, the two girls had quickly helped him get washed and dressed. They'd somehow managed to scrounge up some money and bought him a well-fitted Confucian robe made from a light, soft material. It was a dull, dark gray color, but the stitching on the cuffs, collar, and hem was neat and precise; the needlework was exquisite. They knew that Wu Xingzi didn't like to be dressed too conspicuously, and so there were no patterns or other ornamentation on the robe. However, the material itself gleamed gently on his body.

Even if he believed himself to be an ordinary man from the countryside, Wu Xingzi had to admit that the robe gave him a gentle and stylish air. He had never worn anything so good in his lifetime. In that instant, he couldn't decide where to place his limbs. He sat stiffly in front of the copper mirror, letting Mint comb his hair.

After some time, he finally forced the words out. "Wh-where did these clothes come from?"

"Hmm? Do you not like them, Master?" Mint pressed her lips together, trying to persuade him the moment she opened her mouth. "Master, the capital isn't like Horse-Face City. If you don't dress a little nicer, people will look down on you. You're such a good person—I cannot let you suffer such indignity."

Normally, Rancui would accompany Wu Xingzi during their outings. Even if some people were surprised at his appearance, disdaining this plain, simple man who looked shy and bashful, their facial expressions would not reveal their feelings. Today, though, Wu Xingzi was going on a hike with Ping Yifan. Ping Yifan was also a rather ordinary person, so Mint and Osmanthus were a little worried. They were afraid that Wu Xingzi would be ostracized by the capital's bigwigs.

Wu Xingzi understood what she meant, of course, and he couldn't help smiling ruefully. The girls had been reading too many novels. In the stories involving gifted scholars and beautiful ladies, there were often those of noble status who considered everything beneath them, their demeanors cruel and ruthless. However, talented people could be found everywhere in a place like the capital. The higher their position, the more aware they were that they had to disguise themselves, presenting a humble and courteous front. Even if the other party was currently down on his luck, there was never any guarantee that would always be the case. Even prominent and wealthy families had fallen to become poor and humble ones before. In the aristocracy, it was better to have more friends than enemies.

The rule of the reigning emperor was very strict, and the governance was well regulated; no one family was very much more powerful than the rest. At the very most, it was the son of the Protector General—Guan Shanjin, the Great General of the Southern Garrison—whose power tended to go unchecked.

As he thought about Guan Shanjin, Wu Xingzi's heart began to pound, but he quickly suppressed his emotions. What he was anticipating the most right now was still the hike with Ping Yifan. Ever since the day of the gathering, Wu Xingzi would unconsciously think of Ping Yifan's face and demeanor, especially those hands of his holding the flute. The green of the flute contrasted beautifully with the fairness of his skin, dazzling Wu Xingzi's eyes and mind.

Whenever Wu Xingzi got drunk, he invariably forgot what had happened. When Hei-er and Rancui had insinuated that he'd displayed affection toward Ping Yifan, Wu Xingzi was so embarrassed that he dared not see anyone for the next two days. He had no idea why Ping Yifan wasn't scared away. Instead, he'd taken the initiative to invite him for a hike... Could it be that Ping Yifan returned his affections?!

Oh my! Wu Xingzi's cheeks flushed red, and he dared not look at his face in the mirror. Clothes might make the man, but there was no way to make such an ordinary man refined and elegant.

Noticing Wu Xingzi's blushing face, Mint secretly stuck her tongue out at her sister and sighed in relief. Naturally, Wu Xingzi didn't notice.

Ping Yifan arrived a quarter of an hour earlier than their arranged meeting time. Wu Xingzi had yet to fill himself up, still stuffing half a bowl of porridge into his mouth. He blinked at Hei-er with bulging cheeks when he came to announce Ping Yifan's arrival.

Ignoring the risk of choking, he hurriedly swallowed down the porridge. "P-Ping-gongzi is here?" he said, a little hoarse. "Quick, invite him in!"

"Yes, sir," Hei-er said.

Just as he was about to turn around, Wu Xingzi suddenly called out, "Has Ping-gongzi eaten yet?"

"Uhh..." Hei-er hesitated. He knew very well that Guan Shanjin— the man beneath Ping Yifan's mask—had probably just satisfied his hunger with a mantou on his way here.

If he hadn't invited Wu Xingzi for a hike two days from the gathering—and if he hadn't molded the Ping Yifan persona to Wu Xingzi's preferences—Guan Shanjin would have come here to flirt two days ago. How could he have waited until today? He couldn't wait another quarter of an hour!

"It's still so early, he most likely hasn't eaten yet... Please invite Ping-gongzi to come share a meal. Mint, bring another set of cutlery." Wu Xingzi's entire being was suffused with light, his eyes so bright that Hei-er feared for the future. However, not a single twitch could be seen on his face, and he left silently to invite the man in.

"Master, shall we cook a few more dishes?" Osmanthus asked considerately.

"Yes, yes, that would be good."

Wu Xingzi felt distressed looking at the almost-empty plates, most of which only had gravy left. He had finished up the majority of the dishes, and only two big buns and half a bowl of steamed egg remained. What was wrong with his head, to invite someone to eat with him? There were only leftovers—how mortifying!

Mint and Osmanthus knew Wu Xingzi well. Mint immediately went to the kitchen to start cooking, while Osmanthus deftly tidied away the plates on the table to make it seem as though Wu Xingzi had yet to start eating.

When Ping Yifan appeared, Wu Xingzi happened to be wiping his mouth. He had been afraid that throwing away the steamed egg was a waste, so he swiftly swallowed what was left—along with a lot of air. Upon seeing Ping Yifan's amiable face, he belched uncontrollably.

The silence was deafening. A hint of amusement curled around Ping Yifan's lips, but he did not say anything. Wu Xingzi turned red from head to toe, wishing desperately for a hole to bury himself in.

"You..." Wu Xingzi coughed twice. As the master of the house, Wu Xingzi had no choice but to brace himself and welcome the guest in. "Ping-gongzi, come quickly. Take a seat. You haven't eaten, have you? I've asked the girls to prepare some food. Shall we eat together?"

"Mr. Wu has yet to eat as well?"

"I've already..." Wu Xingzi clamped his lips before he finished the sentence. Rubbing his nose, he gave Ping Yifan a smile, seeming to think that his pretense had been maintained. "Not yet, I'm about to eat... You've come at the perfect time, Ping-gongzi."

"I'll unashamedly steal a meal off you, then." Ping Yifan cupped his hands together, sitting down very naturally next to Wu Xingzi.

The old fellow froze, his body tensing up nervously. He wrung his sleeves nonstop, his brain as messy as burnt porridge. He opened his mouth, but he was unable to say a word, and cold sweat broke out upon his forehead.

However, Ping Yifan was completely at ease. He quietly tilted his head and studied Wu Xingzi with a trace of amusement in his gentle eyes. Wu Xingzi's heart was already disordered, and now he was even more lost. However, a sweetness slowly welled up within him.

Fortunately Mint was quick, and she soon returned with three dishes and a plate of steamed buns. Wu Xingzi's appetite was voracious; now that the initial surprise of Ping Yifan's arrival was past, he was inexplicably hungry again. The breakfast proceeded very smoothly.

After the meal, Ping Yifan led Wu Xingzi up to his carriage. Along the way, he introduced him to some of the scenery in the capital. His voice was as pleasant as the spring breeze, and Wu Xingzi's heart fluttered as he listened to him with relish. He wished that they would never arrive at Qingyun Peak; it would be lovely to stay like this forever.

Suddenly, the carriage jolted violently. A little unsteady, Wu Xingzi toppled into Ping Yifan's arms. He quickly scrambled to withdraw, but Ping Yifan held him gently, patting his back in consolation.

"Are you hurt?"

A heated breath grazed past his ear, making it turn red, and he shook his head shyly. He hungrily but covertly inhaled Ping Yifan's scent. The aroma of white sandalwood threaded with orange blossom was extremely familiar. His eyelids closed halfway. Feigning nonchalance, he nuzzled into Ping Yifan's chest with the tip of his nose.

How could such a clumsy attempt at subtlety escape Ping Yifan? His eyes showed a glimmer of amusement, but it was quickly covered by a trace of darkness. A few moments later, a gentle calm returned to those eyes.

Patting Wu Xingzi's back again, Ping Yifan pulled up the curtain of the window. Someone outside immediately leaned over, whispering, "Master, it's Lord Yan's family in front of us."

"Lord Yan?" Ping Yifan's voice was a little surprised, and Wu Xingzi could not help but look up curiously. "You're referring to Lord Yan—Yan Wenxin?"

Yan Wenxin? Wu Xingzi's thin body gave a violent shudder, attracting Ping Yifan's attention.

"What's wrong?"

"N-nothing..." Wu Xingzi immediately lowered his head, his voice shaky. "L-let's not go to Qingyun Peak today."

"Why?" Ping Yifan seemed not to sense that anything was wrong. "I've asked Manager Rancui about it—he said that you've been wanting to try the vegetarian dishes at Chongxu Temple for a long time. Since we're here already, are we really not going up to have a taste?" Vague amusement could be heard in Ping Yifan's voice, sending tingles through Wu Xingzi.

"True, true..." Absentmindedly, Wu Xingzi nodded. Perhaps this Yan Wenxin was not the Yan Wenxin from his past who gifted him a cheap perfume sachet... After all, it wasn't a very unique name, and Yan Wenxin might not have become an official in the capital...

Wu Xingzi was deceiving himself. Yan Wenxin had married the daughter of the ex-Minister of Revenue. With such a powerful father-in-law, he had easily built a stable career after twenty-odd years in the court.

"We're not far from the thousand steps," Ping Yifan said. "Why don't we disembark and walk up from here?"

Wu Xingzi couldn't refuse Ping Yifan's request. He felt conflicted for a moment, but he still acquiesced to the person he liked. He nodded. "Let's do it, then."

However, in less than a quarter of an hour, Wu Xingzi regretted agreeing to it.

When they came out of the carriage, he had glanced toward the carriages in front of theirs without thinking. The carriages were not lavishly decorated, probably because they were here to pray at Chongxu Temple. The men on the few horses around them were dressed in fine clothes, and all of them were quite young. Some of them were not even twenty yet—most likely the youngest in their families, riding their horses here to take care of their elders.

Amongst them was someone with a very striking face and charming, almond-shaped eyes, and whose skin was as smooth and delicate as cream. This was actually a lady dressed in men's clothing. Her appearance was delicate and gentle, but she also had an exuberant, heroic air around her. With this radiant aura, she urged her horse this way and that. For a girl from a noble family, she was drawing a little too much attention.

Wu Xingzi could not resist glancing at the young lady again. In a barren place like Qingcheng County, he'd never seen such an independent and unorthodox girl. Even the women of Horse-Face City, who were strong enough to hold up the sky, were completely different from the girl in front of him. Truly, there were remarkable people everywhere in the capital.

"Xuan-er, come here."

A low, gentle voice with a hidden stateliness and dignity re-sounded from the carriage at the very front, carried by the wind into Wu Xingzi's ear.

As though struck by lightning, he turned to look, wide-eyed, in the direction of the voice.

CHAPTER 4

TO MEET AGAIN

Wu Xingzi rubbed his nose, looking at Ping Yifan again. This gentle gaze hooked its claws into Ping Yifan's heart. He sighed. "Wu Xingzi."

"Eh?"

"Don't look at me like that."

With the way Wu Xingzi was looking at him, Ping Yifan was almost unable to contain himself anymore; he wanted to crush him into his embrace.

THE CURTAIN OF THE CARRIAGE lifted, revealing a refined, handsome man with a small beard that added a touch of dignity to his face.

"What's your courtesy name?" this thin, good-looking man asked gently.

"Ah, I don't have one. Us villagers don't really care about such matters..." An eighteen-year-old Wu Xingzi hung his head. It was unclear whether the tips of his ears were reddening from shyness or unease.

"Shall I give you one, then?"

"Uhh... H-how can I trouble you so?"

"Hmm... Why don't we go with Chang'an? Your father named you Xingzi, so he must have wanted you to live a long life, safe and sound, right?" The man smiled. His eyes were filled with tenderness as he looked at Wu Xingzi.

"Chang'an..." Wu Xingzi nodded with a blush. He felt a little hesitant. "Thank you for thinking of a name for me, but I'm afraid that this courtesy name would not be of much use."

He was the adviser to the village now. Other than a few close elders, everyone else called him Adviser Wu. He did not have any friends from the same generation who were close enough to use a courtesy name for him. The only elders who addressed him by name were Old Liu and Auntie Liu.

"It doesn't matter. I'd like to call you by this name." As the man spoke, he gently brushed some stray strands of hair from Wu Xingzi's cheek and tucked them behind his ear. "Chang'an... Eternal peace."

"Mr. Wu?" A familiar and pleasant voice brushed past his ear with the speaker's breath. Wu Xingzi shuddered, pulling himself out of his memories, and turned his head to look at Ping Yifan absentmindedly.

"Ah..."

"Does Mr. Wu know Lord Yan?" Ping Yifan seemed a little confused.

Wu Xingzi immediately shook his head. "No, no, no, I'm only a poor man from a small village. How could I know an official from the capital?"

Wu Xingzi didn't realise how uneasy he looked. He unconsciously dug his fingernails into his palms. None of these tiny details escaped Ping Yifan's eyes, but he didn't point them out.

"Mr. Wu is too humble." Going along with him, Ping Yifan held his hand. "Lord Yan is the Minister of Personnel, and he's greatly trusted by the emperor. He has a fair bit of power in the capital, and most of the officials show him some respect. It's best we don't accidentally offend him. Let's just go around his carriage."

Wu Xingzi agreed wholeheartedly. "Ah, yes, yes. You're right." Part of him was still focused on his memories of Yan Wenxin, but most of his attention shifted to the hand tightly holding his. It was an exquisite hand, broad and well-defined. The skin was as fair as jade; no matter how one looked at it, it seemed as though it was the beloved work of a master sculptor. Although there were a few calluses, Wu Xingzi was no less entranced.

In contrast to its appearance, the hand was rough to the touch. It did not feel like the hand of a scholar, but of a military man. It was warm, dry, and powerful, and it almost entirely swallowed up Wu Xingzi's own hand.

To have a man he liked show such affection, Wu Xingzi was up in the clouds. Even while walking, he felt like he was floating on air. The incandescent smile on his face was irrepressible, and the shock of seeing Yan Wenxin was temporarily thrown to the back of his mind.

Ping Yifan was very familiar with Qingyun Peak. Yan Wenxin's entourage evidently planned on taking the private path up the back of the mountain, so he and Wu Xingzi took a small detour through a side trail and quickly reached Qianyun Stairs. Now was not the time to let Yan Wenxin see Wu Xingzi—today's meeting had been a complete coincidence.

Although it couldn't be seen on his face, Ping Yifan felt very frustrated. His hand tightened further around Wu Xingzi's, as if he was afraid that the man next to him might run away if he wasn't paying attention.

On the other side of the mountain, Yan Wenxin was reproaching his daughter. He and his wife were deeply in love, and he never even took a servant to bed, never mind any other concubines. The couple had given birth to two sons and two daughters, a perfectly balanced family.

His oldest daughter had married a few years ago, and his youngest daughter was thirteen this year. Pampered to the point that she was now self-absorbed and wildly unruly, she lacked the gentleness and restraint that a young noblewoman should have. She often dressed up in male garb, running wild in the capital; she had such a good rapport with the other boys in her extended family that she would just throw her arms around their shoulders and run off to drink. She was a massive headache for Yan Wenxin.

Although he had hired many governesses and female tutors to teach this daughter of his, she was the apple of his wife's eye, and his wife shielded her daughter well. Her three older children were all married with their own families, so her youngest was the only child left by her side. As long as she didn't get herself into any serious trouble, Yan Wenxin's wife did not allow him to admonish their daughter.

Thus, Yan Wenxin would not reprimand her—but an occasional lesson was still required.

When her father stopped her, Yan Caijun reluctantly rode her horse back to him, pouting. "Dad—"

"Look at you, so careless and rash," Yan Wenxin rebuked her with a frown. "I let you ride a horse today to help keep watch over the elders of our family, but if you're going to continue being so reckless, you should just come back into the carriage."

"All right, I know, Dad. I'll behave." Yan Caijun stuck her tongue out. Although she was wild and rowdy, she was no fool; she wouldn't push her father's limits. In any case, she had played enough for now, so she stayed sedately by her father's carriage.

Yan Wenxin hadn't only called his daughter over to reprimand her. When he pulled up the curtain just now, he had noticed a plain and simple carriage behind them. Not able to recognize whose it was, he was a little concerned. "Whose carriage is that in the back?"

"Hmm?" Yan Caijun turned and gave it a glance before shrugging. "I don't know. I didn't hear anyone talking about them. They must be ordinary folks. If they're court officials or from noble families, how could they not come and greet you?"

"Shh! Little girls should not speak nonsense. Send someone to investigate it." Yan Wenxin lowered the curtain, his brow creasing deeply in thought.

Seeing how seriously her father was taking this, Yan Caijun dared not ignore his request. She waved at her oldest cousin nearby, and they exchanged a few words before the young man rode his horse to the back of the line.

Unfortunately, the search was in vain. Other than the driver of the carriage, he couldn't see anyone. The driver's lips were tightly shut—all questions were skillfully deflected, and all he managed to find out was that the carriage owner was a born-and-bred capital man. He couldn't get any information about where the man lived or what his name was. Although Yan Caijun's cousin felt rather frustrated by the lack of answers, this carriage was hardly anywhere it shouldn't be, and neither the driver nor the owner had bothered anyone from the Yan family. In the end, he could only let the matter rest.

After hearing his report, Yan Wenxin fell silent.

After Ping Yifan and Wu Xingzi left the carriage together, they slowly strolled down a side trail not too far from the main path.

It was nearing noon, and the summer sun was somewhat scorching. In only a few steps, Wu Xingzi's face flushed with the heat, and beads of sweat rolled down his face. Despite this, he didn't find the walk challenging. Northern heat was different from southern heat, and it was easy for Wu Xingzi to adapt. Furthermore, he had Ping Yifan accompanying him. Even if the path was on fire, he would be willing to walk down it forever!

"Just tell me if you feel tired. It's fine if we go back to the carriage," Ping Yifan said.

Wu Xingzi's face was red from the heat. Feeling his heart ache a little, Ping Yifan took a handkerchief out and wiped Wu Xingzi's sweat away.

"I'm not tired, don't worry." Wu Xingzi shook his head continuously, tightening his hand around Ping Yifan's. "A walk is good. This way, we'll be able to eat a little more food later."

Ping Yifan laughed at Wu Xingzi's words, and tapped the man's plump nose. "All right, then. Since you wish to eat a little more, I'll just have to accompany you to the end. The Qianyun Stairs have nine hundred and ninety-nine steps—just try your best. If you can't climb them, don't force yourself. I'll carry you on my back, hmm?"

Ping Yifan's hum was like a little kitten, batting at Wu Xingzi's ears and his heart. He hurriedly covered the burning tips of his ears, shyly nodding his head.

The Qianyun Stairs were not an easy climb in the slightest. Not only did the stairs cover a great distance, but they were steep as well, and the heat from the sun was intense. After six hundred steps, Wu Xingzi couldn't take it any longer; he stopped and panted heavily. Drops of sweat clustered in his eyelashes, and Ping Yifan wiped his face for him.

"Shall I carry you?" Ping Yifan asked, not for the first time.

Wu Xingzi looked at Ping Yifan's refined appearance and shook his head. "No, you're quite tired yourself, aren't you?" he said. "Let's just take it slow." If Guan Shanjin had been the one accompanying him, Wu Xingzi thought, he would have immediately nodded.

Ping Yifan frowned slightly. He decided not to ask again, picking up Wu Xingzi. "Do you want me to carry you up like this, or do you want to climb onto my back?"

Wu Xingzi nearly shrieked in surprise. As he looked down from the steep stairs, his head started to spin. Being lifted up like this made him feel like they were going to fall off the steps.

"Y-y-you..." Wu Xingzi didn't dare struggle. He gripped tightly onto Ping Yifan's shoulders, his lips turning white from fear.

"Hmm?" A hint of a smile curled around Ping Yifan's lips. He deliberately jolted the man in his arms, and Wu Xingzi yelped and quickly shut his eyes, not daring to look at his surroundings.

"Don't be scared. I've practiced some martial arts—I have very steady footing."

"O-oh, is that so..." Wu Xingzi forced himself to open his eyes a little. He gasped a few times, and his body trembled uncontrollably. He couldn't feel the heat at all now; his limbs had gone completely cold. "I-I'll climb on your back instead!"

Wu Xingzi could tell that Ping Yifan had no intention of letting him refuse. For the last few hundred steps, he would have no choice but to climb onto Ping Yifan's back and be carried up.

"Good boy." Ping Yifan carefully put him down, then tapped his nose dotingly. "Since you like me, you don't have to keep your distance."

This was not a matter of keeping his distance! But Wu Xingzi felt a little embarrassed to mention it—he could hardly tell Ping Yifan that he was only afraid it was too much for him, and the two might end up falling down the stairs. If Guan Shanjin was the one carrying him... But Wu Xingzi hurriedly suppressed that thought, pushing away the mental image that had begun to surface. He already liked Ping Yifan; why bother thinking about someone from his past?

Wu Xingzi looked at Ping Yifan crouching down in front of him. The light-colored robe stretched across his back, which was a lot broader than he'd first thought. Carefully, he clambered on. One of Ping Yifan's hands snaked around, supporting his buttocks and patting them lightly. Wu Xingzi's face flushed bright red in embarrassment. He'd never expected that Ping Yifan would be so daring.

Why did Ping Yifan's "good boy" sound so very familiar? But the question immediately disappeared from his mind.

Ping Yifan's footsteps were a lot steadier than Wu Xingzi expected, too. Before too long, Wu Xingzi relaxed, and he pressed his face into the man's shoulder. He swayed gently as Ping Yifan walked, a cool breeze blowing past, and he gradually grew drowsy, closing his eyes.

Ah, Ping Yifan smells really good.

Surrounded by a familiar, cold fragrance, Wu Xingzi tightened his grip on Ping Yifan's shoulders. The man in front of him was absolutely wonderful. Why had the heavens blessed him so? Coming to the capital had really proved fruitful. Although he'd have to return to Qingcheng County a few months from now—and he did not think that Ping Yifan would be willing to leave the capital for him—this was already enough.

Ping Yifan's footsteps were very steady, even while carrying a man on his back. They reached the top of the Qianyun Stairs in no time at all, arriving at the door of the temple.

Ping Yifan could hear that the man on his back had fallen asleep. The slow, steady breathing brushed past his ears, reaching into the depths of his heart.

A subordinate following them walked forward, quietly asking, "Master, shall I ask for a guest room so Mr. Wu can rest?"

"Mm. Go ahead." Ping Yifan nodded, then suddenly stopped the subordinate before he left "Get the kitchen to set some food aside as well. Once Mr. Wu is awake, he'll be able to eat."

"Understood, Master. Please leave it to me."

Not long later, a Taoist priest in charge of receiving devotees came back with the subordinate, quickly arranging a quiet guest room for them. Before leaving, he promised to save some food for the two guests.

The guest rooms in Chongxu Temple were elegantly constructed, and the bamboo furniture was well arranged. The bed was much wider than normal, meant for both meditating and lying down. In the summer, a mat was spread across it for a refreshing coolness.

Ping Yifan carefully put his passenger down. Wu Xingzi shifted slightly, about to awaken, but fortunately Ping Yifan didn't end up disturbing him, and he continued to peacefully sleep.

Pulling a thin blanket over Wu Xingzi, Ping Yifan sat by the bed and studied the other man for some time. Finally, he leaned down, pressing a kiss on the old fellow's lips like a dragonfly flitting across water.

"Haiwang..." It was a low and gentle murmur, barely detectable. But in Ping Yifan's ears, it was a shocking thunderclap.

He hurriedly retreated, observing Wu Xingzi carefully to make sure he truly was asleep. He saw the old fellow bite his bottom lip, then smile in satisfaction and nuzzle his cheek into the blanket.

"Ah, you silly old thing..."

Wu Xingzi slept all afternoon. When he woke up, Ping Yifan asked for someone to bring in the food.

Sure enough, the vegetarian dishes of Chongxu Temple proved worthy of their sterling reputation. It was the standard set of three dishes and a soup, and a basket of steamed dumplings. The food was cooked in canola oil and tasted refreshing and light. On the table were plates of stir-fried eggplants, tofu meatballs, fried bean sprouts, and a bowl of lotus leaf soup. The stock that was used to prepare the soup was a secret, but its flavor was rich and refreshing. It didn't carry a bitter vegetable taste, and the fragrance of lotus flowers lingered after drinking it.

Wu Xingzi was famished. He buried his face in his bowl and shoveled food into his mouth, not stilling his chopsticks for a single moment. Well-prepared vegetarian food didn't leave an oily feeling in one's mouth; one would only feel comfortable and pleased, satiated without feeling uncomfortably full. Wu Xingzi had ample room in his stomach to enjoy this meal to the fullest.

Ping Yifan did not have as strong an appetite, but seeing how much the man in front of him enjoyed his food, he went for an extra bowl of rice. There wasn't even gravy left on the plates in the end: it had all been poured over Wu Xingzi's rice and eaten up.

"Shall I help rub your belly?" Ping Yifan's smiling face glowed. He had already placed his hand on Wu Xingzi's stomach as he sprawled lazily across the bamboo mat, and he began to gently rub at it.

"Thank you, thank you…" Wu Xingzi's eyes closed halfway. The intimate gesture tinged the tips of his ears pink, but he didn't stop Ping Yifan.

Merely rubbing his belly wouldn't be enough to aid digestion, so Ping Yifan offered to take Wu Xingzi on a stroll around the temple. At this time of day, most of the priests and devotees would be resting in their rooms. The sun was beating down so heavily that their skin felt scorched, but Wu Xingzi paid no attention to the heat at all, eagerly following Ping Yifan to explore the entire temple.

Chongxu Temple covered an expansive area. Although some wings of the temple and ritual areas were closed to the public, they still spent nearly two hours walking through the grounds.

Back in the guest room, a large bowl of cold sour plum drink was ready and waiting on the table. As they each drank a bowl, coolness washed through their bodies from head to toe. Wu Xingzi shuddered in delight, exclaiming at how good it felt.

"Let's return to the capital," Ping Yifan said. He'd still looked very refined drinking the sour plum drink, and he took a while to finish it. He then pulled out his handkerchief and wiped his mouth with it. Ping Yifan completely captivated Wu Xingzi—no matter what he said, Wu Xingzi would smile and nod along.

When they left, Ping Yifan did not take him back down Qianyun Stairs. Instead, his carriage had been brought around to the private path at the back of the mountain.

Before they left the temple, a little disciple ran up to them, carrying a food basket. "This is a small gift from my shifu!" he called out. "Please accept it."

Wu Xingzi accepted the basket with reverence and awe. "I hope we haven't troubled you. Please help us convey our thanks to your shifu."

Ping Yifan immediately helped him up into the carriage, but he didn't get in himself, instead turning to exchange a few words with the disciple. Wu Xingzi was unable to make out their conversation from inside. Instead, he speculated on what sort of goodies might be in the basket.

When Ping Yifan boarded the carriage, Wu Xingzi had already sniffed out that the basket contained dumplings. Midway through the journey, Ping Yifan asked Wu Xingzi to go ahead and open the basket, and eat the items within. However, Wu Xingzi thought he ought to bring these excellent dumplings back for Mint, Osmanthus, and Hei-er to try, so he held himself back.

Chongxu Temple's vegetarian dumplings were famous throughout the land, and it wasn't easy to get one's hands on them. Wu Xingzi had no idea what method Ping Yifan had used to talk the disciples of Chongxu Temple into letting them take some away.

When he asked, Ping Yifan's lips quirked up. "It's not me who has such great skills of persuasion, it's Lord Yan Wenxin." He sighed. "I don't know what Lord Yan is planning. I'm merely a commoner, and you aren't from the capital. This show of courtesy is really rather frightening."

When he heard Yan Wenxin's name, Wu Xingzi lowered his head, mumbling a few words of agreement. He didn't notice the gloom flashing through Ping Yifan's eyes.

Back in the capital, the evening lanterns were already lit. Ping Yifan sent Wu Xingzi back to Rancui's residence. He first got out of the carriage, then helped Wu Xingzi out. He seemed a little reluctant to part from him, and walked him all the way to the door.

"Mr. Wu, I wonder if you'd be willing to listen to a qin recital with me seven days from now?" Ping Yifan finally asked, when Wu Xingzi stepped inside the doorway.

"A qin?" Wu Xingzi's eyes brightened, and he nodded enthusiastically. "Of course I'm willing! May I know which musician you'll be taking me to see, Ping-gongzi?"

"Qingzhu Lane's Bai-gongzi."

Wu Xingzi cried out in delight, and his entire being seemed rejuvenated. "Bai-gongzi's qin! Ah, ah, I'll attend—I'll definitely attend!"

During the Peng Society gathering at the Lianxiang Residence, Bai-gongzi's *The Tree to Heaven* had truly mesmerized Wu Xingzi.

He thought that he would never be fortunate enough to get a chance to hear him play again, but the heavens had smiled upon him.

"I hear that Bai-gongzi doesn't play his qin for just anyone."

Bai-gongzi's personality was as strong as his talent. It wasn't that Bai Shaochang was bad tempered exactly, but he was arrogant. As a musician, he had been immersed in the art of the qin since childhood. He did act a little haughtily, but he was not completely blind to worldly desires. Even though he was hailed as Great Xia's best qin player, he would play in all sorts of places, without a care for the status of his audience members. He played his qin for anyone who appreciated music.

It was rumored that the son of the current Duke of Zhenguo had wanted to invite Bai Shaochang to his residence to play a song for him. The Duke of Zhenguo and the Protector General were known as Great Xia's two sharpest blades, or perhaps the country's gods of war. Although the Duke of Zhenguo was slightly less powerful than the Protector General, one of his footsteps was still strong enough to leave aftershocks in the capital.

As for the son of the Duke of Zhenguo, he could only be described as a prodigal son. He wasn't a bad person, and he did have a sense of propriety. However, his one vice was his indulgence in debauchery. It was well known, as well, that when it came to the six arts—rites, music, archery, charioteering, math, and writing—he had no interest. When he invited Bai Shaochang to play the qin for him, it was evident to everyone that the qin was not the reason for the invitation, but rather the man playing it.

It was evident to Bai Shaochang too, who sternly rejected him on the spot. But he ended up bringing trouble on himself with this refusal. The son of the Duke of Zhenguo was born with a golden spoon in his mouth; no matter how grand Bai Shaochang's reputation was, no matter that the emperor had bestowed upon his father a plaque inscribed "Top Qin Player," or that his father now only played for the emperor, the Bai family was still made up of commoners. With only qin skills, and no riches or power to speak of, Bai Shaochang had the gall to embarrass the Duke of Zhenguo's household. The duke's son would not tolerate it.

He hadn't been obsessed with the musician originally, but now he was consumed with the need to claim Bai Shaochang as his own.

At first, his invitations had been polite and courteous, accompanied by gifts. However, when the steward bearing the gifts had been rejected twice at the door, fury took over the duke's son. Never in his life had he ever met someone so ignorant about what was good for him. Born in an aristocratic and powerful family, the Duke of Zhenguo's son had always received whatever he demanded. Among his peers, the only one who dared ignore or disrespect him was Guan Shanjin. Who else had ever embarrassed him like this before? Rage consumed him, and the Duke of Zhenguo's son dragged Bai Shaochang away from the streets of the capital in broad daylight.

Bai Shaochang was truly stubborn. Even after he was dragged to the Duke of Zhenguo's residence, he was not afraid, nor did he give in. He would never play the qin there. But the Duke of Zhenguo's son had no plans to listen to him play. He only wanted to have his way with this aloof, untouched man—but in the end, he still didn't succeed; in a cloud of shame, he sent Bai Shaochang back home.

The common folk speculated endlessly on what exactly had transpired in the residence. The most commonly agreed-upon hypothesis was that Bai Shaochang, about to be taken advantage of by the Duke of Zhenguo's son, had whipped out his personal dagger and threatened to kill himself. The duke's son was a bit of a spoiled brat, but he had never taken anyone's life before. In that instant, people imagined, he had been scared sober; he dared not push himself on Bai Shaochang any further. Instead, he let the man go.

From that moment on, Bai Shaochang almost never played the qin in public again. He stayed at home for quite some time, closing his doors to all visitors.

Rancui had mentioned that he was fortunate to have Bai-gongzi agree to attend the Peng Society gathering. Wu Xingzi never expected that Bai-gongzi would be willing to play the qin there as well.

Ping Yifan was aware of the rumors around Bai Shaochang, and he laughed at Wu Xingzi's remark. "After the Duke of Zhenguo's son abducted him, Bai-gongzi did seclude himself for some time," he said. "Over the past two years, he's been sending out three invitations every ten days, inviting people with a keen appreciation for music to listen to him play. There are so many rich people in the capital—who wouldn't want an invitation?"

"How did you end up getting invited?" Wu Xingzi realized how rude that sounded as soon as it left his mouth. His ears red, he fumbled for an explanation. "I know that you're a good person, and someone who appreciates music! I didn't..."

Ping Yifan wasn't bothered. Smiling, he tweaked Wu Xingzi's nose. "This is all thanks to the Peng Society. My skill is truly too lacking to be shown in public like that, but unexpectedly, Bai-gongzi had some appreciation for my flute playing. He sent me an invitation."

"Ah, your flute playing is excellent! I liked listening to you play." Wu Xingzi did not understand how he could be so daring—even rash—when facing Ping Yifan. No matter what Ping Yifan did, he liked it all; he wished that he could dig out his heart and present it to the man.

"I'm honored that you don't disdain it." Ping Yifan hooked his little finger around Wu Xingzi's little finger.

It was such a tiny gesture, but Wu Xingzi had never ever done something so affectionate with Guan Shanjin. He trembled slightly. He wanted to take his hand back, but the end, as though possessed, he found himself curling his finger around Ping Yifan's.

"I'll come pick you up seven days from now, at nine in the morning."

It was already quite late. Although they had a late lunch, vegetarian food tended to make one hungry faster. Ping Yifan didn't want to delay the man's dinner, so he decided to take his leave.

Wu Xingzi felt reluctant to part. "The thing is, *I* didn't receive Bai-gongzi's invitation. Wouldn't it be rude for me to just accompany you like that?"

"You don't have to worry. The invitation says I can bring a companion. Bai-gongzi used to like making friends through music. Before the scare from the Duke of Zhenguo's son, it wasn't difficult to get a chance to listen to him play."

Ping Yifan patted the back of Wu Xingzi's hand before pinching at his palm. "Go on in; you should get something to eat. Mint and Osmanthus must be waiting for you already. You shouldn't let the girls go hungry, right?"

"Ah, yes, yes..." Wu Xingzi nodded continuously, but his feet didn't move. His hand was tucked into Ping Yifan's coarse, dry palm, which exuded a pleasant warmth. There was a thin layer of sweat from the day's heat, but Wu Xingzi was still reluctant to let go.

Ping Yifan laughed lightly as he pinched Wu Xingzi's hand again. "It's only seven days! It'll pass in the blink of an eye."

Even if I do nothing but sleep for the next seven days, I would still need to blink seven times before the day would arrive!

Wu Xingzi nodded glumly. He released his hand from Ping Yifan's hold, watching the man get back into the carriage and leave.

Ah, what's wrong with me? We spent the entire day together, and he's only just left—but I'm starting to miss him already.

Wu Xingzi stood by the door for quite some time. He closed the door and looked back a few times before returning to his temporary place of residence.

"Oh? You're back?" Rancui asked. He wore a gauzy crimson outer robe over an ivory-colored inner robe patterned with clouds. He lay on his side on a daybed, leafing through an accounting book. Under the candlelight, his eyelashes looked sharp and distinct, casting a shadow over his eyes.

They were close friends now, and Wu Xingzi was no longer surprised at Rancui's penchant for lounging. In the past, Rancui would try his best to embody what he thought a manager should act like. Now, as long as he was at home, he would never sit when he could lie down. Even the room Wu Xingzi was temporarily staying in had a daybed just for Rancui.

"Yes." Wu Xingzi nodded, giving the basket in his hand to the girls. "These are vegetarian dumplings from Chongxu Temple. Share them among yourselves, Manager Rancui, and Hei-er."

"Chongxu Temple's vegetarian dumplings?" Rancui interjected, surprised. Using his accounting book to block his smirk, he said, "Ping-gongzi sure is resourceful. Today is neither the first nor the fifteenth of the month, yet he was able to get a basket of dumplings from Chongxu Temple."

Chongxu Temple's most noble devotee was the emperor himself; the temple had no need to do anyone favors. No one dared insist on having their way, lest they be seen as disrespecting the emperor. One truly had to be tired of their life to be so impudent.

"No, it wasn't Ping-gongzi." Wu Xingzi's smile was a little bitter. Sitting down by the table, he poured himself a cup of tea.

After wetting his throat, he finally said, "The dumplings are a gift from Lord Yan."

"Lord Yan?" Rancui lifted a brow, sneaking a glance at Hei-er.

The man standing silently in a corner of the room shook his head the tiniest amount, signaling that this was not an intentional part of his master's plans.

Rancui pressed on. "You met Yan Wenxin today?"

Wu Xingzi's expression immediately dimmed. His back, which had been more upright as of late, hunched over again. He curled up into a ball—it was as if he'd reverted to being the man he was before he started collecting *The Pengornisseur*: Qingcheng County's meek adviser, counting down the days to his death.

Seeing him like this, Rancui put his accounting book aside and rose from the daybed to pat Wu Xingzi soothingly on the back.

Not too long ago, Wu Xingzi had confided in Rancui about his past with Yan Wenxin. Rancui was an intelligent man, and he had seen many cases of tragic romance; he understood the place Yan Wenxin held in Wu Xingzi's heart. It was a wound that seemed to have mended on the surface, but still bled underneath. If the necrotic flesh was not cut away, the wound would never fully heal.

This was also why Rancui was willing to cooperate with Guan Shanjin's nonsense, even though the general was worse than a toddler when it came to matters of love. He was bold and resolute, his possessiveness so strong that there was no standing against it. If anyone would be able to completely clear the wound in Wu Xingzi's heart, so that no one would be able to cast so much as a shadow upon it ever again, it would be this man.

However, the Great General of the Southern Garrison seemed to have lost all his brain cells, insisting on pretending to be a man named Ping Yifan to get close to Wu Xingzi. But when he thought about how much trouble Guan Shanjin would be in when the deception was revealed, Rancui was privately delighted. As soon as he got wind of it, he instructed the Peng Society to give Guan Shanjin's plan their fullest support.

Rancui again patted Wu Xingzi's hunched shoulders in comfort. "At least Ping Yifan was with you the entire time, right? Did he not persuade you to eat these dumplings?"

"Ah, he did. But they're so precious, I thought I should bring them back to let everyone have a taste." When he talked about Ping Yifan and about food, the gloom on Wu Xingzi's face receded a fair bit. With a light blush, he quietly told Rancui, "Ping Yifan has invited me to listen to Bai-gongzi play the qin seven days from now. What do you think I should wear? What about the outfit I wore to the Peng Society gathering? Ah, right, that set of clothes wasn't cheap, was it? I have to pay you back."

"There's no need for that. That set of clothes was something I had laying around that didn't fit me. If you like it, keep it. Otherwise it'll just sit at the bottom of my trunk for the moths to eat."

In truth, that outfit had been sent over by Guan Shanjin's men—the materials and craftsmanship were the best in the capital. But why would Rancui ever tell Wu Xingzi that? He had no intention of even hinting at the truth, because he liked being a thorn in Guan Shanjin's side.

"No, no, that's too much! It belongs to you, after all..." Wu Xingzi frowned uneasily, silently counting how much he could take out from that tiny coin pouch of his.

"There's really no need. We're friends! Would you pay for a gift from your friend?" Rancui waved him off magnanimously, then revealed a small, wicked smile. "If it bothers you that much, though, you can simply do me a favor."

"Of course, just tell me."

"You can owe me for now. When the day comes that I need your help, just remember to give me a helping hand." Rancui smiled, his fox-like eyes curving into crescents. Not too far away, Hei-er shuddered.

Qingzhu Lane was in a slightly more remote part of the capital. It was near the old town, with many workshops and old stores located in nearby streets. It might not have been at the center of the city, but it was not a quiet and tranquil place.

Most of the people living along this lane were bamboo craftsmen. The street was narrow and long, only wide enough to accommodate two handcarts pressed side by side. It was impossible for a carriage to pass through it, as it would block the street entirely and obstruct the craftsmen from their work.

Most of the houses in the old town were long and narrow structures. Even with their main doors open wide, the entrances still seemed cramped. Inside their doorways, the houses looked dim and gloomy. Each house was built directly adjacent to the next, and windows could only be found at the back. Because of the cramped conditions, craftsmen worked right at their doors, some even outside their houses.

Many wondered why the Bai family would settle down in a place like this, and why they'd never moved somewhere more spacious and serene. No one had managed to figure it out. People who wanted to visit the Bai family had to step out of their carriages at the entrance of the lane and make the rest of the journey on foot, which was about a half hour's walk. There, at the end of the lane, on the left, was the Bai family's residence.

Compared to the rest of the houses in this alley, the Bai residence was more spacious—nearly seven times the size of the other narrow houses along the lane. A small, exquisite courtyard surrounded the house and wrapped around the side, with clusters of bamboo growing in haphazard clumps. Instead of an old pine tree welcoming guests at the door, there was an old osmanthus tree. In the autumn, it would be entirely covered in blossoms, and the scent of osmanthus traveled down Qingzhu Lane.

I built my hut within where others live, but there is no noise of carriages and horses.[5]

Ever since the son of the Duke of Zhenguo snatched Bai Shaochang off the streets two years ago, the Bai family had declined to receive all but their most intimate friends—with the exception of the qin session every ten days. Wu Xingzi could not believe his good fortune to attend such a sought-after recital.

Ping Yifan had mentioned that this time, Bai-gongzi invited three guests, and that he wasn't sure who the other two guests were. Bai Shaochang was standoffish, but that didn't mean he only invited people from rich and powerful families. Instead, he often invited musicians from various troupes, teachers from music schools, or even female entertainers from the Nanfeng Pavilion.

When the two men reached the Bai residence, the other two guests had yet to arrive. There was still half an hour left until the agreed-upon starting time. The attendant of the Bai residence was a young man in his twenties. He looked honest and serene, but his eyes were sharp. He respectfully led Wu Xingzi and Ping Yifan into the outer hall for tea. Despite looking Wu Xingzi over a couple extra times, he didn't ask any questions; he quickly withdrew from the room, allowing the two to relax.

Wu Xingzi sipped his tea, observing the ordinary-sized room.

---

5 The first lines of Drinking Wine #5 (饮酒其五), a poem by fourth-century poet Tao Yuanming (陶渊明), depicting peaceful solitude.

The furnishings were simple yet elegant. Due to the proximity of the neighbors, laughter and the chatter of craftsmen could be faintly heard. Combined with the rustling of the wind and the buzzing of the cicadas, it was not unpleasantly noisy. Instead, the ambient sounds were quite peaceful.

Today, Ping Yifan was a lot quieter than he had been when they last met. With lowered lids, he drank his tea, looking just like a painting. Wu Xingzi couldn't resist peeking at him, lost in his admiration of Ping Yifan's long, thick eyelashes.

A wave of heat swelled up within Ping Yifan, and he sighed. "What's wrong?" Putting down the teacup in his hand, he turned and looked at Wu Xingzi. "Aren't you tired of staring at me like that?"

At Ping Yifan's long-suffering smile, Wu Xingzi shrank into himself, turning his face away in embarrassment. "Eh? Did we come too early?"

Ping Yifan stared at Wu Xingzi in amusement, but he didn't question him further. "No, we're not too early. If we'd arrived a bit later, I'm afraid we would've ended up bumping into the other two guests outside."

"That's true..." Was there some sort of meaning behind those words? Wu Xingzi rubbed his nose, looking at Ping Yifan again. This gentle gaze hooked its claws into Ping Yifan's heart. He sighed. "Wu Xingzi."

"Eh?"

"Don't look at me like that."

With the way Wu Xingzi was looking at him, Ping Yifan was almost unable to contain himself anymore; he wanted to reveal his true identity and drag the old man into his arms for a good cuddle. However, now was not the time. The person he was waiting for was about to arrive, and he could not allow all his careful planning to go to waste. He had to force down the passion surging up within him.

"Ah?" Wu Xingzi blinked. He realized that his ogling had been rather impolite, and the tips of his ears gradually reddened. "I-I'm just a little nervous."

This was not a lie. Although the Bai residence was a simple home, it was still an unfamiliar place, and Adviser Wu felt a little shy.

Ping Yifan was aware of this. He struggled internally for a moment, then clasped Wu Xingzi's hand and squeezed it. "Don't be nervous. Bai-gongzi won't eat you up, hmm?"

His hand felt hot, and it took no time for a thin layer of sweat to cover his palm, but Wu Xingzi could not bear to let go, holding Ping Yifan's hand tightly. They didn't speak any more, silently drinking their tea. Just as they finished, the attendant came at the perfect time to invite them toward the qin building.

The qin building stood in the middle of a bamboo forest behind the Bai residence, and was a structure that was three stories high. The top floor had no walls. In the summer, bamboo curtains were strung from the ceiling. The thin, delicate bamboo strips swayed gently in the wind. As the sun shone through the designs on them, they projected beautiful pictures of people listening to the qin onto the woven bamboo floor. The scattered light was like golden sand.

Bai-gongzi was already seated in front of his qin. When he saw the two of them, a small smile appeared on his face. He stood up, cupping his hands in welcome. "Mr. Ping, Mr. Wu."

They hurriedly but politely cupped their hands back.

Bai Shaochang was not one for conversation—he was bad at small talk. He didn't speak any further with the two men. Instead, he signaled for his servant to lead them to take their seats on some cushions.

Just as Ping Yifan was about to help Wu Xingzi sit down, the second set of guests arrived. It was another pair of men. One was dressed in a set of dark robes, tall and handsome. A pair of seductively charming eyes happened to meet Wu Xingzi's, and the two men froze.

"G-Guan... Guan Shanjin..." Wu Xingzi swallowed the rest of his words. He raised his hands to rub his eyes in disbelief. He was afraid that he had seen incorrectly; his eyes nearly fell out of their sockets. *Why is Guan Shanjin here?*

He jerked his head toward the man standing next to Guan Shanjin. Unsurprisingly, it was Mr. Lu's white-robed figure. The sight felt like a knife stabbing into Wu Xingzi's heart, and his thin body shuddered violently.

A mere day without seeing each other felt like the passing of three autumns. This time, it was as though they had been separated for thousands of years. Lu Zezhi had accompanied Guan Shanjin for every one of those thousands of years. Did Wu Xingzi still have any place in Guan Shanjin's heart? By now, the general probably couldn't even remember his shadow!

Despite this, Wu Xingzi could not drag his eyes away. Carefully, he looked at Guan Shanjin's brows, Guan Shanjin's eyes, Guan Shanjin's lips, and... After the intense pain in his heart faded, what came next was confusion. Something...seemed to be off about Guan Shanjin. Wu Xingzi couldn't put it into words; he only felt that he had lost any desire to get close to the man. That little hook that always caught his soul like a fish seemed not to exist anymore.

Guan Shanjin clearly had not expected to meet Wu Xingzi here either. When he recovered his wits, the first thing he did was glance over at Ping Yifan, who had his arm around the old fellow's waist. Next, his strong browline creased slightly, and annoyance appeared on his face.

In comparison, Mr. Lu's expression was as calm as ever. He even gave Wu Xingzi a friendly smile. "Mr. Wu, how have you been?"

"Ahh... I've been eating well, sleeping well, and my legs are well. Thank you..." Just as he finished answering, he staggered and nearly fell onto the cushion. This came as no surprise: before he caught sight of Guan Shanjin, he had been about to sit down on the cushion, legs bent. After seeing the general, he had maintained that awkward posture between sitting and standing. If not for Ping Yifan considerately supporting him, he would have seriously embarrassed himself.

"Oh, is that so?" Mr. Lu considered himself a veteran of verbal exchanges with Wu Xingzi, and he knew that this old fellow in front of him was...unique. Receiving a reply was like this was no surprise to him.

Guan Shanjin solely doted upon Mr. Lu, the apple of his eye. Everyone in the Protector General's residence flattered and fawned over him. However, the Protector General himself and his wife were unable to put aside their prejudices toward him. Despite their best efforts, however, they had been unable to withstand Guan Shanjin's persistence, and they could only treat Mr. Lu courteously. Lu Zezhi now lived his life in comfort.

Tightening his hold around Guan Shanjin's arm, he turned to look at Ping Yifan. This young man had an ordinary appearance, with a gentleness that seemed smoothed by water. From his clothes, he could gather that this man at most came from a middle-class family, and was an adequate match for Wu Xingzi. Lu Zezhi's smile became even more sincere and gentle. "This is Mr. Wu's partner?"

Partner? Wu Xingzi widened his eyes, his face flushing red in an instant. His head shook like a rattle; he was so anxious that he turned incoherent. "No, no, no! Uhhh... Umm, uhh..."

Ping Yifan narrowed his eyes at Lu Zezhi and pressed his index finger against Wu Xingzi's lips. "Shh. Our relationship matters only to the two of us, hmm?" Caressing the crease of Wu Xingzi's lip with his rough finger, he carefully helped him to his seat. He could not be bothered to speak even a word to the others, and no one saw the sneer flashing across his face.

"Teacher, let me help you." Guan Shanjin did not pay any attention to Wu Xingzi and Ping Yifan. He helped Lu Zezhi over to the cushions, and they took their seats.

Lu Zezhi gave Guan Shanjin and Wu Xingzi a few more glances. A faint smile curled around his lips, and he regained his usual haughty elegance. Wu Xingzi was no one to be worried about. At least the ugly old thing knew when to retreat—he hadn't wasted his forty years of life acting like a fool.

Now, the one who posed a bigger threat to him... Mr. Lu's eyes secretly turned toward the man sitting in front of the qin.

The last guest had not brought along any companion. He was also someone who looked rather familiar... Looking closely, Wu Xingzi saw it was Yan Wenxin.

Wu Xingzi's eyes went round once again. He could not believe it. Had he misread the calendar? Was it bad luck for him to leave the house today? Guan Shanjin *and* Yan Wenxin, under the same roof?! He averted his eyes in unease, but he couldn't help sneaking looks at Yan Wenxin.

At Chongxu Temple last week, they'd been a little too far apart, and Wu Xingzi hadn't been able to see him clearly. Now, in this small room, they sat nearly face to face. The lines of Yan Wenxin's features were distinct under the summer sun. Although his hair had turned gray and a long beard covered half his face, Wu Xingzi was able to quickly match his eyes to the younger man from his past. It felt as though nothing had changed; he was still that warm and pleasant person, and the lofty aloofness ingrained in his bones still made him seem like a god of the peach blossoms.

Noticing Wu Xingzi's undisguised stare, Yan Wenxin didn't seem offended. Instead, he gave a friendly nod of his head, his kindly yet sharp eyes curving along with his smile.

Wu Xingzi shifted his eyes away in misery. His fingertips felt icy cold. Even though he had immediately recognized Yan Wenxin, he could tell Yan Wenxin had long forgotten who he was... Perhaps he had aged too much, though. After all, they had not seen each other for over twenty years.

As the host, Bai Shaochang noticed all the exchanges between his guests. However, he seemed to not be bothered in the slightest. He calmly addressed each guest, then bowed his head and began to play his qin.

The sound of the strings was melodious and pleasant to the ears, like music from the heavens. It was like jade beads falling onto a silver plate, or the harmony of a hundred birds. The qin tended to exude a trace of cold, metallic solemnity, but in Bai Shaochang's hands, it sounded as sweet as a spring breeze. Although Bai Shaochang seemed distant, if the man was anything like the sound of his qin, one had to imagine great passion and kindness were concealed beneath the surface.

Despite the rare opportunity to appreciate such excellent playing, however, none of Bai Shaochang's guests's hearts were in the music.

Ping Yifan kept his face impassive, but he was fixed on Wu Xingzi's every move. He watched as the old fellow kept glancing at Guan Shanjin, his expression very subtle. It was unclear whether he felt relief or regret, but his attention was quickly taken over by Yan Wenxin.

When Wu Xingzi had secretly admired Guan Shanjin, he knew how to somewhat conceal his actions. However, the way he looked at Yan Wenxin was utterly undisguised, to the point where it could be considered offensive. It was likely that he himself did not realize his brazenness.

Yan Wenxin was unaffected. Despite the overt nature of Wu Xingzi's gaze, he paid no attention. After their initial greeting, he seemed to be completely focused on Bai Shaochang's music, and his expression matched the melody completely. If Ping Yifan hadn't deliberately paid attention, he wouldn't have noticed how the other man was currently observing him. *Hmph. What a crafty old dodger.*

Guan Shanjin was even more distracted. Bowing his head, he fidgeted with Lu Zezhi's hand. In Wu Xingzi's eyes, he seemed to be showering Lu Zezhi with warm and tender affection, but both Ping Yifan and Yan Wenxin had noticed how absent the Great General of the Southern Garrison seemed.

Perhaps due to the worries on his audience's minds, Bai Shaochang's tranquil mood was affected. His music gradually became a little disordered, and his playing culminated in a string of his instrument breaking.

Bai Shaochang's brows knitted slightly. A drop of blood instantly beaded up on the tip of his finger, staining a small section of the string red.

"Be careful, Bai-gongzi." Although it was only a perfunctory reaction, Yan Wenxin was still the first to say something. Next to them, a servant had already picked up a bottle of salve to tend to his master's wound.

Bai Shaochang shook his lowered head. "I have been discourteous."

"How can you say that? I'm afraid it is we listeners who have affected the clarity of your mood," Yan Wenxin said as he surveyed the rest of the guests. The moment he met Yan Wenxin's eyes, Wu Xingzi's face flushed red. He bent his neck immediately, regret filling his expression.

Ping Yifan pinched his hand, speaking up in an apologetic tone. "What Lord Yan said is true. Everyone says that when playing his qin, Bai-gongzi places great emphasis on clarity of mind, concentration, and focus. Seeing it for myself today, it's just as they said. I am truly ashamed."

"No, no, Ping-gongzi." Bai Shaochang pressed his lips together, his face a little pale. The cut on the tip of his finger was a bit deep, and it was unlikely he'd be able to play well if he tried to continue this recital. As such, he pushed the qin away, stood up, and gave a courteous bow. "I, Qiuxiao, wasn't a good host today. I sincerely apologize. I hope that all of you will be willing to accept my invitation for another recital once my finger has healed."

"You are too courteous, Bai-gongzi."

His guests all chimed in with various courtesies, and the gathering ended like this, with the guests all somehow receiving another invitation.

Bai-gongzi was the first to say his farewells and leave the courtyard. However, he had no intention of rushing his guests off. He instructed his family's attendant to take care of them. After some snacks and tea were served, a few children came in. They were all under the age of ten, and each carried a musical instrument. There were flutes, pipas, xuns, and even a zither.

They watched as the attendant personally packed away Bai-gongzi's qin. Two deft servants tidied up the stand where the qin had rested. The children all sat down on their respective seats, and one by one, they started to play.

Although the father and son of the Bai family were accomplished qin players, they were also skilled with other instruments. Bai-gongzi in particular was extremely gifted—it seemed he'd been born with an innate talent for music. No matter what instrument he picked up, he was comfortable playing it. His skills in other instruments could not be compared to his level of excellence with the qin, but were still easily comparable to other famous masters of music.

He had accepted a few children as students, although they were not referred to as his disciples—Bai-gongzi was a qin player, so if he accepted disciples, he would have had to teach them how to play the qin. Instead, Bai-gongzi had taught each of the children to play a different kind of instrument, and let them perform during banquets hosted by the Bai family. He had never taught any one of them the art of the seven-stringed qin.

All the children performing in front of the audience were Bai-gongzi's students. Despite the children's ages and their weaker fingers and lungs, they had been trained since they were little. The sound of their music was already above average. Accompanied by the summer sun, a cool breeze, and lovely scenery, it was pleasing to the audience's ears. Like a rain shower after a long drought, it made the listeners feel refreshed and alive.

Wu Xingzi listened for a while, and then, once again, he peeked at Guan Shanjin.

Seeing Yan Wenxin had caused Wu Xingzi too much of a shock; for a moment, he had been unable to collect himself. Ping Yifan could understand this. In Wu Xingzi's mouth was a tidbit that Ping Yifan had personally fed him, yet his sneaky eyes never strayed from Guan Shanjin. Ping Yifan frowned, and he gave "Guan Shanjin" a harsh glare.

The Guan Shanjin currently lavishing affection on Lu Zezhi stiffened abruptly. All his hair stood on end, and in no time, he broke out in a cold sweat. Despite the suffering he was presently enduring, he still had to pretend nothing had happened. He exchanged a hint of an icy smile with Ping Yifan. His attitude seemed full of scorn, yet people who understood his disposition well would realize that he was somewhat fearful of the plain-looking man in front of him.

None of this escaped Yan Wenxin's attention. With lowered eyelids, he sipped on his tea with no hint of a reaction, yet many thoughts ran through his mind.

"Hmm... Is he ill?" Wu Xingzi mumbled softly.

When Ping Yifan heard that, a trace of hostility flashed past his warm eyes. "Who's ill?"

"Ahh..." Wu Xingzi realized that he had accidentally voiced his thoughts out loud. He covered his mouth awkwardly.

Ping Yifan sighed softly, grabbing Wu Xingzi's hand gently and pulling it to his lips to press a kiss to it.

"Ah, don't do that... There are many people around," Wu Xingzi protested, his face bright red. For now, Guan Shanjin was shoved to the back of his head. He almost didn't remember who the man was.

"Hmm? You don't like it?" Ping Yifan leaned over and tugged Wu Xingzi into his arms, then wickedly kissed his palm twice more.

Wu Xingzi liked it a lot, but he wasn't bold enough for such public affection! When he was with Guan Shanjin, all of their intimacy had taken place in private. At the very most, Rancui, Hei-er, and the two maidservants had caught a glimpse. They had never been blatant about it. Wu Xingzi tried a few times to tug his hand back, but failed. He gave up and hid his head away, pretending to be dead.

This was exactly what Ping Yifan wanted—for Wu Xingzi to avert his gaze from Guan Shanjin and Yan Wenxin.

Fortunately, Guan Shanjin did not stay long. After having some tea and a bite to eat, Lu Zezhi started to look fatigued. The younger man pampering him noticed this. He spoke quietly into Lu Zezhi's ear, then stood up and said his farewells to the group.

As the Great General of the Southern Garrison and the son of the Protector General, Guan Shanjin paid no attention to a pair of commoners like Ping Yifan and Wu Xingzi. He had no reservations about putting on airs; even his farewells to Yan Wenxin, the Minister of Personnel, were very perfunctory. He didn't want to stay for a second longer than he had to.

Before their departure, Lu Zezhi glanced over at Wu Xingzi again. His mouth curled up in a faint, graceful smile, as if to say, *Look at this poor dog that lost its master.*

It was unclear if Wu Xingzi understood the implication, as the old fellow was still staring in a stupor at Guan Shanjin. However, both Ping Yifan and Yan Wenxin picked up on the pitying smile.

Ping Yifan lowered his lids, concealing the disgust in his eyes. Gently, he spread apart Wu Xingzi's palm with his hand. After tweaking each of the older man's fingers one by one, he interlaced their fingers together.

There was no change in Yan Wenxin's expression. Under the cover of light and shadow, he eyed Wu Xingzi from head to toe, then used his teacup to hide the slight smile on his lips.

Since Guan Shanjin had already left, Ping Yifan was not in the mood to linger. The reason he'd brought Wu Xingzi here today was to test him a little, but he also knew that the old fellow liked listening to qin music. That was why he had accepted Bai Shaochang's invitation. Why else would he have spent so much effort pulling off this sham?

However, the refreshments provided by the Bai family had yet to be finished, and they were truly delicious. They were not especially fussy—just some simple steamed cakes. Some were rose flavored, some were decorated with pine nuts, and some were coated in a layer of sugar. The steamed cakes were soft, tender, and fluffy, and the aroma of milk and dough was present in every bite. The cakes were not overwhelmed by the rosewater or the pine nuts; the flavors all melded together perfectly.

The sugar coating on the cakes was the kind that was presented to the emperor, with fine, glittery, translucent crystals. The Bai family could only have gotten it from the emperor himself. These pastries alone showed how highly the Bai family viewed their guests.

Wu Xingzi loved to eat, and he didn't like to see things go to waste. He couldn't resist eyeing the cakes left behind on Guan Shanjin and Lu Zezhi's table. His obvious reluctance to leave the snacks uneaten amused Ping Yifan greatly. He curled a finger under Wu Xingzi's chin, turning his head to face him as he laughed. "They say a person can be so good-looking that they're a 'feast for the eyes.' Does that mean that my looks cannot compare to some pieces of steamed cake?"

The words were teasing, but the sour jealousy behind them was so thick that its stench permeated the entire room. *How could such a comparison be made?!*

Enchanted by the man next to him, Wu Xingzi momentarily forgot about those pieces of steamed cake that didn't belong to him. Obediently, he opened his mouth and accepted the bite that Ping Yifan fed him.

Observing how intimate the two men were, Yan Wenxin stroked his beard. "This young lad looks rather unfamiliar. Where are you from?"

Wu Xingzi obviously did not think he was the "young lad" in question. However, hearing Yan Wenxin strike up a conversation made the steamed cake in his mouth turn to wax. Despite being a touch loftier and more aloof, that bright, clear voice was still as gentle and warm as it had been twenty years ago.

Ping Yifan—who had no choice but to accept the label of "young lad"—was not pleased. However, he did not reveal it in his expression. After pushing a cup of tea into Wu Xingzi's hand, he lifted his head and cupped his hands at Yan Wenxin. "I was born and raised in the capital. I'm just a commoner—I have yet to achieve anything of significance. It's natural you find me unfamiliar, Lord Yan."

"Young lad, you look hale and hearty, and your appearance is agreeable as well. How could you not have achieved anything?" Yan Wenxin himself was born in a poor and humble family, so he understood the mentality of penniless young men. Every man in the lower class dreamed of breaking free from the shackles of poverty. Who would be content to muddle through a life of mediocrity? And which of those young men ambling along in mediocrity would have the ease and confidence of this young lad in front of him? He was neither humble nor servile when facing an important court official. To give such a perfect reply—leaving no room to seek fault in it—yet still leave cracks to tempt others to probe further... This behavior could only be learned in the aristocratic circles.

"I'm unscholarly, and I don't care much for the teachings of sages and wise men," Ping Yifan said. "I have taken the path of trade, but I'm merely a man who profits off of others. How could I be so bold as to become familiar with Lord Yan?"

Hearing the man's response, Yan Wenxin burst out into laughter. "Young lad, you're too humble. The Great Xia dynasty does not look down on merchants and traders. It's said that every trade has its master, and I can see that you're not a fish in a small pond." Seeing that Ping Yifan was about to give another courteous reply, Yan Wenxin gave a wave of his hand. "Ah, I am good at reading people. Young lad, you can skip all the empty pleasantries. You say that you were born and raised in the capital—may I know which area?"

"Around the winding Liantang Path in the south of the city. Considering your nobility, Lord Yan, I'm afraid you'd be rather unfamiliar with the city's south." Ping Yifan's words were laced with a trace of mockery. Since Yan Wenxin had already made his point, Ping Yifan no longer needed to maintain a submissive and overawed attitude.

"The city's south..." Yan Wenxin stroked his beard, smiling. "I may not be as knowledgeable as you with regards to the area. However, compared to the other court officials, I'm somewhat familiar with it."

"Oh, Lord Yan truly cares for the people." Ping Yifan returned a smile. He had no intent to chase after the bait in Yan Wenxin's words. He lowered his head, asking Wu Xingzi, "Are you hungry yet? It's about time for lunch. The Bai family should invite us to stay for a meal—or would you rather go somewhere more interesting?"

Wu Xingzi had just finished his refreshments, and his appetite had been stimulated. Rubbing his belly, he said, "Let's not disturb Bai-gongzi any further. Rancui says a roast duck shop just opened a few days ago—I'd like to try it."

"That's settled, then. We should quickly make our farewells before the attendant invites us to a meal." Ping Yifan deftly stood up before helping Wu Xingzi to his feet. "In any case, the Great General of the Southern Garrison is no longer here. It's all just things from the past—why do we have to get so hung up on them?"

"Ah..." With his thoughts exposed, Wu Xingzi blushed. Just as he wanted to settle Ping Yifan's concerns, a thought suddenly flashed in his head: Ping Yifan's words sounded jealous. At any other time, Wu Xingzi would be embarrassed, yet secretly revel in it—after all, only when a man's heart was set on the other would he be so envious. But why had this jealousy surfaced? Was it simply that Ping Yifan did not like Wu Xingzi looking at other men...or did he know about the previous love affair Wu Xingzi shared with Guan Shanjin?

If it was the former, Wu Xingzi had snuck far more looks at Yan Wenxin than at Guan Shanjin. Ping Yifan certainly didn't seem to hold any jealousy toward Yan Wenxin. Although he did give Yan Wenxin a few verbal jabs, it was because of his annoyance at being questioned and his displeasure at interacting with a court official.

No, no, no. Reflexively, Wu Xingzi shook his head. He must be overthinking things... News about his torrid affair with Guan Shanjin had, at the very most, only spread around Horse-Face City for a few days, then again in Qingcheng County. In the end, it had been overshadowed by news of Guan Shanjin going to Yue Manor to snatch the groom. There was no reason to suspect that any gossip had made its way to the capital. Wu Xingzi didn't believe that Guan Shanjin would allow such scandalous rumors to circulate while his affections were focused on Mr. Lu. He figured that no one would dare to spread any gossip in the capital about the Great General of the Southern Garrison's private matters unless Guan Shanjin had deliberately allowed it.

Wu Xingzi had been in the capital for quite some time already, and Rancui was very well-informed about local happenings. If he had heard something about it, he would have definitely let Wu Xingzi know.

Then, the meaning implied in Ping Yifan's words...

"What's wrong? Look at how dazed you are." Ping Yifan pinched his nose with a hand around his waist. The cool scent of orange blossoms mixed with white sandalwood surrounded him.

"No... I'm just hungry..." Wu Xingzi forced a smile out, then looked down, as though he was being bashful.

Ping Yifan pinched at the soft skin around his waist. "Ah, why do you never put on weight?" he sighed.

Ping Yifan led Wu Xingzi away from the qin building, without saying goodbye to Yan Wenxin.

Yan Wenxin didn't mind being snubbed. Not too long after, the Bai family's attendant passed along Bai-gongzi's invitation to lunch, and he accepted it with pleasure.

CHAPTER 5

DOUBTS ABOUND

One may know a person for a long time without seeing his true nature... Wu Xingzi could not help but think of Ping Yifan again. They had only met three times—why had he fallen for him so quickly? Was the person he liked truly Ping Yifan, or was it Guan Shanjin's shadow?

"However, people can do foolish things for love. The deeper one's feelings are, the more foolish they become. Sometimes, we can see how deep a man's affections run by seeing how willing he is to be a fool."

To be a fool... Wu Xingzi refilled his own cup of tea, glumly emptying it down his throat.

W U XINGZI HAD BEEN an adviser for half his life. He was not a sheltered scholar with no experience of the world. Although Qingcheng County was a small place, people still lived there—and people always had complicated relationships.

A new magistrate would replace the previous one every six years, and Wu Xingzi had worked for four of them. In the whole of Great Xia, you would find nobody else more knowledgeable of the matters of Qingcheng County.

The position of adviser was not an official one established by the court; it was often a teacher hired by the magistrate himself to assist with general affairs. Without an adviser, the magistrate would run into a lot of problems trying to get work done. The true power of an adviser was not small in the least, and being able to peacefully remain the one and only adviser of Qingcheng County for so many years was enough to prove that Wu Xingzi was not an idiot. On the contrary, he was much more capable and intelligent than he seemed. It was just that his disposition was so innocuous—he was like a pot of water that never boiled no matter how long it was left over the flames. He was so peacefully placid and bashful that he seemed as though anyone could bully him.

Wu Xingzi was quite distracted throughout lunch. The food at the newly opened roast duck shop was delicious indeed, and customers had been swarming it for several days now. It wasn't easy to get a table during mealtimes, so it was hard to say how Ping Yifan had managed to get the best seats in the house, right next to the window. Ping Yifan himself didn't eat much, though. His full attention was on feeding Wu Xingzi.

The pancakes were fluffy, the sauce was a perfect balance of sweet and salty, and the duck skin was crisp and not greasy. With Wu Xingzi's appetite, it wouldn't be a problem for him to finish the entire duck. He ate up more than half the dishes on the table.

Ping Yifan then invited him to sail across the lake to lift his spirits, but Wu Xingzi rejected him, saying that he felt unwell. He returned home, with a farewell that was a little perfunctory despite Ping Yifan's concern for him.

Back at his lodgings, Wu Xingzi sat in his room in a daze, carefully combing through every detail of his interactions with Ping Yifan.

He had fallen for Ping Yifan so quickly. He thought about his past affections for Yan Wenxin—he had merely watched him from afar, admiring his beauty. Although the man had left an indelible mark on his heart, it had still taken a few months for Wu Xingzi to truly fall for him.

This was not the case with Ping Yifan. When they first met, he'd still been pining for Guan Shanjin. Even if the object of his affection had changed, he should need some time, shouldn't he? However, on his first glance at Ping Yifan, he'd felt an uncontrollable desire to get closer to him. Wu Xingzi had originally believed that he liked Ping Yifan because he was talented but not showy, and his disposition was as warm and kind as a spring breeze. He was attracted to him like a moth to the flame, and he didn't even pause to think about it, latching onto Ping Yifan without any hesitation.

But they had only met a total of three times: once at the Peng Society gathering, once at the trip to Chongxu Temple a few days ago, and for a third time today... Was it really possible to fall for a person so fast?

Ping Yifan's scent was identical to Guan Shanjin's; Ping Yifan's hands, after some careful consideration, were no different from Guan Shanjin's either—dry, warm, and rough, but they looked like a jade carving. They stirred desire within Wu Xingzi's heart. And those little actions of his were familiar, too: Guan Shanjin also liked to pinch his nose and play with his hands. The strength he exuded, the doting expression on his face... Every detail was shockingly familiar. So...had Wu Xingzi fallen for Ping Yifan because this unassuming man was similar to Guan Shanjin?

No... Covering his face, Wu Xingzi gave a bitter, self-mocking laugh. Perhaps he'd known from the start exactly who was behind Ping Yifan's face. That familiar, faint fragrance... How could he ever forget it?

Wu Xingzi laughed and laughed, tasting an acrid saltiness on his tongue. He wiped his face, only to realize that it was wet with tears.

In a trance, he stared at his damp palm. Not too long ago, Ping Yifan had been intimately holding his hand, intertwining their fingers. The man made him feel that there was no need to hurry over deciding if he should return to Qingcheng County, and that the capital was a nice place. If they kept on spending time with each other, they might really walk down the path of becoming life partners. Wu Xingzi had been alone for more than half his life, and he now finally had someone he wanted to share it with.

There was a knock at his door. Wu Xingzi hurriedly wiped away the traces of tears on his face. "May I come in?" Rancui asked, standing at the door with a faint smile. "I heard from the girls that you came back early today, and that you seemed to be troubled."

"Come in..." Wu Xingzi nodded, his voice a little hoarse.

Rancui carefully observed him from head to toe, his gaze finally stopping at Wu Xingzi's reddened eyes. He sighed lightly. "I've brought along some pine nut candy—would you like to share?" Rancui sat down next to Wu Xingzi, retrieving a bulging package wrapped in a handkerchief from his wide sleeves. A sweet smell filled their noses as Rancui unwrapped the bundle. Each piece of candy glittered like a gem, looking incredibly tempting.

However, Wu Xingzi didn't move. He still could not calm himself. Staring at Rancui as he sucked on a piece of candy, he quietly asked, "Rancui, does Ping Yifan really exist?"

"Huh?" Rancui raised a brow, his reply a little muffled. "Why are you asking? Is there something wrong with him?"

"Umm..." Wu Xingzi rubbed his nose. His posture, which had finally straightened up after all this time, hunched over again. He looked like a withered stalk of grass. In his heart, Wu Xingzi already had a guess, but he lacked any real evidence. And evidence would be hard to obtain—after all, "Guan Shanjin" had attended today's recital with Mr. Lu. Ping Yifan had sat next to Wu Xingzi the entire time. If these two men were one and the same, then who had been the fake at the recital: Ping Yifan or Guan Shanjin?

No matter which way he thought about it, it must have been a tedious affair to pull off. What reason would Guan Shanjin have to do something like this? But on the other hand, if Ping Yifan was real, and Guan Shanjin was also real, how could there be two people in this world who were so similar? How did Ping Yifan know Guan Shanjin's secrets? Wu Xingzi thought that he could see through the whole matter, but after some careful pondering, he twisted himself into confusion again.

"As manager of the Peng Society alone, and not just as your friend, I can guarantee that Ping Yifan exists." Rancui shoved a piece of pine nut candy into Wu Xingzi's mouth. Although he didn't know what had happened over at the Bai residence or how badly that idiot Guan Shanjin had slipped up, now that Wu Xingzi was starting to suspect something, Rancui needed to quickly decide how much he should reveal.

"He really exists...?" Biting into the candy, Wu Xingzi eyed Rancui. He wasn't the least bit reassured, and his thoughts were even more muddled now.

"Yes, there is a Ping Yifan in the capital. He lives along Liantang Path in the south of the city. He is twenty-five this year, and he owns a store selling a variety of goods."

Rancui took out a copy of *The Pengornisseur*, flipping to Ping Yifan's page with familiar ease. Pointing at the man on it, Rancui said, "He's also a long-time client of the Peng Society. The moment he reached adulthood, he dropped by our office. His character is decent, and he has never been late paying the membership fee. Although he was born from a poor family, his family were common folk and not slaves. His ancestors were scholars, but unfortunately, his family's status declined over the years. He did not walk down the path of a scholar and seek an official rank, but his store is doing very well."

And his pengornis is excellent, too, Wu Xingzi added privately. He stared at *The Pengornisseur,* lost in his thoughts. On the page, Ping Yifan's portrait was a little blurry. This was a slight deviation in quality compared to the drawings of other members—almost as if they were trying to hide something.

Wu Xingzi carefully reached out and covered the upper half of Ping Yifan's face, but he could not say exactly how similar the likeness was to the man in real life.

"I saw Haiwang today," Wu Xingzi said.

"Oh?" Rancui rested his elbows on the table, supporting his chin with his hands. A glimmer of malicious glee could be faintly detected in his eyes. "He received Bai-gongzi's invitation as well? How interesting."

"Interesting?" Confusion appeared on Wu Xingzi's face. He hadn't at all been in the mood to listen to the qin today, nor had he paid much attention to Bai-gongzi. He only remembered that Bai-gongzi had broken one of the strings of his instrument.

"Lu Zezhi was there too, right?" Rancui asked, smiling. Without waiting for Wu Xingzi's response, he continued, "There's no doubt that he was there. Although the private matters of the Protector General's residence never escape its doors, my boss has his connections, and I've heard some things as well. They say that the son of the Protector General insists on marrying Lu Zezhi and no one else, but the duke and his wife refuse to allow it. I hear that they accused Lu Zezhi of having impure intentions. A teacher for a day is a father for life—he's essentially committing incest." Rancui laughed until he was nearly breathless. He quickly poured himself a cup of tea, sipping at it and catching his breath.

"But since Haiwang likes him, he'll not let Mr. Lu feel wronged," said Wu Xingzi.

When he thought of how Guan Shanjin had doted on Mr. Lu today, he felt a tinge of anguish. Yes, that must have been the real Guan Shanjin. How else could he display such affection? Mr. Lu had stayed by Guan Shanjin's side for so many years now—it made no sense for him to sit next to an imposter and be none the wiser. Despite the suspicions remaining in his heart, Wu Xingzi decided he must be overthinking it. He was not Guan Shanjin's beloved, so why would the general go to such lengths to get close to him? His emotions steadied considerably at this thought, and his appetite improved. He picked up a few pieces of the pine nut candy and started eating.

"I don't know how Lu Zezhi feels, but it's not the only thing he has to worry about." Rancui pursed his lips. "The duke's wife is Guan Shanjin's mother, and there's no reason she'll let her son destroy his own future. They can accept having a son-in-law instead of a daughter-in-law, and they don't care about his age or family background. But the man must have good character. He doesn't need to be able to improve the family's status, but he needs to not drag them down. In her eyes, Lu Zezhi is dragging their family down and then some. After all, the duke's wife is from the same hometown as Mr. Lu—she is thoroughly aware of his background and his character."

"Weren't the Protector General and his wife quite satisfied with Mr. Lu? Before Mr. Lu, no one could manage to teach Haiwang, right?" This was something Guan Shanjin had said himself. Ever since then, Wu Xingzi understood that Mr. Lu was someone special to Guan Shanjin, not merely his teacher.

"A ten-year-old child is different from a man of twenty-seven," Rancui replied with an enigmatic smile. "Guan Shanjin likes people who are honest and pure, and not overly intelligent. He himself is too smart for his own good, and if he has another intelligent person sleeping next to him, he'll grow tired of him in a flash. But that doesn't mean he wants a fool."

With Rancui's eyes on him, Wu Xingzi suddenly felt a little restless. He decided to just look down and silently stuff himself.

Rancui had no intention of forcing him to talk, so he breezily continued, "The duchess prefers Bai-gongzi."

Wu Xingzi choked, spitting tea and crumbs of candy from his mouth. Thankfully, Rancui was nimble enough to dodge the spray. Wu Xingzi coughed forcefully, both tears and snot flowing down his face.

After some time, he finally caught his breath. He hastily used his sleeve to wipe his face, his reddened eyes wide. He couldn't believe what he'd heard. "The Duchess of Huguo plans to matchmake Bai-gongzi and Haiwang?"

"Mm-hmm," Rancui hummed, sprawled across his chaise lounge and waving his hand lazily. "I feel that they're quite compatible. Just look at Bai-gongzi—he matches Guan Shanjin both in looks and talent! He's even more pure than Lu Zezhi, like a true immortal that has never been tempted by worldly desires, or like a lotus untainted by the mud it grows from, pure and natural without trying to please anyone. Compared to him, Lu Zezhi is the mud."

"But... Haiwang..." It was impossible for Guan Shanjin's affections to change so easily! After all, he'd adored Lu Zezhi for many years! In his heart, Wu Xingzi felt that the two men had taken great pains to be together, so they were the most compatible.

"One may know a person for a long time without seeing his true nature," Rancui said with a chuckle.

One may know a person for a long time without seeing his true nature... Wu Xingzi could not help but think of Ping Yifan again. They had only met three times—why had he fallen for him so quickly? How did they meet each other so coincidentally? Was the person he liked truly Ping Yifan, or was it only Guan Shanjin's shadow?

"However, people can do foolish things for love," Rancui added. "The deeper one's feelings are, the more foolish they become. Sometimes, we can see how deep a man's affections run by seeing how willing he is to be a fool."

To be a fool... Wu Xingzi refilled his own cup of tea, glumly emptying it down his throat.

After Guan Shanjin sent Lu Zezhi back to his residence, he did not show him any further tenderness or concern. In fact, he did not even eat his lunch with him, casually brushing him off with the excuse of having to deal with work. He turned and left immediately; even his courteous farewells sounded perfunctory.

This exquisite residence was staffed with about a dozen attendants. In the upstanding household of the Protector General, this was essentially the only area that housed such a large staff. Even the house used by the duke and his wife only had four attendants.

The Protector General's household had very strict rules. They were a military family, and the Protector General of each generation needed to enter the battlefield and fight for his own status. There was no harem of concubines squabbling and arguing, and not a single person would dare to chatter or share tidbits of gossip after a meal. This huge compound was so quiet that it felt as though Lu Zezhi was the only one there.

He could hardly put on the expression of a resentful spouse, but he also couldn't help feeling bitterness within his heart. Guan Shanjin did dote upon him and make him promises—however, he didn't spend much time with him, and the way he treated him had gradually become more superficial as of late. The most intimate actions that occurred between the two of them were a few dispassionate hugs— there was not even a single kiss.

When he faced Wu Xingzi, Lu Zezhi had been able to suppress the frustration within himself. For his own dignity, he had to put on a good show. Now that he was back in the Protector General's residence, he could no longer conceal the undeniable sadness in his heart. He knew that his current status put him in an awkward place, and the duke and his wife made no attempt to disguise their disdain for him. The only person he could rely on was Guan Shanjin.

Only a few short months had passed, yet Guan Shanjin's adoration and doting toward him had faded considerably. Mr. Lu overheard that the duke and his wife intended to set up Guan Shanjin with Bai Shaochang—today's invitation must not have been just a simple invitation to listen to Bai Shaochang play, but also the musician's response.

Sitting in a chair, Lu Zezhi squeezed a half-empty teacup so tightly his palm turned red. He could not allow himself to go down this path of hopelessness. Bai Shaochang's looks and the way he carried himself were indeed the kind Guan Shanjin would usually appreciate. Lu Zezhi understood that he could not compare to Bai Shaochang, and if Guan Shanjin and Bai Shaochang truly became a match, the general would immediately abandon him. After all, the bloodline of the Protector General was famous for loyalty; their hearts only beat for one person. There was no reason to keep an additional person around.

Gritting his teeth, Lu Zezhi came to a decision. He summoned the servant whom he had brought from Horse-Face City—a person who had accompanied Lu Zezhi for the longest time and whom he trusted the most ever since Hua Shu was cast out.

"Help me pass a message to Lord Yan. Tell him that I'll consider his suggestion, but he has to give me some form of assurance."

"Master, Lord Yan and the general do not get along with each other, and this is..." The servant was a little hesitant. "It won't be good for you if the general finds out."

Although the common folk hadn't heard anything about the animosity between Yan Wenxin and Guan Shanjin at court, every court official, aristocrat, or businessman with a bit of power was aware of it. Ever since the Great General of the Southern Garrison returned to the capital, Yan Wenxin had bothered him continuously, both openly and in secret. Guan Shanjin had his father's protection at court, so for now, his responsibilities had not been taken away from him; however, he was still being set aside, so he was now a man of leisure.

When a man's ability was too great, his superior would become anxious. It was no wonder Guan Shanjin had not returned to the capital for so long.

If disaster struck within his own home, one could only imagine how upset Guan Shanjin would be.

Lu Zezhi pursed his lips. "We'll just have to make sure the general doesn't find out. I'm only helping him probe Lord Yan for information. After all, Lord Yan has already come seeking me. He's surely planning something against the general, so why don't I turn his trick against him? However, we must not let the general know about it before we've succeeded—we don't want him to worry. Once we have Lord Yan's assurance, we'll make it up to the general when Lord Yan falls into the trap I lay for him."

In truth, Lu Zezhi had selfish motives in trying to investigate Lord Yan.

"As expected, Master is truly intelligent. I'm only a servant, lacking in experience and vision. Madam will one day understand Master's devotion toward the general. How can Bai-gongzi or anyone else even compare to one of your fingernails?"

Lu Zezhi secretly reveled in the servant's flattery. He curled his lips up in a small smile, waving his hand. "Hurry up and go. Be careful, and don't let anyone else other than the two of us know about this. Lord Yan's guarantee must be in writing, understand?"

"Understood, Master. Please don't worry." After all, he had been assigned to Lu Zezhi by Guan Shanjin. He was quick and cautious when leaving the Protector General's residence, and no one else saw him.

After Guan Shanjin left Lu Zezhi's courtyard, he headed straight to the study. When he pushed the door open, someone was already waiting for him there. Hearing his footsteps, the man looked up from a book in his hand, greeting him with a grin. "Hey, General, you're back! Did you enjoy listening to the qin?"

It was Man Yue. He was dressed casually, partially reclined on a soft daybed next to the window with his shoes off. A cool wind blew through the open window, and he was enjoying a book, a jug of iced fruit wine, and some strips of meat jerky. Needless to say, he was very comfortable.

"Don't call me General," the fake Guan Shanjin grunted gloomily. He no longer spoke in the pleasant-sounding voice he'd used before— he sounded a lot lower and even a little hoarse. Without hesitation, he dropped into the chair across from the daybed.

"Your acting is quite passable," Man Yue praised, clicking his tongue. Pouring out a cup of fruit wine, he tossed it over. The fake Guan Shanjin caught it steadily without spilling a single drop, and gulped down the wine with a dejected look that had never appeared on the real version of that face. A heavy sigh escaped him.

"What's wrong? Did you not enjoy pretending to be the general?"

"Guan Shanjin" glared at Man Yue, reaching up to his face. As the mask was removed, a young and coarse-looking face was revealed under it. Upon closer inspection, it was Fang He—without his customary beard. He was one of Guan Shanjin's four closest bodyguards. A few red spots dotted his bronzed skin, and they felt so unbearable that he couldn't stop scratching at them. His previously awe-inspiring looks had become foolish and comical, and Man Yue burst out into a fit of loud, rude laughter.

"Man Yue, you...*ugh*. Do you have any medicine?" It took Fang He great strength to stop himself from leaving scratch marks all over his face. He was truly quite unfortunate. Despite being a tough, rough-looking, and muscular man, he had sensitive skin; whenever he wore the resin mask for too long, bumps and rashes appeared on his face. If he failed to apply any medication, his face would swell, and in half a day, his face would be as bloated as a pig's head. However, he was unlucky enough to be the guard who drew the short straw. He had no choice but to wear the mask and pretend to be Guan Shanjin, faking devotion and passion toward Lu Zezhi.

Guan Shanjin's four bodyguards were of similar height and stature to him, and as long as they didn't have to get undressed and into bed, they could easily fool people upon first glance. Even the Protector General's wife had made mistakes once in a while. If needed, the four of them would sometimes pretend to be Guan Shanjin to handle matters. Fang He was very familiar with this pretense...although having to dote on and pamper Lu Zezhi was new.

"Here, take it." Man Yue pulled out a flat box from his robes and tossed it to Fang He. "I didn't know your skin was as sensitive as a girl's," he teased. "Come here, let me touch it."

"Fuck you," Fang He said, glaring daggers at Man Yue as he carefully applied the medicine to his face.

Man Yue stopped making fun of him, and his expression turned serious. "How was the gathering today?"

"The general wanted to chop me up with a knife." Fang He's shoulders collapsed, and he sighed heavily. "I'm afraid I've inadvertently exposed myself—I think Yan Wenxin might have been able to tell something's wrong."

"Yan Wenxin can absolutely tell that something's wrong, but you don't have to worry. The general is well aware of that possibility, and he didn't expect you'd be able to handle that old fox. You just have to remember that people can be too clever for their own good. We don't have to worry about what we've revealed—it all depends on what he thinks he saw." Man Yue tore a piece of jerky and put it in his mouth, flashing a mysterious smile.

Fang He was more brawn than brains. He wasn't a fool, but such complex schemes were beyond him. He just did whatever Man Yue told him to.

"Did Lu Zezhi really not realize the general next to him was fake?" Fang He was curious about this. They all said that Lu Zezhi had deep affections for Guan Shanjin, that he did not regret those feelings, and that he was willing to endure all criticism for the sake of his beloved. Fang He felt rather uncomfortable with all of it.

"Lu Zezhi can't bring himself to realize it." Man Yue pursed his lips mockingly. "For all these years, the general has basically kept him as a pet. Even if it's a cage made of gold, it's still a cage—being cooped up for that long will suppress any great ambitions. In fact, Lu Zezhi has always *wanted* to be kept like a pampered pet.

"In the past, he still had a spine. He knew how to scheme and plan. But all the general's coddling has turned him into a useless piece of garbage. He'd never be able to survive if he left his cage now, so why try to leave it? His sole desire is to be taken care of forever, living a comfortable and worry-free life with someone to dote on him. No matter how unbearable things are now, nothing compares to the assurance of having peaceful days ahead of him."

"You mean that even if Lu Zezhi suspects that I'm a fake, he'll just pretend not to notice? As long as he remains in this cage, all of his feelings and affections are a means to an end?" Fang He's expression revealed the disgust he felt. He spat a few times, and his mood plummeted even more.

"The general himself is partially responsible for this problem," Man Yue reminded him with a shrug. "But you have to keep calm. It doesn't matter much whether Lu Zezhi realizes it or not; he'll convince himself that you're the real general either way. However, if Mr. Wu discovers something, he will definitely find an opportunity to ask about it."

Fang He trembled a little in dread. He'd noticed the look in Wu Xingzi's eyes at the Bai Residence. That was more than simple reminiscence or affection; it was a questioning look...

"If Master wants to deal with Yan Wenxin, he should just deal with him directly. Why does he need to go to all this effort?" Of course, this was only a casual gripe. Yan Wenxin was a top official of the court; his network of power was a complicated affair, and Fang He knew it, no matter how thickheaded he might be. If they wanted to yank a crafty, scheming man like that out along with his roots in one breath, Fang He couldn't afford to complain too much.

"The Protector General and his family have produced upstanding court officials for generations," Man Yue said. "If they dare touch Yan Wenxin, the order must've come from above, so they have to take things step by step and deal with the matter carefully. In any case,

Yan Wenxin is a crafty old fox—he's genuinely difficult to deal with. The general has a tough job ahead." Man Yue jabbed the book in his hand up toward the sky. This hint could not be any more obvious. Fang He's muscular body shrank into itself, and he scratched at the red spots on his face again.

"The general has yet to return?" he asked.

"He needs to commit himself to the act. The general is temporarily staying at Ping Yifan's residence. You'll have to excuse him—and prepare yourself." Not without sympathy, Man Yue reached out and patted the air in consolation—then burst out laughing again. After the medicine was applied, the red spots on Fang He's skin became red patches. On his rugged face, the effect was extremely comical.

What could Fang He do? He had no other choice but to sit there with red blotches all over his face as he quietly discussed the next steps with Man Yue.

A carriage stopped in front of the official residence of the Minister of Personnel, located along Wuyi Row. The driver jumped down and knocked forcefully on the gate. When he heard the sound of approaching footsteps, the driver turned back to help his employer out of the carriage.

The one who opened the gate was a youth around thirteen or fourteen years of age. This youth had an oval face and sharp chin, along with a pretty nose and lips, and eyes and brows like works of art. When the middle-aged man dressed in scholarly robes disembarked from the carriage, the youth's tongue stuck out playfully—and despite the guilty half step back that followed, the man noticed such impudence.

"Making trouble again." The man—the current Minister of Personnel, Yan Wenxin—frowned unhappily. Taking a few steps forward, he rapped his knuckles on top of the youth's head. "You're not a child anymore. Stop wearing boys' clothing all the time! Your mother has really spoiled you."

"Ah, Dad, it's so much easier to move around in boys' clothing! I haven't come of age yet—I promise I'll be obedient in the future." The youth was Yan Caijun, the girl who loved dressing up as a boy. She had just wanted to sneak a peek at who the visitor was, but ended up being caught by her father instead.

"Shouldn't you be working on your embroidery right now?" Yan Wenxin glared at his daughter, feeling defeated. His youngest daughter was bold and intelligent, like him. She knew exactly when to yield, but never missed an opportunity to push the limits. *If only she were a boy,* Yan Wenxin thought.

His two sons both had sedate and gentle personalities like his wife's. They ought to be able to progress smoothly in court, but it would be hard for them to truly excel without their father's ambition. Still, they would have easy lives by relying on their family.

"It's too boring. Mom chased me out because I stretched out the embroidery stand."

From the way Yan Caijun's eyes sparkled, Yan Wenxin could tell his daughter had done it on purpose. "Go back and apologize to your mother. If you're feeling too antsy for embroidery, you can go and study instead. Tomorrow, I'll test your recitations." Yan Wenxin waved his hand to chase his daughter away. However relaxed the barrier between men and women in Great Xia might be, there was no reason for a noble and aristocratic young mistress to run wild and parade herself around all over the place.

"Which book should I memorize from?" the girl whined, but she didn't dare ignore her father's instructions. She pouted her lips and puffed out her cheeks as she walked to the study.

"Hold on," Yan Wenxin suddenly called out to her. Yan Caijun's eyes lit up, and she bounced back to her father placatingly.

Yan Wenxin shook his head, giving another knock to his daughter's brows. "Ask Huaixiu to come to my study. If you can't memorize the text by tomorrow, your punishment will be to copy every book at home. You won't be allowed to leave the house until you're done."

"Aagh!" Yan Caijun screamed in frustration.

"Hurry up." Yan Wenxin nudged his daughter's shoulder before he turned around and strode to his study.

Yan Caijun didn't dare delay when it came to her father's orders. She rushed off to pass the message to Huaixiu.

Fifteen minutes later, there was a quiet knock on the door of Yan Wenxin's study. Yan Wenxin was seated by the table, looking at some letters. "Is that Huaixiu?" he asked in a low voice. "Come in."

The door to the study opened. In the doorway was a young man dressed in plain green clothing, with a straight, slender figure. "Yifu," he called out respectfully.[6] Only then did he enter the study, closing the door firmly behind him. With a slightly unsteady gait, he walked over to Yan Wenxin, bowing deeply.

"Yifu, is there something you need?"

This young man was Yan Wenxin's adopted son. He had been a beggar as a child. At first he'd lived with an old homeless woman, but she died soon after she took him in, leaving him cold, hungry, and all alone. Just as he was about to freeze to death, Yan Wenxin happened to come across him.

At the time, Madam Yan had already given birth to their eldest son, and she was pregnant with their second. Seeing how pitiful the child was, Yan Wenxin picked him up and brought him home.

---

6   *Yifu (義父) means adoptive father.*

At first, he planned on raising him as a servant, but when Huaixiu was three or four years old, Yan Wenxin noticed that the child was very clever and ambitious. Knowing how docile both his sons were, he'd been pondering if he should adopt someone he could raise as a blade to protect the Yan family. With this in mind, he decided to officially adopt this boy, changing his name to Yan Huaixiu.

Today, Yan Huaixiu was Yan Wenxin's confidant. Any matters that Yan Wenxin could not deal with openly, Yan Huaixiu dealt with in the dark.

"Take a seat." Yan Wenxin smiled gently at his adopted son, gesturing at a stool next to him. "Have you investigated the things written in these letters?"

Yan Huaixiu did not sit down. Instead, he kept his body bent in a respectful bow as he replied, "Yes, I've investigated every single one. Everything written inside is true."

"Oh." Yan Wenxin nodded, then he repeated himself. "Take a seat."

This time around, Yan Huaixiu sat down on the stool. He hung his head low, and he didn't look his adoptive father directly in the eyes, the perfect picture of humility and obedience.

Yan Wenxin looked at his adopted son's head of dark hair, his full forehead, his ivory skin, and the smooth expanse of his exposed nape—the man gave off an indescribable sensuality.

"I'm very assured by how you handle matters." Yan Wenxin reached out and patted Yan Huaixiu lightly on the shoulder. "You don't have to be so reserved around me, son. You weren't like this when you were a child! You've become more and more distant as you've grown older. Have I been too strict?"

Yan Huaixiu hurriedly lifted his head. "No, no, you've always treated me well, Yifu!" His expression was anxious, and his eyes were filled with respect and devotion. He seemed deeply afraid that

Yan Wenxin would not believe him. "It's just that I am your servant, Yifu, so how can I..."

"Ah, don't say things like that. I'm well aware of the sacrifices you've made for the Yan family. Even those two brothers of yours are not as capable as you. Without you as my right-hand man, how could I keep such an unshakable grip on my position at court? You need to think more highly of yourself." Yan Wenxin again patted his adopted son's shoulder.

"Many thanks for your praise." Yan Huaixiu stood up again and bowed toward his adoptive father, only to be pressed back into his seat.

"I bumped into Ping Yifan at Bai-gongzi's little concert today." Now that pleasantries were out of the way, Yan Wenxin went straight to the point. He tapped the letters with his finger. "This Ping Yifan—his identity is completely legitimate. There's nothing that particularly stands out."

The letter detailed Ping Yifan's identity and background. Everything from his birth to his past four generations of ancestors was listed clearly in these pages.

"Yes, there's no issue at all with Ping Yifan's identity," Yan Huaixiu replied. "One of his ancestors, four generations past, was an imperial scholar, and his family was considered an intellectual one. However, as his family lacked a social circle in the capital, he was assigned a position in a small county in the south. His achievements were ordinary, and he only returned to the capital after his retirement. By Ping Yifan's grandfather's generation, their family was already in decline. He barely managed to pass the provincial examination to prop up the family, working as a secretary in Chengtian Manor. As for Ping Yifan's father, he didn't even manage to attain the basic rank of scholar. He was reduced to living in Liantang Path, writing romantic novels for a living, and he didn't manage to have a son until his old age—Ping Yifan."

Yan Wenxin nodded. "Mm. These things are all noted down in the letter," he said, confirming his adopted son's attentiveness.

When Ping Yifan was born, his father was close to fifty, while his mother was younger than his father by about twenty years. She had been a beggar before, and seemed to have some sort of mental illness; she was a little foolish, and she had issues recognizing people. However, as she had a very delicate and fair face, Ping Yifan's father brought her home and convinced her to marry him with lies and coaxing. Nearly a decade later, she gave birth to Ping Yifan. The reason for the delay was unclear; perhaps Ping Yifan's father was afraid that her body was not clean. After all, she had been roaming through the streets for years.

As Ping Yifan began to understand more about the world, his father grew ill and passed away. At the time, Ping Yifan had just reached thirteen years of age.

His mother could not be relied upon, and so he, still a child, had to support his family himself. Studying was clearly not a practical use of his time, so he applied to work as a sales assistant in a shop selling sundries. By the time he reached his twenties, he owned his own shop, and it was considered one of the more reputable shops in the capital.

But how could a man with such an ordinary life have attracted the attention of Yan Wenxin, the Minister of Personnel and one of the emperor's favorite officials?

Yan Wenxin was more concerned about something else. "Say, what did Ping Yifan rely on to achieve such success at a young age?"

Yan Huaixiu glanced at his adoptive father. "Are you asking me, Yifu?" he asked, hesitant.

"Of course." Yan Wenxin stroked his beard, smiling brightly at his adopted son.

"I've confirmed it. The current Ping Yifan is not that Ping Yifan from Liantang Path," Huaixiu said. "When Ping Yifan was sixteen, he left for the south with a group of traveling merchants to seek out some rare and interesting items for the owner of the shop where he worked. Later on, all contact with him was lost. When he returned to the capital, he was nineteen years old, and he didn't meet up with any of the people he once knew. After he took his mother away, he opened his own shop, but no one knows where he got the money to do it. It wasn't until the Peng Society gathering a few days ago that he appeared in public again."

Huaixiu took out two drawings from his pockets and spread them out in front of Yan Wenxin. On the left was a drawing of a young man around fifteen or sixteen years of age. His face and eyes were round, with delicate looks that were quite pleasing to the eye. The drawing on the right was the face of the Ping Yifan whom Yan Wenxin had seen not too long ago. He looked calm and ordinary, pleasant like the spring wind, and his eyes seemed rather dull. However, they had a good shape to them, and they made him seem warm and approachable. A pair of alluring eyes like that would attract many people.

Yan Wenxin tapped on the left portrait, then the right. A man could look different as he aged, but the change in appearance from age sixteen to twenty-five was usually not this drastic. At most, he might grow into his features and look a little more mature. It did not make sense that the shape of his eyes would change completely.

The sixteen-year-old Ping Yifan had round eyes which looked lively and clever; the twenty-five-year-old Ping Yifan's eyes were shaped like almonds and were charming, gentle, and steady.

"So there are intelligent people among the southern barbarians."

Yan Wenxin folded up the two drawings, carefully tucking them away. He now held the people of Nanman in higher regard.

The current Ping Yifan was actually an illegitimate son of the previous Nanman king. Many years ago, he had taken over Ping Yifan's identity, planting roots in the capital to keep an ear out for news about Great Xia and accumulate wealth for Nanman.

As Ping Yifan's shop dealt with sundries, it was not suspicious for him to have a group of traveling merchants working for him. When he occasionally pulled out interesting new trinkets, he could use the excuse that he had traded for them. His business had expanded in recent years. Furnishing troops with rations would present no problem for him.

If Guan Shanjin hadn't been keeping watch over the border, many of Great Xia's territories might have been swallowed up. Thanks to Guan Shanjin, though, the wealth and riches Nanman had amassed were useless to them. It was well-known that the Great General of the Southern Garrison was not a man to be trifled with. He was difficult to predict, no matter what approach Nanman tried. His attacks were like thunderbolts striking down from the sky, and his defenses were impenetrable.

Yue Chonghua had managed to make a tiny crack in that wall, but he had been dealt with in the blink of an eye. Right now, the men of the Yue family were still on their way to the northwest region, and it was unknown how many of them would survive the journey. And of those who survived, who could say which of them would last beyond a year?

The one working with Yue Chonghua had been Yan Wenxin.

He had been eyeing the resources that could be reaped from Nanman for a long time now. It was well-known that both the iron and salt trades were under government control, so there was a lot to be gained there. Nanman produced both salt and iron, but Guan Shanjin held very tight control over these resources. The Nanman king was infuriated, but unfortunately, there was no way for him to make his way past the obstacle of Guan Shanjin. The king could only gaze at his hoard and sigh.

"So has he received information about the matter in Horse-Face City already?" asked Yan Wenxin, frowning.

He clearly wasn't eager to bring up this failure from a few months ago. He had kept himself behind the scenes when it came to the Yue family's cooperation with Nanman—although that cooperation had been exposed by Guan Shanjin, it was unlikely that the matter could be linked to Yan Wenxin himself. All the same, though, having a trade route close so suddenly after he'd spent years building it bothered him. This was also the reason he had been deliberately meddling with Guan Shanjin at court. However, Yan Wenxin dared not make any aggressive moves lest he alert his opponent.

Guan Shajin was as ostentatious and willful as a wild horse. It was impossible to control him. The emperor turned a blind eye to whatever he did—Guan Shanjin conducted himself as he pleased at the southern border, all but acting like a dictator there, and the emperor allowed it without ever taking offense. And now that Guan Shanjin had finally returned to the capital to give his reports, the emperor made no move to reassert his own authority by divesting Guan Shanjin of that military power. It seemed he planned to let Guan Shanjin return to the south to keep guarding against Nanman.

Yan Wenxin dared not underestimate this young man, and he knew it was impossible to bribe him. Guan Shanjin wanted for nothing. As the Great General of the Southern Garrison and the son of the Protector General, he was deeply trusted by the emperor and did not lack power or wealth. He had a third of Great Xia's powerful army behind him. There was no way for Yan Wenxin to win him over with sweet words or favors.

It was said that to understand a person's morality, one must observe their marriage and the way they dealt with things. However, the Protector General and his entire lineage were famed in Great Xia for never accepting concubines, so there was no strife within his residence. Six or seven years ago, Guan Shanjin had openly declared that his interest lay only in men, and he had no intention of marrying a woman and continuing the family line. This declaration was the reason the emperor could still tolerate Guan Shanjin's arrogance. Seeing that he was from a politically influential family that held great power, no one else was more reassuring to the emperor than General Guan.

As for Guan Shanjin, although he was arrogant, he was careful not to push boundaries. He understood the emperor well, and he never once tried to test his limits. Some fools only saw Guan Shanjin's brazen attitude, but they never saw his clever sophistication in handling matters.

To Yan Wenxin, Guan Shanjin was the most difficult enemy to deal with in all of Great Xia. It would be a challenge, but he had to come up with a way to get rid him. If he wanted to reap the benefits of a private alliance with Nanman, he had to tear down every shred of Guan Shanjin's power in the south.

Huaixiu was a clever man, and he could see his adoptive father's displeasure. After a period of silence, he said, "Ping Yifan should already know about the matter in Horse-Face City. After how the Yue family was dealt with, Nanman has also suffered a great loss."

"They must be panicking now. Has someone been sent to get in contact with Ping Yifan yet?" Yan Wenxin sneered. In his eyes, this failure was entirely Nanman's fault.

The Yue family had indeed been the best merchants in Horse-Face City, but it had been a clear mistake to seek out such a conspicuous collaborator. There was no need to even mention the utterly inadequate job Yue Dade had done of educating his children. No one in the capital would dare covet anything that belonged to Guan Shanjin, but the third daughter of the Yue family had been stupid enough to try it.

"When Guan Shanjin returned to the capital, he sealed off all the paths that could be used to deliver messages between Nanman and Great Xia," Huaixiu said. "He even planted a saboteur next to the Nanman king. For the past few months, things have been restless within Nanman, so the king was not in the mood to contact Ping Yifan." He hung his head, his expression full of self-reproach.

The people he had sent to the south had all been caught. If he hadn't tied up all his loose ends so quickly, he might have been tracked down and caught. And he had paid a great price for his escape. He had spent many years carefully maintaining this network, but now it was all for nothing. He'd lost a great sum of money.

Yan Huaixiu had only been able to gather information about Nanman through various other means. However, he still couldn't uncover the identity of the saboteur that Guan Shanjin had planted, or what he planned to do next.

Naturally, Yan Wenxin did not think Guan Shanjin would stop there.

"As I expected, he's a ruthless man." Yan Wenxin rapped the table, unable to conceal the irritation in his tone. Guan Shanjin's methods were vicious, but Yan Wenxin was hardly some prey animal awaiting slaughter. Currently, it was hard to tell who would emerge victorious.

"Since there are no issues with Ping Yifan's identity, that's perfect. Do you still have the token of trust you received during your transaction with Nanman?"

"Yes, Yifu. I still have it. No one other than me will be able to get their hands on it."

"I see. Take the token and go look for Ping Yifan."

For now, while Nanman had no way to make a move, it was the perfect opportunity for them to operate. If they could directly rope in Ping Yifan, they would have Nanman by the throat. Once his men took over the land beyond the southern borders, there would also be no fear even if the people of Nanman tried to riot.

"Yes, Yifu." Yan Huaixiu cupped his hands together and withdrew immediately. This time, he was determined to properly carry out his adoptive father's instructions.

Once Huaixiu was gone, Yan Wenxin again spread out the two drawings of Ping Yifan, studying them carefully. He paid close attention to the older Ping Yifan. Those facial features gave him a sense of unease—they hinted at a vague impression of someone else, but he couldn't put his finger on who that person was.

A knock once again sounded on the door of his study, followed by the attendant's voice. "Lord Yan, Mr. Lu has sent someone over to request a meeting."

Lu Zezhi had sent someone over? Yan Wenxin was stunned for a moment, then stroked his beard and smiled. "Invite him in, quickly."

In no time, the attendant brought Lu Zezhi's personal servant to the study. The servant seemed bright and intelligent. He did not lift his head up after bowing.

"My master has sent me to inform you that after careful consideration, he has decided to consent to the matter you proposed," he said. "However, my master hopes that you can make him a written promise."

"Oh? He agreed? I never would have expected it." Yan Wenxin raised a brow. He had seen Lu Zezhi a few times, and had no lasting impression of the graceful man dressed in white. It was true that Lu Zezhi was handsome, but he was not memorable. Whenever Yan Wenxin tried to recall the man's appearance, the image in his head was blurry and indistinct. He had no idea why Guan Shanjin liked Mr. Lu so much.

Yan Wenxin's response sent a strange jolt through the servant. He looked up, glancing at Yan Wenxin before quickly looking back down, pretending that nothing had happened.

Yan Wenxin paid no mind to the servant's nervous jitters. "What promise does he want?" he asked with a lazy smile.

"My master says it all depends on Lord Yan's sincerity." This reply was very clever. It was as though no request had been made, but the intention could not be clearer.

With Lu Zezhi's current status, what sort of help did he need from Yan Wenxin? The man at his side was Guan Shanjin, the Great General of the Southern Garrison himself!

"My sincerity?" Yan Wenxin chuckled, stroking his beard. "Mr. Lu is quite subtle."

Yan Wenxin was implicitly scorning Lu Zezhi for his small-mindedness and awkwardness. He was curious how Guan Shanjin could have come to cherish this man so much.

"Lord Yan, my master awaits your response."

"What an eager servant! Mr. Lu sure has trained you well. Look at how loyal you are! Naturally, I'll show my sincerity, but I also have two things I'd like to ask you. If you can give me the answers, I'll gladly present to your master the sincerity he seeks." Yan Wenxin's gaze toward the servant hid none of his disdain. A master's character could be seen through his servants, and this Lu Zezhi was truly intriguing.

"Please, ask anything you like, Lord Yan."

"Let's tentatively assume that you know what the agreement is between your master and me." Yan Wenxin saw how the servant shivered slightly, shifting about in unease. He already understood what was going on. "Why would Mr. Lu consent to this? The person at his side is the son of the Protector General. Guan Shanjin can already give him whatever he needs."

This question left the servant momentarily speechless. His head hung lower, his chin almost touching his chest.

"Is Mr. Lu not worried that if the matter is exposed, Guan Shanjin would no longer dote on him?" Yan Wenxin rapped his knuckles on the table. A fierce shudder ran through the servant. He retreated a couple of steps, and he still had no response.

"Cat got your tongue? Or is answering my questions beneath you?"

"No, I-I... Even if I were to have all the courage in the world, I wouldn't dare not to answer you..." The servant wiped at his sweat, his breathing becoming more rapid.

Yan Wenxin no longer pushed him. Instead, with great composure, he picked up his teacup and took a sip before casually flipping through a book of poetry.

After quite some time, the servant seemed to have calmed himself down. He stammered, "M-my master understands all this, but... things may not always go in the manner one would hope, and my master needs some help. Although a large tree does provide ample shade, if one attaches oneself to just one tree, one sometimes has to suffer from the freezing wind and the scorching sun."

Yan Wenxin laughed, tamping down the threatening aura he'd been giving off. "Your words are rough, but the logic behind them is not. Mr. Lu has trained you well."

"Mr. Lu trusts me. I cannot disappoint him."

Yan Wenxin deftly ground up some ink and picked up a brush.

After writing a few sentences down on paper, he blew the ink dry and folded it up.

"Take this back to your master and tell him it is proof of my sincerity. I'm aware which tree Mr. Lu wants the most. Since he's helping me, I can also help him maintain his preferred place in the shade."

The servant stepped forward and received the note respectfully, carefully tucking it into his clothes. "On behalf of my master, I thank you, Lord Yan."

"No need for such courtesies—I am grateful to Mr. Lu for his help." Yan Wenxin smiled at the servant, then instructed his attendant: "See him out."

The servant did not stay any longer. With great trepidation and awe, he left, following behind the attendant. Before he walked away, Yan Wenxin saw him pressing down where the note was hidden.

The study was silent once again. Yan Wenxin slowly sipped on the tea that the emperor had gifted him, his eyes lowered in thought.

It rained over the next few days, the temperature dropping a few more degrees each time. Summer in the capital was nearing its end, and the autumn breeze gradually arrived.

Before he realized it, Wu Xingzi had been in the capital for over two months. He often went on short trips with Ping Yifan, and they explored all the famous sights and attractions around the capital.

Today was a rare day that Ping Yifan had not invited him out. Wu Xingzi allowed himself to laze about for half the day, only getting out of bed when it was close to noon. Pulling a slightly thicker robe around himself, he sat by the window and rested his chin on his hand as he gazed at the rain.

Lunch was quickly served, with four dishes in total: two vege-tarian, two meat-based. These dishes were accompanied by a bowl of tofu soup with vegetables. After setting the table, Mint called out, "Master, quick, come and have your lunch. You didn't have any breakfast—you must be starving."

Wu Xingzi agreed, but he did not move. He was a rare picture of laziness, a teacup in his hand. The originally steaming tea had already turned cold, yet less than half the cup had been drunk.

Osmanthus waited for some time, but still did not see her master come to the table. Walking over to him, she urged, "Master, there are fresh lotus roots today, and jiejie has fried some. Take a sniff—don't they smell good?"

"It does smell pretty good. Mint's culinary skills keep improving," Wu Xingzi praised the girl with a smile. Only then did he stand up from his chair.

"Isn't that so? You have been eating outside with Ping-gongzi a lot lately, Master. There are so many great chefs in the capital—if we don't improve our skills, how can we be worthy of working for you?" Mint covered her smile, the teasing in her voice causing Wu Xingzi to scratch his nose in embarrassment.

"Girls, come and have lunch with me," Wu Xingzi said, feeling a little apologetic. Ever since he met Ping Yifan, he had been neglect-ing the two girls at home.

Ping Yifan liked bringing him out on excursions. Once they became more familiar with each other, he would often come by and pick him up early in the morning, and didn't bring him home until after sundown.

Just now, Wu Xingzi had belatedly noticed that the two girls had made a small plot for gardening at some point, with a trellis and eggplants.

Mint and Osmanthus did not actually share a table with their master. Standing by the side, they would occasionally dish out more food for Wu Xingzi, chattering away as they spoke with him. While doing so, they shared all the rumors they had heard in the capital.

"Master, do you know of a court official named Yan Wenxin?" When she mentioned the man, Mint's face flushed red. Her smile vanished, and her cheeks puffed in anger.

"Yan Wenxin?" Wu Xingzi was startled, nearly dropping the fried lotus root from his chopsticks. "Isn't he the current Minister of Personnel?"

"Yes, that's him!" Osmanthus's voice was furious, her brows furrowing. "This Yan Wenxin—who knows what his problem is? He seems to really dislike our general. *Hmph!* If it wasn't for the general guarding the southern borders, how could these officials in the capital lead such carefree lives?"

Born in Horse-Face City, Mint and Osmanthus revered Guan Shanjin like a god. If anyone dared to say a negative word about him, both girls would roll up their sleeves on the spot and give that person a good thrashing.

"What did he do?" Although Wu Xingzi had been living in the capital, he had spent most of his time with Ping Yifan. He was truly unaware of current events.

And also...he wasn't sure if it was deliberate or not, but Ping Yifan had never mentioned Guan Shanjin or Yan Wenxin since their chance meeting at Bai Shaochang's place. The younger man rarely mentioned anything that had to do with the capital—at the most, he gave short explanations about the specialty dishes on their table. Wu Xingzi had learned that there was a special cellar in the northern outskirts of the city where vegetables were planted using water from a hot spring, so that people could have summer fruits and vegetables even in the dead of winter.

"Ugh, it makes me angry just speaking about it! Yan Wenxin had the audacity to accuse the general of being disloyal to the emperor, and said that was why he stayed at the southern borders for five years and refused to return to the capital!"

The girls spat at Yan Wenxin.

The most important reason that Guan Shanjin remained at the southern borders for so many years—other than his disinterest in the courtly power struggle in the capital—was that actually, Nanman was not at peace at all. On the surface, they had declared themselves subjects to Great Xia, but in truth they were suppressing their anger, planning on rising up again as soon as they had the chance. Without Guan Shanjin defending the borders, there was no guarantee that Horse-Face City would have been able to enjoy a peaceful existence.

It was stated clearly in the laws of Great Xia that if there was no war, the head of the army would have to return to the capital every two years for a debrief, and Guan Shanjin had defied this law twice. Although the emperor neither urged him to come back nor punished him, his failure to return was still a strike against him. This was exactly what Yan Wenxin was using against him at court, colluding with the censorate, the Minister of War, and other court officials who supported him to submit dozens of accusations to the emperor.

Since the Protector General's line of ministers had always been upright and never formed factions within the court, the Protector General and his son stood alone. A few days ago, Guan Shanjin had finally been stripped of his title; he was no longer the Great General of the Southern Garrison. The emperor even wanted to place him under house arrest for him to reflect on his actions. Only the heavens knew how long this house arrest would last.

The once-mighty general, son of the Protector General, had fallen in the blink of an eye.

Hearing this made Wu Xingzi lose his appetite. "Is Haiwang not returning to Horse-Face City?"

"We don't know." Mint and Osmanthus spoke simultaneously, both wearing frowns on their little faces. They had only heard about this on the streets, and they were unclear on any further details. However, the general was a clever man. He would be able to get out of this predicament and return to Horse-Face City!

Wu Xingzi nodded. He put down the chopsticks in his hand, rubbing his chest. He no longer had any interest in the food. He sat there blankly, and the girls didn't know what he was thinking.

A moment later, he suddenly asked Mint, "Is Rancui home?"

Mint nodded. "The manager is home." She had just sent over a plate of freshly fried lotus roots to accompany the manager's meal.

"You should go ahead and finish everything—there's no need to wait for me to come back and eat. I have something to discuss with the manager." Wu Xingzi stood up and hurried off without waiting for the girls' response.

Rancui was currently eating lunch. He didn't have an abnormally huge appetite like Wu Xingzi, but there were quite a number of dishes on the table. At the same table was Hei-er, who currently had his head bowed as he deboned fish for Rancui. Seeing that focused look of his, Rancui could not help but be amused. He already had two pieces of deboned fish in his bowl, the tender white flesh gleaming with a dark green sauce. It looked delicious, and he couldn't help eating a couple more mouthfuls of rice with it.

When Wu Xingzi arrived, Rancui was already half full.

"Mr. Wu," Rancui called out warmly. "Quick, have a seat. Shall we have lunch together?"

He gave Hei-er a kick under the table. Hei-er, who was currently drinking his soup with his head lowered, immediately wiped his mouth and stood up. Deftly, he placed a new set of cutlery in front of Wu Xingzi, then quietly removed his own cutlery and stood in the corner of the room.

"I-I'll just have some soup..." Wu Xingzi had wanted to refuse, but his stomach, failing to live up to expectations, growled loudly. Blushing, he wrapped his arms around his stomach, then sat down and ladled a bowl of soup to soothe his empty belly.

The dishes Rancui had were more exquisite than the ones Wu Xingzi loved to eat. The soup was a thick, clear broth made from bamboo mushrooms. The mushroom was soft but still had a bite to them, and paired with seafood and shellfish, the soup slid down and warmed his belly. In moments, Wu Xingzi became even more ravenous. He'd missed breakfast, after all—how could a man who loved to eat so much endure his hunger any longer? Despite the troubles weighing on his mind, he still managed to sweep the dishes on the table clean.

Smiling, Rancui filled up Wu Xingzi's bowl. He was in no hurry to ask why Wu Xingzi had come by. In case Wu Xingzi was not yet full, he asked a servant to bring over two more plates of food, as well as some steamed buns. He ate a piece of candied lotus root as he sat with Wu Xingzi.

When they were finally done with the meal, Rancui feigned nonchalance as he asked, "Did Ping-gongzi not invite you out today?"

Ping Yifan? Wu Xingzi hadn't expected Rancui to mention Ping Yifan before anything else. Dazedly, he replied, "He said that the rain today is too heavy, and it wouldn't be good if I caught a cold. Anyway, he has a group of traveling merchants stuck in the rain, and he needs to go handle the situation. He probably won't be able to see me for the next couple of weeks."

Wu Xingzi sighed, feeling somewhat sad to part from the man.

Rancui covered his mouth with his hand. He appeared to be blocking a sudden bout of dry coughing, but in truth, he couldn't hold back his sneer—he nearly rolled his eyes, too. The excuse was truly ridiculous, and Wu Xingzi was probably the only one who'd be willing to believe it. Today was not the first day the rain had fallen. It had been raining for quite a few days now, and Ping Yifan had taken Wu Xingzi out anyway.

"And why did you want to speak to me?" Rancui asked, drinking some tea to soothe his throat.

Wu Xingzi frowned thoughtfully, trying to decide where to start. Rancui did not hurry him, knowing that Mint and Osmanthus must have said something to do with Guan Shanjin. Why else would Wu Xingzi wear such an expression? He wasn't sure if Wu Xingzi had come by to confirm the rumors or to ask him for help.

"Rancui." A moment later, Wu Xingzi gritted his teeth, looking as though he was ready to risk it all. "Do you have any sort of drug that can make people tell the truth?"

This question startled even Hei-er in the corner, who usually managed to remain stoic. Staring at Wu Xingzi in amazement, he opened his mouth to say something, only for Rancui to hold up his hand and stop him.

Rancui was surprised as well. He watched Wu Xingzi's uneasy yet determined face for some time before slowly opening his mouth to speak. "You're asking for a truth serum?"

"Yes." Wu Xingzi nodded, rubbing his sweaty palms on his knees. He quickly added, "The drug cannot be too strong—I'm afraid that it'll be bad for the body. Just enough to lower someone's barriers a little so they'd be willing to speak some truth... That's all."

"I do have such a drug," Rancui replied, "and the effects aren't strong, either. For four hours after ingestion, the person will answer any question, and then they'll fall asleep. If you don't want him to remember, just dose him again with a different drug. Although the truth-telling effect of the first drug only lasts two hours in that case, he will not remember anything on waking." Rancui tapped his chin with a finger, then smiled. "I'm curious. On whom do you plan to use the drug, Mr. Wu? Is it Ping Yifan?"

Wu Xingzi hunched into himself and shivered a little. His forehead was covered in a thin layer of sweat, and his hand went to scratch his nose.

Just when Rancui thought that he did not plan on answering, he heard Wu Xingzi's low and muffled response. "It is Ping Yifan..."

Hei-er was a well-trained martial artist, and his hearing was much more sensitive than the average man's. He could hear Wu Xingzi's answer clearly, and it made him somewhat anxious. "Mr. Wu, why do you want to give this drug to Ping Yifan?" he asked.

Rancui was unable to stop Hei-er. He rolled his eyes at him as if to say, *what a fool.*

Wu Xingzi already suspected that Ping Yifan had a rather complicated identity, so he must have been pondering for a while before finally asking for this drug. Wasn't Hei-er just confirming Wu Xingzi's suspicions, asking a question like that? If Ping Yifan's identity was real, why would Hei-er show a fraction of concern over it?

The subordinate was just as foolish as his master, Rancui thought. How did this group of idiots defend the southern border? He felt bad for Man Yue—he seemed to be the only one of this band of oafs putting in any effort.

As expected, Wu Xingzi's head sank low when he heard Hei-er's question. His hands tightened into fists in his lap. "I-I plan on becoming life partners with Ping Yifan, even if I never return to Qingcheng County. Even if I spend the rest of my days in the capital, it wouldn't be so bad. However, I would like to confirm Ping Yifan's intentions. I'm afraid that..." Wu Xingzi clenched his jaw, and didn't finish his sentence.

Hei-er's face darkened even further. He knew that Wu Xingzi had only ever liked three men in his entire life. He had shared no fate with the first two men, but he was still willing to present his heart. Hei-er was shocked for a moment.

"Becoming life partners with Ping Yifan..." Rancui's slender fingers tapped lightly on the table. Seeing Wu Xingzi was nervous enough to turn pale and clammy, Rancui pushed over the plate of candied lotus roots. "Calm yourself down and try this. This is something I specially bought from the House of Taotie. They only sell two pounds' worth a day, and the ingredients used to make them are all of the highest quality. You'll love it."

Wu Xingzi picked up a slice and placed it into his mouth. However, it tasted somewhat flavorless to him. He kept glancing at Rancui with damp eyes, deeply afraid that the manager would not agree to help him. After all, drugging a person was rather despicable. However, he was unable to come up with any other plan. This was his only option.

Seeing Wu Xingzi nibble at the candied lotus root with his two front teeth like a mouse, Rancui smiled. "I thought that you had come looking for me to ask about Guan Shanjin. The two girls must have already informed you about him, yes?"

Wu Xingzi's head drooped lower and his body shrank even more, as if to hide from Hei-er's prying eyes. He nodded hurriedly. "I-I heard about it... The Minister of Personnel, Lord Yan, along with the censorate, submitted dozens of accusations against Haiwang. He has been dismissed from his position, and he's under house arrest in the Protector General's residence." Not much worry could be detected in his solemn tone.

Seeing that Hei-er wanted to speak again, Rancui shot him a frown, forcing the tall, muscular man to swallow his words. Hei-er's face darkened even further, his negative feelings practically pouring off him in waves.

"Mint and Osmanthus do have quite a good grasp on current events," said Rancui. "It's no secret that Yan Wenxin dislikes Guan Shanjin. The year General Guan returned from the northwest region, he'd attained countless military achievements. Songs spread in the capital of his glory: 'With General Guan in the northwest, we need neither the heavens nor the earth to protect us.' The emperor gave Guan Shanjin the cold shoulder for quite some time back then. If you have a sharp knife, you have to use it, but you need to have some sort of insurance against it—and of course a wife and children are the best sort one could ever have." Rancui laughed. He drank some tea, pretending that he did not notice how entranced Wu Xingzi was by listening to him.

"At that time, there wasn't a noble family in the capital who didn't want to form a connection with Guan Shanjin. Not a connection with the Protector General, but with his son. The Protector General was as stubborn as a mule and always went his own way at court. Although he was a military man, he was very clever and knew exactly how to handle other people. However, Guan Shanjin clearly was not the sort of man willing to hinder himself. In the entire court, he was the only one young enough to fight—and quite skilled at it. If the emperor wished to continue ruling Great Xia, he had no choice but to use Guan Shanjin.

"And of course Yan Wenxin knew that, too. That year, his daughter was only thirteen, but he still sent her portrait to Guan Shanjin. Yan Wenxin made many moves in private as well. He is the Minister of Personnel, and he had his finger on the pulse of the whole court. If he had Guan Shanjin's power over the army in his hand as well, he would essentially have power over the entirety of Great Xia."

"Yes, yes... Yan Wenxin is truly intelligent." Wu Xingzi nodded along, agreeing firmly. He was completely engrossed in the story. "What happened next?"

Was Wu Xingzi treating this like story time? Rancui chuckled, glancing over at a very tense Hei-er. He sipped his tea and continued, "After that, Guan Shanjin only had Lu Zezhi in his heart, but you already knew that. The Protector General's son has a million negative traits, but he does have *one* thing to recommend him—his loyalty. When he is set on someone, he doesn't easily change his mind. He spread the word that he would only be willing to spend the rest of his life with a man. He didn't want a wife and children, even if it meant his family's lineage ended with him."

"Ah..." Wu Xingzi sucked in a breath, then exhaled lightly. His eyes were still wet, but Rancui could not read his thoughts. He only saw Wu Xingzi nod. "Haiwang is someone who takes responsibility," he said, his voice soft.

What an earnest compliment. Rancui had to stop himself from rolling his eyes. What responsibility? The general was clearly an idiot! He had Lu Zezhi in his heart, yet he still flirted and philandered, and Rancui had lost two Peng Society members as a result. Now, with Guan Shanjin's attentions fully focused on a certain someone, was the object of his affection still not obvious?

"Whether he is someone who takes responsibility or not, I'm not sure. However, it was clear that he offended Yan Wenxin." Rancui pursed his lips, lowering his voice. "Think about it—Yan Wenxin is a vicious, scheming man. How could he just give up because Guan Shanjin did not like girls? He didn't only have a daughter—he had two sons, and a foster son, too."

Rancui paused here, but Wu Xingzi was already stunned. In order to accomplish his objective, Yan Wenxin even planned to push his sons on Guan Shanjin? How old had Yan Wenxin's sons been back then? It didn't bear thinking about! One must have been fifteen, and the other only thirteen! Guan Shanjin certainly would not have gone for them. He seemed to prefer older men... Besides, Guan Shanjin was just as vicious: he didn't want to lose to Yan Wenxin in any way.

These were all Rancui's personal opinions. He had said everything that he needed to say, and he didn't forget the reason why Wu Xingzi sought him out. Standing up, he walked into his bedroom. When he returned, he carried two paper bags in his hands, one green and one pink. He placed both bags on the table.

"Here. In the green bag is the truth serum. It's colorless and tasteless—you can mix it in wine, tea, or food. After it's ingested, it will take effect in less than ten minutes. For the next four hours, there will be no lies or deception. After those four hours he'll fall asleep, and he'll be fine upon waking up.

"If you don't want him to remember that he has been drugged, remember to mix the drug from the pink bag into the green one. The drug in the pink bag tastes a little bitter, so it's best to stir it into wine. Although the effect of the truth-telling drug will then

last only two hours, I guarantee there will be no issues for you after that." After this exhaustive explanation, Rancui smiled and pushed the bags toward Wu Xingzi.

Wu Xingzi struggled internally as he looked at the two bags. In the end, he picked up only the green bag with the truth-telling serum. His fingers hovered above the pink bag for a moment. Then, he pushed it back to Rancui.

"Some things should be remembered."

Hearing the meaning implied in his words, Rancui held back a smile.

ᴛᴡᴏ Hᴇᴀʀᴛs ᴀs Oɴᴇ

"I will definitely listen to what my father said. My parents left this world early, but in the brief time they were here, they were steadfast in their love for one another. That is all I want—to give my heart to one man, and to have his in return. Since your heart belongs to another...I don't want it."

Guan Shanjin was astonished. He hugged Wu Xingzi tightly, wishing he could subsume the older man's entire being into his blood and bones.

"My heart only belongs to you. If you want it, take it. In this life, I will never give it to anyone else. There will never be another."

THE DAY AFTER WU XINGZI asked Rancui for the truth serum, the rain stopped as well.

Wu Xingzi woke up early in the morning, going to the market to buy some groceries with Mint and Osmanthus. When he returned home, he went to the kitchen, tinkering around for a bit and preparing some simple homemade dishes, which he packed up neatly in a box. He then borrowed a carriage from Rancui and went of his own accord to look for Ping Yifan, accompanied only by Hei-er.

Ping Yifan lived at the edges of Liantang Path, where there were a mix of residences and stores. The shop which had kickstarted his family fortune was situated right along Xuanwu Street in the southern part of the city, selling goods imported from the south. Ping Yifan's home was in a compound behind the shop.

The shop boy at the store recognized Wu Xingzi, as he had visited a few times before. Seeing him walk in with a box of food, the boy greeted him warmly. "Mr. Wu, are you here for our boss?"

"Yes, is he around?" Wu Xingzi, about to commit a morally reprehensible act for the first time in his entire life, broke out in a cold sweat, tightening his grip around the handle of the box. It was a miracle that he managed to make the smile on his face look natural.

"The boss is around. Please head inside." The shop boy knew that the man in front of him was essentially equivalent to his boss's spouse. Naturally, he would not stop him.

Wu Xingzi nodded. He turned around to wave at Hei-er, signaling that he could head back. Then he took a deep breath. After a moment's hesitation, he stepped inside.

Ping Yifan had woken up late today. When Wu Xingzi came in, he had only just finished taking a bath, and he was now sitting in the yard to dry his wet hair in the sun. He held a book of accounts in his hands, looking very focused. However, with his loose hair, he didn't seem as meek as usual; instead, he looked a little more alluring.

Unsurprisingly, Wu Xingzi was entranced by the beauty in front of him. With slightly reddened cheeks, he stared for a moment before calling out, "Ping Yifan."

"Hmm?" Ping Yifan had heard him enter, but he chose to play along. The old fellow breathed lightly and walked lightly, like an old, lazy cat. Without his permission, Ping Yifan's heart softened into a puddle, and he did not spend any effort wondering why Wu Xingzi would arrive here out of nowhere.

Looking up, he smiled at Wu Xingzi. His eyes then fell to the box of food in Wu Xingzi's hands. "What did you bring?"

"Just some small things." Wu Xingzi walked over with the box, awkwardly looking at the stone table covered in letters and ledgers.

Ping Yifan had never concealed any of his business from Wu Xingzi, and it seemed that he had no intention of hiding it away now, either. He watched Wu Xingzi with a bright smile.

"It's almost noon. I've made a few dishes, and I even asked Rancui for a jar of fruit wine. Shall we share?"

"Oh? You cooked?" Pleasant surprise spread across Ping Yifan's face, and he casually bundled up the documents on the table and placed them on a chair next to him. "I've never eaten your cooking before."

Ping Yifan helped Wu Xingzi take the food out from the box and place it neatly on the table. Then he pulled the older man into his arms, pressing a kiss onto his cheek.

"Ah, we're in broad daylight..." Wu Xingzi was easily embarrassed. Shyly, he pushed at Ping Yifan a couple of times, but he couldn't suppress his desire for intimacy. Soon, he reclined obediently in Ping Yifan's arms, allowing the man to caress him.

It wasn't anything intense, though. Although the couple had known each other for more than a month, and they intended to become life partners, their relationship had been very chaste. The occasional cheek kisses were the most intimate actions they shared; Ping Yifan usually just held Wu Xingzi's hand or wrapped an arm around his waist.

Wu Xingzi craved more. What he'd gotten up to with Guan Shanjin had been so wet and messy it could have saved Great Xia from ten years of drought—but he was far too timid to take the initiative. Being constantly surrounded by the scent of white sandalwood and orange blossoms like this, he felt like he was about to explode.

That was one of the reasons why he wanted to use the drug on Ping Yifan. He had nothing else to lose; he might as well give it a try.

Once he clarified who Ping Yifan was, he could resist his desires more easily. After all, without this familiar scent and warmth, Wu Xingzi wasn't the kind of man who craved sex—his pengornis pictures and his right hand were enough to sustain him.

Wu Xingzi had prepared two vegetarian dishes, two meat dishes, and a cold dish. His cooking wasn't fancy, but the ingredients were fresh. Ping Yifan enjoyed the food a great deal, and he had a little more wine than usual, too. By the time he realized that something wasn't quite right, he was already so intoxicated that he couldn't even move a finger.

"You..." Ping Yifan stared at Wu Xingzi in disbelief. He had never needed to guard himself against the man in front of him before. The drug hit him fast and hard—he tried to use his inner force to block the drug from spreading through his body, but it was already too late. However, no matter how severe the effects of the drug were, they could not compare to the astonishment of having been drugged by Wu Xingzi—of all people!

Ping Yifan tried his best to support his feeble body, his unblinking stare boring a hole through Wu Xingzi's head.

"A-are you all right? Does it hurt?"

Wu Xingzi had never used a truth serum before, and seeing Ping Yifan break out in sweat and become unsteady on his feet made him anxious. "I-I only gave you a truth-telling drug—how did things turn out like this? I'm going to get a physician!"

He turned around, wanting to hurry off.

"A truth-telling drug?" Ping Yifan instantly felt a sense of relief. He grabbed onto Wu Xingzi's arm, pulling the older man back to him. "Don't worry, this is normal."

His breathing was a little heavier, but he was no longer worried. He could not blame Wu Xingzi for it. Even if he had been given poison, perhaps... There was nothing he could do but shrug his shoulders and accept it.

One would, at most, feel a little uncomfortable when the truth serum took effect. As he waited for Yan Wenxin to fall into his trap, he'd made a habit of stationing a few hidden guards around himself. However, they had all withdrawn today when Wu Xingzi arrived. If they were to see Wu Xingzi running off in a panic and returned to find him lying on the ground, drugged, there was no telling what they might do to Wu Xingzi—and Ping Yifan was not willing to let the man next to him suffer in the slightest.

"This is normal?" Wu Xingzi repeated cautiously. When Ping Yifan nodded in affirmation, he patted his chest and returned to his seat, carefully watching the man in front of him.

For a long moment, neither man spoke. The only sound in the room was Ping Yifan's heavy, addled breathing.

Ping Yifan's face was pale and sweaty as he gritted his teeth and tried to bear with the drug's effects. Wu Xingzi's heart ached at the sight. He used his sleeve to wipe away Ping Yifan's sweat, then tilted a teacup to his lips so he could drink a few sips of tea. After confirming that the effects of the drug were indeed temporary, and that Ping Yifan was not harmed in any way, Wu Xingzi let out a deep sigh of relief.

Once he'd recovered somewhat, Ping Yifan was the first to speak. "Why did you...?"

Wu Xingzi did not react in his usual bashful manner; he frowned slightly, his expression stern. He gazed at Ping Yifan with wet eyes, as though he could see right through him. Slack-jawed, Ping Yifan couldn't ask anything else.

"Ping Yifan, who are you exactly?" Wu Xingzi got straight to the point. Ping Yifan knew at once that things weren't going to end well.

If Wu Xingzi was asking, he must already have made a guess. He just wanted to confirm it. Ping Yifan chuckled bitterly to himself. He'd thought his disguise was perfect, but this soft old quail already suspected him...

Under the influence of the drug, Ping Yifan knew that he could not lie. His mind was muddled and his limbs were weak and achy. His vision was hazy; he felt as though he was dreaming. He was starting to become unsure whether he was awake or not.

Ping Yifan's mouth opened as he emitted a weak cough. But he was a high-ranking general, so he did have some slight resistance against this sort of drug. He bit his lip harshly, using all his resolve to keep from answering.

Wu Xingzi watched as Ping Yifan bit his lips bloody with the effort of forcing himself to keep quiet. His heart twitched in pain. That face, so similar to Guan Shanjin's, was twisted and terrifying. Rivulets of sweat rolled down his face, collecting on the tip of his nose and chin before dripping down to soak the lapels of his robe. Ping Yifan kept his eyes tightly shut, refusing to spill a single word, enduring the pain until his entire body trembled.

"Why do you choose to suffer?" Wu Xingzi sniffled, on the verge of tears. He could not bear to see Ping Yifan torment himself like this, but Rancui hadn't given him an antidote. What could he do to prevent this pain from lasting for four hours? Even the strongest person could be tortured to death like this. Reaching out, Wu Xingzi lightly stroked Ping Yifan's ashen face, soothing him in a gentle voice. "Haiwang, I know it's you."

The man under him jerked violently. His cloudy eyes fixed upon Wu Xingzi in shock. His bleeding lips moved, mumbling vaguely. In the end, he still said nothing.

"You don't trust me?" Wu Xingzi asked. Immeasurable guilt

weighed upon his heart, and he was beginning to regret what he'd done. But he had no choice. Even though it was a method that harmed both of them, it had to be done.

This time, Ping Yifan wasn't able to resist the drug. He shook his head slightly. It was because he trusted Wu Xingzi too much that he fell victim to his ploy. It was because he trusted Wu Xingzi too much that he'd let the drug get this far, to the point where he was barely able to resist it. If anyone else had drugged him—even Man Yue—he would have immediately noticed that something was wrong and withdrawn. He would have fought back. He would have given the other person something to remember him by.

Wu Xingzi sighed again, helping Ping Yifan—no, he knew that this was Guan Shanjin—wipe the sweat from his face. He stared at him blankly for a moment, his head spinning, but he could not think of a better way to make Guan Shanjin speak.

It didn't surprise him that Guan Shanjin was resisting so strongly. After all, a general stationed at the border who could not resist a truth serum would be easily defeated under its influence. Guan Shanjin must have been trained to resist the effects of such a drug. Although Wu Xingzi wanted to hear the answers from Guan Shanjin's mouth, it was surely going to be a difficult task.

But he refused to give up. He asked a series of simple, insignificant questions, but Guan Shanjin kept stubbornly frowning, his eyes squeezed shut. His body occasionally quivered and jerked, and Wu Xingzi shuddered along with him. Ultimately, Wu Xingzi could no longer bear it.

He sighed heavily and wiped Guan Shanjin's face again. He poured a cup of fruit wine. "I put the drug in the wine," he said. "You know that I'm a lightweight, and you've seen me get drunk twice. You haven't let me drink again since, so I decided to drug the wine."

Wu Xingzi smiled as Guan Shanjin stared at him vacantly. "Haiwang, let's both be honest with each other, all right?"

The young man jerked, looking like he wanted to reach out to smack the cup out of Wu Xingzi's hand. However, he was a second too late. The moment Wu Xingzi finished talking, he tilted his head back and emptied the cup. He choked and coughed, his eyes reddening. Looking determinedly at Guan Shanjin, he said, "We should have an honest conversation with each other."

Wu Xingzi's eyes were as red as an albino rabbit's, making him look both pitiful and adorable. Guan Shanjin sighed, no longer forcing himself to resist the drug's effects. Trembling, he reached up and removed the mask.

As expected, under the mask was Guan Shanjin's face.

"When did you figure it out?" Tossing the mask casually on the table, Guan Shanjin carefully pulled the older man into his embrace. "I underestimated you..."

Compared to the somewhat hoarse voice he put on for Ping Yifan, Guan Shanjin's natural voice was smoother and gentler, but it was not a significant difference. Still, when combined with the mask, the two identities did seem completely different.

Wu Xingzi pressed lightly on the corners of Guan Shanjin's eyes with the tip of his finger, then traced the beautiful curves of his face. By the time he'd touched Guan Shanjin's face all over, his eyes were red and close to weeping. Guan Shanjin's heart ached terribly over it.

"Don't cry... This is my fault," he said. "I shouldn't have deceived you. I won't hide anything any longer—just ask me what you want to know." He kissed the tip of Wu Xingzi's nose in consolation, then kissed the corner of his mouth, nearly giving into the temptation to press the older man down and tangle their tongues together.

"You can't hide anything regardless." Wu Xingzi snorted lightly. He was gradually falling under the effect of the drug himself; his gaze grew hazy as he cuddled into Guan Shanjin's arms, panting.

He could feel his body weaken under the drug's influence, his brain turning blank and his tongue thickening. As he murmured aloud, even he himself could not clearly hear his words. It felt as though he was drifting up into the clouds, floating along in a dream. He realized that in this moment, if he were to say anything, it would be nothing but the truth—there would be no way for his brain to concoct any lie or deceit.

He narrowed his unfocused eyes at Guan Shanjin. "Say," he mumbled, "where did the Murong Chong of pengornises come from? It was so pink and adorable." That drawing played a huge part in his falling for Ping Yifan at first sight; the image had taken a firm hold of his heart.

Murong Chong? Guan Shanjin froze, but he quickly understood what Wu Xingzi meant. He couldn't stop himself from breaking out into laughter. He pulled the old quail's hand up to his lips and gave it a nip. "The thing you wanted so desperately to ask me about...was a pengornis picture?"

"Mm. I really, truly liked that drawing, although it can't compare to yours... Where did it come from?" Wu Xingzi was still Wu Xingzi. Ever since the first time he laid his eyes on the vibrant world of pengornises, they had become the most important part of his life. Now that he had taken the truth serum, he could no longer hide it.

"I asked Man Yue to just draw it based on my own anatomy."

Although it wasn't really a big deal, Guan Shanjin still blushed a little. If this was an ordinary circumstance, he might not even have been willing to answer honestly; it was too embarrassing.

Wu Xingzi blinked slowly and his lips curled up in a smile. "You got Man Yue to draw your pengornis? You pulled it out and showed it to him?" Wu Xingzi's mouth straightened a little, his eyes falling very naturally downward. Unfortunately, he could only see his own languid legs and hips. After all, he was tucked firmly in Guan Shanjin's arms.

"No. Why would I have to show it to Man Yue? Doesn't *The Pengornisseur* already feature a drawing of my cock? I instructed Man Yue to copy that one. And I was afraid that you might recognize it, so I made him add some color to disguise it."

It truly was a wonder how a shy old thing like Wu Xingzi had developed such an astonishing talent for judging cocks. He might actually be better at recognizing people by their pengornises than by their faces. His sharp eyes could notice any discrepancies, so he was able to identify that Ping Yifan's and Guan Shanjin's cocks were one and the same.

"The coloring was so lovely." Wu Xingzi praised Man Yue's art skills. His mind wandered back to the image of Ping Yifan's pengornis, and the memory of secretly enjoying the drawing at night made his face flush red.

Now that the matter of the cock was clarified, it was time to ask about its owner. "Why did you pretend to be Ping Yifan?" Wu Xingzi asked.

Still embracing Wu Xingzi, Guan Shanjin twitched. His knee-jerk reaction was to refuse to answer.

Wu Xingzi's entire body was limp. He reached out with a trembling hand to pat Guan Shanjin's arm soothingly, and the man behind him soon exhaled slowly and relaxed his tense muscles.

"I pretended to be Ping Yifan because I wanted to lay a trap for that old fox Yan Wenxin, as well as..." Guan Shanjin hissed in pain, trying to resist answering. It wasn't so much that he was intentionally trying to *hide* the truth—rather, he felt it was just too embarrassing to say out loud. Unfortunately for him, the drug was very powerful. Dejected and unwilling to let Wu Xingzi worry over him, he gave an honest answer.

"I just don't want you to be tempted away by other men," he admitted. "That little troublemaker Rancui is always hoping to shove you at any man out there so you'll spend the rest of your life with him. Isn't it true? The moment your heart calmed down, he gave you a copy of *The Pengornisseur*. Tell me yourself—before you came to the capital and met Ping Yifan, how many letters did you send through the pigeon post, hmm?"

The lilt the end of Guan Shanjin's question tickled Wu Xingzi's heart. He hummed a couple of times, unable to stop himself from nuzzling into Guan Shanjin's warm, broad chest.

Feeling Wu Xingzi wriggling against him like that set Guan Shanjin aflame with desire. He couldn't suppress his urges; he bent his head down to kiss and suck the old fellow's tender lips. Their tongues intertwined, and Guan Shanjin kissed Wu Xingzi so fiercely that he felt his eyes stinging. When Guan Shanjin finally released his trembling tongue, Wu Xingzi struggled to catch his breath; his entire being felt like a puddle of water.

Wu Xingzi had only just caught his breath, but Guan Shanjin couldn't help himself. He started kissing the older man again. The soft and clinging kiss seemed endless, and Guan Shanjin truly wished that he could just swallow the old man up.

"Ah... Stop kissing me..." Wu Xingzi gently pushed Guan Shanjin away, no longer able to endure it. He still had so many questions he wanted to ask—he couldn't let all his efforts go to waste! The effects of this drug were so severe, he didn't want to give it to Guan Shanjin a second time! He needed to make full use of these next four hours.

Guan Shanjin understood. Although he would have preferred to just skip over the whole honesty part and fuck Wu Xingzi senseless, he knew that if he really wanted to tuck this old fellow under his wing and dote on him forever, he could not avoid this conversation. If Guan Shanjin refused to talk, he would be the one left empty-handed, and all his previous efforts would've gone to waste.

After a fierce nip to Wu Xingzi's lip, Guan Shanjin pressed his forehead against Wu Xingzi's, their panting breaths mingling. "You can keep asking me questions. Hurry up and finish."

His self-control was wearing thin under the influence of the drug, and it was hard to say how long he could persevere. Although he'd been meeting Wu Xingzi every day, he was afraid of exposing his identity. He was also jealous of Wu Xingzi's affection for Ping Yifan. Therefore, Guan Shanjin had forcefully suppressed his desires using his inner strength. Now, his lust was hitting him like an avalanche, and his sweat was not entirely due to the drug's effects.

Wu Xingzi took a few breaths. When he saw Guan Shanjin lean in for another kiss, he hurried to interrupt. "Why do you want to lay a trap for Yan Wenxin? Did it start in Horse-Face City?"

"Yes... I was already dealing with Yan Wenxin back in Horse-Face City. Now, this information cannot go beyond this courtyard—it's best that you forget everything you hear, hmm?" Guan Shanjin gently caressed Wu Xingzi's face, waiting for him to nod his promise before he continued. "The one who wants Yan Wenxin dealt with... is the emperor. You know that my family has always produced uncorrupted officials; we are loyal only to the man on the throne, and by extension to Great Xia itself. In recent years, Yan Wenxin has prospered within the official court, and he holds boundless wealth and power in his hands."

"But doesn't the emperor value him a great deal?" Wu Xingzi asked. He still remembered how Rancui and Hei-er had spoken of Yan Wenxin. He was the highest-ranking official at court and the Minister of Personnel, powerful enough to influence all the other officials. He was held in the emperor's utmost trust and esteem. If not for the fact that the majority of the military served under Guan Shanjin, Yan Wenxin would have been the most powerful man at court—he could even stage a coup. He had both the ambition and the skill. The emperor seemed not to have noticed the threat in his midst.

Guan Shanjin sneered. "If Yan Wenxin is a cunning old fox, the man on the throne is a fox so cunning he has cultivated human form. Originally, he supported Yan Wenxin because he wanted the use of his talent, his competence, and his mind. Yan Wenxin was vicious yet keenly restrained, and he would be a powerful addition to the emperor's arsenal. However, a man like this can never be tamed, and he was bound to bring chaos, and of course the emperor knew that very well.

"The son of the Protector General needs to first gain military accomplishments before the emperor decides if he is fit to inherit the title. It was only once I returned to the capital from the northwest region that I gained my official title as Heir to the Protector General. The emperor took that opportunity to gain clear insight into the sort of person Yan Wenxin was. The emperor also silently approved the years I spent in the south and refused to return to the capital—the intention was to let me rest for a while. But it turned out that Yan Wenxin could even spread his influence beyond the south, so it was a pleasant coincidence that I was there to counter him."

Wu Xingzi's eyes opened so wide that he looked quite foolish. He'd never expected that there would be so many twists and turns to the situation. A moment later, he raised a shaky hand to press it against Guan Shanjin's mouth, feeling troubled. "So... So all this time, what you were hiding from me was something so important, but I've drugged you... Don't say anything more. I won't keep asking."

He was truly frightened. It wasn't because he was afraid of knowing these secrets or of attracting trouble toward himself—he was worried that Guan Shanjin would be further implicated. Under the influence of the drug, though, Wu Xingzi could not control his mouth. He heard himself keep on talking. "But Zaizong-xiong wasn't that sort of person before. We spent some time together in the past, and he truly wishes to work for the interests of the country."

"Hmph. So he cheated you out of your money and used a cheap perfume sachet to steal your heart?" Thinking of it made Guan Shanjin's heart feel bitter and sore. Mixed emotions swelled within him. Of course Wu Xingzi would have fallen for other men in his lifetime—it was impossible to expect that he'd spent all this time just waiting for Guan Shanjin. Hadn't Guan Shanjin himself once had Lu Zezhi in his heart, too? However, it was clear just from the way he spoke up for him that Wu Xingzi's feelings for Yan Wenxin were different.

"The last time he saw you, he didn't even recognize you, and you're still thinking about him?"

"No, it's not like that..." Wu Xingzi blinked innocently. He held no remaining feelings for Yan Wenxin, but Yan Wenxin was still someone he'd cherished in the past. Their interactions and meetings were all sweet memories. Back then, Yan Wenxin had eagerly told Wu Xingzi about his ambitions. To Wu Xingzi, it felt as though Yan Wenxin was a ray of sunlight shining directly upon his heart, dispelling the gloom of his parents' deaths. Even though their connection turned out to be a lie, it had once been of great help to him. He stammered out an explanation, telling Guan Shanjin that years had gone by and things had changed; he only felt some slight sadness upon seeing Yan Wenxin again. After that he'd been completely focused on pondering the connection between Ping Yifan and Guan Shanjin, as well as the relationship between Guan Shanjin and Lu Zezhi. He had no time at all to even think about this person who had left him twenty-odd years ago.

Hearing this, Guan Shanjin felt that his jealousy was no longer as acrid, and the ache in his heart had even turned to joy. He leaned over to resume kissing and caressing the older man.

"I know you want to ask me about Lu Zezhi." This time, Guan Shanjin did not need Wu Xingzi to bring up the topic. He was well aware of the greatest issue still keeping the two of them apart.

At the sound of Lu Zezhi's name, Wu Xingzi immediately stiffened up in Guan Shanjin's arms, and his kiss-flushed cheeks paled abruptly. His head sank so low that it was practically buried in his chest. Guan Shanjin felt ashamed. Tightening his embrace to soothe Wu Xingzi, he gently patted the older man's thin back.

Just as the general was about to say something, Wu Xingzi spoke up first. "Haiwang, I am fond of you. It's not a casual type of fondness, but the kind that makes me want to spend the rest of my life with you. Even Zaizong-xiong never made me want this. I really feel too much for you... I know that Lu Zezhi is the one in your heart, not me—so I left..."

His gentle voice sounded very earnest. Even though the drug was making him mumble a little, each and every emotional word echoed in Guan Shanjin's ears. Absently, he looked at the old quail in his embrace, suddenly feeling as though sparks from a falling star had landed on his arm. When he looked closer he realized that a few teardrops had fallen there—Wu Xingzi was silently weeping.

The heat from the tears had vanished instantly, but they fell like the hot ashes of a meteor, burning into Guan Shanjin's blood, traveling into his heart. In his chest was a pain that he had never felt before. Guan Shanjin hugged the older man tightly, deeply afraid that Wu Xingzi would again disappear without a trace. If it were to happen again, Guan Shanjin would truly fall into madness.

"My father only had my mother. When I was younger, he told me that it was enough for a man to love just one person forever... After all, can a man's heart be sliced into many parts?

"In the past, my father attained the rank of imperial scholar, and he was assigned to the Hanlin Academy. At that time, he was only eighteen, and he enjoyed great literary fame. Although he never went into detail, I always thought that there might even be people in the capital who had heard of him before. He had not planned on marrying so early.

"Still, when he met my mother, it was love at first sight. His heart could not be split; it was wholly given to my mother. My mother had been sold into the capital in order to help her family, so she was not a free citizen. It was impossible for her to marry my father as his official wife; at most, she could be his concubine. My father refused to slight my mother that way, so he decided to give up his official position. After getting rid of my mother's lowly status, he brought her back to his hometown, Qingcheng County, and settled there."

This was the first time Wu Xingzi had shared the private details of his family. Guan Shanjin had guessed that the status of Wu Xingzi's father was more complicated than he let on; the man could not have merely been a simple private teacher. However, he'd never expected that the situation would be something like this.

Wu Xingzi looked up, his eyes still red. Despite the cloudiness from the drug, there was still a fixed determination in them. "I will definitely listen to what my father said. My parents left this world early, but in the brief time they were here, they were steadfast in their love for each other. That is all I want—to give my heart to one man, and to have his in return. Since your heart belongs to another...I don't want it."

People's desires often contradicted one another: Fulfilling someone else's might mean giving up on your own. Wasn't it human nature to be selfish?

If Wu Xingzi looked deep inside himself and reflected on his actions—his departure from the general's estate, his insistence on believing that Guan Shanjin and Lu Zezhi held mutual affection for each other, or even when he fell for Ping Yifan—the root of everything was his selfishness.

When it came to love, Wu Xingzi wanted everything or nothing at all...which was why he eventually threw away that perfume sachet Yan Wenxin gave him.

Guan Shanjin was stunned. It was as if he was seeing the old quail's true character for the first time. Wu Xingzi did have a good temperament; he sought nothing and asked for nothing. But everyone still had something of a temper, and if it flared up, they could end up hurting others.

Still, after he processed his astonishment, waves of indescribable joy crashed through Guan Shanjin. He hugged Wu Xingzi tightly, wishing he could subsume the older man's entire being into his blood and bones.

"My heart only belongs to you," he told him. "If you want it, take it. If you don't, I'll just smash it. In this life, I will never give it to anyone else."

Wu Xingzi was shocked to hear such a passionate promise. Guan Shanjin's words were so sweet it was as if Wu Xingzi's heart was submerged in honey. However, when he thought about that beautiful, white-robed man Guan Shanjin used to dote upon, the smile on his face froze. "What about Mr. Lu? After all, you snatched him from his wedding."

Guan Shanjin knew it wouldn't be possible to gloss over this matter so easily—and so he answered, albeit a little unwillingly. "I'm only using him. Lu Zezhi doesn't have any true affection for me. What he loves is my lavish doting and the free and easy life where he doesn't need to lift a finger. I did have feelings for him before, but it's in the past now.

"There are some relationships that can only happen in a certain window of opportunity. Once that opportunity is missed, they will never come to fruition. That's the reality of my relationship with Mr. Lu; he was up high on a pedestal and I dared not touch him. We kept dragging on like this until I met you—and he no longer mattered.

"Don't put any blame on yourself. What happened isn't anyone's fault. Feelings cannot be forced, and I will always be true to my feelings." Guan Shanjin had always stuck to his guns. He would either conceal his emotions to the very end, or, if it was advantageous to him, he would take the opportunity to reveal everything.

"But why did you..."

Guan Shanjin bent over, kissing Wu Xingzi to stop him from finishing his question. He fiercely caught Wu Xingzi's soft little tongue with his, sucking on it for a moment before letting go. "It was all because of you," he replied, panting. "Yan Wenxin isn't an easy old fox to catch, and his methods are vicious. How can I not worry about you being thrust into danger? The moment an error is made, that old man will use you against me. I have no choice but to keep Lu Zezhi by my side—it's for your own safety."

The words "no choice" made Wu Xingzi feel slightly rueful. "Are you going to continue making use of Mr. Lu?"

"Yes." The moment Guan Shanjin finished responding, he pressed a finger against Wu Xingzi's mouth, not letting him say another word. "I can't tell you anything more than that. Don't ask me any more questions, all right? You only need to know that you are my heart's desire, and your safety is of utmost importance to me. Even if I were to do everything over again, I would still make the same decisions. I've wronged you by making you unhappy, but that is the price of keeping you safe."

The words were stark and unromantic—but a blush still spread across Wu Xingzi's face and ears as he listened to them, his breathing quickening. The purpose of the truth serum was to lower someone's defenses. It was a drug that revealed one's heart...and there was only one sordid thing his heart truly desired.

A sudden soft lick to his palm made Guan Shanjin's heart skip a beat; he narrowed his eyes in understanding. This wanton old thing really had impeccable self-restraint. If they both kept trying to keep their desires in check, though, it wouldn't be good for either of them.

What had to be said had already been said—and Guan Shanjin's body had adjusted to the drug's effects. His limbs were no longer weak. He deftly lifted Wu Xingzi and walked into the bedroom, kicking the door shut.

There was decidedly not just a truth-telling element to the drug Rancui had provided. He was the manager of the Peng Society—no one would believe that the drugs he had on hand had no aphrodisiacal components to them. The drug coursed through their bodies demandingly, bringing all their heart's desires to the surface.

Guan Shanjin panted heavily, his forehead covered in sweat from the effort of holding himself back. It only took a few small steps, but by the time they made it to the bedroom, the fronts of both of their robes were soaked. Wu Xingzi huddled in his arms like a spoiled, pampered puppy. With a burst of energy, he nuzzled his nose into the younger man's broad chest, inhaling deeply like a besotted fool. He couldn't stop himself from mumbling about how good Guan Shanjin smelled. The general could only keep on enduring his lust as it spread through his body like wildfire.

The old quail had always been open-minded when it came to sex; in fact, he could be downright depraved. It was yet to be seen how much more lascivious Wu Xingzi might become under the influence of the drug. Guan Shanjin found himself looking forward to it.

Ping Yifan's bedroom was decorated very simply. It was even more humble than a room that cost one copper coin per night at an inn. That being said, the blanket on the huge bed looked soft and comfortable.

Guan Shanjin stumbled and collapsed onto the bed with Wu Xingzi squirming in his arms. At this point, even the back of the general's robes was drenched in sweat, making the scent of white sandalwood and orange blossom noticeably stronger—it quickly permeated the cramped room. Wu Xingzi's fleshy nose twitched. Just inhaling the other man's scent made him feel like he was about to melt into a puddle.

At first, he teased Guan Shanjin breathily, with phrases like "You smell so good," "Can I lick you?" or even "You're poking me!"

The words spilling from Wu Xingzi's mouth made Guan Shanjin so hard that it hurt. His cock looked as if it could burst through his clothes and injure the man in his arms.

By now, however, Wu Xingzi was beyond words. He clung onto Guan Shanjin's shoulders, his head settling in the crook of Guan Shanjin's neck as he gave tiny gasps and muffled moans. His heated breaths were like scorching sparks against Guan Shanjin's skin, making him tighten his grip on Wu Xingzi. No longer trying to stay level-headed, he stripped the old quail naked. Under his robes, Wu Xingzi's smooth and soft skin glowed with a sheen of sticky sweat.

"Take off your clothes, too—*ah*, the friction hurts," Wu Xingzi said.

The drug's influence made their skin more sensitive. Guan Shanjin was wearing Ping Yifan's clothes, and although the material and craftsmanship were satisfactory, the fabric was still rather coarse. They could not begin to compare to the clothes tailored for the son of the Protector General, and as they scraped roughly against Wu Xingzi's skin, the older man wailed and twisted about.

"That crafty Rancui..." *Has done a wonderful job.* Bearing with the pain, Guan Shanjin did not finish his sentence. He hurriedly removed his clothes, but with Wu Xingzi kissing his lips and rutting against his body it was impossible to undress properly. Unwilling to let him go, Guan Shanjin gave up and tore his own clothes off.

Their ragged clothes blanketed the floor. After so many months apart, Wu Xingzi and Guan Shanjin were finally in the same bed again, exposed to each other in more ways than one. Firm, defined muscles stood out underneath Guan Shanjin's smooth, porcelain skin. Wu Xingzi raked his gaze over him, his eyes filled with rapture as he admired the man's broad shoulders, his narrow waist, his tight buttocks, his long, powerful legs...and of course, his magnificent pengornis. With trembling fingers, he reached out and grabbed hold of the member he'd missed for so long, saliva pooling in his mouth and almost drooling from his lips.

"So where does it rank on your list of pengornises now?" Guan Shanjin asked, allowing Wu Xingzi to carefully inspect his cock, up close and personal. He'd recently bathed, and he smelled clean and fresh. Along with the musk of a hale and hearty man, the scent completely intoxicated the horny old quail.

"Number one," Wu Xingzi answered without hesitation. "It's definitely number one. No one can compare." In the past he would have felt shy, but under the effects of the truth serum he had long forgotten what the word "shy" even meant.

"Oh? Not even Ping Yifan?" Guan Shanjin's question reeked of jealousy. On the surface, the general seemed not to care about Wu Xingzi's affection for Ping Yifan at all, but in his heart, he could not let the matter go. He would never be able to forget how Wu Xingzi had invited Ping Yifan to share his grave the first time they met!

Hmph! Ping Yifan is nothing but a counterfeit!

After some hesitation, Wu Xingzi replied cautiously, "He can't compare." The drug had a much greater effect on him than Guan Shanjin. He had no wits about him other than his instincts. Although the answer was pleasing, Guan Shanjin was extremely possessive, and that brief moment of hesitation made him huff unhappily.

"Were you thinking about lying to me?" he asked, crooking a finger under Wu Xingzi's chin. Wu Xingzi rubbed his cheek against his prized pengornis, his little pink tongue wetting his lips. His tongue almost brushed against the sizeable head of the general's cock a few times. Guan Shanjin's hunger was nearly unbearable; he prodded Wu Xingzi's mouth with his cock, causing Wu Xingzi's soft lips to swell slightly.

"No... I wasn't..." Wu Xingzi chased after the huge, delicious dick as it rubbed against his lips. Before he could finish his sentence, his mouth was stuffed full of cock.

An indescribable satisfaction filled him as he finally tasted Guan Shanjin's pengornis. Wu Xingzi had not yet mastered the art of sucking cock, but he still skittishly licked the drops of fluid gathering at the tip. Next, he loudly sucked on the head before swallowing more of the cock down.

Guan Shanjin breathed heavily. He had wanted to take the opportunity to provoke Wu Xingzi into talking dirty, but Wu Xingzi's mouth felt too good. It was warm and wet and he knew how to suck. Even if that soft little tongue of his was somewhat unskilled, it was beyond shameless. Wu Xingzi teased the general's cock with his lips, then curled his tongue and slid it up the pulsating vein. Guan Shanjin groaned in pleasure, his long fingers sliding through the old fellow's hair. Gripping onto the back of Wu Xingzi's head, he shoved his thick cock all the way inside Wu Xingzi's mouth.

"Mmph!" With the colossal cock suddenly in his throat, Wu Xingzi gagged, a few broken moans escaping. He pushed at Guan Shanjin's thigh, wanting to catch his breath. However, the man had lost his mind with passion, and Wu Xingzi's gentle pushes brought out his beastlike nature. Half kneeling, he shoved himself further into Wu Xingzi's mouth, stretching out the old fellow's throat and tightly trapping his tongue in place. Wu Xingzi's mouth was nothing more than a sheath for Guan Shanjin's cock; all he could do was allow the man to thrust furiously into him.

Guan Shanjin had been suppressing his desires for so long that he was a starving, savage wolf. He thrusted wantonly into Wu Xingzi's mouth, making his cheeks bulge out. The older man choked and whimpered, tightening his grip on Guan Shanjin's thighs so much his fingers nearly went white. The cock in his throat made him choke until tears flowed from his eyes; it made for a salaciously pitiful picture. His throat bulged each time the general's cock entered it, practically impaling his slender neck.

Guan Shanjin looked down at Wu Xingzi's debauched state, noting that his teary eyes were as red as a rabbit's. He wished that he could just fuck this man to death so Wu Xingzi could never run away from him again. He roughly shoved his cock into Wu Xingzi's mouth, his full balls slapping against his chin, turning Wu Xingzi's skin red with the force of it.

After a few more dry heaves, Wu Xingzi went limp, no longer able to either resist or welcome the general's thrusts. He would still move his mouth occasionally, though, sucking Guan Shanjin's cock a little and making him moan. Guan Shanjin would then pull Wu Xingzi's head further down onto his cock, wishing he could just thrust straight through his throat.

Probably because he had been suppressing his lust for so long, Guan Shanjin could not last very long. In less than half an hour, Wu Xingzi felt the cock in his mouth stiffen even more as it jabbed viciously into him.

Guan Shanjin tightened his grip on the back of Wu Xingzi's head, pulling him close and coming into his mouth. The scorching seed was thick and abundant, spattering against Wu Xingzi's sensitive throat. He shuddered and choked, thinking he might actually suffocate like this. Some of Guan Shanjin's cum even spilled out through his nose, smearing across his face with his drool and tears. He ended up swallowing most of it right into his belly; for a moment, it felt as though he'd eaten a full meal.

Guan Shanjin pulled his cock out of Wu Xingzi's mouth, gently stroking his swollen lips before pressing a kiss to them. He did love the old quail, after all. "Does it hurt?"

"It hurts..." Wu Xingzi frowned a little, feeling somewhat aggrieved. His throat was sore and his voice was extremely hoarse. Guan Shanjin's heart ached. Just as he was about to get off the bed to bring Wu Xingzi some water, though, two arms wrapped around him tightly, preventing him from leaving.

"I'm only going to get a cup of water for you. Doesn't your throat hurt?" Guan Shanjin lowered his head to comfort Wu Xingzi. Wu Xingzi looked at him with wet eyes. His entire body was flushed red as he rubbed his thighs together, and it was evident that his little cock had spilled, too.

"My dirty darling." Guan Shanjin laughed gently, fondling the little prick with his fingers. He immediately understood what Wu Xingzi wanted.

There was no hurry to get water. Right now, desire thrummed through both of them, and Wu Xingzi's desperate hole was hungry to be filled. One only had to look at the bed to see that there was already a large wet patch staining the sheets. Neither of them could be bothered to consider anything as insignificant and unnecessary as gentleness.

"Come inside..." Wu Xingzi pulled at Guan Shanjin, shyly spreading his legs and revealing his hole. Unsurprisingly, the long-unused hole had regained its tightness. It looked as though it was winking with passion. As it opened up just enough to fit a pinky finger, lewd fluid dripped out.

"Where?" Having already found release, Guan Shanjin was a lot calmer than Wu Xingzi. Leaning down, he kissed the older man's lips, coaxing his tongue out and sucking on it. Quietly, he grunted, "It's bitter. All I can taste is myself."

It sounded like a complaint, but it was followed by a number of soft, lingering kisses. The general kissed Wu Xingzi into bleariness, until his eyes lost focus. All that mattered was tangling his tongue with Guan Shanjin's.

Guan Shanjin finally pulled away, panting. He looked at Wu Xingzi with a wicked smile. "Quick, tell me—where do you want me to put it? If you don't tell me, I won't know what to do."

"Huh?" Wu Xingzi's eyes were half lidded. The tip of his tongue slid past his swollen, red lips as he curled his legs around Guan Shanjin's firm, narrow waist.

"Didn't you tell me to go inside? Say it clearly—where do you want me?" Reaching out, Guan Shanjin tucked Wu Xingzi's fair, slender legs around his waist, and his once-again erect cock nudged the winking hole.

Wu Xingzi gasped loudly, tightening his legs as he writhed on the bed. He moaned and groaned as he sought relief against Guan Shanjin.

"This little thing must have been ravenous," Guan Shanjin said.

Each time Wu Xingzi drew himself closer, Guan Shanjin retreated a little, maintaining a negligible distance. Another trickle of lewd fluid dribbled out of Wu Xingzi's hole. "Come on, push yourself inside," he pleaded pitifully. "I'm starving."

"I know you are, but you haven't given me an answer yet. Where do you want me to push inside?" Guan Shanjin affectionately drew his fingers around Wu Xingzi's face, then pinched his fleshy nose. "Say it plainly, hmm?"

Wu Xingzi had no patience. He twisted about, lifting his thin waist. "I need something down there. Quick, come soothe it..."

"Down there... Here?" Guan Shanjin asked, grinding the head of his cock against the wet, hungry hole, making the old fellow tilt his head back and moan brazenly.

"Fuck me, Haiwang... Fuck me, please..."

"This, here, is your slutty hole. Now tell me what you want me to fuck, hmm?" Guan Shanjin did not relent, insisting that Wu Xingzi say something naughty. The old fellow had always been very open in his actions, but his mouth was very shy. The truth serum presented a rare opportunity—how could Guan Shanjin let it go to waste?

Wu Xingzi looked at Guan Shanjin with teary eyes. After a moment of hesitation, he finally opened his mouth. "Please fuck my slutty hole, Haiwang," he said bashfully. "I need it."

"Good boy." Guan Shanjin's faint smile was as warm as spring. Wu Xingzi's heart pounded as he gazed at him, and he felt as though he was melting.

Having waited long enough, Guan Shanjin gripped his cock in one hand and Wu Xingzi's hip with the other. He rubbed against Wu Xingzi's leaking hole a few times before thrusting his cock halfway inside.

"Mmmm..." Wu Xingzi shuddered, his hole bearing down so forcefully that Guan Shanjin could not move. The general panted heavily, bending down to nip at his lover's neck. His scorching palm stroked Wu Xingzi's ass soothingly, but it took some time before he finally relaxed. Guan Shanjin then impaled Wu Xingzi with the rest of his length.

"Ah—!" Wu Xingzi shrieked at the sudden, immense pressure on the sensitive spot inside him. His little cock instantly spurted cum onto Guan Shanjin's abdomen.

Seeing the sticky fluid, Guan Shanjin smiled, his eyes narrowing. He wiped the mess away. "Smell it: my body is now saturated with your sinful scent," he said gently. "Now that I've been marked by you, you have no choice but to acknowledge me."

Wu Xingzi whimpered shyly. Looking up with unfocused eyes, he twisted his hips, urging the general on. "Hurry up..."

"My dirty boy," Guan Shanjin murmured as that soft, warm, tight sheath caressed his cock. Having just experienced an orgasm, Wu Xingzi's body twitched and shuddered with oversensitivity; it felt like countless little mouths were sucking on Guan Shanjin's skin.

Guan Shanjin grasped Wu Xingzi's hips and pulled him down onto his cock until a visible bulge appeared in Wu Xingzi's tender belly.

"Ah..." Wu Xingzi shut his eyes and arched his slender neck. A weak, quivering moan escaped his mouth. He felt so much pleasure that he could hardly bear it.

Now that he could finally devour Wu Xingzi, Guan Shanjin started to fuck him earnestly. The slapping noises of flesh against flesh and the squelching sounds of bodily fluids filled the room as they fucked. Wu Xingzi's soft moans quickly turned into tearful gasps, mingling with the younger man's gentle laughter.

"Ahh... *Ah—*!"

Guan Shanjin gripped Wu Xingzi's hips tightly as he fucked him hard and fast. Guan Shanjin was a man of martial arts; his strength was formidable, especially at his hips. In their past encounters, he'd gone easy on the older man; afraid of injuring him by fucking him too hard, he'd always controlled himself somewhat. Now, under the influence of the truth-telling drug mixed with either an aphrodisiac or a hallucinogen, his savage nature took over. After the first few courteous thrusts, he let go of his restraint, fucking into Wu Xingzi as deeply as possible.

Guan Shanjin's long, thick cock reached all the way to Wu Xingzi's belly, the shape of it bulging through the skin. But Guan Shanjin was not yet satisfied. He drove into him harshly a couple more times, then caressed the bulge with his hand. Feeling such sensations both inside and out, Wu Xingzi was fucked until he was left shuddering, his eyes rolling back and his tongue hanging out. His half-hard prick leaked fluid nonstop.

Each time the general's massive, veiny cock pulled out of Wu Xingzi's body, his hole would clench down after it. His hole was quickly fucked loose, shaping itself to fit around Guan Shanjin's cock. Wu Xingzi was pressed against the bed, his legs dangling apart in a fucked-out haze of pleasure. He struggled to think, and he didn't even have the strength to wrap his legs around Guan Shanjin's waist.

When Guan Shanjin saw Wu Xingzi's mouth hanging slack with his tongue out, he couldn't resist bending down and kissing him. His entire body covered Wu Xingzi's as he sucked forcefully on that little pink tongue of his in an intimate, syrupy-sweet kiss that filled the room with the sounds of sucking and nibbling. If he really tried, he could almost reach the back of Wu Xingzi's throat. Wu Xingzi was left mewling and whimpering; he trembled and shook his head, not knowing whether he wanted to draw closer or pull away.

As he passionately kissed Wu Xingzi, Guan Shanjin did not neglect his work lower down. He fiercely pumped his hips, the head of his cock hitting the swollen, sensitive spot inside of Wu Xingzi with perfect accuracy. Wu Xingzi was both terrified and ecstatic as he called out impassioned nonsense, by turns pleading for mercy and begging for more. The words were all swallowed up into Guan Shanjin's mouth, and in no time at all, Wu Xingzi could barely breathe. His body started spasming, his toes tightly curling up in bliss.

Unable to withstand Guan Shanjin's fucking, he came once again. This time, Wu Xingzi fainted straight away. Then, at long last, Guan Shanjin released his mouth. He lovingly licked away the tears from Wu Xingzi's face, the head of his cock still grinding into the spot inside him. Then, he flipped the unconscious man right over.

With such a vigorous action, Guan Shanjin fucked Wu Xingzi awake. The older man opened his mouth, a moan tumbling from his throat. He quietly wept; he had no idea if he was being fucked to death or if he'd died already.

"Be good." Guan Shanjin bit his tender nape, not letting go. He raised Wu Xingzi's hips, pressing his palm against the slight bulge of his belly. Without waiting for Wu Xingzi to catch his breath, he fucked fiercely into him once again. In this position, Guan Shanjin could thrust even deeper, and it was easier for him to put even more power behind his thrusts. Wu Xingzi felt as though he was about to be pierced clean through.

With his head pushed into the bed, his mouth hung open and saliva drooled from his lips. He couldn't even make a sound as his hole greedily welcomed the other man's cock, leaking all the while. It was truly in too deep. Wu Xingzi's insides quivered and spasmed; his red, swollen entrance could not have looked any less enticing.

Wu Xingzi was fucked into a stupor. Shuddering, he touched his belly, feeling the pressure from the cock inside of him against his palm again and again. Something warm spattered out of his cock, soaking his belly and the bedclothes underneath.

Feeling Wu Xingzi come, Guan Shanjin did not stop his relentless pounding. His motions became even more demanding, pushing Wu Xingzi into an endless orgasm. As Wu Xingzi clamped down on his cock, Guan Shanjin panted heavily, his handsome face turning somewhat savage in the peak of his pleasure. He looked beautiful and beguiling, yet also like a demon about to devour his prey.

With how tightly Wu Xingzi's ass was clenching his huge, thick cock, Guan Shanjin could barely move. He aggressively gripped Wu Xingzi's waist, driving himself even more roughly into the man's body, making Wu Xingzi's shuddering muscles lose their resistance and turn slack.

Guan Shanjin was near his climax as well. He left a brutal and slightly bloody bite mark on the back of Wu Xingzi's soft, fair neck as he worked his hips to push himself as deep inside Wu Xingzi as possible. Wu Xingzi's round, perky buttocks were now red and swollen from the repeated impact of Guan Shanjin's thighs. At long last, Guan Shanjin came with a roar.

Wu Xingzi whimpered at the sensation of Guan Shanjin's cum inside of him. His belly felt heated, and the sheer amount of semen inside him made his belly look as though he was three months pregnant. He trembled, unable to catch his breath, slipping into unconsciousness once again.

Lying atop Wu Xingzi, it took Guan Shanjin quite some time to finally calm down. After he pulled out his half-hard cock, a mix of his semen and Wu Xingzi's fluids trickled out of Wu Xingzi's swollen, gaping hole, staining both of their legs. The bedclothes beneath them were in a particularly tragic state.

Guan Shanjin was a little tired. Not wanting to part with Wu Xingzi, he decided to just embrace the man and fall into bed, their limbs tangling intimately as they both drifted off to sleep.

Wu Xingzi slept deeply. Despite how sticky his body was and how wet the bedclothes were underneath him, he still slept comfortably in Guan Shanjin's arms.

As for Guan Shanjin, he had always been mindful of cleanliness. After a short nap, he woke up, then called for a servant to bring in hot water. After he cleaned them both up, he changed the bedding, then wrapped his arms around the older man once again and lay down to rest.

CHAPTER 7

THE FICKLE MAN, OR THE FICKLENESS OF RELATIONSHIPS?

"Master looks lovely dressed up like this," Mint teased Wu Xingzi happily, making him flush red, a little flustered. "If the General were to see you, he wouldn't be able to tear his eyes away."

Wu Xingzi understood that the girls were worried that he might still be holding onto this affection of the past. How could that be? Apart from the fact that they had not met for twenty years, and that Yan Wenxin had let him down, he and Guan Shanjin had recently confirmed their feelings for each other. His heart was still immersed in that honeyed, sugary-sweet dream. A person's affections didn't just change that quickly.

SPENDING THE NIGHT WITH Wu Xingzi had given Guan Shanjin a pleasant respite from his duties, but he still had to get back to them—Yan Wenxin had already made his move.

Now that Yan Wenxin had successfully taken away the general's job, his next step would involve drawing the two hundred thousand soldiers Guan Shanjin had once commanded over to his side.

Guan Shanjin could not hold back his sneer. Yan Wenxin's greediness truly knew no bounds. The soldiers he had trained were not so easily ordered around.

Although the general knew very well what his opponent had in mind, he had no concrete evidence. If he struck too early, that old fox was sure to find a way to survive, and all the meticulous arrangements Guan Shanjin had been making would be for nothing. Despite understanding these circumstances, he still felt annoyed.

Guan Shanjin tightened his embrace. It had taken so much for him to finally become intimate with Wu Xingzi again, and he didn't want to let the man go so easily.

Seeming a little uncomfortable in Guan Shanjin's arms, Wu Xingzi sniffled a couple of times, then opened his eyes blearily. Not yet fully awake, he stared at the bare, muscular chest in front of him in puzzlement. Guan Shanjin had spent half his life in the military, so his physique was outstanding. His pectoral muscles were firm but not bulging, and his skin was very fair; the pressure from Wu Xingzi sleeping against him had turned part of it pink. It was breathtakingly beautiful.

A blush quickly spread on Wu Xingzi's face. Absentmindedly, he drew his fingers across that patch of pink skin. He felt the muscles flex immediately, and the arms around him tightened even further. His heart pounded and he quickly withdrew his hand, trying to pretend that nothing had happened. Wu Xingzi was sure there would be consequences for flirting with the young and virile Guan Shanjin—his body still ached, and if they were to repeat what they had just done, he might not be able to withstand it.

Guan Shanjin laughed and tapped the end of Wu Xingzi's fleshy nose. "Look at you—are you afraid that I'll eat you up?" he joked. "You're so scrawny, you won't even be enough to floss my teeth with."

Wu Xingzi giggled. Now that the conversation turned to eating, his stomach abruptly rumbled. He quickly held onto his thin belly, not daring to look toward Guan Shanjin. Now was clearly a good opportunity for affection; the two of them had finally shared their hearts with each other. Why did his stomach always get in the way?!

Guan Shanjin wasn't surprised, though. After all, it was mealtime. Although he wanted to continue tenderly holding Wu Xingzi, he also could not bear to let the man go hungry.

"I'll get someone to prepare lunch. Eat your fill before you go back." Embracing Wu Xingzi as he got up from the bed, Guan Shanjin lovingly helped him dress and put on his shoes. Wu Xingzi wanted to refuse his help, but the general waved him off. Blushing, he could only allow Guan Shanjin to do what he liked.

Every breath he took held the pleasant scent of incense; Wu Xingzi felt like he was dreaming. He stared at Guan Shanjin, looking at his brows, his face—everything.

The impassioned gaze was almost too much, even for Guan Shanjin; he reached out and tapped Wu Xingzi's eyelids. It gave the old quail quite a start, making him nearly tumble backward in embarrassment.

"What are you looking at?" Guan Shanjin asked. Sighing, he once again pulled Wu Xingzi into his arms. His chest felt empty without Wu Xingzi there.

"I'm wondering...if I'm dreaming." Wu Xingzi's brows furrowed slightly, his expression serious and his eyes a bit anxious. "Maybe I didn't get the truth serum from Rancui at all, and I never tricked you into taking it. Maybe everything that happened was just a pleasant dream."

"Even if it's merely a dream, isn't that a good thing? I was all yours before you woke up." Guan Shanjin tilted his head down and kissed

Wu Xingzi's forehead before continuing to sweet-talk him. "If this is your dream, it's my dream as well. Perhaps our entire lives are nothing but dreams. If that's the case, why don't we live well in this dream? It would be a pity to waste it, would it not?"

That made sense, but Wu Xingzi still worried. Without the effect of the drug, he'd returned to being that down-to-earth adviser from a tiny village. Content with his lot in life, he dared not dream of more. Even if he were to go mad from loneliness, he would silently endure it. "What if I suddenly wake up?"

"Then I'll wake up with you." As he smiled, Guan Shanjin's eyes curved into crescents. Pulling Wu Xingzi's hand, he placed it on his chest and patted it. "Why? Will you not want me anymore once you wake? Then I have no choice but to cling onto you."

"Ah... How could I not want you...?" Guan Shanjin's words had turned Wu Xingzi's ears and cheeks red. His self-pity melted away like the remnants of snow in March.

Intimately twined together, the two men chatted aimlessly. Wu Xingzi shivered as Guan Shanjin tucked him into his embrace and left new kiss marks on his neck. If it hadn't been for the servant bringing in their lunch, the two men might have ended up back in bed.

The cook in the Ping household was rather skilled. The home-cooked dishes were a mix of meat and vegetables. Every grain of rice was shiny, distinct, and smooth as a pearl, and everything on the table was to Wu Xingzi's liking. Despite Wu Xingzi's huge appetite, he did feel somewhat stuffed once he'd finished the food.

"If you like, we could have lunch together from now on," Guan Shanjin suggested, gently rubbing Wu Xingzi's stomach. Wu Xingzi bashfully agreed.

Guan Shanjin had said that he could only dispense with his disguise when he was inside Ping Yifan's residence. Until Yan Wenxin was caught, the general would need to continue wearing Ping Yifan's mask outside.

The only reason Wu Xingzi liked Ping Yifan was because he didn't dare to let himself have feelings for Guan Shanjin. Now that he and the general had confirmed their mutual affection, Wu Xingzi felt awkward looking at Ping Yifan's face.

Whether the general was in disguise or not, many tasks awaited him. Although he wished to continue whiling away the time with Wu Xingzi, he could not do as he pleased. The day was still young, but Guan Shanjin needed to send Wu Xingzi back.

"I'll have someone pick you up tomorrow, hmm?"

Wu Xingzi felt a prickling pain in his heart as he watched Guan Shanjin put on Ping Yifan's mask. He opened his mouth to say something but held back the words.

Just as Wu Xingzi got into the carriage, Guan Shanjin pulled the curtain aside and entered. "Don't send any more letters through the pigeon post, all right? You can keep the pengornis drawings you've received...but how about you throw away Ping Yifan's?" He stopped to bite Wu Xingzi's lips before adding, "If you dare to keep Ping Yifan's pengornis picture, I'll light all your favorite phalluses on fire."

"Ah..." Wu Xingzi was unable to avoid the general's attack. Guan Shanjin invaded his mouth, voraciously sucking on his tongue. Only when Wu Xingzi could barely breathe was his mouth released. However, Guan Shanjin was still unsatisfied; he pecked at his lips until they were swollen.

"Oh... Don't..."

"Be good." Guan Shanjin was domineering and possessive by nature—he didn't care if the older man could endure it or not. Even back before Guan Shanjin and Mr. Lu were established as a "couple," he still kept Mr. Lu all to himself, refusing to let anyone else catch a glimpse of him. Now, Wu Xingzi was his in body and soul—all he wanted was for him to be by his side. "I will settle things with Yan Wenxin as soon as possible. Once it's over, we'll return to Horse-Face City and live there together."

"Mm…" The kisses left Wu Xingzi's head in a daze and his tongue a little numb. Still, he obediently kept his mouth open, allowing Guan Shanjin's tongue to conquer his. He felt ready to melt into a puddle.

The servant finally had no choice but to grit his teeth and call out a trembling reminder to the general. "Master…"

The servant was one of Guan Shanjin's personal bodyguards in disguise, so he was well aware of the man's temper. He also understood that Mr. Wu was essentially Guan Shanjin's wife, and that to interrupt their affectionate moment was akin to tugging at the whiskers of a tiger.

But he had no choice! Thirty minutes had passed, and the sounds of kisses were still coming from the carriage, along with Mr. Wu's soft, indistinct moans. Yes, this was a back alley, but there were still a lot of people passing by. He couldn't withstand so many prying eyes!

If his master were to realize that so many people had heard the sounds Wu Xingzi was making… The servant's shoulders hunched inward, trembling. He took a deep breath and forced himself to speak up again. "Master, we'll be late if we don't send Mr. Wu back now."

Yan Wenxin's adopted son, Huaixiu, would be meeting with Ping Yifan today. It was nearly time for the appointment, so no matter the consequences, the servant had to drag his master away from the carriage.

Guan Shanjin snorted unhappily. A moment later, he finally pulled the curtain open and came out, closing it behind him so adroitly that no one could see the other man inside the carriage. Once he was on the ground, Guan Shanjin instructed the driver to leave.

The servant pretended not to notice the bulge in Guan Shanjin's trousers.

A few days later, Guan Shanjin was rather busy. Rumors about the Protector General and his son spread like wildfire in the capital; everyone was hitting them while they were down.

Guan Shanjin's previous status within the capital was reflected directly in the number of people who wanted to tread on him now. There were even storytellers in taverns openly speaking of Guan Shanjin engaging in an indecent relationship with his teacher, Lu Zezhi. These establishments were always packed with people, and the gatherings further smeared the reputation of the Protector General's estate.

As per usual, Wu Xingzi had no idea whatsoever that this was occurring. He had never been the sort of man who listened to idle gossip. Guan Shanjin had specially warned him earlier that there might be some adverse gossip about the Protector General's estate spreading through the capital soon, besides, and in order to keep Wu Xingzi from feeling despondent, he had asked him to not pay any attention to it.

Hence, Wu Xingzi kept his ears shut, paying no heed to such chatter. He obediently ensconced himself inside Rancui's residence, whiling away his days as he waited for either Guan Shanjin or Ping Yifan to come calling for him when he had free time.

Today, Wu Xingzi and his two serving girls were tilling soil in the yard. Wu Xingzi was not the kind of man to wait around idly. Knowing he would probably be spending quite some time in the capital yet, he'd obtained Rancui's permission to draw out a small plot of dirt to grow some chives, cucumbers, cabbages, and other vegetables.

Yesterday, the three of them went out to buy some seeds and sprouts. After they spent the entire morning in the garden, the yard in front of the residence now looked rather delightful, with the seeds and sprouts planted in neat rows. The tender, freshly watered shoots looked very cute under the waning summer sun.

"Aiyah, we should have planted these cabbages a few days later. I've heard that cabbages grown through a frost are tastier," Mint said, wiping away the sweat on her face. Not realizing that there was soil on her hand, she ended up smearing her forehead with dirt. Osmanthus looked at her sister, and she could not help but cover her mouth and laugh.

"Ah, there will be plenty of opportunities next time," said Wu Xingzi. While shopping, he'd even found some black pepper seeds. He remembered from his time in Horse-Face City that Guan Shanjin tended to prefer spicier food, so Wu Xingzi couldn't resist bringing some of the seeds home. Once the seeds grew, he could use them to fry up some dishes for the general. The thought pleased him greatly.

"Master, you've worked all morning and you're covered in sweat. You must be uncomfortable. Shall we heat up some water for you to clean yourself up?" Osmanthus asked her master, who was much more passionate about farming than she or her sister were. As for herself, she had just washed her face, hands, and feet with the water collected from the well.

"Ah, there's no need. The weather is still warm—I can clean up with water from the well."

"All right, then. Please wait a moment." Mint didn't care that her face was still dirty. She picked up the bucket, planning to go collect more well water for Wu Xingzi. Right after she left the yard, Hei-er arrived.

"Hei-er? Why are you here?" It had been a number of days since Wu Xingzi had last seen Hei-er; he welcomed him warmly. "Is Rancui looking for me?"

"No." Hei-er felt a little distressed at the mention of Rancui's name, but his complexion didn't show his blush and his expression showed even less—Wu Xingzi didn't notice at all. "Lord Yan—Yan Wenxin—has sent an invitation for you to meet him at Tianxiang Restaurant at fifteen minutes past one this afternoon."

"Y-Yan Wenxin?" Wu Xingzi stuttered out, not expecting to hear this name. He hunched his shoulders and shivered. He opened his mouth, wanting to refuse the invitation, but he forced the words back down. Hanging his head, he hesitantly asked, "Wh-why is he inviting me so suddenly? What did Haiwang say?"

Hei-er's brows creased slightly. "The general doesn't know." Disguised as Ping Yifan, Guan Shanjin had been working very closely with the Yan family. Not even Hei-er knew what his master's plans were.

A few days ago, Man Yue had told Hei-er to deal with everything at his own discretion, then disappeared. None of them seemed to plan on addressing any of the rumors circulating on the street. Hei-er had tried to get information from Rancui, but that little fox was so canny, Hei-er's head was muddled by his confusing words.

Rancui was present when Yan Wenxin's invitation was delivered. He had even accepted the invitation immediately, telling the errand boy that there was no need to worry—Wu Xingzi would definitely be there. This bothered Hei-er a great deal, as Guan Shanjin certainly would not want Wu Xingzi to interact with Yan Wenxin in any capacity. Hei-er was well aware of the history between the two men, too, so he was even less inclined to let Wu Xingzi meet Yan Wenxin alone.

"He doesn't know...?" Wu Xingzi said. Unconsciously, his eyes fell to the vegetable plot.

"If you're unwilling, I'll refuse it on your behalf," said Hei-er.

"Ah, it's not that I'm unwilling..." Wu Xingzi sighed, giving Hei-er a discomfited smile. "I'm just a little bothered. Did he recognize me and want to catch up with an old friend? Or is it because of my connection to Ping Yifan, and he wants to pry information from me?"

Of course, it could be both: that he recognized Wu Xingzi, and seeing how intimate he was with Ping Yifan at the Bai residence, he wanted to take the opportunity to probe his mind for useful details.

Wu Xingzi could not describe how he felt. If Yan Wenxin did recognize him, how was he going to explain what happened in the past? Being recognized was the more troublesome option! Wu Xingzi would much prefer that Yan Wenxin only knew him as Ping Yifan's partner.

"What do you intend to do, then, Mr. Wu?"

"I might as well go meet him. After all, it's been twenty years..." Wu Xingzi was quite curious what Yan Wenxin's motive was, and his desire to know gnawed at him.

"I'll be protecting you from the shadows," Hei-er said. "How about letting the two girls accompany you in the open?"

Since Wu Xingzi had already made his decision, Hei-er would not try to persuade him to change his mind. As one of Guan Shanjin's personal bodyguards, though, he could not follow Wu Xingzi openly. Although appearances made it seem that Hei-er had betrayed Guan Shanjin by bringing Wu Xingzi out of Horse-Face City, he still had to remain cautious.

"Then I'll have to trouble you." Wu Xingzi gave Hei-er an appreciative smile. After they agreed upon a time to leave, Wu Xingzi headed back to his room to clean up.

The invitation had arrived at thirty minutes past eleven; such tight timing showed this hadn't been planned very thoroughly in advance. All the same, Wu Xingzi still dressed up properly, donning his rarely worn Confucian robe. The fabric was very lightly colored, like a bubbling brook in May.

"This is the first time Master has worn this color," Osmanthus said with quiet admiration.

Wu Xingzi usually dressed in colors that would not easily show stains. The few light-colored outfits in his wardrobe had all been purchased for him recently by Ping Yifan. The materials used were delicate, with exquisite stitching; Wu Xingzi had never dared to wear them before.

Dressing up like this gave a simple elegance to his ordinary-looking face. The image he portrayed was that of a pleasant breeze, refined and graceful.

"Master looks lovely dressed up like this. If the general were to see you, he wouldn't be able to tear his eyes away," Mint teased.

Wu Xingzi flushed red, feeling a little flustered. "Ah, little girls shouldn't speak such nonsense," he said, tugging at his lapels and retreating a few steps to look at his reflection in the copper mirror. Lost in thought for a moment, he took out a perfume sachet and hung it on his waist, then finally nodded in satisfaction.

"But the one you're meeting is Yan Wenxin! What a shame, letting him see this for free." Both of the twin girls' faces scrunched up at the thought of Yan Wenxin. They had heard too many things on the street; they wished they could just pummel him on sight.

Wu Xingzi smiled faintly, but he didn't respond to the girls' words. Unconsciously, his fingers shifted to the perfume sachet.

He hadn't told Mint and Osmanthus, but the year he had deliberately dressed up to send Yan Wenxin off on his journey, the color of his robe was very similar to the one he was wearing now...except that robe had been old, its stitching simple, and it was made of a much coarser material.

Back then, Yan Wenxin had been dressed in a Confucian robe the color of ink. In Wu Xingzi's mind, the memory of Yan Wenxin's black-cloaked figure shouldering a satchel of books was as clear as if it were yesterday. He had walked with him almost a half day's travel away from Goose City before reluctantly letting Yan Wenxin depart, then stood in place and watched as the man slowly disappeared down the path to the capital, his tall, slender figure slightly hunched from the weight on his back.

At the time, Wu Xingzi had thought they would meet again in a couple of years. He could never have imagined that instead it would be twenty cold winters. It had reached a point where Wu Xingzi was certain they'd never see each other again.

He could see that Mint and Osmanthus were holding themselves back from speaking. He smiled helplessly and rubbed his nose. "He's a top official at court, after all. We can't show any disrespect."

Wu Xingzi understood the girls were worried that he might still be holding onto this affection of the past. But how could he? Disregarding who it was who'd let him down twenty years ago, he and Guan Shanjin had recently confirmed their feelings for each other. His heart was still immersed in that honeyed, sugary-sweet dream. A person's affections didn't just change that quickly.

By the time Wu Xingzi and the two girls finished getting ready, there was not much time left, so they headed out in a hurry.

Wu Xingzi was planing on walking to Tianxiang Restaurant. Although it was quite a distance away from Rancui's place, there was still enough time if they didn't delay. However, when he arrived at the gates, Rancui was already standing there waiting for him. His charming eyes swept up and down Wu Xingzi's body, and he gave him a meaningful smile.

"You're heading out, Mr. Wu?" he asked.

"Ah, yes." Feeling awkward under Rancui's gaze, Wu Xingzi reflexively straightened out his clothes. "If we don't leave now, we'll be late. We can't let Lord Yan wait for a commoner like me."

"No, you look fine," Rancui said with a wave of his hand. "You're meeting Lord Yan, after all, so you should look your best. You're a close friend to the manager of the Peng Society, and you're Ping Yifan's lover as well. Don't let people look down on you—you deserve to have a little pride."

"Exactly." Wu Xingzi nodded, agreeing. Just as he was about to make his farewells, Rancui spoke up again.

"Please, take the carriage with me. I have to go to the Peng Society anyway. I can drop you off along the way." Rancui knocked on the door, and someone immediately opened the gates and greeted him respectfully.

The carriage outside the gate was not the simple, small one Rancui normally used. It was a lot larger and more exquisite, gleaming under the sunlight.

Wu Xingzi's eyes widened; he was stunned for a moment. Then, coming back to himself, he waved his hands frantically. "Th-this... This is t-too..."

Even when Guan Shanjin was doting on him in Horse-Face City, he had never been invited to ride in such a luxurious carriage! This carriage might cost more than his little house in Qingcheng County!

"It's to show off a bit so others don't look down on you. Furthermore, Yan Wenxin will have his guard down around an old fellow townsman with affections long past."

The words were spoken so plainly that Wu Xingzi understood what was being insinuated. He looked down at his luxurious clothes. That shining, glittering carriage was not too outrageous in comparison.

"Then I'll have to trouble you, Manager Rancui."

"Please go ahead, Mr. Wu." Rancui held an arm out in invitation. He let Wu Xingzi, Mint, and Osmanthus board the carriage before he slowly made his own way up with the help of the driver.

The roads in the capital were well maintained, and the carriage was solid and steady. They quickly arrived at Tianxiang Restaurant, barely feeling any bumps or jolts along the way. The fragrance of delicious food wafted into the carriage through the curtains; Wu Xingzi's nose twitched as he took several deep breaths.

"I'll come pick you up in about four hours," Rancui said. "If Lord Yan departs first, you should have a meal at Tianxiang Restaurant. The most famous dishes here are the steamed rose dumplings and Heaven's Duck. It's sweet and salty, bursting with flavor, and excellent by itself or with rice. Since you're already here, don't miss out on it!" He lazily waved goodbye to Wu Xingzi and the two girls as he reclined in the cushioned seat. His fox-like eyes drooped, seeming as though he was struggling to open them. A little worried, Wu Xingzi wondered if Rancui hadn't slept well last night.

In the end, he didn't ask. Adviser Wu's ability to seek good fortune and avoid calamity was still pretty decent. Hei-er's face inexplicably flashed through his mind, and he had a vague idea why Rancui may have lost sleep.

Upon entering Tianxiang Restaurant, he was warmly welcomed by a waiter. "Hello, sir, are you here for a meal or for tea?"

"Ah, I have an appointment..." Before Wu Xingzi could even mention Yan Wenxin's name, recognition dawned on the waiter's face, and he became even more enthusiastic.

"You must be Mr. Wu, yes?"

Wu Xingzi nodded, a little confused.

The waiter smiled kindly. "Please follow me. Lord Yan has told us he is expecting an important guest. He's waiting in the Changle Room at the back garden. Mr. Wu, here, please."

"Ah..." Wu Xingzi's palms were starting to sweat. He furtively rubbed them against his thighs. He could hardly even walk straight; he felt like a big, clumsy duck stumbling into the imperial gardens.

Mint and Osmanthus were calm and steady in comparison. Without making any obvious movements, they stepped up and supported Wu Xingzi. The girls' round, bright eyes darted everywhere, taking in their surroundings.

Tianxiang Restaurant occupied quite a large plot of land, separated into two courtyards. The courtyard in the back featured a picturesque little stream and a bridge, reminiscent of towns in the south, and it was as beautiful as a poem. Small pavilions were scattered around, exquisite yet not too pretentious. Compared to the clamor and noise in the front garden, this one was more serene; the pavilions were clearly meant to be used by the capital's top officials.

The Changle Room was situated in an even more tranquil area, surrounded by swaths of bamboo trees. The light breeze that rustled through felt as if it could blow all dust and weariness away.

The waiter knocked on the door. Before he could speak, the door opened, and out came a handsome young man with a gentle and refined air about him. He was dressed in a white robe tied with a red silk sash, and the cuffs and collar of his robes were embroidered with a faint pattern, elevating his elegant demeanor and ethereal appearance.

Wu Xingzi felt himself take two steps back. The person in front of him was decidedly not a servant of the Yan estate. Dressed like this, he had to be a member of the family. Having someone like this answer the door for Wu Xingzi was unlikely to be a sign that Yan Wenxin held him in high regard, and it seemed instead that he was deliberately trying to overpower him. Wu Xingzi had spent half his life involved in bureaucracy—he immediately surmised that Yan Wenxin had not recognized him, and that today's invitation surely had to do with Ping Yifan.

"Is this Mr. Wu?" the young man asked. His smile was very friendly, and his gentle voice was musical and pleasant to the ears. However, Wu Xingzi could not relax. His heart leaped into his throat, and his back felt cold and clammy.

"I'm Wu Xingzi. With the utmost respect, I'm honored to have received this invitation." Wu Xingzi made an extended bow, and he could not conceal the anxious quiver at the end of his sentence. He didn't know why he was so nervous.

A light laugh came from within the room, and the young man revealed an affable look of amusement. "You're too courteous, Mr. Wu. Lord Yan only wishes to have an exchange on equal standing— there's no need to be so formal."

Twenty years ago, they had many such exchanges, but today... Wu Xingzi did not have the courage.

With difficulty, Wu Xingzi straightened up. The waiter had long been sent away. The young man in white turned, going in first and gesturing for Wu Xingzi to follow. Finally, Wu Xingzi shakily wiped away the sweat on his forehead.

He sighed. The top official of the capital was hardly someone a commoner like him could even dream of getting close to. He truly wished that Guan Shanjin was by his side right now.

A voice drifted out from inside. "Please, Mr. Wu, come in." It was not the young man in white. Gentle and dignified, the voice made Wu Xingzi's heartbeat stutter: it was Yan Wenxin.

He hesitated for a moment. At long last, taking in a deep breath, he braced himself and entered. There was no turning back.

Although it was not his first time seeing him again, Wu Xingzi's breath caught and his face turned ashen as he laid eyes on Yan Wenxin. The sight was so familiar, and yet so foreign.

Unlike the previous two times they crossed paths, the man in front of him did not have the stately air of an important official. Instead, he was dressed in a simple, unembroidered robe made of coarse material, the color a dark blue. Still, the basic clothes could not dampen his elegant presence.

Yan Wenxin smiled and politely poured Wu Xingzi a cup of tea, his eyes half lidded. "It's been a long time, Chang'an."

Wu Xingzi stumbled, feeling as though he had traveled back twenty years. He stood there, dazed.

Somehow, Wu Xingzi managed to sit down in the seat across from Yan Wenxin. Lifting the teacup, he gulped down the entirety of its contents.

Chang'an was the courtesy name Yan Wenxin had given him, and only Yan Wenxin had ever used that name. During the time they were together, it was how he had always addressed him. Chang'an— everlasting safety and peace...

Wu Xingzi looked at Yan Wenxin with a complicated gaze. Many questions ran through his head at once. Had Yan Wenxin sought him out because of Ping Yifan? Why had he given him that perfume sachet?

Why was he calling him Chang'an again? These questions tumbled through his mind nonstop, but in the end he was unable to ask even a single one.

"This is a cloud tea from Liu'an. Do you like it?" Yan Wenxin took no notice of Wu Xingzi's hesitation. His tone was warm and friendly, as though their separation of twenty years had never happened. It was as if they were not even in the capital, but back in that little town twenty years ago. Although the peach blossoms were gone, the same two people remained.

"It's lovely, it's very lovely..." Wu Xingzi drank another cup of tea.

Huaixiu, who had been standing by the side, had brought Mint and Osmanthus away at some point. When he returned, he placed an exquisitely crafted container in front of Wu Xingzi.

"This is a snack that I had someone make at home. Why don't you try it?" Yan Wenxin opened the container as he spoke. When Wu Xingzi glanced inside, he gasped.

Inside were a few small pieces of round pastry; half were fried and half were baked. All of them had a peach blossom print on top, and a light pink color peeked through the skin. Each pastry was only a quarter the size of one's palm, a perfect, bite-sized piece. The fragrance of the pastries filled their noses: a hint of peach blossom.

This snack was called Spring Rendezvous, and the meaning was quite obvious. It was a flaky pastry made with lard and peach blossoms, and in the middle was a thin layer of malt syrup with peach blossoms mixed into it. The flavor was rich and decadent, and the texture was thick yet did not stick to the teeth. Eating this extremely delicate and flaky pastry felt like savoring an entire peach orchard.

This snack was a signature of an old pastry shop in Goose City. It was delicious and made with good ingredients, but it was not something that could be considered a fine delicacy—its price made it affordable to the people. The fried version was cheaper, with seven of them selling for one copper coin. The baked version was a lot more expensive—just two of them cost eight coins.

Twenty years ago, Wu Xingzi would always bring along seven pieces of fried Spring Rendezvous to visit Yan Wenxin. He would eat three himself and give Yan Wenxin the other four. Even the bitter, hastily made tea they drank tasted a lot better when paired with the pastry.

As Wu Xingzi and Yan Wenxin ate the fried pastries, they would discuss poems and essays. Their time spent together was shrouded in gentle sunlight, and even though they were poor and their days were simple, it felt like they were immersed in honey.

Wu Xingzi suddenly recalled one of those days. It had been raining, and the season was close to winter. Although Qingcheng County did not grow cold very quickly, the wind would turn bone-chilling during these bouts of rain.

That day saw the last batch of Spring Rendezvous being fried. The shopkeeper put up a notice, stating that their store of peach blossoms had been used up, and the sale of this pastry would be stopped until the peach blossoms bloomed again next year. On the street, people snatched up the remaining pastries, leaving only one behind. In a rare, uninhibited moment for Wu Xingzi, he shouted, "I'm buying it!"

The shopkeeper jerked upon hearing his shout, nearly dropping a tray of freshly baked mung bean cakes.

Figuring out how this lonely little pastry should be priced was a bit of a puzzle. The shopkeeper was familiar with Wu Xingzi, so with a wave of his hand, he packed it up and gifted it to him. Grabbing the still-hot pastry, Wu Xingzi ran down the street with an umbrella in his hand. Because of his work at the magistrate's office, he had ended up arriving at Goose City a little late today, and he was very anxious that Yan Wenxin would worry.

As expected, when he neared Yan Wenxin's little house, Wu Xingzi saw a tall and slender figure by the door, leisurely standing under the eaves. It was unclear which direction he was looking.

"Zaizong-xiong, I'm late!" Wu Xingzi hurried over. Not looking where he was going, he stumbled into a shallow ditch and nearly fell flat onto the ground.

Yan Wenxin noticed him. "Watch out!" He rushed forward, holding out his hands, and managed to pull Wu Xingzi into his arms.

"Ah!" The tip of Wu Xingzi's nose bumped into Yan Wenxin's shoulder. In an instant, his entire face ached. His eyes turned red and tears threatened to spill out.

However, he did not have the time to rub his aching nose. His eyes, full of regret, were fixed on a little wax paper bag lying in the ditch... Spring Rendezvous, now soaked with dirty ditch water.

Not stopping to steady himself, Wu Xingzi hurriedly bent down, wanting to pick the paper bag up. However, Yan Wenxin stopped him.

"Forget it. Since it's already dirty, why don't we offer it to the heavens and the earth? Worms and ants and gnats are living things, too. Feeding them will bring you good fortune." Yan Wenxin undid his front lapels, tucking Wu Xingzi's cold and wet hands inside. "Hurry up and come in. Look at how cold your hands are. Why aren't you taking care of yourself properly?"

Warmth seeped through Wu Xingzi's hands and traveled upward, turning his face red.

"It's fine. I'm very healthy," he mumbled. "Zaizong-xiong, you don't have to worry about me."

Yan Wenxin turned back to look at him, then brought him into the house and handed him a cup of tea. "I'm happy to dote on you," he said sternly.

Wu Xingzi was stunned at first, then shyness overtook him. His fingers trembled, almost to the point where he could not hold onto the cup. He gulped it down before finally looking up with a blush. "I'm also happy to treat you well..."

Yan Wenxin did not respond, and Wu Xingzi was too shy to say anything more. Bowing his head, he quietly listened to the rain pattering outside. In the small, quiet room, it seemed as though they were the only two people in the entire world. It was not frightening—instead, the tranquility made them feel assured.

A moment later, Yan Wenxin sighed deeply, then smiled. "When I emerge successful from the imperial examinations, I'll take you out to buy an entire basket of baked Spring Rendezvous. We can try it together, Chang'an."

"Ah..."

Wu Xingzi had thought that he'd long forgotten all these memories of the past, but it turned out that they were still fresh in his mind.

The next year, Yan Wenxin had headed to the capital for the examinations, but in the end, he still was unable to buy a basket of Spring Rendezvous. Yan Wenxin owed the county a sum of money, and Wu Xingzi was earnestly saving up his entire salary—save for the amount he needed to live—to pay off Yan Wenxin's debt. Even the fried pastries that cost one coin for seven pieces were too expensive, so of course he never ate another pastry like it again.

Five years after that day, the eldest son of the pastry shopkeeper opened a shop in some big city up north. Apparently, the business ended up proving incredibly popular. Wanting to have his parents nearby so he could support them, the son moved his entire family away.

"I had thought that in this lifetime, I'd never have the chance to eat this again," Wu Xingzi exclaimed quietly as he carefully picked up a piece of pastry. He hesitated for some time, and then finally took a tiny bite with his front teeth like a mouse.

The baked pastry's outer crust was made up of layers of dough as delicate as silk. It was soft and flaky, but it did not crumble when bitten into; it melted the moment it landed on Wu Xingzi's tongue. It was neither too sweet nor too sticky, and the fragrance of peach blossoms suffused his senses.

So this was what the baked version of Spring Rendezvous tasted like. It was no wonder that two of them were worth eight coins.

Yan Wenxin saw that Wu Xingzi enjoyed it tremendously, so he picked one up to savor as well. Another bout of silence elapsed as Wu Xingzi ate one piece after another. In the blink of an eye, he finished the entire box.

"Chang'an is the same as always," Yan Wenxin said with a light laugh, reminiscing. "You have quite the appetite, but because of me, you always had to suffer and hold yourself back. I felt so guilty, but I didn't want to say anything to upset you. Now that times have changed, though, I have no right to dote on you anymore."

He gave another sigh.

Smiling bitterly in response, Wu Xingzi took out a handkerchief to wipe away the grease on his hands. In his heart, he had also made a plan.

"Zaizong-xiong...did you seek me out merely so we could reminisce?"

"Hmm?" Yan Wenxin smiled at him. There was not even the slightest trace of surprise in his expression. Instead, he looked rather frank. "Naturally, it's not just to talk about the past. You've always been clever, Chang'an. You see the world more clearly than anyone else. We have not met for twenty years, and I was the one who let you down. If it was merely to reminisce, how could I have the face to come meet you?"

Just like that, their past was glossed over. Wu Xingzi felt like millions of needles pierced his heart at once. His usually mild and gentle face turned a few degrees icier, and he grew weary and listless.

"So Zaizong-xiong still remembers," Wu Xingzi sighed. "It's all in the past. You don't have to worry about it."

He knew that Yan Wenxin wanted to ask him about the past twenty years, but to Wu Xingzi, the past was in the past—what was the point in asking about it? Ultimately, Yan Wenxin had still let him down, and the debt between them could never be settled. To discuss it further would be fruitless.

If Wu Xingzi were to fall into disarray because of the past, his meeting today with Yan Wenxin would be a waste. However, suddenly learning that Yan Wenxin had not forgotten their past interactions made Wu Xingzi a little angry. Still, with his gentle temperament, his anger was easily suppressed.

Yan Wenxin did want to use their past to take hold of Wu Xingzi's heart, but it didn't bother him that Wu Xingzi didn't take the bait. The person in front of him had a mild disposition—it would hardly take much further effort to manipulate him.

He waved his hand, signaling for Huaixiu to withdraw. Then, he filled both their cups with tea. "You're very forgiving, Chang'an. I'm truly ashamed of my actions. It was I who left you back then. When I achieved second place at the examinations, I should have written a letter to you to share my joy. However, I got lost within the prosperity of the capital, and my teacher wished for me to marry his daughter. Looking back, I was truly blinded by my selfish desires. Over the past twenty years, I kept remembering you... But what's the point in saying all this?" Yan Wenxin smiled bitterly. The dignified mien he'd cultivated standing in his high position for so many years dissipated entirely—he even seemed a little melancholy.

Wu Xingzi felt warring emotions as he listened to Yan Wenxin go on and on, and bitterness welled up in his throat.

"As long as you're living well now, Zaizong-xiong," Wu Xingzi said. He did not understand why Yan Wenxin was acting this way; he could only give a few words of comfort.

"Have *you* been living well?" Yan Wenxin asked, his gaze full of concern and affection. Wu Xingzi was almost entranced.

"It's not too bad..." After all, he had the Lanling Prince of pengornises by his side.

"I saw you at Bai-gongzi's place recently, but you were with someone, so it was not an ideal situation to greet you. Please do not hold any anger toward me for that."

"No, no, of course not. I just figured you didn't recognize me. After all, it's been twenty years..." Moreover, both Ping Yifan and Guan Shanjin were there. How could he have spared any attention for another person?

"I'm afraid I might offend you with what I have to say next, Chang'an. Please pardon me." Yan Wenxin stood up and gave a slight bow.

Wu Xingzi hurriedly stood up and returned the courtesy. Secretly, he was astounded. Were they finally going to talk business? Wu Xingzi inexplicably felt a little thrill of excitement. No matter what he and Yan Wenxin had shared in the past, it had been irrelevant for a long while now. Now, Guan Shanjin and Yan Wenxin were at odds, and Wu Xingzi had never sided with an outsider before.

"Zaizong-xiong, please don't stand on ceremony. If you do have any advice, I'm all ears."

"Ah, you truly haven't changed at all, Chang'an," Yan Wenxin exclaimed again. His expression then turned serious. "I have to ask. That day, the man next to you—Ping Yifan... Are you in a relationship with him?"

"Uhh..." Wu Xingzi's face flushed red as he recalled the sweet moment he shared with Guan Shanjin recently.

When he went home, he'd tidied up his selection of prized pengornises. He obediently followed Guan Shanjin's demand, tossing Ping Yifan's Murong Chong of dongs into the fire, although he deeply regretted having to do it. That pink prick had been painted to perfection!

Afterward, he took Guan Shanjin's pengornis picture and placed it properly up on top of all the others. He felt a great sense of relief; everything had returned to its rightful place.

Even if Yan Wenxin were to live two lifetimes, he would still never be able to guess that Wu Xingzi was fixated on phalluses. Yan Wenxin merely thought that Wu Xingzi was feeling shy about Ping Yifan; clearly, his feelings ran deep.

"So that's how it is." When Yan Wenxin's brows creased together, his expression became even more serious. He deliberated for a few moments before continuing. "Do you know Ping Yifan's identity?"

"Huh?" *You'd be shocked to find out exactly how much I know.* Picking up the teacup, Wu Xingzi took a sip, working hard to put on a vaguely troubled expression. "Of course I'm aware. He was born and raised in the south of the capital—in Liantang Path. His family has suffered misfortune, but their reputation is spotless. He's a businessman... Is there a problem?"

"No, there isn't. In Great Xia, there is a man named Ping Yifan, and his background is exactly as you said. However, about a dozen years ago, he traveled beyond the southern border and went missing for a period of time." With that, Yan Wenxin suddenly fell quiet and did not continue. He silently poked at the red clay stove that was heating up the water. The charcoal was white and the fire within it crackled lazily.

Yan Wenxin had perfected this skill of baiting. Although Wu Xingzi had prepared himself for this meeting, he was still so enticed he could barely suppress his curiosity.

"What do you mean, Zaizong-xiong?" he asked impatiently.

"I don't mean anything," Yan Wenxin said. "I am merely curious about this matter. Has Ping Yifan ever spoken to you about it before?"

On the surface, the conversation seemed casual; Yan Wenxin was just curious about what had occurred. But Wu Xingzi was no fool. How could he *not* detect the provocation in Yan Wenxin's words? He frowned, shaking his head and putting on an expression of disbelief. "He never mentioned it before. That period of time is probably not something he wants to recall—and isn't he doing perfectly well in the capital now?"

"You're right. He is living well in the capital at the moment." Yan Wenxin's eyes curved with his smile, and he changed the topic. "You haven't had Spring Rendezvous in a long time. Shall I get my people to prepare some for you to bring home? You can share it with Ping Yifan."

Wu Xingzi hurriedly refused. "How could I trouble you?"

"It's not any trouble. If not for your great efforts in the past, how could I have made it to the capital to take the imperial examinations? This is only a small token of my regard." Yan Wenxin waved his hand, summoning Huaixiu back. Quietly, he instructed Huaixiu to go back to the residence and ask the kitchen staff to prepare two more boxes of the pastries.

Wu Xingzi swallowed his saliva. He was on guard against Yan Wenxin's wiles, but he would never be on guard against delicious food.

While they waited for the pastries, the two men spent another two hours alone. Yan Wenxin did not make any further mention of Ping Yifan's past, but instead shared anecdotes about famous people in the capital. His low, gentle voice sounded just like it had in the past, and Wu Xingzi could not keep himself from becoming spellbound.

When Huaixiu returned with the boxes of Spring Rendezvous, Wu Xingzi saw the beautiful young man lean into Yan Wenxin's ear and whisper something. Wu Xingzi was not curious about what he was saying—his entire attention was focused on the freshly baked pastries. Unable to stop himself, he picked up a piece to eat; it was exceedingly scrumptious.

"You're sure about this?" Yan Wenxin exclaimed.

Wu Xingzi jumped in shock at the sudden outburst, and he nearly choked. Quickly, he drank some tea to soothe his throat.

"Yifu, it's definitely true."

Were they expecting him to ask about their conversation? Wu Xingzi's eyes widened as he considered it for a moment. In a somewhat sheepish manner, he asked, "What's wrong?"

"This...is just some idle chatter." Yan Wenxin's face showed a hint of a sneer. "You've heard of the Protector General's son, yes? You must have met him that day at Bai-gongzi's place."

"Ah, I know about him. He used to be stationed at Horse-Face City." He even had a little red mole on his inner thigh, right by his groin. Wu Xingzi was familiar with him indeed!

"Huaixiu heard that Bai Shaochang has moved into the Protector General's estate. The Protector General's wife plans to let her son and Bai-gongzi join in marriage." Yan Wenxin snorted coldly. "Seems like this is their last-ditch effort."

Bai Shaochang was going to marry into the Protector General's estate? Wu Xingzi froze, and his expression grew troubled.

"What is Chang'an thinking about?" Yan Wenxin did not understand his expression, and so he had no choice but to ask.

"Ahh... I was just wondering... Bai Shaochang is a man. Who's going to be the wife?"

Ultimately, no one spoke up to answer this question.

CHAPTER 8

No One Knows a Son Better than His Mother

"All right, you should go back. Since you've decided to spend the rest of your life with him, stop treating him like a bird in a gilded cage. Mr. Wu isn't a simple man—don't underestimate him."
She wasn't sure exactly how much of her advice her son took in.
Guan Shanjin gave an informal nod of his head. He did not underestimate Wu Xingzi; he only wanted to shield him from any and all harm.

I T WAS ONLY AFTER he bade farewell to Yan Wenxin that Wu Xingzi learned Mint and Osmanthus had been forced to remain in another room. The girls sure were trusting. They figured that Yan Wenxin was a top official of the court, and if he truly had any malicious intentions, he would not have sent such an open invitation.

With this in mind, they happily remained in the room, snacking and drinking tea. They even packed up some honey cakes and apricot tarts in their handkerchiefs to share with Wu Xingzi.

Wu Xingzi and the girls met back up at the entrance of Tianxiang Restaurant. Wu Xingzi handed a box of Spring Rendezvous to the girls before instructing them, "You two can head back first! I'm going to meet Ping Yifan. There's no need to worry about me."

Yan Wenxin's intentions had been very clear. Although Wu Xingzi did not know why the man wanted to sow discord between him and Ping Yifan, the pastries were still piping hot and he hadn't seen Guan Shanjin for a number of days now—he should take this opportunity to see him!

"It's too far to walk to the south of the city from here. Why don't we head back first and borrow a carriage from Manager Rancui?" Mint suggested, covering her smile. She knew that Wu Xingzi was so eager because he greatly missed the general.

The reminder left Wu Xingzi blushing and scratching at his nose. "That's true. You girls are always so meticulous."

It took about half an hour to walk back to Rancui's place, and he easily managed to borrow a carriage once he was there. Mint and Osmanthus knew that Wu Xingzi did not wish for company when meeting with the general, so they stood by the gates and sent him off.

During the journey, Wu Xingzi was in a joyful mood. Afraid that the pastries would cool and become less flavorful, he tucked the box against his chest to keep it warm. A hot Spring Rendezvous was fragrant and delicious. Guan Shanjin had been working hard the past few days; he deserved to have a sweet treat.

After some time, Wu Xingzi suddenly realized that he was humming to himself. His face flushed instantly. He was a grown man—old enough to have had a number of children or even grandchildren at this point—but here he was, acting like a foolish, emotional youth.

Wu Xingzi lifted up the curtain and peeked outside. The carriage couldn't go as fast within the city, but why did the rumbling of the wheels sound so very slow?

The driver of the carriage noticed him looking, and turned around to ask if Wu Xingzi had any instructions. Shyly, Wu Xingzi bit his lip and shook his head before retreating and continuing to incubate his box of pastries. The box was all warm and toasty.

More time passed, and the sound of the crowd outside grew louder. Soon, the carriage stopped.

The driver lifted up the curtain, his expression a little odd. "Mr. Wu, we're here."

With his mind occupied by Guan Shanjin, Wu Xingzi did not notice the driver's strange behavior at all. He eagerly jumped off the carriage with his box of goodies, and he looked up to see Guan Shanjin wearing the mask of Ping Yifan. Delighted, he started to approach, only to come to an abrupt stop. The smile on his face stiffened and his eyes widened a comical amount.

Ping Yifan was not alone outside the shop. Next to him stood a woman in a veiled hat. Although her face was concealed by thin, gauzy fabric, her tall and graceful figure was still plain to see. Just standing there, she looked like a branch of flowers covered in dew.

Ping Yifan was a lot taller than the woman. In order to listen to what she was saying, his body was slightly bent toward her, and his head was bowed. He looked very attentive and vigilant, keeping an eye out for any danger lurking around her.

The lanes in the south of the city were narrow, and there were many passersby. Periodically, people carrying goods or holding onto baskets walked past, and if any of them happened to come a little close to the woman, Ping Yifan would immediately hold his hand out to protect her. He seemed rather familiar with her.

Wu Xingzi didn't know if he should approach or not. Did the woman know Ping Yifan, or did she know Guan Shanjin? Should he present himself as the man's friend or as his lover? Was there enough Spring Rendezvous to be shared among three people?

The driver had already left with the carriage. Wu Xingzi remained, hiding by the corner of the wall, unsure what to do next. Ping Yifan was still whispering with the woman, and they seemed to have no intention of stepping into the shop. It looked like the woman would not be staying for long, so all Wu Xingzi needed to do was wait.

However, the woman speaking to Ping Yifan quickly noticed Wu Xingzi looking at them. She glanced over at him, then tugged on Ping Yifan's sleeve.

This was awkward. Distressed, Wu Xingzi retreated into his little corner. However, no matter how thin he was, he was still a fully grown adult. How could this corner conceal him, especially in broad daylight?

When Ping Yifan saw him, a confused expression momentarily appeared on his face. He strode over, and Wu Xingzi did not have any time to run away.

"Why did you come by yourself?" Guan Shanjin asked quietly as he covertly surveyed their surroundings.

"I-I... I came to give you some snacks."

Guan Shanjin stood very close to him, almost burying Wu Xingzi's face in his chest. The familiar scent was intoxicating; Wu Xingzi felt his body go weak.

"Snacks?" Guan Shanjin noticed the box of pastries in Wu Xingzi's arms. His heart melted, and his lips curved up in a smile. "What snacks? Just look at how you're treasuring them."

"Ah, these are truly treasures! The pastry is called Spring Rendezvous, and it's so mouthwatering! Quick, try one. They've only just been made—they're still hot." As if presenting precious gems, Wu Xingzi carefully opened the box. Picking out a piece, he held it up to Guan Shanjin's mouth. "Here, try one. You've been working hard lately, and you should have something sweet as a reward."

Needless to say, Guan Shanjin didn't refuse. Not only did he eat the pastry right from Wu Xingzi's fingers, he even sucked on them, his tongue twining around the digits where the taste of the pastry lingered. Wu Xingzi tensed and shivered in response.

"What goodies are these?" a pleasant, gentle voice interrupted. Wu Xingzi jerked in shock, almost falling backward. If Guan Shanjin hadn't nimbly wrapped an arm around him, he was bound to have collided straight into the wall.

It was the woman in the hat. She had drawn closer to them at some point. Her facial features and red, smiling lips could vaguely be seen through her veil, and she was beautiful—just as gorgeous as Guan Shanjin, in fact.

"I-it's a pastry called Spring Rendezvous..." Despite her indistinct features, Wu Xingzi felt that this woman seemed friendly, and he was no longer as shy.

"Oh, isn't this the legendary pastry from Xianlin Restaurant? There's twenty per box, and a box costs five taels," the woman exclaimed when she looked into the container. "I remember that this pastry is called Seeking Spring, but it's not as interesting a name as Spring Rendezvous."

"A box costs five taels?" Whether the pastry was called Seeking Spring or Spring Rendezvous, that cruel, heartless price horrified Wu Xingzi. "Miss, would you like to try one? Perhaps it's not the same thing. This is a snack from my hometown, and two of them only cost eight coins."

"Miss? Hah! What a sweet tongue you have, calling me Miss." The eyes of the woman curved in a bright smile as she gleefully grinned at Guan Shanjin. "You've even said that I'm past my prime. I do wonder who gave you such a poisonous tongue."

Rudely, Guan Shanjin rolled his eyes at her, then picked up a piece of pastry and shoved it at her. "Mr. Wu is being courteous. He's a gentle soul—don't scare him."

"How did I scare him? I didn't even reveal my face," the woman in the hat mumbled. Lifting up her veil, she revealed a pair of petal-like lips. "Fan-er, come, feed me."

"Tch, you're so lazy." Despite the complaint, Guan Shanjin was careful and gentle as he placed the pastry into her mouth. "How is it?"

After tasting it carefully, the woman replied, "It's exactly the same! The last time I managed to eat Seeking Spring was all thanks to the Grand Secretary's wife. They sent a box of these over to curry favor with your father. There was also a box of fried pastries called Meeting Spring. Those are a lot cheaper—one box for two taels."

Two taels? Wu Xingzi's eyes widened. He couldn't believe his ears. Did that mean that he had eaten upward of five taels today?

"Uhh... Uhh..." Wu Xingzi gasped, his hands trembling as he shoved the box at Guan Shanjin. "Quick, eat it. You can't let five taels turn cold."

Guan Shanjin didn't know whether to laugh or cry. He had yet to ask Wu Xingzi where the pastries came from, so how could he wolf them down just like that?

"You want me to eat standing by the road?" He pinched the old fellow's cheek, then accepted the box with one hand and caught Wu Xingzi's hand with the other. "Let's go inside first. You have to explain it to me. Who gave you these pastries?"

"Zaizong-xiong." Wu Xingzi had no intention of hiding it.

Before Guan Shanjin could respond, the woman in the hat exclaimed in shock, "Zaizong-xiong?! That name sounds so familiar... Isn't it Yan Wenxin's courtesy name...? Ah, you know Minister Yan."

"Shh! Can't this be said inside the house?" Although there were no spies around, Ping Yifan did not have high enough social status to discuss top officials of the court in public.

Realizing that she had been careless, the woman hunched down a little and apologized. Sullenly, she followed the two men into the yard at the back of the shop.

When the three of them sat down in Ping Yifan's residence, the woman took off her veiled hat, and Wu Xingzi finally saw her features clearly.

With just one look, he was astounded. Wu Xingzi was born in a small, rural village, and he had never seen such a beauty in his life. She had an oval face with thin, shapely brows, and her almond-shaped eyes glimmered with emotion—it was as if her eyes could speak a thousand words. She looked at him with a bright smile, which made him feel shy.

He kept feeling that this face looked somewhat familiar... Wu Xingzi turned his head away, avoiding the woman's gaze. However, he could not resist tilting his head back to secretly study her. Accidentally meeting her eyes, the old fellow cowered, hurriedly lowering his head to avoid offending the beautiful lady.

"Ah, this child is so amusing. Look, his ears are turning red!" The woman covered her laugh with her hand, reaching out with the other as if to pinch Wu Xingzi's ear. Seeing this, Guan Shanjin immediately held his hand out to block her.

"Child, why are you always so possessive? You can't even let your mother touch her future son-in-law?"

The woman...was the wife of the Protector General, and Guan Shanjin's mother. This noble lady was elegant and beautiful at fifty years old, and still as lively as a young maiden.

"Mother?" Wu Xingzi jerked his head up, staring at the Protector General's wife in disbelief.

Yes! The woman's facial features were very similar to Guan Shanjin's. It was just that as a man, Guan Shanjin's features were a bit harsher. In addition to that, perhaps because of his personality, there was a sharpness and seductiveness to Guan Shanjin's handsome beauty. The outer corners of his eyes trailed upward, sharp enough to pierce a person's heart.

That was happening right now: Guan Shanjin looked at Wu Xingzi with a faint smile, making the old fellow's body and limbs turn limp and soft. All he wanted to do was lean on Guan Shanjin.

"Slow down, now. Although I'm not the untactful sort, these five taels are about to turn cold. Are we not going to eat them?" The Protector General's wife could see that this pair of lovers were about to fall into each other's embrace. They actually managed to completely ignore a lovely lady like her. Just look at the poor pastries in the box—they were practically about to cry!

"Yes, yes, yes. Haiwang, M-Madam, quick, have some. It'd be such a pity for them to turn cold." Wu Xingzi immediately regained his senses. With a disconcerted expression, he pulled back his hand from Guan Shanjin's shoulder and opened the box.

The Protector General's wife waved her hand warmly. "Just call me Mother. You will become Haiwang's partner in the future, won't you? Calling me Madam makes it seem like you're an outsider." She picked up a piece of Spring Rendezvous, then addressed Guan Shanjin. "Son, hurry up and bring out your treasured tea to soothe your mother's throat. We've been standing outside for an hour and you haven't even served a single cup."

"Why are you so good at ordering people around?" Guan Shanjin complained, frowning. However, he still stood up and walked into the house to prepare the tea.

Now that her son had left, the Protector General's wife smiled even more warmly at Wu Xingzi. This left the shy adviser completely bewildered, and he nearly fell off his chair.

"How old are you?"

This first question was a harsh blow to the adviser straight out of the gate. Wu Xingzi's face paled a little, but still he answered honestly. "I'm forty."

"Forty..." The Protector General's wife nodded, then picked up another pastry and asked, "Where are you from?"

"I was born and raised in Qingcheng County."

"Qingcheng County? Hmm... I've heard of it. It was probably around forty-odd years ago when I knew of a top scholar from Qingcheng County. He had yet to reach twenty years of age. It was a pity that he only stayed in the capital for two years, as it seemed he would be joining the emperor's cabinet. The emperor appreciated him a great deal, and so did my father. He said that not only was he very knowledgeable, he also possessed a rare excellence of character. If he hadn't resigned and headed back to his hometown, Yan Wenxin would probably not have been able to reach his current status."

"Ah... That top scholar...w-was my father..." Wu Xingzi did not expect to hear about his father; it made his eyes sting a little.

The father in his memories was very stern and rarely laughed. It was only when he saw Wu Xingzi's mother that he would reveal a bashful smile and shining eyes.

Wu Xingzi knew that his father loved him. The man did his very best to teach him to be a good person and instructed him on philosophies written down in books, but his father never forced him to seek titles in examinations. The provincial examination had been something Wu Xingzi wanted to participate in for himself.

Wu Xingzi dared not forget a single principle his father instilled in him. He'd followed them carefully his entire life; he would not stray from his father's teachings. Unfortunately, though, he didn't know much about his father. He only found out that his father had received top honors in the imperial exam because his mother had told him about it. Perhaps, to his father, the days spent hand in hand with his mother were happier and more real to him than praise and merits bestowed upon him by strangers.

"Yes, that's right. Jin-er called you Mr. Wu just now." The Protector General's wife had a sentimental expression on her face, carefully studying Wu Xingzi from head to toe. "I was only a little girl that year, around five or six years old. But I can still remember that man's appearance. Your eyes are very much like his."

"Ah, is that so?" Wu Xingzi lifted his hand to touch his face. He didn't really know which parent he took after in appearance. His father was clearly refined and handsome, while his mother was pretty and delicate; his own looks were just so plain.

"Mr. Wu, as a mother, I have to ask—what do you like about Jin-er? This son of mine is heartless and has been since he was a child. He does respect his father and me, but that's only due to the filial duty a son ought to have toward his parents, and nothing more than that. I spent many, many years trying to help him open his heart. The amount of effort I spent was more than enough to birth another Monkey King from the Mountain of Flowers and Fruit."

She sighed, her face turning serious. "Jin-er treats you differently, Mr. Wu. I know that you drugged him before, and not only did he fall for it, but he did not even get angry in the slightest. Instead, he felt that he was in the wrong. If you truly were colluding with others to harm Jin-er, he would still jump into the trap with no hesitation and willingly shatter himself into pieces for you."

Wu Xingzi trembled slightly. He understood why the Protector General's wife wanted to say such words to him, but he was unable to suppress the sweetness and joy welling up inside him. Did Guan Shanjin truly hold such deep affection for him? Ah, it was fortunate that he had asked Rancui for the truth serum. If the two of them hadn't been forced to bare their feelings and thoughts to each other, they would have wasted so much time.

"Mr. Wu, what exactly do you see in Jin-er?" The Protector General's wife's previous playfulness and friendliness was gone, replaced by the awe-inspiring dignity of the noble class.

Wu Xingzi's mouth gaped open. After a moment of hesitation, he finally mumbled, "It's mainly his pengornis."

Of course, the Protector General's wife knew what a pengornis was.

She and her husband had worried themselves sick over their son's future happiness, afraid that he really was set on that crooked Lu Zezhi. After much consideration, they decided to sign their son up with the Peng Society.

It had to be said that *The Pengornisseur* was truly a sight to behold; the Protector General's wife was satisfied with every entry in its pages. However, they had never heard of starting relations through the pigeon post before. As a mother, the Protector General's wife had to vet the process first. Thus, using her son's name, she sent out a number of letters. She was left stunned for quite some time by the various phallic illustrations she received in the mail in return.

There was nothing more for her to be concerned about. Men were so very straightforward when it came to making friends; she figured there was bound to be a cock that caught her son's eye. But she never could have imagined that it would be the other way around.

"As his mother, I won't be able to comment on other issues, but regarding that particular aspect... The men of the Guan family are unlikely to be an embarrassment to their ancestors." The Protector General's wife bit into a pastry, her expression perfectly placid. She felt a lot more at ease—she no longer doubted the honest temperament of the man in front of her.

This time, it was Wu Xingzi who was left stunned. The Protector General's wife was truly a remarkable woman.

Although Wu Xingzi and the Protector General's wife were not speaking loudly, Guan Shanjin was very skilled; he could still hear most of their conversation. He was worried that his mother would say something inappropriate to Wu Xingzi, so although he was inside while they were out in the yard, he eavesdropped. At that moment, he did not know if he should step outside again or not.

Putting aside how confident his mother sounded, the issue of Wu Xingzi liking Guan Shanjin's pengornis more than the man attached to it caused unpleasant feelings to rise within him.

He took out the tea leaves and instructed the servant to prepare a stove and hot water before slowly returning to the yard, sitting down between his mother and Wu Xingzi.

Since it was important for a couple not to go to bed angry with each other, Guan Shanjin had to clarify things immediately. "It's mainly my pengornis that you like, hmm?"

Wu Xingzi's eyes widened. "Y-you heard us?" He felt a chill run down his spine, his hair standing on end as a wave of guilty panic crashed through his heart.

"Mm." Guan Shanjin tossed the tea leaves at his mother, smiling as he studied Wu Xingzi's petrified expression. "Why? Did you forget what you just said? You're quite daring, saying something like that right in front of my mother." He pinched the old quail's cheek, leaving three red marks that took some time to fade.

"Th-that's not what I meant..." Wu Xingzi hurriedly pressed a hand to his cheek. Although Guan Shanjin did not use much strength, the pinch still stung a little, and Wu Xingzi knew that the man in front of him was jealous again. Why was the general's jealousy so easily provoked?

"Then what did you mean? Is there nothing else about me that you like?" Guan Shanjin's tone was very aggressive. He did not feel that there was anything odd about being jealous of himself constantly.

The general was sitting right next to his mother and yet completely ignoring her. She secretly rolled her eyes at her son's hopelessly foolish question. This son of hers had always been innately wise and immensely gifted. Even as a child, he had been somewhat of a genius. Who knew he would be such an idiot when it came to matters of love?

"No, there are many things I like about you other than your pengornis!" Wu Xingzi tried to explain, a bright blush on his face. Guan Shanjin might not mind that his mother was right there, but he did! He wasn't shameless enough to discuss such things right in front of his future mother-in-law!

Guan Shanjin, however, was relentless, insisting that Wu Xingzi make himself clear. "What things?"

"Uh... Uhh..." Wu Xingzi shot a glance at the Protector General's wife. The lady had her head bowed as she ate the pastries, pretending not to see anything.

"Hmm?" Guan Shanjin blocked Wu Xingzi's view. Even out in broad daylight, this man was easily distracted by the sight of others. *Hmph!*

"D-don't be like this." Wu Xingzi's ears burned, ready to burst into flames at any moment. "Th-there are many things that I like about you, like...like...your face."

"*Pfft!*" The Protector General's wife clamped her hand over her mouth, managing to prevent herself from spitting out the contents. Her beautiful eyes, focused on Wu Xingzi's face, could not conceal her amusement.

"Mother!" A bit embarrassed, Guan Shanjin raised his voice a little.

"I have to say, Mr. Wu recognizes quality! Your face is really not too bad—it's very much like mine." She was quite pleased.

"Yes, yes, you and your mother have very similar facial features." Wu Xingzi eagerly nodded in agreement. Receiving a fierce glare from Guan Shanjin, he slowly hung his head, not understanding what he had done wrong.

"So, if I were ugly, you wouldn't like me?"

Huh? "How could that be? I like Ping Yifan's face, too." Wu Xingzi shook his head, waving his hands and quickly declaring his loyalty. Unexpectedly, Guan Shanjin's expression darkened further, making Wu Xingzi feel even more at a loss. He wanted to seek help from the Protector General's wife, but Guan Shanjin was blocking his view; he couldn't see a single hair on the lady's head.

"Ping Yifan?" Guan Shanjin sneered. He recalled how Wu Xingzi had dared to invite Ping Yifan to share his grave during their first meeting! That crappy little plot of land! Guan Shanjin hadn't lain there even once yet—who did Ping Yifan think he was?!

Wu Xingzi wanted nothing more than to cry. He had no idea why Guan Shanjin was so angry. Was Ping Yifan not Guan Shanjin as well? Was Guan Shanjin's penis not a part of him? And Guan Shanjin's face was really, really handsome!

"D-don't be angry. Has Zaizong-xiong been making your life difficult lately?" Wu Xingzi drew closer to Guan Shanjin, shyly patting his hand to soothe him. "Have something sweet to calm yourself, all right? Sh-shall I stay and keep you company tonight?"

Hearing these words, the sour jealousy in Guan Shanjin's heart faded a great deal. The old fellow was so dedicated to him—how could he reject such an offer?

"You've certainly learned how to make someone feel better," Guan Shanjin snorted lightly.

A servant brought over the heating stove along with the tea set. Now in a better mood, the Protector General's son started preparing tea.

"I meant what I said." Wu Xingzi rubbed his nose, finally heaving a breath of relief. He still remembered that time during Lunar New Year when Guan Shanjin tore his pengornis pictures! "You wanted me to burn Ping Yifan's pengornis drawing, and I did."

"Good boy." Guan Shanjin could not be any more pleased. He affectionately stroked Wu Xingzi's nose, then reached out and tugged the other man into his arms. "Feed me another piece of pastry. Did Yan Wenxin really dare to use something so trifling to tantalize you?"

"Ah, it is really delicious! Twenty years ago, it was the most famous snack in Goose City. Later on, though, the shop owner packed up and moved up north with his relatives, and I never ate it again." As Wu Xingzi spoke, he carefully picked up another piece and fed it to Guan Shanjin.

The man's soft tongue flicked past his fingers. Wu Xingzi's body tingled as his fingers were sucked on. With a bright red face, he hunched into himself. "Don't do that! Your mother is here."

"Don't mind me—continue as you usually would." The Protector General's wife kindly waved her hand. "I'm just having a bite to eat and cup of tea. I'm happy to see that Jin-er is living well." This was the first time she'd seen her son be so loving toward another person. It was truly a great comfort to her. In the past, when Guan Shanjin's priority had been Lu Zezhi, he had never acted like this with him.

Since his mother had essentially given him permission, Guan Shanjin dispensed with formalities. He openly cuddled and flirted with Wu Xingzi, making the old quail thoroughly flustered. Wu Xingzi wanted to refuse him, but at the same time, he wanted to draw closer. In the end, he just pretended that the Protector General's wife wasn't there, burying his face in the crook of Guan Shanjin's neck. His entire body flushed red as he essentially played dead in the general's arms.

The Protector General's wife—who'd finally managed to get her hands on some tea—looked on disdainfully. She knew that her son must be doing this deliberately. Other than getting jealous of himself, he was even being spiteful toward his own mother. All she did was ask her future son-in-law what he liked, accidentally unearthing a pengornis in the process.

How did she end up giving birth to someone so foolish in the matters of love? However, when she thought about her own husband... Fine, this was something her son inherited from his Guan ancestors. It could not be avoided.

No matter how forgiving the Protector General's wife was, she couldn't stay there and watch her son nibble on his lover's lips. Rubbing her nose, she bade them farewell.

Finally, Guan Shanjin seemed to remember his duty as her son. He instructed Wu Xingzi to remain waiting in the yard, and saw his mother off.

The Protector General's wife did not take a carriage, having made her way here on foot. Guan Shanjin wanted to prepare a carriage for his mother, but she stopped him. "Just walk part of the way with me. I'm about to suffocate staying cooped up at home all the time! It sounds glorious to be the Protector General's wife, but it's not a status that allows one to relax easily."

Although the Protector General's wife came from an aristocratic family, she'd always had a lively personality. When she was young, she liked to dress up as a boy and explore the world outside. Her family had tried various times to stop her, but after failing repeatedly, they simply allowed her to do as she liked.

Her parents had thought that their daughter would only be able to marry down, but it just so happened that in a border town, she met the man who was at the time the son of the Protector General. The two fell in love at first sight and quickly started a life together, startling her entire family.

Having carried the status of the Protector General's wife for so many years, she had to be dignified, demure, and dainty. Acting so elegantly all the time was exhausting. Now that she had an opportunity to relax outside, she didn't want to go back so quickly.

"Father must be waiting anxiously for you," Guan Shanjin said, but his mother saw right through him. He was obviously thinking about his own spouse waiting for him, and it was clear that all he wanted to do was go back and take him to bed.

She snorted. "Don't brush me off. Since your father has allowed me to come out alone, he knows I will not be home so soon. There are some things we must discuss as mother and child. Don't try to hide by pretending to be ignorant." She caught her son's hand, about to share some private words.

Guan Shanjin resigned himself to the situation. No matter what, his mother would always hold a special place in his heart; he couldn't just pull his hand away and leave.

"I'll listen obediently, then."

"Have you told Mr. Wu that you've invited Bai Shaochang into the family?" The news of this matter had spread quickly through the capital. Everyone knew that the Bai family was highly favored. In fact, even the emperor held them in high regard. Despite their status as ordinary citizens, their thoughts and opinions did hold a certain weight in the city.

Now, though, the emperor had tossed Guan Shanjin to the side. Not only was his command over the army taken away, but he was removed from his position as well. If not for being the Protector General's only child, he might even have lost his position as heir.

People were speculating that to regain his status, Guan Shanjin had struck up a relationship with Bai-gongzi, asking him to become his official spouse.

Guan Shanjin's forehead wrinkled in displeasure. "No, and there's no need to, either. This matter will be over with very quickly. Bai Shaochang already has someone in his heart; he won't actually fall for me. I'm just taking advantage of this opportunity."

"Son, I do not understand. You're clearly very intelligent, but why are you so utterly foolish in matters of love? Other than being gifted in *that* category, you Guan men really have no ability to seek partners for yourselves. No wonder Mr. Wu only likes your pengornis!" When it came to disparaging her son, the Protector General's wife had never held back. With a few sentences from her, her son's already unsightly expression darkened even further.

"He likes other things," Guan Shanjin objected, his voice grim.

"Oh, yes, your face. I remember." Through her veiled hat, the Protector General's wife smiled at her son.

"What exactly are you trying to say?" Guan Shanjin's tone was a lot less polite now. His mother's affront had him feeling dejected.

"I'm just trying to tell you that although you have your own plans regarding Bai Shaochang, you should still inform Mr. Wu. This will prevent him from feeling any upset."

Furthermore, since Yan Wenxin had sought out Wu Xingzi and even gave him the boxes of pastries, it was possible he had already revealed some of the gossip to Wu Xingzi to try and get a reaction.

"Wu Xingzi is not the petty and small-minded sort." Guan Shanjin paid no heed to his mother's words. He had always held sole control over his personal operations, and he did not wish for his partner to be entangled in such matters in the slightest. It would make it seem as though he were incompetent.

"Whether he is small-minded or not, I don't know, but..." The Protector General's wife sighed, speaking seriously. "With Lu Zezhi as an example, you should be considering things carefully."

Her words were very straightforward. The Protector General's wife had known Lu Zezhi before he was even twenty. A young man who once held some sort of integrity was rendered entirely useless by her son's doting, and she did not wish for history to repeat itself.

Guan Shanjin remained silent. He knew that Wu Xingzi and Lu Zezhi were different. However, when he recalled what Wu Xingzi had said a few days ago under the influence of the truth-telling drug, he felt a mysterious pain in his heart.

"Fine, I'll consider sharing some details with him." Guan Shanjin finally relented a little. By now, the two had reached the edge of the city's southern sector. "Don't spend too much time walking about. If Father doesn't see you in four hours, I'm afraid he'll go crazy. Go home as soon as possible."

"Aren't there still four hours left?" The Protector General's wife casually waved him off. "All right, you should head back. Since you've decided to spend the rest of your life with someone, don't treat him like a bird in a gilded cage. Mr. Wu isn't a simple man—don't underestimate him."

She wasn't sure exactly how much of her advice her son took in.

Guan Shanjin gave an informal nod of his head. He did not underestimate Wu Xingzi; he only wanted to shield him from any and all harm.

After sending his mother off, Guan Shanjin returned to the shop, only to be held back by the shop manager giving him various reports. It was nearly two hours before he was able to return to the yard.

From afar, he could see Wu Xingzi's thin body sitting alone in the pavilion. On the wooden table sat a variety of snacks and a pot of tea. There was steam wafting from the pot; it must have been recently refilled.

Typically, Wu Xingzi never ignored food. If there was any food in front of him, he would want to at least have a few bites, regardless whether the timing was appropriate or not. People from small towns were never willing to let food go to waste.

Right now, though, the old fellow was only holding his teacup. Guan Shanjin didn't know if the tea within had already cooled, or if the cup was empty. He was just sitting there fiddling with the cup, but nothing spilled.

Guan Shanjin was a little curious, so he didn't hurry forward. He stood at a distance and quietly studied Wu Xingzi.

Although the yard was furnished according to Ping Yifan's style, Guan Shanjin was still the one using it. The items that seemed extremely plain and simple exuded an air of subtle elegance. It was this very habit that had confirmed Yan Wenxin and Huaixiu's speculations about Ping Yifan's identity.

Wu Xingzi sat there for a while, then suddenly stood up and put the teacup down. He glanced over in the direction Guan Shanjin was hiding, but he clearly didn't notice him there. There was a path that led outside paved with high quality Yuhua stones. They were sturdy, yet smooth and comfortable, causing no sound when one walked on them. However, when rain fell upon the stones, a soft, gentle tinkling would echo from them, creating a captivating atmosphere.

Perhaps feeling uneasy due to the long wait, Wu Xingzi walked a couple of laps around the pavilion. Then he turned himself around and walked another two rounds, before finally stopping by the Yuhua stone path. His brow was slightly creased, as if he was deep in thought. After some contemplation, he cautiously stepped upon the path, then quickly retracted his foot, walking another lap around the pavilion.

In the past, Guan Shanjin might not have been able to understand what Wu Xingzi was thinking. However, things were different now. Every single one of Wu Xingzi's actions was absolutely adorable in Guan Shanjin's eyes.

Wu Xingzi was probably worried that Guan Shanjin had met with trouble outside, and he wanted to go out and take a look. However, he was also worried that he guessed wrong and would end up disrupting Guan Shanjin's personal business. What would he do then? Consequently, he hurried back to his pavilion. The snacks on the table had not been touched at all.

Who knew what kind of terrifying possibilities were milling around in that old quail's head? Guan Shanjin's heart melted completely.

The general was too powerful, and he was used to taking care of people. Although his parents, his elders, his friends, and his family cared for him, no one thought that Guan Shanjin was a man who needed to be doted on or adored. When Lu Zezhi had yet to understand him, he had treated him like an ordinary child at first, doting on him like he would other children. Unfortunately, though, once he discovered that Guan Shanjin was more predisposed to doting on others, their relationship reversed completely. Lu Zezhi felt no sense of unease at accepting Guan Shanjin's affections, and he clung onto Guan Shanjin like a vine wrapping around a tree.

Wu Xingzi was different. This old fellow knew that Guan Shanjin was powerful, reliable, and capable; he knew that when Guan Shanjin treated someone well, he would insist on spoiling and pampering that person to no end. Wu Xingzi did not refuse Guan Shanjin's pampering, but he also tried his very best to stretch out his own thin arms and return the general's doting.

Guan Shanjin was unable to put how he felt into words. He only knew that he could never let go of Wu Xingzi as long as he lived. If he were to be parted from this timid old quail, where was he going to find someone else to dote on him?

CHAPTER 9

THE STORM APPROACHES

"A few days from now, Guan Shanjin will be taken to jail."

Wu Xingzi's eyes widened. He gripped tightly onto Guan Shanjin's clothes, momentarily at a loss for what to do.

His heart aching, Guan Shanjin stroked Wu Xingzi's cheek. "It's not a major concern. This is something the emperor and I decided on together. Don't make that face, hmm?"

"You've discussed it with the emperor?" Wu Xingzi's grip on Guan Shanjin's clothes tightened. "...You decided to go to jail yourself?"

Guan Shanjin was surprised—Wu Xingzi had hit the nail on the head. His brow furrowed slightly; in that moment, he was unable to respond.

GUAN SHANJIN STRAIGHTENED his robe and, once he'd confirmed that there was no one else in the yard other than his own bodyguards, he removed Ping Yifan's mask. As he slowly stepped out from his hiding spot, Wu Xingzi happened to be looking in his direction. His face immediately brightened, and he clumsily wiped his palms on his clothes and rushed over to him.

"What took you so long? Did something happen?"

"I spoke with my mother for a while, then the store manager held me back to tell me some things." Guan Shanjin made his way over to

Wu Xingzi, reaching out with a long arm to pull the older man into his embrace. "Did the wait make you anxious?"

"Ah..." Wu Xingzi obediently leaned into his chest, nodding his head frankly. "There's something I'd like to speak to you about, but you didn't come back. I was worried that Yan Wenxin had..." He shuddered. His recent meeting with Yan Wenxin had left him still somewhat fearful.

"Don't worry—Yan Wenxin does not doubt Ping Yifan's identity." Guan Shanjin massaged Wu Xingzi's furrowed brow. "Just look at you," he teased. "You're not a young man anymore, and you like to frown so much. Are you deliberately reminding me to be respectful to my elders, so I won't be too aggressive when I flirt with you?"

Wu Xingzi hurriedly reached out and rubbed his own face, his expression a mix of bashfulness and nerves. "It's only because I'm worried about you. I don't usually frown like this."

"Don't worry, even if your face turns as wrinkled as a pickle, I'll still like it." Guan Shanjin bowed his head to kiss Wu Xingzi's face.

The old fellow's shoulders trembled slightly, a blush instantly spreading across his face. Guan Shanjin's heart completely melted at the sight. He tightened his arms around Wu Xingzi and kissed him, only stopping when the older man gasped for air, his eyes turning red.

"Why did you suddenly start..." Wu Xingzi did not mind engaging in such acts of intimacy during the day; in fact, he secretly welcomed it. However, this yard was so exposed, and there were bodyguards hidden all over. Guan Shanjin had even said himself that this yard wasn't suitable for any outdoor sexual activities.

"I want to see what this pickle tastes like," Guan Shanjin said. Although his beauty was otherworldly, he had spent a lot of time in the army. When he wanted to act crass, he held nothing back.

Wu Xingzi was mortified. He mumbled softly once or twice, then hung his head and played dead. Watching the old fellow grow shy, Guan Shanjin stopped teasing him. Lifting him up in his arms, he brought him indoors, where he squeezed both of them into a chair and tangled their bodies together.

"What did you want to talk to me about?" Guan Shanjin fiddled with Wu Xingzi's thin, calloused fingers. He must've been working in the yard a lot lately. His calluses from writing had faded, but the calluses from farming had thickened.

"Oh." Wu Xingzi patted the back of Guan Shanjin's hand lightly, wanting to free his fingers, but Guan Shanjin refused to let go. He smiled and brought the adviser's hand to his lips, pressing kisses to it. His meaning was obvious—either Wu Xingzi said what was on his mind, or Guan Shanjin would not stop at just a few kisses.

Wu Xingzi's fingers soon turned red from kisses, and he shrank into himself and trembled. A look of helplessness clouded his eyes.

"Just now, you sent...you sent the Protector General's wife—"

"Mother," Guan Shanjin interrupted him.

"Huh?" Wu Xingzi blinked, stunned. "You want me to call you Mother?"

He seemed to realize his mistake as soon as the words left his lips. He stared at Guan Shanjin in distress.

Guan Shanjin did not know how to react. Clearing his throat, he answered with feigned seriousness, "If you insist on calling me Mother, I'll allow it. However, I would much prefer that you call my mother that."

"Ah, that will be so embarrassing..." The Protector General's wife was only a few years older than Wu Xingzi. She was close enough in age to be his older sister, not his mother.

"You'll have to call her that sooner or later anyway. In front of my mother, you proclaimed your devotion to my cock and my face, but now that she's left, you're regretting your words?"

"But your cock is so nicely shaped..." Wu Xingzi quickly clamped his hands over his mouth. Unfortunately, he was too late.

Guan Shanjin studied him with a faint smile, then aimed a smack at Wu Xingzi's round buttocks. Although he didn't put much strength into it, and only a muffled sound could be heard through his clothes, the old fellow was still absolutely abashed. Wu Xingzi waved his hands. "Slow down, slow down!" he exclaimed hurriedly. "I still have something to say!"

"I'll slow down. Go ahead." Guan Shanjin eagerly kneaded Wu Xingzi's soft buttocks, his expression full of tenderness. His movements were slow and leisurely; Wu Xingzi's mouth fell slack, his entire body on fire.

"Don't be like this..." He wanted to reach out and stop Guan Shanjin's salacious conduct, but he had to admit that the kneading and caressing felt lovely. The man's palms were broad and warm; one hand was big enough to cover nearly half of his buttocks. Guan Shanjin would squeeze them together, then spread them apart, using just the right amount of pressure at just the right pace. Wu Xingzi was on the verge of melting.

He had always been very direct in bed, and he never had much restraint when it came to his desires. He let out a few soft moans, almost entirely forgetting what he'd wanted to say. He felt his hole start to twitch, and all he wanted now was for Guan Shanjin's cock to soothe the ache.

"What exactly do you want to tell me, hmm?" Guan Shanjin pulled the other man down onto his lower half, grinding his slowly hardening cock against Wu Xingzi's soft inner thigh and letting Wu Xingzi's prick rub against his firm, muscular abdomen.

"Ah..." Wu Xingzi panted, his eyes glazing over as he leaned his head on Guan Shanjin's shoulder. "More... Harder..."

"Dirty darling." Guan Shanjin smiled, his eyes curving. In no time at all, he deftly removed Wu Xingzi's trousers, revealing his fair, slender legs. At the same time, the general took out his half-hard cock and rubbed it against Wu Xingzi's sensitive perineum. The old fellow mewled, intoxicated; he muffled his trembling moan against Guan Shanjin. Heated air brushed against Guan Shanjin's ear, and the feeling could not have been any more provocative.

"This little cock of yours is so adorable." Guan Shanjin's fair skin was now tinged with a hint of red, tiny beads of sweat gathering on his temples. He skillfully played with Wu Xingzi's pengornis where it was pressed against his abdomen.

Although Wu Xingzi's cock was not big—it was a little more delicate than the average man's—it was clean, pink, and cute. The hole at the tip of his cock was closed tightly, just as shy as its owner. However, it was shy only in appearance. As soon as it was touched, the little prick quickly lost all its inhibitions.

Guan Shanjin liked to toy with Wu Xingzi's little pengornis—at times he would stroke its tender head with his calloused fingers, causing the tip to gape open slightly and leak drops of precum; sometimes he would use his broad, warm palm to stroke up and down the shaft. He had all sorts of depraved tricks up his sleeve, always able to massage Wu Xingzi's balls at the perfect moment, followed by a hard squeeze at the root of his cock. His ministrations made the old fellow tremble and howl as his orgasm was forcefully held back, the slit at the tip of his cockhead twitching pitifully.

"You still can't handle me touching you like this?" Guan Shanjin teased, bringing his hand, was wet with precum, to Wu Xingzi's lips. In a low voice, he coaxed, "Here, lick it. Tell me how it tastes."

But that was his own precum! Wu Xingzi still had a tenuous grasp on his senses. He glanced at Guan Shanjin's face before glancing back at his beautiful hand, blushing in shame. Face completely red, he stuck his tongue out. Right as he was about to lick Guan Shanjin's finger, though, he quickly retracted his tongue, grabbing his own clothes and wiping away the juices on that hand.

Guan Shanjin did not stop him. He only smiled as he watched a mortified Wu Xingzi wipe at his hand. Wu Xingzi was still licking his lips with the tip of his tongue, painting quite the sultry picture.

"Say, what does this taste like?" Wrapping an arm around Wu Xingzi's slender waist, he tugged him closer to his chest. Wu Xingzi's prick left a wet smear against Guan Shanjin's firm stomach.

Guan Shanjin turned his head, putting his mouth on one corner of the fabric Wu Xingzi was gripping, deliberately making loud sucking noises.

"Ah... Don't be like that... Don't, it's dirty..." Wu Xingzi flushed even redder. Tears welled up in his eyes; he was both nervous and turned on. He tugged at his clothes with some strength, wanting to take them back. However, Guan Shanjin was biting onto his robes with so much force that he could not free the material. Wu Xingzi's eyes reddened in his anxiety.

Once he'd left a wet patch of saliva, Guan Shanjin finally released his teeth. "It's the taste of sex." Immersed in the sensation, he licked his lips. "There's a hint of sweetness to it, too."

Wu Xingzi froze; the tip of his tongue again slid across his lips, as if tasting something. With a single glance, Guan Shanjin could see that the lustful old fellow was wondering how it tasted.

Very quickly, Wu Xingzi's eyes widened, as if his own thoughts frightened him. Hanging his head, he tried to slip out of Guan Shanjin's arms. But Guan Shanjin had a firm grip on his waist;

he held him there tightly. As a result, Wu Xingzi's pengornis ground firmly against Guan Shanjin's powerful muscles, and he ended up making his body go slack with the pleasure. Sprawled in the younger man's embrace, he jerked and shuddered, quite a bit of cum escaping from the tip of his dick.

Every breath he took was filled with Guan Shanjin's scent. There was the familiar scent of orange blossom and white sandalwood, as well as a distinctly masculine musk. Like a drug, it muddled his mind, and Wu Xingzi only wanted to cling and rub himself against Guan Shanjin's body. His hole itched, hungrier than ever to be filled.

Guan Shanjin seemed to be in an excellent mood today—there was no sense of urgency or roughness like all those previous times. Although his breathing was heavy and his face was flushed, he was still calm and composed as he teased the man in his arms. He jerked Wu Xingzi's cock, making him tilt his head back in pleasure and moan, exposing his pale, slender throat.

Guan Shanjin's hand was big and broad, and it was so hot that it felt almost scalding. Wu Xingzi unconsciously started to thrust his hips, fucking into the younger man's grip.

Guan Shanjin chuckled quietly as he watched Wu Xingzi helplessly writhing and grinding against him. He increased his efforts, quickly bringing him to orgasm. With a shriek, Wu Xingzi collapsed into Guan Shanjin's chest, panting and trembling.

Before Wu Xingzi could recover, he was suddenly flipped around. He was moved from Guan Shanjin's embrace onto the chair, his legs straddling the armrests on each side, leaving his hole exposed. He quivered in fright, his hole contracting as he shivered, causing a wave of desire to wash through the general.

"H-Haiwang…" Wu Xingzi wanted to pull his legs back together.

He didn't mind exposing his private parts in bed, but he did not have the courage for an exhibition like this!

Guan Shanjin held a firm hand against Wu Xingzi's belly, restricting Wu Xingzi's movements. Struggling a few times, Wu Xingzi grew exhausted and gasped for air. He had just reached his release; his limbs were still weak and soft. His mind was dazed; putting his thoughts into words was beyond him. He could only look at Guan Shanjin pitifully.

"Be good..." Guan Shanjin smiled teasingly, then crouched down. All Wu Xingzi could see was the top of Guan Shanjin's head. This made him panic a little, and just as he was about to call out, his oversensitive cock was suddenly enclosed in soft, wet heat.

"Ah—!" Wu Xingzi squealed loudly. Blushing a bright red, he quaked in place. His legs tensed up over the armrests as the pleasure rushed straight to his head.

His cock was enveloped in Guan Shanjin's mouth. The warm, wet cavity tightened around him as Guan Shanjin sucked voraciously. The general's tongue pushed Wu Xingzi's cock to the roof of his mouth so he could suck on it even harder, nearly sucking out the man's soul along with it.

Wu Xingzi mewled and whimpered as his cock jerked and twitched relentlessly. He tried his best to reach out and push the general away from his crotch, but with the position Guan Shanjin had left him in, there was no way his hands could reach that wicked head.

After a few sucks, Guan Shanjin's tongue became even naughtier. It deftly twined around the little prick, stroking the shaft with each sucking motion. Eventually, the tip of Guan Shanjin's tongue prodded the slit at the tip of Wu Xingzi's cock.

Wu Xingzi twisted his hips and howled, feeling he was about to be sucked to death. Guan Shanjin's tongue was able to dig into the slit slightly, and some of his saliva even slid inside. Tingles shot through Wu Xingzi's body; he didn't know what to do. His calves tensed tightly and all of his toes curled up.

"Haiwang, Haiwang... Please, stop, hurry up and stop—!" Wu Xingzi cried and begged, but Guan Shanjin didn't seem to hear him. Instead, he gently scraped his teeth against the sensitive head of Wu Xingzi's cock. Wu Xingzi's eyes rolled to the back of his head, and all he could do was whimper. His face was smeared with tears and sweat as his tongue lolled out of his mouth.

Guan Shanjin truly adored this little cock in his mouth. It was rock-hard, yet the skin was velvety-soft, a delicious interplay of sensations. The cockhead happened to reach the perfect spot right before his throat, so it was not too uncomfortable for him to swallow Wu Xingzi's entire length. Sucking loudly, Guan Shanjin played with the pengornis in all sorts of sinful ways.

The old quail was left twitching and speechless, his head falling backward. Spurts of cum erupted from the tip of Wu Xingzi's cock, only to be swallowed down Guan Shanjin's throat. The general refused to let go, reaching out and teasing Wu Xingzi's little balls.

"Mm—!" Wu Xingzi's moan was stuck in his throat. He could barely catch his breath. Having just orgasmed, it was impossible for him to come again right away. The hole at the tip of his cock twitched a few times, and a clear, sticky fluid seeped out from it. Wu Xingzi felt like a little boat in a storm, rising and falling with the swells. The pleasure was like a huge wave, lifting him up higher and higher. He thought he'd reached the peak, only for an even larger wave to come and sweep him away.

Wu Xingzi drooled, his tense body twitching as an ache burned in his lower back. The slit on his cockhead gaped open, yet nothing came out. Guan Shanjin took this opportunity to dig his tongue in further.

Wu Xingzi's grip on the armrests was so tight that it felt like he could crumble them. His mind blanked out until he erupted in a wail, forced to reach his peak again; he convulsed so strongly that Guan Shanjin could barely hold him down.

Guan Shanjin loved seeing Wu Xingzi dazed and covered in fluids because of him, with his mouth open and his tongue lolling out. The general's cock was even more excited; the crotch of his trousers was extremely tight, with a wet patch forming where the head of his cock pressed against the fabric.

Wu Xingzi wasn't a young man, and Guan Shanjin didn't know how his body would be affected after being brought to climax three times. He stood up and lifted Wu Xingzi into his arms, so he could sit himself down in the chair with Wu Xingzi on his lap.

Wu Xingzi had yet to recover from his orgasm, and he was still trembling slightly. He nestled into Guan Shanjin's arms like a delicate kitten, inhaling Guan Shanjin's deliciously cool fragrance along with the smell of sex.

After patting Wu Xingzi's completely limp hips, Guan Shanjin undid his own trousers. The moment his colossal cock was freed, it slapped against Wu Xingzi's round, plump buttocks. Wu Xingzi's hole twitched and his body shuddered violently.

Wu Xingzi's mind was still hazy, so he hadn't realized what Guan Shanjin wanted to do. Panting, he huddled into Guan Shanjin's chest. His mind was still a jumble even as his buttocks were parted. Soon, a thick, hard, hot cock pushed its way into his warm, wet hole.

"Ah—!" Wu Xingzi squeaked. Instinctively, he pushed at Guan Shanjin's chest. Despite how wet and eager his hole was, the sudden intrusion of the thick shaft was still more than he could bear. His pleasure still had yet to dissipate, and it was being pushed to the limit once more; every single hair on Wu Xingzi's body felt extremely sensitive.

Holding onto the curves of Wu Xingzi's waist, Guan Shanjin tugged him down further onto his cock until his entire length was sheathed. The old fellow's trembling moans were sweet, lush, and obscene; they were like the little claws of a kitten, pitifully scratching against Guan Shanjin's heart.

Wu Xingzi had always been thin and scrawny. He had been sleeping and eating well during his time in the capital, and finally developed a bit of meat on his bones—when Guan Shanjin held him in his arms, he no longer felt as bony. However, his waist was still very slender, as if the slightest bend could break it. With just one arm, Guan Shanjin was able to encircle more than half of Wu Xingzi's waist.

In truth, apart from the plumpness and perkiness of his backside, nothing else about Wu Xingzi's body was particularly attractive. Still, his appearance always whipped Guan Shanjin's desire up into a frenzy. The general wanted nothing more than to bundle him up and swallow him into his belly to ensure no one else could have him.

"My dirty darling, won't you move by yourself a bit?" Guan Shanjin thrust his hips upward, chuckling as he sucked Wu Xingzi's earlobe.

"Ah..." Wu Xingzi supported himself on the younger man's shoulders. His thighs were so weak that they felt like limp noodles; his muscles quivered nonstop, and he could not even properly kneel. He had no energy at all to hold himself upright. However, he was afraid that the general would not be able to wait and would start frantically fucking him. His own cock still couldn't get hard again, and if he was fucked that forcefully, he might end up pissing himself again. It was broad daylight—he wanted to maintain at least a little of his dignity!

He had no choice. He shakily forced himself up with trembling legs. After letting Guan Shanjin's cock slide out a little, he sucked in a breath and sat back down. The stiff cockhead unerringly found that sensitive spot inside him, provoking the utmost pleasure.

Moaning aloud, Wu Xingzi gasped for air. He shifted his body and lost all his strength, falling right into Guan Shanjin's lap. Guan Shanjin's heavy balls smacked directly against Wu Xingzi's plump buttocks as his cock slid even further inside.

"*Ahh*—! I-it's so hot..." Whimpering, Wu Xingzi hugged his belly, pressing his palm against the bulge forced out by Guan Shanjin's cock. Groaning in pleasure, Guan Shanjin gripped Wu Xingzi's waist and began to fuck him roughly.

The intense thrusting caused Wu Xingzi's eyes to roll to the back of his head, and his cries left him breathless. "Slow...down..."

But Guan Shanjin didn't have the slightest intention of easing up. Now that he was finally inside Wu Xingzi, Guan Shanjin was like a crazed beast. His thick, hard cock was wrapped in a warm, wet sheath, its muscles clenching and convulsing around him. There was no greater pleasure than this. All he could do was follow his instincts, seeking to push himself even deeper.

The thrusts jolted Wu Xingzi incessantly. Wailing, he sprawled across Guan Shanjin's broad chest, his face smeared with saliva and tears. Wu Xingzi's body twitched and jerked along with every savage snap of Guan Shanjin's hips. His tongue hung loose from his lips; he thought he was about to break.

The general's cock was truly worthy of its title as the Lanling Prince of pengornises. It was fierce, vigorous, and unyielding; it felt like it was going to fuck right through him. Wu Xingzi's belly would periodically bulge out, showing where Guan Shanjin's cock was inside of him. His poor prostate felt swollen from the relentless attack.

"My filthy darling." The rims of Guan Shanjin's eyes were red from pleasure. He was an untamed beast, yet when he lifted Wu Xingzi's chin up he was as gentle as if he held the world's most precious treasure. His heart overflowed with love for this man, so much so that he didn't know what to do with himself.

On the receiving end of Guan Shanjin's fierce, deep thrusts, Wu Xingzi gave him a teary-eyed glare of grievance. "You scoundrel..."

Wu Xingzi could not have looked any more enticing. Guan Shanjin lowered his head, sucking the older man's tongue in a firm, satisfying kiss. Their lips melded together and their tongues danced; Guan Shanjin's kiss was just as brutal as the thrusts of his hips. He swept his tongue across the inside of Wu Xingzi's mouth, then curled it against Wu Xingzi's, sucking and nibbling. Next, he slid his tongue further inside, almost as if he was trying to reach Wu Xingzi's throat. The kiss left Wu Xingzi whimpering and wailing, and by the time Guan Shanjin pulled back a little to nip his kiss-swollen lips, he could hardly breathe.

Wu Xingzi was on the verge of fainting. But for Guan Shanjin, one kiss was not enough. He held onto Wu Xingzi's chin, refusing to wait for Wu Xingzi to catch his breath before pressing another deep kiss against his mouth. His cock did not rest, either; each thrust was stronger than the last. Wu Xingzi's hole had loosened up by now, slick dripping from it continuously.

Suddenly, Wu Xingzi's body tensed. After a moment of stiffness, he flailed and jerked wildly, almost falling off of Guan Shanjin's lap. Guan Shanjin's muscular arms tightened, holding Wu Xingzi firmly against his chest.

Guan Shanjin felt a warm wetness where their bodies were joined. Looking down, he discovered that Wu Xingzi had pissed himself again. The old fellow kept spasming for quite some time. His eyes became completely unfocused as Guan Shanjin continued fucking him hard.

Seeing Wu Xingzi's condition, Guan Shanjin did not dare go too far. As such, he did not deliberately drag out his pleasure. Before Wu Xingzi returned to his senses, he quickly thrust in a few hundred times more. This caused the old quail to start whimpering again— only then did Guan Shanjin thrust inside for the last time, spurting hot come into Wu Xingzi...

It turned out Guan Shanjin had gone a bit too far after all. After Wu Xingzi lost consciousness, he didn't regain it until nine o'clock the following morning.

Upon waking up, he was still very bleary. He sat there groggily on the bed, and he only fully returned to his senses after Guan Shanjin sat him in his lap and carefully fed him a bowl of porridge.

"Is the porridge tasty?" Guan Shanjin had prepared rice porridge with sliced fish. Each piece of fish was so delicate that it melted in Wu Xingzi's mouth, with a fresh, sweet flavor. Finely chopped cabbage leaves were also mixed into the porridge, their color a bright, fresh green. The porridge tasted excellent, and it went down easy. After all, it had been personally cooked by Guan Shanjin.

Wu Xingzi nodded, blushing, and shyly allowed Guan Shanjin to feed him the entire bowl of porridge. With his belly now warm, he felt a lot more awake. However, his stomach still felt empty—he could easily eat another four or five more bowls.

Guan Shanjin knew Wu Xingzi's appetite well. Just a single bowl could never relieve even a little of the old fellow's hunger. Seeing Wu Xingzi's cheeks regain their rosiness, Guan Shanjin pinched his fleshy nose. "I'll go fetch another bowl of porridge for you. We'll have some other dishes once your belly's warmed up, hmm?"

Wu Xingzi nodded his head obediently. He could smell a fragrance wafting from Guan Shanjin that excited his appetite; the sweetness that welled up within him was impossible to suppress. He could tell by this scent that the man next to him had woken up early in the morning to prepare food for him.

After Guan Shanjin brought Wu Xingzi another bowl of porridge, he asked him to eat it by himself while he headed back to the kitchen. After a bustle of activity, he brought out all the dishes he had prepared. There were ten dishes in all, featuring everything from chicken and duck to fish and vegetables, all prepared according to Wu Xingzi's preferences.

After two bowls of porridge, Wu Xingzi's belly woke up too, and he discovered that he was ravenous. It shouldn't have been a surprise, considering he hadn't eaten a meal since his meeting with Yan Wenxin. No matter how delicious Spring Rendezvous was, it was only a snack—barely enough to even fill the gaps between his teeth.

Then the two of them engaged in some daylight debauchery. If it hadn't been for the two bowls of porridge, Wu Xingzi's belly would have ached from hunger.

Guan Shanjin laughed when he saw Wu Xingzi greedily licking his lips. "Come on, it's been a long time since I've cooked for you. Quick, try some. See if it's just as good as before."

Wu Xingzi nodded. Sitting right up against Guan Shanjin, he picked up his bowl, and started to sweep the table clean.

Although the table was filled with a variety of food, it was nothing to Guan Shanjin and Wu Xingzi. In less than half an hour, the plates were empty. Even the gravy from the dishes had been emptied into Wu Xingzi's bowl to accompany his rice. He rubbed his belly in satisfaction, taking a sip of his freshly brewed cup of tea.

"Oh, you," Guan Shanjin said, pleased that his cooking was appreciated so much. He pulled out a handkerchief and wiped Wu Xingzi's mouth before summoning a servant to clear the plates.

The dessert after the meal was almond tofu that Guan Shanjin had specially bought from a well-known, century-old establishment in the capital. It was simple and plain, with nothing fancy added to it. The tofu was the color of snow, and it looked rather adorable. Its delicious scent spread through the room.

Wu Xingzi finished two cups of tea before picking up the bowl of almond tofu and starting to eat. The taste of almond was strong and so was its scent. His eyes closed halfway as he sighed in pleasure. Guan Shanjin didn't have as hearty an appetite, so he pushed his bowl of almond tofu over to Wu Xingzi.

Satiated, Wu Xingzi burped—then covered his mouth, a little embarrassed, and snuck a glance at Guan Shanjin.

Guan Shanjin did not laugh at him. He had always been biased; when it came to those he doted upon, every single one of their flaws was adorable. "Will you accompany me on a stroll around the yard?" he asked.

Wu Xingzi nodded and accepted Guan Shanjin's outstretched hand, lacing their fingers tightly together.

The afternoon sun was not too hot. The Double Ninth Festival[7] was coming up; the temperature was starting to dip quite a lot at night.

The two strolled around the yard hand in hand. Although neither of them spoke a single word, warmth and sweetness filled their hearts. They gripped their clasped hands a little tighter.

"What did you want to tell me yesterday?" Guan Shanjin asked abruptly.

---

7   Celebrated on the ninth day of the ninth month.

Wu Xingzi blanked out for a moment, his face turning pink. "Ah... Wasn't it yesterday, in front of your mother, that I said that I liked your pengornis and your face?"

Guan Shanjin looked down at him, amused. "Why? Are you regretting it now?" he teased.

He had known from the very beginning that Wu Xingzi liked his cock. If not for the prized pengornis passed down to him through the Guan family line, he would never have been able to capture this salacious thing.

To his surprise, Wu Xingzi nodded. The smile on Guan Shanjin's face crumbled in an instant. The first thought that came to his mind was to set the Peng Society on fire, then find all the pengornises that had seduced Wu Xingzi and destroy them!

Completely unaware of the bloodthirsty brutality raging inside the man next to him, Wu Xingzi stopped walking. Earnestly, he held onto both of Guan Shanjin's hands. There was a shy expression on his face, but his words were honest: "Actually, what I like...is you. As a whole. The good and the bad—I like everything about you. It has nothing to do with your pengornis."

It was such a sudden, clumsy confession, but Guan Shanjin felt he had swallowed a mouthful of honey. Even his heart was overcome with sweetness. He stood dazed for a moment. Then, unable to control himself, he revealed a foolish grin. If the Protector General's wife were to see the look on her son's face right now, she might have thought he'd hit his head.

Looking at Guan Shanjin's silly appearance, Wu Xingzi pressed his lips together in a smile. The two men gazed at each other, neither of them willing to drag their eyes away.

"When all this is settled, I'll take you back to Horse-Face City." Guan Shanjin pulled Wu Xingzi into his arms. He desperately yearned to absorb him into his bloodstream, yet his actions were still very careful. "If you don't wish to spend all your time in my estate, you can go to the magistrate's office to look for a job. I hear that Horse-Face City is in need of an adviser. What do you think?"

"Mm." Wu Xingzi returned the hug, nuzzling his face into Guan Shanjin's chest.

The two of them were surrounded by a warm, intimate atmosphere. How perfect would it have been if this moment could last forever? Unfortunately, Guan Shanjin was not the sort to linger in his feelings. Before long he settled his emotions, releasing Wu Xingzi and taking half a step back.

Wu Xingzi looked up at him, not understanding. When he saw Guan Shanjin's apologetic expression, though, he knew that there was something serious that needed be discussed.

"A few days from now, Guan Shanjin will be taken to jail."

Wu Xingzi's eyes widened. He gripped tightly onto Guan Shanjin's clothes, momentarily at a loss for what to do.

Guan Shanjin stroked Wu Xingzi's cheek, his heart aching. "It's not a major concern. This is something the emperor and I decided upon together. Don't make that face, hmm?"

"You've discussed it with the emperor?" Wu Xingzi felt as though he had been rudely woken up from a dream. His face was ashen, and his grip on Guan Shanjin's clothes tightened. "...You decided to go to jail yourself?"

To Guan Shanjin's surprise, Wu Xingzi had hit the nail on the head. His brow furrowed slightly; in that moment, he was unable to respond.

Wu Xingzi was not fooled. The look on Guan Shanjin's face told him that his guess was correct! In order for things to go off without a hitch, Guan Shanjin had to go to jail.

Wu Xingzi's heart throbbed with pain. After a moment of hesitation, he stammered, "C-can... Can..." *Can someone else go instead?* But in the end, he didn't finish his question.

Guan Shanjin knew that as the commanding general, he would have to take risks when necessary. Otherwise how could he be worthy of his soldiers' loyalty? With the emperor and Man Yue on the outside watching over everything, what reason did Guan Shanjin have not to enter the jail himself? Even if Yan Wenxin had arranged for some sort of interrogation while he was imprisoned, Guan Shanjin would be the only one who could deal with it.

But Wu Xingzi's chest brimmed with anxiety, and he was unable to give any words of comfort. He didn't realize it, but his eyes reddened a little.

Looking at Wu Xingzi made Guan Shanjin's heart hurt. He hurriedly pulled the older man into his arms and patted him in comfort. "Don't worry. I've fought my way out of battles and wars. What sort of injuries and hardship have I not suffered before? Yan Wenxin's claws are not embedded that deeply in the jail. Even if he arranges some form of interrogation, it's nothing to worry about. Don't worry—don't cry."

The hand patting Wu Xingzi's back was as gentle as a babbling brook and as warm as a spring breeze. He shrank into himself, nodding glumly, but he was unable to put aside his worries. "Do you have any men planted in the jail?" he asked, unable to help himself. "Is it possible for things to go wrong?"

Guan Shanjin laughed lightly, bowing his head and tapping on Wu Xingzi's nose. "The emperor's men run the jail, and I know them well. Naturally, nothing will go wrong," he promised. "You must believe me. If I can't even make it out of jail, where could I find the self-respect to guard against Nanman?"

"That's not how that works..." Wu Xingzi frowned, clicking his tongue. Those two things had nothing to do with each other. The history books were full of generals who guarded the borders but still died in jail or at the hands of their colleagues. But he didn't say so out loud—he didn't want to jinx it.

"Right..." he said instead. "Then what will happen to Ping Yifan?"

"Someone else will take over the role of Ping Yifan for a while. When I go to jail, it will be just about time for him to leave the capital for a trip down south." Guan Shanjin was still holding Wu Xingzi in his embrace, patting him gently. Still, the information he provided sent a chill down the old fellow's spine.

"You mean...Ping Yifan is actually involved with Nanman?"

Guan Shanjin pondered this question for a moment, then shook his head. "Don't get yourself involved. The less you know, the better. Once Ping Yifan leaves, Yan Wenxin will undoubtedly assign someone to watch you. For now, just stay in Rancui's residence—do some farming and reading. I'll have someone bring you that qin I gave you. Once I'm out of jail, you can play a few pieces for me, hmm?"

All Wu Xingzi could do was nod. He had thousands of words in his heart, but he understood that Guan Shanjin would not listen to them. Sighing, he feigned casualness and changed the subject. "It was so unfortunate that Bai-gongzi abruptly stopped playing that day. Will I have the chance to listen to him play again?"

The hand on Wu Xingzi's waist tightened, then quickly let go. Guan Shanjin chuckled quietly. "If you want to listen to the qin, I can just play it for you myself. Bai-gongzi, Hei-gongzi, Huang-gongzi—forget about them all! I'm going to get jealous if you curate a qin musician list on top of your list of pengornises."

"Ah, what are you getting jealous about...?" Wu Xingzi's ear turned red from the heated breath brushing against it. "I'll wait for you to play the qin," he said obediently, glancing at Guan Shanjin. "You must be careful when you're in jail..." He paused, then mumbled, "It doesn't matter what happens to the others. I just want you to be safe and sound."

It might be a little selfish, but it was his undeniable wish.

A jolt shot through Guan Shanjin's chest. A moment later, he hoarsely swore a promise: "I will. There's no need for you to worry."

The two clung to each other for some time.

Guan Shanjin instructed Wu Xingzi not to come looking for Ping Yifan in the next few days. If anything happened, Hei-er would ensure his safety. Then he sent Wu Xingzi home.

Back at Rancui's place, Wu Xingzi was a little distracted. In his room was the qin Guan Shanjin had given him in Horse-Face City.

The plain, smooth surface of the qin was warm to the touch. His hand lingered along the strings before finally clenching into a fist, as though he dared not touch it.

When Guan Shanjin formed a plan, he would carry it out until the end. Wu Xingzi understood that there was nothing he could do to stop him. He had to simply carry on with his days as agreed, quietly waiting for the incident to occur.

As expected, a few days later, a huge wave crashed through the capital.

The son of the Protector General, the former Great General of the Southern Garrison, Guan Shanjin...had been sent to jail for colluding with Nanman.

When the news spread through the capital, Wu Xingzi and the two girls were hunched down in the garden harvesting eggplants, planning to fry slices of them in the afternoon. The twin girls were like sparrows, chattering away about the latest happenings in the capital. In one morning, they managed to cover all of yesterday's ongoing gossip.

Wu Xingzi usually smiled when he listened to the sisters chat away. It had already been a few days since he came back from Ping Yifan's place. There hadn't seemed to be any mention on the streets of any matters of the Protector General's estate—at the very most, all people were talking about was how Bai-gongzi seemed to be very well liked by the Protector General's wife after he entered the residence, and they were now discussing marriage with the Bai family.

Guan Shanjin was usually a popular topic of conversation, but the girls had heard nothing about him. It seemed as though he had completely vanished from the capital.

Seeing that the basket was nearly full, Wu Xingzi lifted it and stood up. "All right, just look at the two of you," he scolded them, laughing. "Aren't your throats dry from all that talking?"

Mint and Osmanthus simultaneously stuck their tongues out at him. Mint had a basket of beans in her hands, and her sister had a basket of cucumbers. They stood up and patted the dirt and dust off their skirts. "It's because Master doesn't like to leave the house." The two girls spared no effort to entertain Wu Xingzi, as they were worried that he was not happy in the capital.

"Well, aren't you two clever?" Wu Xingzi smiled. He reached out and wiped a bit of mud off Osmanthus's face. "Go and wash the vegetables—we'll make stuffed long bean nests and fried eggplants for lunch. I'll go ask Manager Rancui if he'd like to join us for a meal."

"Got it!" Osmanthus immediately emptied the basket of beans into her sister's basket of cucumbers. Then she took away the basket of eggplants from Wu Xingzi, and the two girls swiftly ran off to the kitchen.

Wu Xingzi used what was left of the water to wash his hands and face. Just as he was about to head to Rancui's yard, he unexpectedly came across Rancui walking over with Hei-er.

His heart inexplicably lurched in his chest. Thinking about what Guan Shanjin had told him a few days ago, he gripped the cuffs of his sleeves, his face slightly pale.

Seeing the look on his face, Rancui had a rough idea what Wu Xingzi was thinking. It was likely that Guan Shanjin had already told Wu Xingzi what was going to happen today, so he could save some of his efforts.

"Rancui." Wu Xingzi's voice was very careful, afraid that if he was too loud, he would scare himself.

"Mr. Wu." Rancui still had a tremendous smile on his face, waving the basket in his hand. "Here's some osmanthus cake."

Hei-er took the basket quickly, making a respectful bow toward Wu Xingzi. "Mr. Wu."

"Hei-er." Wu Xingzi smiled nervously and tugged hard at his sleeves. "I was just telling the girls... We've harvested a lot of beans, eggplants, and cucumbers—lunch is going to be very satisfying. I wanted to invite the two of you to come share it. Do Rancui and Hei-er like stuffed bean nests and fried eggplants?"

"How serendipitous. I'm not picky about food—thank you, Mr. Wu." Rancui clapped his hands together. His face was as charming as ever, and his gentle tone soothed Wu Xingzi's nerves.

Hei-er did not speak. He placed the osmanthus cakes directly on a nearby bamboo table where Wu Xingzi liked to relax. The area was simple yet comfortable, with a table and a few chairs.

Rancui warmly took Wu Xingzi's hand and walked over to the table to sit down. He wanted to start the conversation with some inconsequential matters—only for Wu Xingzi to speak up first.

"What happened to Haiwang?"

All right, then. Mr. Wu had always been a very straightforward man. Rancui's mouth was left hanging open for a while before he picked up a piece of osmanthus cake and popped it into his mouth.

"It has only just happened. News will probably spread through the whole capital by the afternoon, and throughout the entirety of Great Xia within a couple of days."

Rancui gestured at Hei-er. Hei-er did not look happy, but when he saw how tense and worried Wu Xingzi was, he sighed quietly and left for the moment.

After Hei-er walked away, Rancui patted Wu Xingzi's hand. His fingers were practically about to dig through the table. "Didn't Guan Shanjin mention it to you? About an hour ago, the emperor had the general thrown in jail for colluding with the enemy, and treason. The trial will be held tomorrow. Due to the severity of the matter, the emperor has assigned a few experienced and loyal ministers to oversee it."

"Is Yan Wenxin one of them?" Wu Xingzi only realized that his voice was trembling once he'd already spoken.

"No, Yan Wenxin is the Minister of Personnel. This isn't under his purview." Rancui picked up another piece of osmanthus cake. When he saw Wu Xingzi relax slightly, he added, a little wickedly, "However, the Assistant Minister of War, the Assistant Minister of Justice, and the Assistant Minister of the Court of Judicial Review are all in collusion with Yan Wenxin. Yan Wenxin has long held control over the departments in charge of Guan Shanjin's trial."

Wu Xingzi shuddered violently. He stood up from his seat, wanting to rush out immediately, but Rancui swiftly held him back. "Mr. Wu, don't be so rash!"

"Wh-what are we going to do? Haiwang told me that everything was under control!" Wu Xingzi's eyes were slightly red; he was about to cry from worry.

Wu Xingzi had worked in the magistrate's office his entire life, and he knew quite a bit about legal proceedings. Justice was extremely important in Great Xia. Every trial had to rigorously adhere to the appropriate procedures, and the laws in Great Xia were probably stricter than any dynasty that came before. But no matter how strict the laws were, there were still many loopholes one could exploit. If Yan Wenxin had any intention to kill Guan Shanjin, the situation could not be any more dangerous.

"Don't be scared. At most, Guan Shanjin will have to endure some superficial injuries. If the emperor doesn't allow it, Guan Shanjin's life will not be in danger." Rancui was very calm as he pushed Wu Xingzi back to his chair. He pursed his lips. "The Protector General's family have all been loyal officials for generations, and although they never formed an alliance with any other officials, they have always been the emperor's right-hand men. No matter how capable Yan Wenxin is, he will never be able to defeat the emperor."

"This is not a matter of winning or losing," Wu Xingzi said, continuously pinching his palm. For the past few days, he had deliberately refused to recall the things Guan Shanjin had told him that day, pretending the general would be fine. No news was the best news.

But reality would not let him hide inside his shell forever. That day, Guan Shanjin had clearly been making light of the dangers, afraid that he would worry him. Still, there was nothing Wu Xingzi could do now but quietly wait.

Rancui and Hei-er stayed for lunch. Wu Xingzi was clearly distracted, though, and he barely touched any of the dishes, just furiously shoveling rice into his mouth. He only stopped once he'd finished five big bowls.

Rancui couldn't bear to watch him like this. He took a sip of wine and sighed. "Mr. Wu, why don't I teach you how to play the qin? When the general gets out of jail, you can play the qin for him and soothe his heart."

Wu Xingzi brightened, remembering the promise he had made to Guan Shanjin. He nodded continuously, agreeing to learn the qin from Rancui. The anxiety in his chest finally abated a little.

The days went on. In the morning, Wu Xingzi would tend to his precious little garden. After lunch, he would take a nap, then go to Rancui's yard and play the qin for two hours. When that was all done, he would return to his own yard and practice playing on his own until dinnertime.

Within the capital, Guan Shanjin's situation changed multiple times a day, and it was all anyone spoke about. The once highly regarded hero had turned out to be a despicable traitor. He took advantage of his position so far from the emperor's eyes, selling his own country to its enemies for his own benefit. He had to be punished—his crime was unforgivable!

At first, Mint and Osmanthus still went out to the streets to get more information. After a few days, they were no longer willing to go out anymore.

The two of them knew very well what the general had done for Horse-Face City, but all these city folk did was slander the general with everything they had. Did any of them bother to ask the citizens of Horse-Face City about any of it? Mint and Osmanthus suppressed their rage, but they wished they could just grab the people vilifying Guan Shanjin and slap them hard!

Guan Shanjin had already spent half a month in jail. Wu Xingzi had injured his fingers slightly by playing the qin so much. Rancui couldn't bear to see it, so he confiscated his qin, telling him he couldn't have it back until his injuries had healed. Wu Xingzi was left with nothing to do but spend the entire day in a daze, sitting in his yard.

One day, Mint rushed in from outside, holding her skirts up. Her little face was bright red, and she was clearly nervous. "Master, someone would like to see you."

"Who is it?"

"It's..." Mint bit her lip and said quietly, "It's Vice General Man."

Man Yue? Wu Xingzi leapt up from his chair, panicked. He knew there was no way Man Yue would visit him during such a precarious time. Something must've happened to Guan Shanjin.

"Quick, let Vice General Man in." Wu Xingzi didn't know where Yan Wenxin might have planted spies. He was so worried that all he wanted was to run out to meet Man Yue, but he had to try his best to breathe and calm himself.

"Understood." Mint nodded her head and bounded out of the yard like a little rabbit.

Wu Xingzi paced around his room, regretting that he had not spent more time persuading Guan Shanjin to be more careful. Yan Wenxin was a vicious man, and he held immense power at court. Guan Shanjin might have had the emperor protecting him, but when it came to luring the enemy, he was nothing but a replaceable pawn.

In jail, Guan Shanjin was alone and without aid. Yan Wenxin was watching him closely with claws unsheathed... *Could it be, could it be...?*

Wu Xingzi was frightened by the wild speculation running through his head. His legs buckled under him, and he collapsed into his chair.

It was then that Man Yue entered the yard.

"Vice General Man?" Wu Xingzi's voice trembled. He looked like a quail huddling into itself in the rain, pale and haggard.

Man Yue was dressed simply, wearing the same smile as always on his round face. "Mr. Wu."

As he cupped his hands toward Wu Xingzi, Man Yue noticed that the poor man was suffering quite a fright, and he quickly poured out a cup of tea and handed it to him. "Don't worry, calm down. If the general knew I'd scared you, he'd flay me alive."

"Thank you, thank you." Shivering, Wu Xingzi accepted the cup of tea and took a few sips, his heart managing to settle down. The smile on Man Yue's face had allowed him to feel more at ease.

Once Man Yue saw that Wu Xingzi's face had regained a bit of color, he sat down next to him and poured himself a cup of tea too, not bothering with decorum.

"Vice General Man..."

"There's no need to be so courteous, Mr. Wu. You can just call me Man Yue." After all, Wu Xingzi was the future lady of the house. If Wu Xingzi kept on calling him Vice General Man, Man Yue wouldn't be able to bear it.

"Yes..." Wu Xingzi was not in the mood to mull over formalities with Man Yue. He only wanted to know if Guan Shanjin was facing any trouble. "Man Yue, why did you come today...?"

"Oh." Man Yue smiled at Wu Xingzi and quickly gulped down the contents of his teacup. After wiping away the sweat on his forehead, he finally said, "It's not a major issue. It's just that the general is worried that you're very anxious over the matter, so he asked me

to come over and inform you that he's well. He says that everything is fine, and that jail is even quite comfortable."

"Everything is fine?" Wu Xingzi frowned. If everything truly was fine, why was there a need for Man Yue to risk being discovered by Yan Wenxin by coming here to tell him that?

Wu Xingzi had ruminated over the entire situation over and over for the past few days. Ping Yifan had something to do with Nanman. Yan Wenxin had framed Guan Shanjin, landing him in jail. The most plausible explanation was that Yan Wenxin and the real Ping Yifan were working together, having illicit dealings with Nanman, and Yan Wenxin had pinned all the blame on Guan Shanjin. The emperor and Guan Shanjin were thus turning his scheme against him, taking the opportunity to dig out evidence of Yan Wenxin's dealings.

Because Wu Xingzi was "Ping Yifan's" lover, Yan Wenxin would certainly want to keep an eye on Wu Xingzi to ensure Ping Yifan didn't betray him. There was no telling how many people were watching Wu Xingzi right now!

Man Yue was a capable and intelligent man—capable and intelligent enough that Guan Shanjin trusted Man Yue with watching his back. There was no way Guan Shanjin would want Man Yue to take the risk of visiting Wu Xingzi. If this meeting was to be discovered by Yan Wenxin's people, their plan might fall apart, and Guan Shanjin would never be able to clear his name.

The more Wu Xingzi thought about it, the more he was sure this was the case, and he grew even more worried. His eyes burned as he stared at Man Yue, yet he was unable to say anything too harsh. He could only ask softly, "Is Haiwang truly fine?"

Man Yue smiled again. "At the very least, he won't die."

This was not the answer Wu Xingzi wanted to hear. His face crumpled.

"Mr. Wu, don't worry. Since I've come to see you, we're not at the end of our rope yet." Man Yue saw the dried fruit and snacks on the table and asked Wu Xingzi if he could have some. With permission granted, he happily started eating.

"You might not be at the end of your rope, but there are still many obstacles in your way, right?" Wu Xingzi asked. He forced himself to calm down, picking up a pine nut candy and chewing it.

"Yes." Man Yue openly admitted to it. His round chin wobbled a little as he sighed. "If we really need to, we can actually force our way through this current situation, but the emperor wishes for us to provide some leeway. It's hard to go against the emperor's wishes."

"Provide some leeway?" Wu Xingzi grew angry, the hand resting on his knee clenching into a fist.

Guan Shanjin had to follow orders and go to jail. Now, in the capital and across most of Great Xia, people spat and cursed at the mention of the Protector General's son. Even if the emperor pulled him out of jail and issued an edict proclaiming Guan Shanjin's innocence, his reputation would never return to its original state!

Why couldn't the emperor provide Guan Shanjin some leeway instead?!

Man Yue glanced at Wu Xingzi. When he saw how aggrieved Wu Xingzi was, his smile became more sincere. He straightened up, looking at him with bright eyes. "Do you know of Bai Shaochang, Mr. Wu—Bai-gongzi?" he asked.

"I do. Hasn't he moved into the Protector General's estate?" Wu Xingzi said. Guan Shanjin had refused to tell him why he was deliberately involving himself with Bai-gongzi. Wu Xingzi couldn't come up with a guess.

"So you know about this." Man Yue frowned a little, studying Wu Xingzi without revealing his thoughts. Still, he didn't see anything other than worry on Wu Xingzi's face. "I thought the general did not share the matter of Bai-gongzi with you, Mr. Wu," he said cautiously.

"Haiwang did not mention it—Yan Wenxin told me," Wu Xingzi replied bluntly.

Man Yue sneered when he heard the name. "Yan Wenxin? That man's reach is quite far." He pursed his lips. "Don't mind it, Mr. Wu. The general and Bai-gongzi share no personal relationship."

"I know." Wu Xingzi nodded seriously. He would never doubt Guan Shanjin's feelings for him or the promises Guan Shanjin made. He was not a fool—Guan Shanjin's sincerity was plain as day. "What happened to Bai-gongzi?"

"Bai-gongzi..." Man Yue sighed deeply, his plump body deflating slightly. "Has Mr. Wu ever heard the gossip regarding Bai-gongzi and the son of the Duke of Zhenguo?"

"Mint and Osmanthus have mentioned it to me before. So there's really something going on between Bai-gongzi and the Duke of Zhenguo's son?" Wu Xingzi was astonished. The rumors had always held that nothing had happened between Bai-gongzi and the Duke of Zhenguo's son. The Duke of Zhenguo's son had even been reproached by the emperor.

"Not entirely." Man Yue rubbed his chin, his tone a little aggravated. "It's true that the Duke of Zhenguo's son, Du Fei, likes Bai Shaochang, but Bai Shaochang hates Du Fei. Obviously, he wouldn't be willing to put on a friendly face for him. The incident where Du Fei snatched Bai Shaochang off the streets *did* happen, but Du Fei did not actually succeed. Someone interrupted his plan partway, and he also lost his chance with the man he admired. He lost both the battle and the war."

"So who was the one who saved Bai-gongzi?" Wu Xingzi had an idea, but he hoped that he was just overthinking things.

Man Yue shot him a look, his lips curling into a smile. "Mr. Wu has guessed it for himself, hasn't he? It was Yan Wenxin."

Wu Xingzi pressed a hand against his chest. He had to take a moment to catch his breath. So it really was Yan Wenxin!

"Haiwang knew very well that the person in Bai Shaochang's heart was Yan Wenxin, but he still moved him into the Protector General's residence on purpose?" Wu Xingzi's soft voice quaked, fire raging within him. "The evidence showing that Haiwang was collaborating with the enemy was secretly planted by Bai-gongzi?"

Man Yue shot Wu Xingzi a surprised glance. He hadn't expected Wu Xingzi to grasp the situation so quickly.

"Yes, the general feigned closeness with Bai Shaochang and left a hole in his defenses for Bai Shaochang to enter. All those letters and messages with Nanman were covertly planted in the secret chamber within the general's study by Bai Shaochang. On one side, Bai Shaochang anonymously wrote a letter to alert the emperor, and on the other, Yan Wenxin 'discovered' the news and disclosed the matter to the emperor. And so our trap was laid."

Wu Xingzi gasped for air, half collapsing in his chair. He was angry, and yet his heart still ached. He desperately wanted to go to Guan Shanjin right now and scold him. How could he have laid a trap that would implicate himself like that? If only one mistake were to occur in the entire process, Yan Wenxin could always find a way to kill him in jail!

"Bai Shaochang refuses to admit that he was the one who did it?"

At this point, Wu Xingzi finally understood everything. From the start, Guan Shanjin's plan had been first to lay a trap for Bai Shaochang, force him to admit who was instructing him to plant evidence, and then take the opportunity to gather oral proof of Yan Wenxin's crimes.

After all, it was true that Ping Yifan had dealings with Nanman. However, Yan Wenxin was very careful; it was always Huaixiu who took part, never him. He never gave himself away. The messages and letters that had been found in the Yue family's manor could not even be linked to Huaixiu.

If there was no genuine evidence that could point to Yan Wenxin being the mastermind, at the very most, he would just lose his right hand: Huaixiu. However, Yan Wenxin had more than one hand.

"There is evidence of Bai Shaochang sneaking into the secret chamber of the study and falsifying the letters and messages, but he refused to admit that he was working for someone," Man Yue explained. "He insisted that he acted alone—he said he was over-whelmed and made a mistake because he was unwilling to become life partners with the general, but his father was forcing him to marry into the family. He claimed he was falsifying evidence and letting the general be captured so that he would be able to go home." Man Yue sneered, hatred visible in his eyes. "Old Mister Bai has shared a personal relationship with the emperor for a long time—the emperor was the one who gifted him the title of Top Qin Player. Who in Great Xia doesn't know Old Mister Bai is special to the emperor? The emperor watched Bai-gongzi grow up, and he has always been softhearted toward the younger generation."

Man Yue's words were filled with a sort of sourness, and Wu Xingzi sympathized.

The emperor had also watched Guan Shanjin grow up, but Bai Shaochang grew up in the sheltered environment of the capital, while Guan Shanjin had been fighting and killing his way through the bat-tlefield since the age of twelve. For the peace of Great Xia, he even willingly became the emperor's pawn. No matter how difficult the journey, how arduous the task, he never once protested. Wu Xingzi's heart truly ached; it hurt so much that he nearly teared up.

"Is there anything I can do?" he asked.

Half a month had already passed; it was no wonder that Guan Shanjin wanted Man Yue to report to Wu Xingzi that he was fine. It was clear that the younger man had wanted to comfort him.

"The general wishes for you not to worry. The identity of Ping Yifan is still useful. Although Yan Wenxin is very cautious, he has far too many irons in the fire—sooner or later, he will end up exposing himself. Until then, I'm afraid that the general will have to remain in jail. But he's living quite well. You don't have to worry, Mr. Wu."

Wu Xingzi's chest was filled with anxiety. How could he *not* worry? If Man Yue were to go back to his duties while Wu Xingzi just kept hiding in Rancui's residence, Wu Xingzi would break out in hives.

Wu Xingzi saw that Man Yue intended to leave, so he hurriedly reached out to stop him. "Hold on, hold on—can you let me meet Bai Shaochang in secret? Perhaps I may be of use."

Now that he knew that Bai Shaochang and Yan Wenxin shared a love affair, it had given Wu Xingzi a hunch. He only needed to meet Bai Shaochang to prove it. If he was right, they could turn everything around.

"Um... The general does not wish to involve you in this matter, Mr. Wu. If something were to happen to you, I'm afraid that the general would end up destroying half of Great Xia." Man Yue stammered out a refusal, his honest face looking quite conflicted—which distracted from the darkness hidden in his eyes.

"It will be fine," said Wu Xingzi, refusing to let go of Man Yue. "If you're able to secretly come see me, you definitely have a way to let me secretly meet Bai Shaochang. Vice General Man, I'm not some foolish youth. I won't cause you guys any trouble." He knew that Guan Shanjin wanted to keep him safe, but how could he stay safe if Guan Shanjin was in danger? He refused to be kept out.

"Uhh... It would be possible to let you meet Bai Shaochang secretly, but what do you plan to do? He's deeply in love. He would rather die than implicate his lover." Man Yue pursed his lips, clearly disapproving of Bai Shaochang's feelings.

"I've seen many people who were deeply in love." Wu Xingzi could see that Man Yue had given in. He continued with a tiny, wry smile: "At court, at the magistrate's office."

Man Yue and His
Memories of Childhood

*"You're going to the northwestern border tomorrow?" Su Yang
asked hesitantly.*

*"Yes, I'm going to the border tomorrow to join my master. Is
there a message you want me to deliver?"*

*"I have nothing to say to him." Su Yang's lips curled. "I-I'm...
worried about you."*

"Worried about what? I haven't even left yet."

*In all these years, Man Yue had never been able to figure out
Su Yang's intentions.*

1

FOR A HUNDRED YEARS, the heirs of the Man family had
always stayed at the side of the Protector General. In the beginning, when the Guan family won the country for the emperor,
the Man family were the Guan family's right arm. The Man family
had always been loyal. After the emperor outlawed private armies,
the children of the Man family entered the imperial army instead,

and continued to either charge forward or plan and scheme with their masters. Either way, they never left their sides.

However, maintaining an army was expensive, and the later emperors all valued brain over brawns. After a while the emperors put aside their worries that major generals would defy the government with their own armies. As long as no harm came from it, the emperor would just pretend not to know there were private armies numbering in the thousands—even tens of thousands—along the borders.

And so the Man and Guan families, whether professionally or privately, were tightly linked. One could even say they were symbiotic, like lips and teeth.

Before Man Yue even turned five, he went with his father to meet his future master. After all, the heirs of the Protector General were always thrown to the army at around twelve or thirteen to fight for their futures. As the heir of the Man family, even if he was a bit younger and it would be a few years before he joined him, his life was destined to be tied to his master's.

The first time Guan Shanjin met Man Yue, it was a warm spring day.

He was having tea with the second son of the Su family, who were imperial merchants. To be honest, Guan Shanjin didn't really like dealing with Su Yang. Guan Shanjin was a cold person by nature, but he was incredibly clever. Although the way he treated everyone was rather insincere, even the Protector General and his wife hadn't noticed that their son's respect and admiration were mostly fake.

The Su family's status was far from that of the Protector General's family, but the emperor held them in high esteem. As a trusted subject of the emperor, of course the Protector General would be on good terms with those the emperor liked. Besides, the head of the Su family was humble and meticulous, and he conducted himself socially with a refreshing brightness. It was good to get to know such people; as the generations went on, the Su and Guan families became close.

Su Yang was an odd one out in his family.

Because they had been imperial merchants for several generations, the Su family's status had always been very stable. They put a lot of effort into educating their children. Not every child could be a genius, but they were all careful and humble, and knew exactly how to read a room. Everyone in the capital was on the same page: Who wouldn't give the Su family two thumbs up and shower them in praise? Clearly, when it came to the imperial merchants, they were at the top.

But for some reason, despite receiving the same education as his brothers, Su Yang was rambunctious and willful. Things didn't improve as he got older; instead, they got worse. He didn't take anyone seriously. To be completely fair, however, he got away with acting like this because he had the skills to back it up.

Before he was ten years old, he could easily understand account books; he even managed to find some issues that would have caused great problems later on. He convinced his eldest brother to open a restaurant that only sold dishes made of tofu. Not only was the taste amazing, but the decor and design of the place also exactly appealed to the rich. In just a few months, it had become one of the most famous restaurants in the city. Every day, they served the rich and wealthy and made buckets of money.

The head of the family realized that in spite of his personality, this boy could practically turn lead into gold, so he just let him do as he pleased. The Su family was powerful enough that they could support at least one person like him.

It came as a surprise, though, when Su Yang was able to befriend Guan Shanjin.

Guan Shanjin didn't particularly like or dislike this friend of his, but Su Yang, who was one year younger, liked Guan Shanjin a lot. He could often be found at the Protector General's estate.

On this day, Su Yang had come to see Guan Shanjin with a box full of snacks. When it came to food, Su Yang was quite talented. Although he never stepped foot into the kitchen himself, he was very creative, and he had a discerning palate. Whatever he ordered the kitchen to make always managed to excite people's appetites and was fit to be served at a restaurant.

The two young men sat in the garden drinking tea and enjoying the snacks. Guan Shanjin was a little distracted, but Su Yang didn't care. He was quite happy to chatter away about the various things that happened recently in the capital without Guan Shanjin's attention.

That was when Man Yue and his father appeared before the two of them.

Man Yue was only three or four months away from turning five. He was tiny, soft, and rosy, and a little rounder than other kids his age. His arms were like plump white lotus roots, and on his round face, even his eyes, nose, mouth, and earlobes were round. A redness shone through his skin, like a tangyuan filled with red bean paste.

He looked quite timid, holding tightly onto his father's robes with his little hands and trying to hide behind him. In order to stick close to his father, he stumbled as he walked, but he refused to let go no matter what. His father tried many times to bring him out of his hiding spot, but was avoided nimbly each time, so in the end he had to give up.

Guan Shanjin took a few extra looks, and decided he liked him immediately.

Su Yang's reaction was much more direct. He stared straight at him with his charming eyes, as though he couldn't bear to look away.

"Young Master." Man Yue's father greeted Guan Shanjin with clasped hands. Then he bent down to tell his son, "You must hurry and greet the young master."

Man Yue was still hiding behind his father's leg, and he only peeked his head out to greet the other boy. "Hello, Guan-gege," he called out softly.

Guan Shanjin hummed in response, then turned to Su Yang. "I have things I need to discuss with Man-shushu. You can head back."

Guan Shanjin was only eight or nine, still just a child, but he already had a powerful aura, and the dignified expression on his small face forced people to take him seriously.

Su Yang made a noise of agreement, then pointed at Man Yue. "What about this kid?"

"He'll be the vice general of the Guan family army when we grow up, so he'll come with me to get to know things," said Guan Shanjin as though this was obvious, ignoring Su Yang's disappointed, unhappy expression.

"I'm staying with Dad," said Man Yue quickly, gripping his father's clothes even more tightly with his chubby little hands. "I won't get into trouble."

"He's too small to understand. He doesn't even know to call you 'Young Master.' Did you hear what he called you? Guan-gege." Su Yang smirked at Man Yue. "What did you say your name was, little fatty?"

Man Yue shrank back—he'd clearly never been called that before. His large, round eyes were immediately filled with tears, but he still answered obediently: "My name is Man Yue. I'm not Little Fatty."

"You're not fat? Have you ever seen a full moon?" Su Yang laughed even harder, still running his mouth with no regard for the fact that Man Yue's father was listening. He was familiar enough with Man Yue's father; he knew that this large, tall, strong, bearlike man had a warm, gentle personality. He wouldn't get mad over a few jokes made by children

"I have," said Man Yue. "The full moon appears on the fifteenth of each month. My mom will sit with me in the yard to look at it." His expression was full of sincerity, but half of his face was hidden behind his father, becoming a half moon.

"Oh, so you should know that the full moon in the sky is round, then. And the little fatty on the ground is also round."

Su Yang left Man Yue speechless. The pink little rice ball opened his mouth as if to say something, but because he was so young, despite all his efforts, he couldn't come up with a single thing. His features slowly scrunched together, as if he was about to cry.

Man Yue's father and Guan Shanjin were right there, but they didn't seem to pay attention to what was going on, which only spurred Su Yang on.

"About to cry? You're so delicate, I can't even say anything a little harsh?"

"No, I don't want to cry." The little pink rice ball pursed his lips, then reiterated in a soft voice, "Man Yue doesn't want to cry."

"Hmph, stupid fatty, do you think I'm blind?" Su Yang curled his lips, resisting the urge to reach out and pinch Man Yue's flushed little face. Those big, sparkling eyes were making his heart flutter, but his words were as ruthless as ever.

"Man Yue isn't dumb or a fatty." Man Yue really looked like he was about to cry, his small pearly teeth digging into his bottom lip. The tip of his round nose was red, and so were the rims of his eyes.

Finally, Su Yang was satisfied. He didn't actually want to make Man Yue cry, he just wanted to tease the tiny thing. He clicked his tongue, then waved a walnut cake in front of Man Yue. "Here, a sweet for you. You can't cry so easily—are you a man or not?"

"I am, I am a man." Man Yue puffed up his chest. The desire for the walnut cake in Su Yang's hand was evident in his eyes, but he was also afraid of this mean gege. He hesitated, too afraid to reach for the cake.

"You're a man and you're too scared to even take a walnut cake?" Su Yang snorted. He narrowed his eyes and said meanly, "If you don't take it now, I'm going to eat it!"

Man Yue finally gathered his courage to walk out carefully from behind his father. He was wearing a light teal-colored robe on his round little body, and he looked like a very full tangyuan. Slowly, he moved toward Su Yang.

Su Yang wanted to pull him into his arms to squeeze him. He had a few younger siblings, and two of them were about four or five. He'd never thought those two little boys were cute—in fact, he was annoyed every time he saw them—so he'd never tried to get close to them.

"Thank you for the cake, Gege." Man Yue stood in front of Su Yang shyly. He was small and his legs were short, so he was only a little taller than the chair—the perfect height to place his chin on Su Yang's knee. From that angle, Su Yang could no longer resist; without even thinking, he reached out to pinch Man Yue's chubby cheeks harshly.

It was just like freshy risen dough! It felt so good that Su Yang pinched him twice more, leaving two marks on Man Yue's face. The child seemed to be in complete shock. His eyes were open wide, as though tears were about to spill from them at any moment, and he was too stunned to react.

"Call me Su-gege." Su Yang wasn't done pinching, but he was afraid Man Yue might actually cry. This little rice ball was so pitiful, he didn't want to scare him away on their first meeting.

Man Yue pouted, but still did as he asked. "Su-gege..." His eyes were focused on the walnut cake in Su Yang's hand.

"Hmph, you're already as round as the full moon but you still can't look away from food. You have to stop eating so much in the future!" Su Yang said, and finally stuffed the walnut cake into Man Yue's mouth.

This walnut cake was the culmination of many attempts (at Su Yang's instruction) by his family's cook. When he opened a sweets shop in the future, he was planning on making it his signature dessert. The walnut paste had been sieved until it was smooth and fine, and melted on the tongue. It wasn't too sweet, and it smelled like osmanthus. Even Guan Shanjin had two pieces, so how could Man Yue resist?

He covered his mouth, opening his eyes wide in shock and happiness. The walnut cake was a dainty little piece, but to a four-year-old, it was still slightly large, stuffing his cheeks completely full. But in just a few bites, most of it had already melted, and Man Yue could feel the sweetness seep from his mouth to his heart.

"How is it? Good, right? Here, they're all yours." Su Yang watched Man Yue's smile, his heart also growing sweeter. He couldn't explain why he liked this little kid, but he shoved the rest of the box of walnut cakes into Man Yue's arms. "Don't eat it too fast or you'll get fat. Then you'll really fly into the sky and become the full moon."

"Thank you, Su-gege, Man Yue will eat it slowly." The little pink rice ball held the box tightly, his round little face blooming into a smile. The marks on his cheeks stood out even more. Su Yang felt a little regretful, but he didn't let it show on his face.

"Are you done?" Guan Shanjin finally spoke up. He glanced at Man Yue, deep in thought, then gave Su Yang a glance. "Go home."

"Okay, okay." Su Yang didn't really want to, but he knew he shouldn't push Guan Shanjin's limits. A little reluctant, he looked at Man Yue. "Man Yue," he couldn't resist asking, "will you come to Guan-gege's house to play in the future too?"

Man Yue stared, eyes wide. He turned to look at his father, then at Guan Shanjin, before responding hesitantly, "Man Yue will be leading soldiers and fighting the war with Guan-gege in the future, so I won't be coming to play. We're going to be heroes."

"Tch, heroes? If you keep plumping up, the only thing you'll become is the moon." Su Yang pinched Man Yue again. "Okay, okay, I'll just assume you'll be here often. Remember to say hi whenever you see me!"

"Okay..." Man Yue bobbed his little head. It was unclear if he was just answering out of courtesy or if he didn't understand.

"Su Yang, you can go." Guan Shanjin had no more patience for Su Yang continuing to waste his time. He called the steward over to see Su Yang out.

Su Yang finally had no choice but to leave.

For the next few days, Su Yang came to the Protector General's estate almost every day to look for Guan Shanjin. He was there so often, he might as well have moved there.

Guan Shanjin couldn't be bothered to ask him why; it was obvious enough. After the day he saw Man Yue, Su Yang's goal was clear, but the poor child was in for it.

Man Yue had been thrown to the Guan family at such a young age so that he and Guan Shanjin could get to know each other. He only stayed with the Guans for half the month and went home for the rest of the time—but to a child less than five years old, no matter how obedient, going from living with his parents as the treasured jewel of his family to being a servant somewhere else was far too much to take in.

Never mind the fact that there was also a mean gege who watched his every move.

Su Yang wasn't evil; he just didn't have the greatest personality, and he was used to getting his way. He liked the soft little Man Yue so much he didn't know what to do. At first he just stuck to teasing, saying a few mean things to make the child feel angry and lost. Man Yue's eyes were always red, but he never let a single tear fall.

After a few months, Man Yue got used to Su Yang's jabs. If he called him fat or dumb, Man Yue would just blink and respond softly, "Su-gege, if you don't like little fatties, Man Yue will stay away in the future."

How could he do that?! Su Yang was furious. If he couldn't see Man Yue, what was the point of running to the Protector General's estate every day? How could the little rice ball be that stupid? But no matter how angry he was, Su Yang couldn't let Man Yue hide from him, so he had to tone it down. He racked his brains to come up with a few unique new desserts and supervised the kitchen during their creation, just to feed them all to Man Yue. As a result, the red bean-filled tangyuan turned into a meat bun.

Su Yang was more smug than ever. Man Yue was now truly chubby, but Su Yang continued to think of new things to feed the kid, all the while becoming more and more toxic. He stopped calling Man Yue "fatty," but other insults still spilled forth from his mouth. After six months of this, Man Yue really did start avoiding him. Guan Shanjin couldn't take it anymore, either, and warned him to stop bothering Man Yue.

The cute little rice ball had turned into a meat bun at the master's house. Man Yue's parents thought their son was breaking the rules, being lazy and gluttonous. In a fit of rage, they made Man Yue kneel in the ancestral shrine for two nights and write a self-reflection report that was over ten thousand words. In the end, they marched Man Yue over to the Guan estate and forced him to confess his wrongdoings. It took a long time before the general and his wife finally convinced Man Yue's family to leave. When they looked Man Yue over, they realized he had gone down a couple of sizes. With the pitiful way he was looking, even Guan Shanjin felt a little bad.

When he suddenly heard the news, Su Yang didn't know how to react. His expression was complicated, as though he wanted to explain something to Guan Shanjin. But when he opened his mouth, nothing came out.

"If you like Man Yue, you should treat him better." Guan Shanjin had no patience for this. His mocking smile was difficult to look at.

"Tch! Me? Like him? Have positive feelings toward that little piglet? Hah! Guan Shanjin, are you blind? Liking that thing would cheapen me." Su Yang jumped in anger with each ruthless, relentless jab. His face was completely red, and his tongue was even sharper than usual.

"A piglet can be sold by his weight, but I couldn't say the same about you, Su Yang." Guan Shanjin waved his hand impatiently to stop Su Yang from running his mouth any further. "I don't care if you like Man Yue or not," he added, his expression turning solemn. "But there are some people you shouldn't truly anger. When you do, their anger might burn you."

Su Yang opened his mouth, then snapped it shut with a noise of frustration.

He was arrogant and willful, but he wasn't stupid. No matter how well the Su family was doing now, no matter how well merchants were treated in Great Xia, they were still just commoners.

He couldn't afford to offend the Protector General's family or their close allies.

He had used his age and rare friendship with Guan Shanjin as a shield and gone too far with Man Yue. Glumly, he gulped down a few cups of tea. Seeing that Guan Shanjin was ignoring him in favor of the book in his hand, Su Yang was so frustrated he could rip his hair out and scream.

After a while, Su Yang grit his teeth and asked, "Man Yue complained to you?"

"Man Yue would do no such thing." Guan Shanjin glanced at Su Yang with a hint of sympathy. For once, he gave a bit of advice. "You need more practice at reading people. Man Yue is not as soft as he looks."

Su Yang snorted in disbelief. In his eyes, Man Yue was a soft child who was easy to bully. He was only five; what could he do?

For two more weeks, Su Yang resisted the urge to bother Man Yue. One day, he came to the Protector General's estate with the elders in his family to bring gifts. As he was about to go look for Guan Shanjin to have tea with him, he ran into Man Yue, who was sitting under a grove of trees in a daze.

Man Yue had gone from a meat bun back to a rice ball, and he had grown a little since two weeks ago. His little cheeks were flushed, tender and delicate, but there was a smudge of mud on his face. He was covered in dirt, and he wore the dark brown robes of a servant. Curled up into a little ball, he looked very comfortable.

Su Yang resisted his urges and tried to walk past him like he hadn't seen him. But only two steps later, he circled back around to stare at little Man Yue from beyond the trees. He was like a wild beast that hadn't eaten for a few months. His eyes were red, and he desperately wanted to pounce on this little rice ball.

Man Yue didn't seem to notice the heated gaze on him at all. He was still young, and he was playing with a ladybug with his small fists. Even though it was just a bug, he was very entertained. Occasionally, he would let out peals of kittenish laughter. He would let the ladybug climb onto the tip of his finger, and just as it was about to take off, he would capture it within his small fist, giggling nonstop.

Su Yang guessed the little fatty had caught the ladybug himself—that must be where the mud on his cheek had come from. He couldn't suppress the urge that rose within his heart. Man Yue rarely ever laughed so lightheartedly in front of him; he was usually nervous and scared. Su Yang tightened his hands into fists and tried to ignore the temptation. But when Man Yue's pout at accidentally letting the ladybug fly away turned into surprised delight as the ladybug flew back, Su Yang pulled apart the branches and stepped forward.

"Little fa...little meat bun." Su Yang's appearance scared Man Yue into shaking. The ladybug he had just recaptured flew away again. This time, it disappeared into the distance and didn't return. Man Yue pursed his lips pitifully, but he didn't complain. Instead, he smiled pleasantly and greeted Su Yang in a soft voice.

"Hmph, you sure know how to entertain yourself. It's just a little bug." Man Yue tensed up, and his smile was no longer as cute and bright. Su Yang didn't like that. His tone turned even sharper.

"Su-gege, don't laugh at me. I just think the little bug is cute..." As he spoke, Man Yue carefully glanced behind Su Yang, as though he were afraid someone else would catch him playing in the trees.

Su Yang was immediately delighted. "What are you looking at? Are you slacking off?" He reached out to pinch Man Yue's cheek, leaving behind a mark on the pink skin. He felt a lot better.

"No, no..." Even though it hurt, Man Yue didn't dare rub the spot. Tears swam in his large, round eyes. He didn't dare cry either.

"I'm being good, I'm not slacking off. Steward Wang said I could rest for a bit and go serve the master a little later."

Seeing the sincere way he was explaining himself, Su Yang felt an even greater itch in his heart, like there were thousands of little bugs crawling around in his chest. His finger twitched, and in the end he couldn't resist grabbing the little rice ball into his arms to squeeze him.

"A-ah... S-Su-gege..." Man Yue's hair had been messed up, there were a few more marks on his arms, and his little face was entirely red from being pinched. He was so shocked he didn't know what to do. He tried to curl in on himself, like a quail. Even though he wanted to defend himself, he was small and weak, absolutely not a match for Su Yang. There was even a row of teeth marks around one of his fingers. Man Yue was so afraid that for a moment he even forgot how to cry—he just stood there, completely frozen.

From head to toe, Su Yang pinched, squeezed, and bit him for a full fifteen minutes before he was finally satisfied. "Why do you smell so good, little meat bun? What scent is that?" He held onto Man Yue, pushing his nose into Man Yue's neck like a dog sniffing at a bone.

Man Yue blinked, wiping away the tears at the corners of his eyes with a shaking hand. "M-Man Yue doesn't smell good," he replied, completely tense. "Su-gege, don't eat me. I don't taste good."

There were teeth marks on his cheeks, neck, and all ten of his fingers. He almost believed that the beautiful gege in front of him was about to swallow him whole. Now that he was recovering from his shock, he started to hiccup.

"Don't be afraid. Even if I want to eat you, I won't do it yet. How old are you now? There isn't even enough of you to fill up the cracks between my teeth." Although Su Yang had heard a few things about romance, at his age he still barely understood any of it. He just liked to bully this little rice ball to the point of tears. With the pitiful way Man Yue looked, he really wanted to take the little thing home and keep him there so no one else would see him for the rest of his life.

Man Yue hiccupped even harder. Did that mean Su-gege would eat him after he grew older and fatter?

"Su-gege, I-I really don't taste good. I won't taste good even after I grow up. Please don't eat me?" As Man Yue gathered his courage to beg, his tears started to fall, and his little body trembled like it was about to come apart. Su Yang's heart broke.

Su Yang did have a sadistic streak, and he did like to bully Man Yue, but seeing how pitiful the little thing in his arms was, with tears streaming down his cheeks, it felt like there were needles stabbing into his heart. Su Yang was at a loss.

"Tch, why are you crying? There's no food in all of Great Xia that my family can't afford; why would I need to eat a little piglet like you? I'm just joking, stop crying!" He clumsily patted Man Yue on the back and tried to wipe away his tears. But still, the little boy wouldn't stop. This time Su Yang was genuinely panicked. His mouth was open, but he couldn't think of anything to say. He was ready to worship this little boy and beg him to stop crying.

Man Yue was so utterly terrified that he couldn't just stop. As he cried, he hiccupped, and his little face went from pale white to bright red. He gasped for breath and cried until a large wet patch formed on Su Yang's chest.

Su Yang didn't dare say any more mean things. He patted Man Yue's small back, repeating over and over again that he was stupid, and that Man Yue should be good. He promised he'd never eat him, now or later, no matter how fat he got. They could even pinky swear on it. If they did, that would be an oath, and no one could break an oath or they'd be struck by lightning.

"Stop crying, stop crying..." Su Yang's throat was dry from all the coaxing. For the first time, he regretted his youthful recklessness, regretted making Man Yue cry. What if the kid really did avoid him from now on?

Man Yue cried his heart out. He was only five. Any other kid his age would be out there butt naked getting into mischief and playing with other children his age. But he was born into the Man family, so he had to carefully learn how to take care of his masters. If he was at all naughty he'd have to kneel at the ancestral shrine.

And somehow he'd managed to catch the attention of the devil himself, Su Yang. Man Yue was at his limit, so once the tears started flowing, it was a full half hour before he was able to stop.

Seeing that he'd finally stopped crying, Su Yang let out a sigh of relief. He pulled out his handkerchief and wiped Man Yue's face for him, but he still had to get a few jabs in. "How come you cry so much? Can't stand a little teasing? Look how ugly you are when you cry like that. Who'll want you in the future?"

"I won't cry anymore once I grow up," Man Yue protested, voice nasally from crying. He still let Su Yang wipe his tears for him, though.

"It's okay to cry once in a while..." Su Yang cleaned Man Yue up, and stowed his handkerchief back in his robes, uncaring that it was now full of tears and snot. He rubbed his nose against Man Yue's slightly cool neck a few times. "You still haven't told me why you smell so good."

Man Yue's scent was incredibly pleasant. It was like the fragrance of flowers, but not quite: slightly sweet and soft, like a piece of rice cake under the sunlight. As Su Yang sniffed him, his jaw ached to chomp down, wanting to take a few more bites. It took a huge amount of willpower to resist.

"I smell good?" Man Yue blinked, his confusion written all over his face. He raised an arm to smell himself, but Su Yang held him tightly, not letting him move at all.

"Are you wearing some sort of perfume sachet?" Su Yang mumbled, rubbing against Man Yue even more forcefully.

"Ah..." Remembering something, Man Yue said softly, "My mom gave me a sachet—it's on my waist." Su Yang immediately reached for it. The child's waist was soft and plump, and his stomach was round. It felt so good in Su Yang's hands. He pinched inch by inch, unwilling to let go, until he finally found the sachet hanging on Man Yue's waist and yanked it off.

The sachet was small, to match Man Yue's size: It was only about half a palm's length. It was made from high quality fabric, clearly a piece from an adult man's clothing. It was a pale, soft grey-blue, and "Man Yue" was embroidered on it with a light-colored thread. The embroidery was delicate and elegant. It was clear how much the embroiderer cared for Man Yue.

Man Yue seemed to want to take the sachet back, but Su Yang could stop him with just one hand. Entranced, he pressed his nose to the sachet. This was the scent he'd been looking for.

"I like it. Give it to me." This was the first time Su Yang had ever wanted something so desperately. Even if Man Yue burst into tears again, he wouldn't return it to him.

Man Yue opened his mouth in shock, but didn't know what to say. He hadn't expected Su Yang to be a thief.

"If you give me the sachet like a good boy, I'll be good to you from now on, how's that?" Su Yang coaxed him with lies, already starting to tie the sachet to his own waist.

"But..." Man Yue pouted, wanting to say something, but Su Yang smiled at him like a fox. Man Yue's shoulders immediately shrank like a quail's. He nodded pitifully. "All right, Su-gege can have it."

Su Yang was satisfied. He kissed Man Yue on the check a few times, then let go of him and floated off to Guan Shanjin's rooms.

Man Yue, left behind, stared after him. After Su Yang disappeared, a brilliant smile appeared on his face.

After acquiring Man Yue's perfume sachet, Su Yang always kept it on his waist and never took it off no matter where he went.

Guan Shanjin clearly recognized it. As soon as he spotted it, his brow furrowed. He stared at his friend's radiantly happy face for a while and snorted, but didn't say anything.

Su Yang liked the smell of this sachet. It was warm and slightly sweet. At first he only wore it when he was awake, but after a while he started placing it by his pillow when he went to bed.

Perhaps it was because of the sachet, but Man Yue no longer hid from Su Yang. He always followed Guan Shanjin around. He was supposed to be Guan Shanjin's servant, but really, he studied both academics and martial arts together with Guan Shanjin. Guan Shanjin seemed to hold the little boy in high regard. It was a common sight to see the both of them holding a military strategy book and discussing it in low voices, or little Man Yue practicing behind Guan Shanjin, waving a wooden sword around.

Su Yang once again started going to the Protector General's estate every day. He knew what times Guan Shanjin rested, and knew Man Yue was always following his master. Every day, he came at exactly the right time with snacks.

On a random day two months later, Guan Shanjin had just finished practicing at the sword. His upper body was bare as he wiped his sweat with a towel. Man Yue was huffing and puffing at his side, red-faced. As they cleaned themselves up, Su Yang sat in a pavilion nearby, sipping his tea. He looked a little under the weather, his complexion a little pale. In fact, upon closer inspection, he looked almost gray.

"What's wrong?" Guan Shanjin asked in a rare display of concern.

"Nothing." Su Yang waved a hand. His sleeve slid down, revealing half his arm.

Catching a glance, Guan Shanjin frowned. "What's wrong with your arm?"

Su Yang had always lived in the lap of luxury. His skin was soft from top to bottom, and not a single scar could be found on his body. But right now, the exposed portion of his arm was covered in little red spots. It was an alarming sight.

"It's really nothing." Su Yang pulled his sleeve down in a hurry, sneaking a glance at Man Yue. It was like he was afraid of scaring the little thing.

Man Yue was busy wiping his face and hadn't seen Su Yang's arm, but at that moment, he just so happened to look up and meet Su Yang's gaze. He blinked and broke into a beautiful smile. Fireworks immediately exploded in Su Yang's heart.

"I brought sweet pea pudding today," Su Yang said. "I made sure to sieve the paste seven times, and the sugar is flavored with the scent of lotus. The fragrances of the sweet pea and lotus won't compete with each other. It should still be cold now, so eat it quickly." He picked up a bamboo toothpick, skewered a piece of pudding, and brought it to Man Yue. Clearly, he wanted to feed it to him.

Man Yue was used to this. After a quick glance at Guan Shanjin, he obediently opened his mouth to accept the pudding. Su Yang couldn't have been more pleased. He reached out to gather Man Yue into his arms, feeding him bite by bite.

Guan Shanjin watched all this for a while, and noticed that Su Yang had another rash under his collar. A few of the spots had already spread to the side of his neck. Soon, clothing wouldn't be enough to cover them. The spots were quite scary, all of them pointy and so red it looked like they were bleeding. The tips were white; if he scratched at them, they would definitely scar.

Guan Shanjin felt his hair stand on end just looking at it. His skin started feeling itchy too.

Man Yue was in Su Yang's arms, so there was no way he didn't spot them too. But the little thing was scarily calm, eating the sweet pea pudding and attentively listening to Su Yang speak. Occasionally he would even chime in with an agreement, only delighting Su Yang more. Out in the open, Su Yang even kissed Man Yue a few times on his soft little cheek.

How interesting.

Guan Shanjin put a piece of pudding in his mouth, the corner of his lips curving upward in an amused sneer as he looked down.

A few days later, Su Yang suddenly stopped visiting the Protector General's estate. At first Guan Shanjin didn't think much of it; he thought Su Yang was annoying anyway. Every day, Su Yang was running around under his nose, and it really grated on his nerves.

But after Su Yang had disappeared for the better part of a month, Guan Shanjin eventually found out his friend was sick. It wasn't anything serious, but it was very tedious. The doctor made many visits and he still hadn't recovered. He would have a fever, then get cold chills, and no matter how many medicines he took or how many ointments he applied, the scary red spots just wouldn't go away. Apparently they were also incredibly itchy, and would break at the slightest touch. Once broken, they would leak, and took three days to scab over. It would definitely scar. The Su family had no choice but to tie Su Yang to the bed to prevent him from scratching.

Finally, the emperor found out about Su Yang's illness and sent some imperial physicians to care for him. The imperial physicians were able to determine that the rash was caused by a plant called silver angelica. After they prescribed him the appropriate medications, his condition improved a lot. But somehow, two or three days later, an even more serious rash spread across his skin. This time, Su Yang's throat was swollen. He was stuck in bed groaning and crying, looking like he was on his last breath.

This repeated four times. Su Yang lost an entire layer of skin before his condition finally stabilized and the rash went away. But it took a toll on him. He probably wouldn't recover without at least ten days of rest, so he wasn't able to go bother Guan Shanjin.

"Poor thing, what did he do to have to go through such an ordeal?" Guan Shanjin's mother sighed. She quite liked Su Yang.

Guan Shanjin didn't say anything, focusing on his food. He had already guessed the reason for Su Yang's suffering.

Once he finished eating, he excused himself to return to his own rooms. Man Yue was in the yard in a horse stance. His face was covered in sweat and half of his clothes were wet, but he remained focused, afraid to slack off.

Guan Shanjin watched the rice ball for a while before saying, "You can stop now. Come back right once you've eaten—I have something to ask you."

"Yes, Master." Man Yue obediently stood upright, wiped off his sweat, and ran off to eat. Guan Shanjin made himself a pot of tea, but didn't drink it. Instead, he dipped his finger in the tea and wrote the words "silver angelica" on the table. He stared as the words gradually faded and disappeared, his lips quirking up in what could be a smile.

Man Yue always ate quickly, and less than half an hour later, he was back.

"Master," he called out.

Guan Shanjin glanced up at him. "Sit." Guan Shanjin pointed at the spot Su Yang normally sat in.

"Yes, Master." Man Yue didn't insist on any pleasantries. He ran over, his little butt wiggling, quickly climbed onto the chair that was half his height, and sat down properly. "Master, what did you want to talk to me about?"

"You know how Su Yang was sick recently?" Guan Shanjin was too lazy to beat around the bush, and got right to it.

"Was Su-gege sick?" Man Yue was clearly shocked. His bright, round eyes blinked in obvious worry. "Then is he better now? Do you want me to go pay him a visit for you, Master?"

Guan Shanjin couldn't help but laugh at how sincere he looked. "You sure are concerned for Su Yang. He recovered a few days ago. He might've lost some skin, but his life is intact... That's not quite right. He was never quite in danger of losing his life, but the illness was very annoying." Guan Shanjin tapped on the table, contemplating. "The imperial physicians said it was caused by silver angelica. It's a common herb, but some people have an intolerance toward it. Once they come in contact with its juice, they'll erupt in rashes, and it's difficult to cure."

"So does Su-gege have an intolerance to the plant?" Man Yu exclaimed, covering his mouth with shock and panic in his eyes.

"It seems like it." Guan Shanjin gave Man Yue a deep look. "But it's strange—Su Yang was sick for quite some time when he was younger because he'd come in contact with it. Ever since then, he's been very careful to never touch it again. He even avoided plants and animals that have a symbiotic relationship with it. Nobody knows how he came in contact with it this time."

"Symbiotic relationship?" Curiosity was written all over Man Yue's face. Guan Shanjin smiled.

"There's a stone fruit that grows together with the silver angelica. Those who avoid silver angelica avoid that fruit, too. There are plenty of desserts in Great Xia that are made with it. That's why Su Yang is so interested in food. He likes to eat, but he can't eat that specific ingredient, so he had to figure things out for himself."

"I see." Man Yue nodded. Then, with a very sincere expression, he looked at Guan Shanjin. "Master, don't worry—I'll remember all of this and help keep an eye out for Su-gege in the future."

"Man Yue, you're smart. Let's not beat around the bush anymore." Guan Shanjin took a sip of his tea, his sharp, arrow-like gaze locking onto the soft, squishy Man Yue. "You already knew Su Yang couldn't touch silver angelica and that stone fruit, right? You've known for a long time now."

Man Yue's eyes opened wide in shock, the perfect picture of innocence. "Master, what are you saying? I don't understand."

"You don't understand?" Guan Shanjin snorted, knocking on the table forcefully. Man Yue shrank into himself in fear. His nose was scrunched, and he looked quite pitiful.

"You're only five, but your actions don't show it. Only an idiot like Su Yang would be fooled. There's no need to play pretend in front of me—it pisses me off. I have plenty of ways of dealing with you."

Now that Guan Shanjin had laid everything out like this, if Man Yue wasn't stupid, he should know what he had to do.

A bright smile broke out on the small, soft rice ball's face, and then he asked, as if unwilling to admit his loss, "When did you find out, Master?"

Just as Guan Shanjin had said, Man Yue wasn't as sweet and harmless as he looked on the outside. He was only five, but he wasn't an ordinary five-year-old.

He had learned to read by one year old, and at three, he had already read the Four Books and Five Classics. It wasn't an exaggeration to call him a genius.

In addition to his thirst for knowledge, Man Yue's thinking was more sophisticated than other five-year-olds'. If someone wronged him, he took revenge. If others treated him kindly, he would repay them. He was able to see things clearly, and he knew how to use his appearance to his advantage to seem more innocent. Su Yang was considered a genius, and had been familiar with the dealings of the marketplace since an early age, but he still fell prey to Man Yue's tricks. If Guan Shanjin told anyone about this, no one would believe him! How could such a soft little rice ball harbor such thoughts? And lay such a meticulous plan?

Guan Shanjin scoffed. "I saw through it from the beginning." The very first time he met Man Yue had been right here, with Su Yang next to him. At that time, Su Yang had been rude to Man Yue, but Man Yue had kept his thoughts hidden well. But Guan Shanjin still spotted the flash of fury and viciousness in Man Yue's eyes. At that moment, he knew Su Yang would pay for it one day, without even knowing what it was he was paying for.

As expected, Su Yang's illness lasted the better part of a year, and Man Yue had finally found some peace and quiet for himself.

"From the beginning?" Man Yue pouted, unhappy. "It was because of that fool Su Yang that you found out, wasn't it?"

"That's because you're still too young and inexperienced. But the perfume sachet was quite brilliant." Guan Shanjin couldn't help but praise him, then filled up Man Yue's tea. "You ground the silver angelica into powder, then covered up its scent with tonka beans and cloves. Then you filled the sachet with other fragrances and hung it on your waist. You knew Su Yang would definitely steal the sachet and keep it on himself, so the rash was only a matter of time. All you had to do was wait patiently."

Man Yue's plan was very simple. Su Yang liked to feed him snacks, and as time went on, Man Yue noticed the desserts that Su Yang brought never contained that stone fruit. That was what gave him the idea.

In order to assist Guan Shanjin, Man Yue had learned all sorts of skills, and read many medical books. He remembered that in one of the books he'd read, the stone fruit and silver angelica were common plants. The stone fruit was used in cooking; it had a subtle taste but was very fragrant, so it was very suitable for desserts. Silver angelica had a mild medicinal effect, so it could be used with almost all other medicines. It had a slight sweet taste, so it helped to make medicines less bitter and to stabilize them. These two plants could be found all over Great Xia, and were hardly rare or uncommon.

But some people were born with intolerances to these two things and couldn't touch, eat, or in some serious cases, even smell them. If Su Yang had such a weak spot, how could Man Yue not exploit it? He'd had enough of Su Yang's sharp tongue; he had no idea why the boy liked to bully him so much.

Just as Guan Shanjin guessed, after finding out Su Yang's weakness, Man Yue went home and begged his mother to make him a perfume sachet. Later, he secretly switched out the fragrances inside. Although he was young, he was smart, and no one ever caught him tampering with the sachet.

Then, he purposefully led Su Yang to find the sachet. Just as he expected, Su Yang tried to coax Man Yue into giving it to him, then stole it anyway. Soon after, the rash appeared on Su Yang's body. Although the scent wasn't as effective as eating it or touching it would have been, and needed time to cause a reaction, it was also why Su Yang never could have figured out it was his beloved sachet that caused his illness.

It was also because he kept wearing the sachet that later, even after the imperial physicians had prescribed him the correct medicine, the rash never fully went away and kept coming back. His condition only improved once the perfume sachet lost its scent.

Of course, this was all according to Man Yue's plan. He just wanted Su Yang to suffer a little; he didn't want to actually hurt him or take his life. The sachet would gradually lose its potency, and because the silver angelica was the weakest scent, it would disperse the fastest. Su Yang would only suffer for a couple of months at most.

Nobody would expect such shrewdness from a five-year-old. Not only had he kept himself completely free of suspicion, but his victim was utterly clueless. To this day, Su Yang still had no idea where he'd come in contact with silver angelica.

"Thanks for your praise, Master." Man Yue happily picked up his tea and took a big sip. He looked around and asked, "You're not going to make me apologize to Su Yang, are you?"

"Apologize?" Guan Shanjin frowned, confused. To him, Su Yang's suffering was all his own doing—it was his fault he'd fallen for Man Yue's trick so easily. Guan Shanjin had warned him several times, yet Su Yang still didn't take it seriously. This suffering was predetermined and unavoidable; Su Yang couldn't blame it on anyone else.

"Because it was my fault he got so sick." Man Yue looked helpless and regretful, staring up at Guan Shanjin with his large eyes.

"If you want to go apologize, then go. You don't need to ask me. But let me say this now: I don't care what you do, but as the future vice commander of the Guan family army, you must remain loyal to me. If you try to test me with these little tricks again, I won't hold back." Guan Shanjin smiled beautifully, then reached out to pat Man Yue's cheek.

Man Yue trembled, a chill rising up his spine. He smiled cutely, then lowered his eyes respectfully, not daring to push his master any further.

As a result of the Su Yang incident, Guan Shanjin and Man Yue somehow grew closer to each other. They were both incredibly smart and had no patience for stupid people who only slowed them down. There weren't many people in Great Xia who could match Man Yue; if it hadn't been for Guan Shanjin, it probably would have been hard to keep him under control. If Guan Shanjin hadn't been just as brilliant, Man Yue probably wouldn't have accepted him as his master. If Guan Shanjin faltered at all, Man Yue wouldn't hesitate to eat him up.

Poor Su Yang. After offending Man Yue, he suddenly became the the object of a power struggle between master and servant. He lay in bed, fighting for his life for six months before he recovered.

By the time he visited the Protector General's estate again, that soft rice ball was nowhere to be found. Man Yue was too lazy to play innocent with him anymore, and his comebacks left Su Yang so furious he was in danger of spitting blood, but he still couldn't do anything to retaliate. He left in a fury, swearing that he'd never speak to this wolf in sheep's clothing ever again, but not even half a month later, he couldn't resist the urge to see Man Yue again. Setting aside his resentment and embarrassment, he shamelessly returned to the Protector General's estate, where he had a lengthy argument with Man Yue.

Guan Shanjin couldn't be bothered to deal with them. Several years passed like this, until Guan Shanjin turned twelve and had to go to the northwest. Man Yue returned to his own home to hone his martial arts skills, waiting for the day when he grew old enough to return to his master's side.

Now it was truly difficult for Su Yang to see Man Yue. It felt like there was a flame burning in his heart, but there was nothing he could do about it. The battlefield on the northwest frontier was dangerous, so he didn't dare bother Man Yue. If he distracted Man Yue from developing his skills and something happened once Man Yue got to the battlefield, he'd never forgive himself. At most, he'd take his servants on a walk around the Man estate, pretending that he could hear Man Yue from outside the walls. Just with that, he was satisfied.

This unfortunate relationship lasted several years. On the day before Man Yue was due to head to the northwestern border, Su Yang couldn't bear his fear and longing anymore. He ordered a servant to set up a ladder outside the Man residence, and he, a spoiled young master, climbed it clumsily, having decided he was going to sneak in to see Man Yue.

Su Yang was extremely lucky: Man Yue just so happened to pass by that area of the wall. He heard someone on the other side huffing and puffing like they were on their last breath, only to see Su Yang slowly make his way to the top. Su Yang hung there like a piece of cured meat, completely still, for a long time.

Man Yue thought those robes looked somewhat familiar, like the kind a certain asshole that he hadn't seen in a few years liked to wear. They were just a little more decorated than before: The cuffs, collar, and hem were all embroidered with silver clouds. In the sunlight, the embroidery gave off a subtle light; it was incredibly eye-catching against the gray-blue fabric.

Man Yue crossed his arms in front of his chest, casually watching Su Yang and his servants as if he had a lot of time on his hands. Though he couldn't see Su Yang's face, he could guess who that was.

Su Yang, on the wall, had finally caught his breath, and was about to close his eyes to jump down when a voice stopped him from his reckless decision.

"Su Yang, don't jump. Don't break a leg here on my property." It was Man Yue. He was standing by the wall, looking up smilingly at the struggling Su Yang. For some reason, he was in a great mood.

"Man Yue?" Su Yang couldn't hide the shock on his face. He never expected that he'd run into the exact person he'd wanted to see right when he managed to flip over the wall. He also hadn't expected that the Man Yue he'd been wanting to see had become even more round than before. Su Yang's heart itched.

Man Yue nodded. "It's me." Seeing how precariously Su Yang was perched on the wall, he felt his heart soften, and he leapt up onto the wall as well. He sat next to Su Yang and put an arm around his waist in case he really fell down and hurt himself. "Why are you trying to sneak over the wall? You do know where this is, right?"

Su Yang felt the soft, chubby hand wrap around his waist, and nearly wanted to jump down from the wall and make a lap around the capital to release the emotions surging up within him. But his face betrayed none of that, and he hmphed quietly.

"Where this is? Isn't this just your backyard?"

"That's right. All the women live here." Man Yue glared at him, knowing he shouldn't have been kind to Su Yang. He didn't know what Su Yang's problem was, always fighting with him.

"The women?" Su Yang was shocked, shrinking in on himself. If he hadn't run into Man Yue, he might've gotten into trouble as soon as he landed on the other side. No one would assume a strange man sneaking into the living quarters of women had good intentions. The Su family couldn't stand to suffer such an embarrassment.

Man Yue glanced at him with a smile, then turned to look at the ladder he had brought and the worried servants below.

"Tell me, why did you suddenly set your sights on the women of my family? My two older cousins both live here, and they're both at the stunning age of sixteen now. Have you taken a fancy to either one of them?"

"Shut up, who do you think I am? If I wanted any woman all I'd need to do is wave them over; why would I need to flip over a wall? Hmph!" Su Yang stuck his chin in the air. His attitude and his eye-catching embroidered robe really made him look like he needed to be taught a lesson.

Man Yue rolled his eyes at him, regretting his moment of sympathy from earlier. "All right, Young Master Su, this servant is ignorant. Please enlighten me as to why you were trying to get over the wall, then."

Man Yue wanted to take back the hand he had around Su Yang's waist, but Su Yang's entire body flailed in place, looking like he was about to fall down at any moment. Man Yue immediately put both arms around him instead, his body almost entirely covered by Su Yang.

Man Yue was only twelve, and not particularly tall. He couldn't compare to the seventeen-year-old Su Yang, who was as tall as a pine tree. If it weren't for the fact that he was skilled in martial arts, he wouldn't be able to hold onto this youth.

"Stop moving, you'll really fall down. My family isn't rich enough to pay for the treasure of the Su family."

"Okay, okay, I won't move..." Su Yang wouldn't try to fight Man Yue at a place like this. Being held made him feel great, and he sneakily reached out to pull Man Yue's smaller frame into his arms.

The two of them sat lovingly together like that on the wall; it wasn't a pleasant sight no matter how you looked at it.

"Tell me why you tried to climb the wall. I don't want to embarrass myself here with you." Man Yue once again regretted his momentary lapse in judgment. He should've just let Su Yang fall and break a leg, and see how his cousins would deal with this pervert.

Su Yang couldn't keep on being stubborn. "I...I...I miss...you... You're going to the northwestern border tomorrow, aren't you?" he asked hesitantly, his pale face slowly turning red.

"Yes, I'm going to the border tomorrow to join my master. Is there a message you want me to deliver?" Man Yue knew Su Yang and Guan Shanjin were friends, and that the war in the northwest was getting worse lately. Man Yue's father had nearly lost his life there; perhaps Su Yang was concerned for his friend?

"I have nothing to say to him." Su Yang's lips curled. He and Guan Shanjin sent each other letters; he knew exactly how his friend was doing on the border. "I-I'm...worried about you," he admitted, frustrated and exasperated.

Man Yue glanced at him, confused. "Worried about what? I haven't even left yet." Man Yue prided himself on his ability to read people, but in all these years, he'd never been able to figure out Su Yang's intentions. If Su Yang hated him, it didn't make sense that he was always hovering around him. If he liked him, why was he always making fun of him? Everyone said Su Yang was arrogant but brilliant, but to Man Yue, Su Yang was just a hilarious person he couldn't understand.

"You're so young, and it's dangerous in the northwest. Why wouldn't I be worried?" Su Yang was like a firecracker, easy to light up. He'd been stammering just earlier, but now he was so angry his eyes were red, as if he'd suffered a great injustice.

Man Yue shrugged. "Worry all you want—that's not my problem." He'd long since gotten used to Su Yang's sudden mood changes, and wasn't sure what his problem was.

"Aren't you afraid? Man Yue, that's the northwestern border. I heard that when it gets to the worst winter months, cannibalism isn't unheard of." Su Yang was angry at Man Yue's indifference, but when he thought about how the person in his arms would be heading to the faraway border to fight in a war, his worry trumped his own temper.

"I know. My dad is there, and Master is there too. I know much better than you what it's like out there."

It was impossible to not be scared. But so what? Man Yue sighed. For once, he revealed that soft, sweet side he hadn't shown to Su Yang in a while and rubbed his face on Su Yang's shoulder. "Don't worry about me, and don't worry about Master. We'll both return safely."

"Who's worried about you..." Su Yang muttered, but his arms tightened around Man Yue.

In the end, Su Yang was still spotted by the young ladies of the Man family. They angrily called him a pervert, until they spotted their own younger cousin and the pervert hugging each other tightly. In a panic, they both fell off the wall...

It was a good thing Man Yue had martial arts training—thanks to that and the fact that Su Yang just so happened to land under him, he came out completely unscathed. The next day, he gracefully left the capital and headed for the northwest.

Su Yang, however, was not so lucky. After he was spotted, the news of him climbing over the wall had spread all over the capital. Not only that, but he'd climbed over the wall not to peek at young ladies, but to peek at a twelve-year-old boy. And he'd been caught in the act! In addition to all of that, as a result of Man Yue falling on him, he'd broken two ribs. It took him another six months of bed rest to recover.

2

Su Yang wasn't a bad person, but he had an arrogant, unfortunate temper. His attitude wasn't because he was spoiled; he was born with it. The shortcomings in his personality had been clear even when he was just a baby.

He had always liked his wet nurse. Unfortunately, that only brought the wet nurse trouble. He could already speak by the time he was just one year old. He was pink and soft, like a doll carved from jade, and everyone who laid eyes on him was immediately smitten. Naturally, his wet nurse cared for him too, treating him like a little deity.

But somehow, from a certain day onward, Su Yang never spoke a single nice word about his wet nurse ever again. No matter what the wet nurse did, one-year-old Su Yang would only ever point out her faults. The wet nurse didn't know what to do—nothing she did pleased him.

In the end even Su Yang's father got involved, and since his son didn't like his wet nurse, he decided they'd just get him a new one. Su Yang's father gave the order and fired the wet nurse. After she left, Su Yang cried for three days, but no one could work out why he was crying. He was still too young to explain himself; all he knew was that his favorite wet nurse was gone.

Later, Su Yang got a personal servant. This servant was a few years older than Su Yang, and he was honest and obedient. He had a simple look about him, always smiling at Su Yang's side and never complaining or grumbling. Su Yang was very pampered, and he couldn't weather even a little bit of suffering. Even when he was supervising the kitchen, he required two chairs: one for sitting in, and one for his feet.

After half a year, Su Yang started running his mouth again. He started complaining about the servant working too slowly or looking too awkward. One had to concede Su Yang had a way with words: He kept finding new ways to ridicule the man's appearance. He could go a whole month without repeating an insult. Before long, things blew up again. The servant was well-behaved, but his grandpa was a longtime trusted servant of the Su family, and of course he cared for his grandson. Once the master of the family caught wind of it, the servant was transferred away, and they barely ever saw each other again.

Su Yang's personality was his biggest shortcoming. He himself couldn't explain why, when faced with someone he liked, he just couldn't control his mouth and ended up spouting all manner of insults. When the other person looked helpless and angry, he felt a secret glee deep inside.

He thought there had to be something wrong with him. Even Guan Shanjin knew to repay kindness with kindness, but he just couldn't.

He met Man Yue when he was nine and immediately took a liking to the little pink rice ball, to the point where he didn't know what to do with himself. Naturally, he tried all kinds of ways to tease and bully Man Yue until Man Yue lost his patience. Later, he realized that Man Yue wasn't a soft tangyuan but a sharp, pointy sesame ball. That's when it occurred to him that the rash that had plagued him for over half a year might've been the work of Man Yue.

He just didn't know how Man Yue had gotten him in contact with silver angelica.

Even so, Su Yang still liked Man Yue, but it was different from the way he'd liked his wet nurse and his servant. Whenever he saw Man Yue, a kind of satisfaction would settle over his heart. When he couldn't see Man Yue, his heart felt empty, like he couldn't muster the energy for anything.

He couldn't say how he got through those years when Man Yue was at the northwestern border. Looking back, he now had ten restaurants, and earned thousands of taels of silver a month. With his enormous income, he was now one of the central pillars of the Su family.

Half a month earlier, Man Yue returned from the northwest. Among the army returning to the capital, his round stature stood out. Compared to three years ago, he seemed to have grown even more in size. Life was tough on the northwestern border; how had he grown even larger? Su Yang sat on the balcony of a restaurant facing the street and spied on Man Yue through the curtains. He felt both reassured and confused.

They had achieved great victory on the northwestern border this time—Nanman had been chased out several hundred miles, and they had killed the Nanman king and several princes. Only the two youngest princes escaped with the protection of their subjects. They wouldn't be able to attack the border again for a while.

The people gathered on both sides of the streets to welcome the Northwestern Army, and a celebratory atmosphere spread throughout the capital. Many unmarried young ladies came out with their servants to peek from the upstairs private rooms of restaurants at the great heroes who had protected their country. In the past, a few marriages had come about like this.

But the Northwestern Army didn't have such luck. As soon as they stepped through the city gates, a murderous aura wafted in with them, along with the faint stench of blood. The tens of thousands of soldiers were covered in dirt, many with unkempt facial hair or crooked scars. Demonic spirits couldn't have looked much worse than these men. But seeing wounds on their faces or even missing limbs was nothing new to the townspeople. It was the empty eyes and unconcealed malice of the Northwestern Army that made this sight so unsettling. All the people's hair stood on end, and they felt more fear than awe.

These men were less like humans, and more like monsters returning from the battlefield. It was like one could feel the ruthless slaughter that had taken place at the border emanating from them.

In such a group of monsters, the round, smiling Man Yue was even more eye-catching.

He looked a little tired, but seemed all right on the whole. His head was half raised, looking into each window of the restaurants lining the sides of the streets. Most of the windows had their curtains drawn, but even in the few that hadn't, he couldn't catch anyone's eye. Man Yue pursed his lips as if he were trying to hide a smile, then pulled on the sleeve of the soldier next to him and whispered something in his ear. That large, tall, expressionless man froze for a moment, then let a small smile spread across his face.

Su Yang's heart quivered. The alcohol on his tongue suddenly tasted bitter and unpleasant. He turned to spit it on the floor, then said to a servant in a nasally voice, "Let's go—what is there to see? Didn't Guan Shanjin go fight in a war? Fine, he didn't injure his face, but why is he still so pale? What was I worrying for all this time?"

"Ah, Master, then...what about the present?" Su Yang's servant was a youth in his teens. Although he was small and short, his movements were swift and sharp. His name was Zuosi.

"The gift for the Protector General's estate can go ahead as planned. Save the gift for the Man family." Su Yang turned back to glance outside the window. Man Yue and the rest of the army had walked further away. All Su Yang could see now was the round shape of the back of his head.

Su Yang felt even more annoyed. He kicked over a table and left in a huff.

Man Yue had only just gotten home. He hadn't even had the chance to take a bath before the steward handed him a letter.

"Who's it from?" Man Yue looked at the handwriting on the letter and smiled until his eyes curved. It was nice handwriting; the strokes were bold, sharp yet soft. The curves were clean but the ends of the strokes were a little weak. A person immediately jumped out in his mind.

The steward sighed and shook his head. "Young Master, you must've guessed already." He just didn't understand why this fellow from the Su family had to stick to the young master like that.

"Su Yang, right?" Man Yue rubbed his chin, curious why Su Yang would write him such an urgent letter. "Steward Wang, you can go; if the Su family sends someone else to look for me, you don't need to stop them."

After the steward left, Man Yue disregarded the bathtub, not caring if the water grew cold, and ripped the letter open. It was indeed from Su Yang. It wasn't long, only two short lines: *After three years of being apart, the full moon is about to spill over. Did you singlehandedly eat all the rations at the border? Who was that next to you today?*

Who? Man Yue paused at the last line, then burst out laughing.

It seemed Su Yang had been in one of those private rooms in the restaurants. Why did he care so much about who was next to Man Yue? Had he fallen for that man?

Man Yue let out a hmph, not planning on replying. He'd see how long Su Yang could wait.

It turned out the answer was half a month.

"Su Yang, why are you climbing my wall again?" Man Yue crossed his arms, looking up exasperatedly at the person sitting unsteadily up on the wall. "And where the women live again? Did you fall for my younger sister or my cousin? Let me tell you, my cousin is already being courted, so don't bring any trouble. And my younger sister is only ten, so you're going to have to wait a few more years."

"Man Yue!" Su Yang gnashed his teeth together, looking rather worse for wear. He was a lot taller than he had been three years ago; now he looked like a string of smoked sausages hanging on the wall.

"Yes?" Man Yue looked at him with a smile, but made no move to help him.

"You..." Su Yang couldn't help remembering his broken ribs from three years ago, and his chest started hurting slightly. Meanwhile, the cause of all his suffering didn't seem to have any intention of helping him this time. How could he not be furious?

"Do you want me to come and help you again?" Man Yue gave an exaggerated sigh. He spread his hands. "It's not that I don't want to help you, but...Second Young Master Su, why do you keep climbing my walls?"

"Who wants to climb your walls?! I'm just...I'm just...exercising!"

Su Yang was embarrassed. He was sure Man Yue had already figured out why he was here and was just laughing at him!

"Okay, have fun then. Don't forget my warning, though: My cousin is already being courted. Don't do anything untoward to the beauty. My younger sister is still young, so please have mercy." Man Yue waved, getting ready to leave.

"Don't you dare leave!" Forgetting he was still on top of the wall in his fury, Su Yang reached out to try to stop Man Yue. His entire body swayed, and he fell toward the ground headfirst.

From just the noises behind him, Man Yue was unconcerned, but when he turned around he was shocked. "Su Yang!" He immediately shot forward to catch Su Yang before he hit the ground. The two of them rolled on the ground, but came out unscathed.

As soon as he caught his breath, Man Yue grabbed Su Yang's collar. "Su Yang, what's your problem?" he yelled. "Did you forget you were on top of a wall? You're a young master who can't carry or hold anything! If you turn yourself into minced meat, how am I supposed to answer to my master?" His heart beat harshly in his chest. He felt like it was about to jump out of his throat. This was the first time he'd lost control like this.

Su Yang still felt a little dizzy, but how could he take that lying down? He grabbed the hand Man Yue had on him, and cursed. "Who said you could just turn and leave?" he muttered. "We haven't seen each other in three years and this is how you treat me?"

Man Yue burst into angry laughter. "Su Yang, do you hear yourself? What kind of relationship did we have even three years ago? You are my master's friend; who are you to me? If it weren't for my master, I wouldn't even bother with you!"

"You've eaten so many of my desserts! Even a dog knows to get closer to the hand that feeds it!" Su Yang was so furious he lost what little filter he had. He knew that in reality he and Man Yue were not close at all. Aside from Guan Shanjin, they had no connection to each other. But to have this fact exposed so openly pissed him off! It pissed him off so much there was a buzzing in his ears, and he had completely forgotten the promise he'd made to himself before climbing the wall that he wouldn't fight with Man Yue again.

Man Yue had never been so insulted in his entire life. He couldn't even keep the smile on his face, and he glared at Su Yang as though he wanted to take a bite out of him. "Nice one, Su Yang—you used to call me a piglet, and now you're calling me a dog? Even if I were a dog, I'd be the Guan family's dog. What does that have to do with you?!"

"You... How dare you get angry at me? Man Yue, have I not treated you well? Why do you keep talking about Guan Shanjin? I'm coming to see you for once; why are you making me angry?" Su Yang had just started regretting his big mouth, but now, hearing Man Yue's response, he was so furious he practically wanted to stomp the ground. He felt so sorry for himself. "Do you think I have nowhere else to be, climbing your wall? It was just to see you..."

"You came to see me to call me a dog?" Man Yue snorted, pushing Su Yang. He got up and dusted himself off. "It's all your fault that I got all dirty. Second Young Master Su, I don't care if you have a hobby of climbing walls. But this is where my female relatives live. Please fuck off."

"I'm not here to take advantage of your relatives! Even if I were, I'd..." Su Yang snapped his mouth shut, swallowing the subsequent words back down.

Man Yue glanced at him, confused. When he noticed how Su Yang was covered in dirt, for some reason, his heart softened again. "You can go take advantage of whoever you want—I don't care."

Su Yang looked like he wanted to open his mouth again, so Man Yue hurriedly stopped him with a gesture and said with a serious expression, "Figure out exactly why you came to find me today. If you just came to make me angry, well, you've already succeeded. I will ask the steward to send you out. From now on, we'll go our separate ways. If you let me see you again, I won't go easy on you. But if you came to speak to me about something else, then speak properly. Perhaps I'll even keep you for a cup of tea."

Man Yue had laid everything out in the open. No matter what Su Yang's problems were, he wasn't stupid. He knew how to assess the situation. He immediately swallowed down all his barbed comments, and finally, after a moment's hesitation, he said awkwardly, "I do have something I want to talk to you about... D-do you want to offer me a cup of tea?"

"Sure, but you aren't allowed to run your mouth again. Deal?" Man Yue was tired of Su Yang's temper, but he couldn't figure out why he kept softening when it came to him. Perhaps it was because Su Yang was Guan Shanjin's friend. People did tend to adopt the likes of the people close to them, after all...

Su Yang nodded hurriedly, then happily got up from the ground and cleaned himself up, returning to his usual appearance of a spoiled young master. If he hadn't been so familiar with Su Yang, Man Yue could've been fooled into thinking he was an even-tempered gentleman.

The area reserved for the women wasn't too large; only the daughters of the main family lived there, and sometimes the unmarried women of the extended family came to stay temporarily. When Man Yue led Su Yang away, they didn't run into anyone else. Soon, they arrived at Man Yue's own quarters, and he invited Su Yang in.

This was Su Yang's first time in Man Yue's room. He was like a villager arriving in the city for the first time, looking all around. If Man Yue hadn't stopped him, he might not have been satisfied until he investigated every corner, including under Man Yue's blankets.

There weren't many decorations in Man Yue's room. A sword and a bow hung on the wall. Other than the bed, there was also a desk, two chairs, and three shelves. One of the shelves held a pair of wood-carved lions, and the other two were filled with books. A trunk for clothes sat in the corner, and a full set of armor sat on top of it. There were some dark marks on the armor, as well as dents and scrapes from weapons—he must've worn it on the northwestern border. Perhaps he was keeping it as a memento?

There was a pot of still-steaming tea on the desk. Next to it was a plate of sesame balls and a plate of almond cakes. Their fragrance spread throughout the room, giving the two men a warm, comfortable feeling.

"Sit, eat." Man Yue offered the pastries as he took a sesame ball himself and popped it into his mouth. "I've instructed the kitchen not to use anything that would trigger your symptoms, so you should be able to eat these fine."

Su Yang was very picky. He hesitated, taking a sip of tea first, then put a piece of almond cake in his mouth. His eyes turned wide in surprise.

"This almond cake..." It was unexpectedly delicious. It melted in the mouth, and the fragrance of almonds flooded the nostrils, mixed with a subtle sweetness and bitterness. It felt like all his pores had opened up and were exuding an almond scent.

"My mother made them." Man Yue smiled smugly. "If you like it then eat up. My mother doesn't bake often—you sure are lucky."

"No wonder, no wonder... I sure am." Su Yang nodded, inhaling half the plate of almond cakes before he could stop himself. Man Yue couldn't help but laugh at the way Su Yang was swallowing them down, and he couldn't help his curiosity either.

"Your family's shop sells almond cakes as their specialty, and it's famous throughout the capital. Even my mother can't stop complimenting them. Why are you acting like you've never tasted an almond cake in your life?"

How could they even be compared? The shop's almond cakes were made by chefs. These were made by Man Yue's mother! If they were made with ingredients he couldn't eat, Su Yang would still eat them even if it meant being bedridden for another half a month.

"Your mother's skills are not worse than the chefs at the shop," Su Yang said indirectly, too afraid of complimenting Man Yue outright.

"Thanks. If my mother knew, she would be very happy." Man Yue didn't have as much of an appetite as Su Yang. He only ate one of each dessert, then sipped on his tea as he stared at Su Yang with his large eyes.

"Why do you keep looking at me?" Su Yang was warm from his staring. Over the years, he'd come to realize that his feelings for Man Yue were hardly simple. Otherwise why would his obsession have lasted so long? Being stared at now, he felt like he was submerged in hot water; he felt comfortable everywhere.

"I'm waiting for you to speak. Why did you come today?" Man Yue had never seen Su Yang smile so stupidly. It was quite funny.

"Oh..." Su Yang rubbed his nose. His earlobes turned red, and his neck followed soon after. He hesitated for a moment, then said, "I wanted to ask...did you fall for someone while you were in the northwest?"

The question was too direct. Man Yue nearly spat out his tea. He stared at Su Yang, shocked, unable to respond.

But Su Yang grew worried. He pressed down on Man Yue's shoulders with both hands. "You really did?" he asked urgently. "Man Yue, do you like men?"

"Huh?" Man Yue, as smart as he was, finally couldn't compute. He stared at Su Yang, completely lost, until he finally remembered to swallow the tea in his mouth. "What?"

"I asked you if you liked men!" Su Yang used even more force, nearly spitting the words out.

"I... Does it matter? Whether I like men or not?" Man Yue really didn't understand Su Yang. He risked all his soft, tender skin to flip over the wall just to ask him this?

"Of course! D-do you really like men? Then...then you really are with someone now?" Su Yang gripped Man Yue's shoulders harshly, completely upset. Although it didn't hurt Man Yue at all, it did feel a little itchy and uncomfortable.

Man Yue shrugged his shoulders, wanting Su Yang to loosen his grip. But it was like Su Yang had suffered a terrible blow. He suddenly stood up and stumbled backward a few steps, his face so pale it was nearly ashen. Suddenly feeling a little panicked, Man Yue tried to reach out to steady Su Yang, but Su Yang nimbly avoided him.

"I see... I see... I was wondering who that was. Why did you joke around and make him laugh?" Su Yang laughed bitterly. His normally charming eyes were dim and lightless; Man Yue's heart ached.

"Make who laugh? Su Yang, are you all right? Sit...sit down and have some tea. Calm down—don't scare me!" Man Yue reached out for Su Yang again. This time, Su Yang didn't avoid him. Dragging his feet, he was pulled back into his chair and a cup of tea was stuffed into his hand. Man Yue squatted down in front of him, staring up at him worriedly. "Come, have some tea. After you drink that, explain yourself clearly. I have no idea what you're talking about." Man Yue rubbed Su Yang's knee affectionately, and Su Yang finally recovered some of his calm. Shaking, he slowly drank the tea in his hand, and he finally felt a little better.

Seeing that he was no longer so pale, Man Yue let out a sigh of relief. But he didn't dare relax just yet. "Let's have a nice little talk and clear things up, all right?" he coaxed him, still squatting in front of Su Yang.

Su Yang nodded. He took a few deep breaths before he asked, voice shaking, "Half a month ago, when you returned to the city, that person next to you. Was he your...partner?"

"Where would I get a partner? Su Yang, don't you remember I'm only fifteen? The law states men can get married at sixteen. Even if I were to do so, I'd have to wait until I was sixteen." Man Yue thought he'd finally caught on to something. Resigned, he rolled his eyes. "Did you think I found a partner in the northwest? We were fighting a war. My life was hanging by a thread from my belt loops. The Yanluo King could have come for me at any moment. Where would I find the time or energy to fall in love? Have you made so much money your brains turned to mush?"

Hearing Man Yue deny it, Su Yang paid no attention to the insults. His eyes sparkled and he seemed to come alive again. "So you don't have anyone?"

"No. Am I supposed to?" This was absurd. No wonder Su Yang wrote that letter half a month ago. It turned out it wasn't that he had set his eyes on someone, it was that he thought... Was he stupid? "If you wanted to ask me who that was next to me when we came back to town, I'll tell you now: That's my colleague. His name is Hei-er. In the future he'll be part of the Guan family army, so we're quite close." Man Yue had never thought there'd come a day where he'd have to comfort Su Yang. He was at a loss.

"Then what did you say to make him laugh?" Su Yang was relaxed now, so he was starting to lose his filter. His little piggy hadn't been lured away by another man, so he'd better keep a firm grip on him.

Knowing he'd managed to calm Su Yang down, Man Yue let out the breath he was holding and returned to his own seat. "I really don't remember... That day when we got into town, I was exhausted. I thought I'd see you up in one of the restaurants, but I never spotted you... Where were you hiding that day?" he asked, curious.

"I... I was in the restaurant Wushuang. When I spotted you entering the city I was relieved." Su Yang rubbed his nose. He leaned over and carefully took Man Yue's hand in his, squeezing it slightly. "Don't you have a conscience? You knew I missed you, yet you made me wait for two whole weeks!"

Man Yue glanced at his hand in Su Yang's, feeling an itch in his heart. He wanted to pull it back but was reluctant to actually do so; he might as well just let Su Yang be happy.

"That's your own fault," he said. "Who could make heads or tails of your letter? And you insulted me right at the beginning. If you can't get used to my face, stop looking at it."

"Who said I didn't like your face? I just..." Su Yang pursed his lips. He'd rather swallow the fruit he was allergic to than say he liked Man Yue.

"Just what?" Man Yue teased, head tilting to the side. The man before him was clearly already grown, but was somehow more foolish than him, a teenager. Somehow, except for that one time when he was a kid, he kept letting Su Yang do as he pleased.

Su Yang couldn't answer, so he hmphed and looked away. But he didn't let go of Man Yue's hand.

Man Yue swung their hands, a little amused. "All right," he teased him, "I know you get embarrassed easily, so I won't ask anymore. But there's something we have to talk about. Just listen."

"Go ahead—I'll listen if I'm happy." Su Yang tightened his grip. Man Yue's hands weren't very smooth, but they were soft and plump and comfortable to hold. He almost didn't want to let go.

"If you want to come find me in the future, stop climbing over the walls. Go through the front door. No one's going to stop you." Never mind whether or not he'd hurt himself climbing over the wall—if Man Yue's sisters or cousins were the ones to discover him one day, Su Yang might not be able to get away without losing a layer of skin. Man Yue didn't want that to happen.

"Fine." Su Yang pouted, but still agreed obediently. "It's not like I'm doing it for fun."

After that, Su Yang really did stop climbing that wall. But he still wouldn't use the front door. Instead he found out exactly where Man Yue lived, and started climbing Man Yue's wall.

Man Yue was smart and capable, but he was resigned when it came to Su Yang, so he let him do as he pleased.

These days, the Northwestern Army was recuperating. Other than reporting to the camp every morning, Man Yue had nothing to do and was bored to death. So he decided he might as well stay home so he could keep an eye on the wall, in case Su Yang showed up and really ended up falling to his death in the Man family residence.

Su Yang climbed this wall for two months without stopping. Before, he was completely weak and helpless, but he'd gotten a lot stronger just from doing this so often.

Today, as usual, Su Yang climbed into Man Yue's rooms with a lunchbox. Man Yue's rooms were a little out of the way, so people rarely came by. The garden wasn't very large, and not a lot was planted;

there was just a patch of well-kept grass. The main room didn't have a side hall, so it seemed lonely and a little too simple. It wasn't easy to even find a spot to sit.

Originally, there were two chairs in Man Yue's room. Then, one day, perhaps because he'd grown tired of Su Yang's daily visits, Su Yang found there was only one chair left. Su Yang was so angry he could feel the veins in his forehead pulsing; he nearly spat out blood. But Man Yue just continued to sit in his chair, eating his snacks happily.

No matter how many times Su Yang complained, trying everything he could think of to get Man Yue to place two chairs in the yard to host him, Man Yue played dumb and refused. In the end, Su Yang ended up bringing his own chair. That way, he could rest a bit and stay a little longer. If the mountain wouldn't come to him, he'd just go to the mountain. Young Master Su might have had a bad temper, but he was flexible.

After that, his servant would carefully flip over the wall as well, carrying a stool. The two of them walked the familiar road to Man Yue's door. As soon as he entered, however, Su Yang was shocked to discover that a chaise lounge had been put in. Man Yue was lying on it, a book in hand, but had fallen asleep.

Su Yang hurriedly blocked his servant's view. With a tilt of his chin, he gestured for the servant to put the chair down and wait outside. Once he'd closed the door, he put the lunchbox carefully down on the table and walked slowly toward Man Yue. In just these few short steps, Su Yang thought half his life had passed. His mouth was dry, his palms sweaty, his breathing erratic. It felt like there were a few birds jumping around in his heart, about to fly out of his throat at any moment.

This was his first time seeing Man Yue so vulnerable.

Man Yue, like his name, was as round as the moon, and he was soft and round everywhere. When he was a little boy he was like a little tangyuan; now that he was older, he was like a steamed bun. But his features were proper and intricate, and very easy on the eyes.

Su Yang stood quietly by the chaise lounge. He was afraid of breathing too hard, in case he woke the person sleeping, but his eyes were fixed on Man Yue, staring at him like a hungry wolf. This was the prey he'd set his eyes on, and he wanted to swallow him bit by bit.

When Man Yue was little, he'd had the pleasant smell of a child. Before he showed his true face, Su Yang had even held him and argued with him. Even back then, he liked him so much he didn't know what to do with himself. Unfortunately, once Man Yue revealed his claws, Su Yang had no choice but to watch from afar. No matter how great the itch, he had to endure it... Until now.

Man Yue was almost sixteen. Did he still smell the way he had as a child?

Su Yang rubbed his hands together. He hesitated for a moment, to check that Man Yue wouldn't wake up just yet. Then, unable to keep holding back, he leaned down and pressed his nose to Man Yue's neck, taking a few deep breaths.

A warm scent spread through his nose, and he felt as comfortable as if he'd eaten a ginseng fruit. Even though Man Yue didn't smell the same as when he was a kid, he was still so soft, and Su Yang really wanted to take a bite.

"Man Yue..." Su Yang backed off reluctantly, quietly calling out to him. Seeing that Man Yue was still sleeping soundly, his nose crinkling cutely in his sleep, Su Yang sat down on the chaise lounge. He pressed his face even closer. "It's a shame you don't smell sweet anymore..." *But I wonder how you taste.*

He sniffed all around Man Yue's neck, his gaze finally settling on Man Yue's lips.

Man Yue was sleeping on his side, so his face was a little squished. Even his lips were puckered, but Su Yang liked Man Yue like this all the same, whether it was his eyes, nose, or mouth—especially his shapely lips. These days, Su Yang often found himself unthinkingly staring at Man Yue's lips. Fortunately, Man Yue hadn't seemed to notice; otherwise he'd definitely stop him from climbing his walls.

That mouth was beautifully shaped, the corners tilting upward like he was always gently smiling. His top lip was very full and cute; it gave the impression that he was always pouting a little bit. On any other man, it might have seemed feminine, but on Man Yue, it just looked good. At least, Su Yang thought so, even back when Man Yue was a child.

Somehow, Su Yang kept getting closer, their breaths nearly mingling together, but he still didn't want to stop. When would he have the chance to get this close to Man Yue again? And perhaps Man Yue was going to run off with Guan Shanjin again one day, leaving him behind to wait bitterly in the capital.

Su Yang didn't know whether Man Yue liked men or women, but there were only men in the army, and Man Yue was attractive. There was a high chance someone would set their sights on his little piggy and steal him away. Su Yang's heart felt like it was being roasted over an open fire just considering the thought, and he wanted to run to Guan Shanjin right now to ask for Man Yue's hand. He'd been raising this little piggy his whole life; he didn't want him to leave his sights for even a moment.

But Su Yang knew he couldn't. Never mind whether or not Guan Shanjin would agree; if Man Yue found out he'd done that, he might just end Su Yang himself. Su Yang was so frustrated his chest hurt.

The older Man Yue got, the more worried he was that he would lose his chance.

"Don't you know you have me worried sick about you, you ungrateful bastard?" Su Yang tapped Man Yue's nose in complaint. "Who will you fall in love with in the future? By the time you can get married, are you going to go find a girl to spend the rest of your life with? Hmph! In your dreams! Don't you dare! You're the piggy I've set my sights on—no one else is allowed to touch you."

Su Yang would never dare say any of this to Man Yue. He knew well that Man Yue was not someone who could be controlled by others. If he got annoyed with someone, Man Yue could avoid them for his entire life. Su Yang could only secretly say these things when Man Yue was sleeping to satisfy his own selfish desires.

Man Yue, perhaps annoyed that there was someone constantly muttering by his ear, furrowed his brows in his sleep and waved a hand toward his ear, nearly slapping Su Yang in the face.

Su Yang immediately scooted backward, staring at the snoring Man Yue angrily but helplessly. This continued for half an hour. It wasn't until Man Yue suddenly let out a quiet laugh that Su Yang came to his senses.

Perhaps he'd dreamt of something funny. Man Yue's brows were curved, his eyes were curved, his lips were curved; he seemed so happy. But Su Yang's neck was sore.

Su Yang couldn't just stay here forever, after all; he was the owner of several restaurants and food stalls. Every day, he found a few spare minutes or at most an hour to climb the wall to see Man Yue. Technically, this was on company time, so he really couldn't stay any longer. Unwilling to wake Man Yue up, Su Yang just left the food box along with a note and departed, unhappy and unwilling.

Before he pushed open the door, his gaze inadvertently landed on Man Yue's lips again.

Su Yang suddenly stopped, a daring thought popping into his mind.

He rubbed his hands together, hesitating for a good while, before taking a deep breath and turning back to Man Yue. He leaned down, close to Man Yue... He was indeed sweet.

When his lips touched Man Yue's, they were just as soft and sweet as he imagined. Su Yang wanted to deepen the kiss so he could swallow Man Yue whole, but he didn't dare. He tamped down on the urge, and stopped himself at just a small taste.

Having stolen a kiss, Su Yang's mood improved drastically. He touched his own lips, as though Man Yue's taste still lingered on them. The little birds in his heart fluttered even more enthusiastically.

He kissed Man Yue's brow affectionately before finally turning to leave. His footsteps were so light, he felt like he was flying.

Soon, the sounds of Su Yang and his servant disappeared from the yard.

Man Yue, who had been deeply asleep this whole time, finally moved. He covered his face with the book in his hand, but it couldn't hide the redness on his ears.

"Shameless pervert..." A low curse came from below the book, but Man Yue was well aware that he only felt a little bit of anger. It was mostly embarrassment and shyness.

He'd never understood why Su Yang had always cared for him so much. Now he knew. That barely-there kiss made Man Yue feel flustered and annoyed, and the heat on his face just wouldn't dissipate.

He took a few deep breaths. It wasn't just his face; his whole body felt hot and tingly, as though Su Yang was still by his side, staring at him like a starving wolf.

"Tch! Man Yue! Get it together!" After a while, he threw away the book and sat up. He forcefully patted himself on the head a few times and managed to pat away some of the heat, but he was still too embarrassed to see anyone.

Flustered, he paced around the room three times. Then he suddenly rushed out from the room and stared at the wall Su Yang climbed every day.

He scratched his head and went back inside, face glum.

The box and note that Su Yang had left behind sat on the table, extremely conspicuous. They were impossible to ignore. Man Yue crossed his arms and stared at them for nearly fifteen minutes before he finally opened the box and ate one of the unknown desserts.

It was chestnut flavored, sweet and chewy... Ah, who would've known Su Yang, with his terrible temper, had such soft lips?

A thought flashed in Man Yue's mind, and he nearly choked.

Coughing, he poured himself a cup of tea, then leaned against the table, panting.

He could run. He knew Guan Shanjin would stay in the capital for a couple of years to reassure the emperor—he could take that chance to travel the world and gain more knowledge...and also avoid Su Yang.

Since he'd already decided, he shouldn't hesitate! Man Yue didn't want to think about why he was in such a hurry, nor how angry and sad Su Yang would be after discovering that he'd left. He just wanted to get away, as far as possible. Once he calmed down, he'd mull everything over carefully.

He quickly packed his bags. His family was very supportive of this decision, so nobody stopped him. Before leaving, though, Man Yue glanced at the box and note that Su Yang had left. For some reason, he packed them up as well. He left the capital under the cover of night, like he was running for his life.

The next day, when he learned that Man Yue had left, Su Yang fainted from anger—and so the Man family finally found out that someone had been climbing their walls to see their son every day.

As for how Su Yang also packed up his bags to chase after Man Yue, and how he ended up unsuccessful—that's another story.

$\mathcal{A}$N INTERVIEW

The mystery behind the plot and characters revealed—
Blackegg reveals her secrets!

QUESTION #4: How do you come up with your plots? Did you come across any difficulties while writing this novel?

A: I've previously shared how I write my stories on Plurk. Essentially, I first decide on my main characters and think about how they interact before seeing what sort of scenes appear in my mind. Do these scenes draw me in? Would they draw the readers in? Are they cute? If I think that these scenes can be used, only then will I start to come up with an outline. Although I made it sound very mystical and mysterious before, it's really not.

I'm the kind of person who really enjoys melodramatic plots. If you were to see my imagination, you'd think I was possessed by Grandma Chiung Yao.[8] I think melodramatic plots are amazing! Melodrama is the reality of this world! Everyone loves melodrama! The only issue is sometimes the way it's written makes the readers hate it.

---

8 Chiung Yao (瓊瑤) is a romance novelist and one of the most popular writers in both Taiwan and mainland China. Her work is notoriously melodramatic.

The novels I love to read the most are either the face-slapping quick transmigration ones, or the face-slapping rebirth ones. They are extremely satisfying, and the face-slapping is so gratifying.[9] So I've come across countless melodramatic novels that I can't stand, which in turn taught me a lot.

I won't mention my personal preferences. If anyone is interested, you can contact me anytime on Plurk and we can chat about these things!

Let's get back to the main topic. As I previously mentioned, I figure out the setting of the novel before I start to write.

For *YGM*, the background is mainly inspired by the Song and Ming dynasties. I did my research on the ranks of the officials, and the kinds of garments, food, and drinks, trying my best not to stray too far from history or create any awkward situations. Sometimes, I would make a few adjustments based on plot requirements, but I tried my best not to deviate too much.

Before I start writing, I usually buy some reference books for study, and so my home is filled with many, many books. My mom is furious with me for filling our place up to the brim with them. I once thought about writing a book about the ongoings between a magistrate and a coroner, and I even bought *Washing Away of Wrongs*, a handbook for coroners in the Song Dynasty. I also bought books about forensic autopsy and true crime as references. However, one of the books had a photo of a corpse that was completely uncensored, and I was so terrified that I couldn't write the story at all. Although I still think about writing a book like that, I never dared to open

---

9   *"Face-slapping" is a slang term used to describe fiction where people who have wronged or looked down on the protagonist are punished by the narrative—their face might not be literally slapped and the protagonist might not be directly responsible, but the readers are gratified by seeing their comeuppance.*

that particular reference again. Yep, this is how I prepare myself to write a book.

Some authors prefer to have a complete outline ready right at the start, including things like what will happen, how the climax should come about, and how the plot should progress. In the past, I started my stories like this as well. In university, I would even write outlines for every chapter, planning out exactly what would happen before I started writing it.

However, as I got more and more used to writing, I realized that this method became a hindrance to me. I would end up restricted by the outline, and I wasn't able to let my words flow freely. My characters and story would easily become very stiff and unappealing, and it felt a little like I was checking off achievements to complete missions in a video game. Making my way toward a planned objective like that is actually very dull. It's not that writing out an outline is inherently bad—this method might be helpful for many people, but it clearly didn't work for me.

The method I use now is just like what I mentioned earlier. In my mind, I would decide on certain key scenes that definitely had to happen. For example, in *YGM*, Xingzi and Guan Shanjin's first meeting and their first time were already decided before I started writing. Lu Zezhi was also created quite early on—pretty much all the scenes involving him had already been decided before I started writing. After all, I wanted to write a story about a man with an unattainable first love who then met his true love. With a setting like that, how were Xingzi and Guan Shanjin going to fall in love? What sort of situations would they encounter? I would let the story present opportunities to me as I wrote.

However, I wasn't writing blindly. Generally speaking, as I'm writing, I periodically draft out new outlines. The endings of these new outlines are also not decided upon immediately, as that would be meaningless—I would only decide on a couple of key scenes and details at the start. As such, while serializing, I would often take a few days off. That was because I was about to finish writing the scenes I already planned, and I needed to start drafting out a new outline.

Of course, this habit has its flaws as well. The worst is that I tend to get stuck on the ending for a very long time. Friends who have been following my works in progress will notice that the further I am into the second half of the story, the more I will disappear and not update. This is because I will be tidying up the entire storyline, as well as imagining all sorts of scenarios and making sure they make sense. The reason for this is that I really can't stand unsatisfying endings and I'm very afraid of writing one, so the closer I get to the end, the harder it is for me to write.

I often go over things nonstop in my head. I actually rewrote the ending to *Pigeon* seven or eight times, and I'm only counting the times that I physically wrote it out. There were even more times where I deleted the whole section in my mind. This resulted in the ending dragging out for another two or three more months before the story was complete, even though it should've been finished in about three to five updates.

It's a good thing that I made the effort to really work out my drafts, though, because now I can confidently tell everyone that *Pigeon* is not a story with a good start but a lousy end. I've made sure to wrap up all the loose ends, character-wise and plot-wise. I certainly wouldn't make them clichéd, or just gloss over their endings. Although that means that I can experience quite bad writer's block—to the point that I thought many readers will no longer be interested in the story—the final product that I present to everyone is a complete story that will not leave them disappointed. This is something I'm very confident about.

QUESTION #5: Who is your favorite character in the story? Which character was the most difficult to write?

A: Ha ha, this is one of my favorite topics—characters.

Normally, I like powerful and pretty tops, and personality-wise, I like them to be a little flawed. As for bottoms, I like them to be ordinary yet tough, or powerful and pretty like the tops.

No matter how a character's appearance or personality changes, many authors have a very distinctive style. I believe that this is something that exists in my writing as well—there will always be one character, maybe even two characters, who can't help but be stubborn to a fault.

I think that's true about me, too. When it comes to principles that are very important to me, I will defend them even if I face negative outcomes, and I still will not retreat. When this characteristic is reflected in emotions, it becomes a sort of paranoia and obsession, but everyone's expression of this paranoia and obsession is different.

In *Pigeon*, at first, Xingzi had a very mild and gentle personality. He always shrank back, lacked self-confidence, and didn't like to argue with others. He was in the habit of isolating himself, and it was as though he had cut himself off from the world. However, as the story developed, I'm sure everyone reading followed along Xingzi's journey with him and gradually discovered that there isn't just one side to a person. I also wanted to make sure his personality wouldn't be forcefully and dramatically changed just because the story required it, and he wouldn't suddenly exhibit out-of-character behavior.

I feel that we're products of our environment, but we also play a part in creating our environment. I believe that the readers will be able to feel this through the story.

And not just for Xingzi. All my characters are roughly handled in the same manner. I don't like to use the plot to shape the characters—I hope that the characters shape the plot.

My favorite character definitely has to be Xingzi! After all, he's the most reasonable character I've ever written, and the most complete one as well. I finished the story because of him, and you could say it's his existence that allowed the story's merit and appeal to shine. Without him, I believe this story would be greatly lacking.

However, Xingzi is not the most difficult character to write in this story. If I really had to choose someone, it would probably be Lu Zezhi.

I originally wanted to say Yan Wenxin, actually, because he's way more intelligent than me. To be honest, toward the end, he was nearly about to succeed. It's no exaggeration at all to say that I really racked my brain for every last brain cell to come up with an idea to finally defeat him.

So why did I say Lu Zezhi is the most difficult? Because Lu Zezhi is a person who is very easy to understand. I believe that once everyone reads the story, they will share the same sentiment. He's selfish and self-serving, and he has both self-confidence and an inferiority complex. Compared to every other character in *YGM*, he's much more like someone who exists in reality—so if he wasn't written well enough, he'd seem very fake and stereotypical. However, if I accidentally ended up going overboard while writing him, he would become either a pitiful, innocent cinnamon roll, or an inexplicably crafty and treacherous character instead. No matter the result, neither of those would be Lu Zezhi, because Lu Zezhi is just an ordinary man.

He's so ordinary that every single one of us has met someone like him before. Making everyone detest him while feeling pity for him at the same time was a really big challenge.

So, did I succeed? I invite everyone to discuss this with me after you finish reading *Pigeon*, and I look forward to it!

QUESTION #6: Finally, please use one sentence to introduce *You've Got Mail: The Perils of Pigeon Post*.

A: A single sentence... Then I'll provide a powerful and concise introduction!

Pigeon is a depiction of men meeting men in ancient times. Anyone can inadvertently develop feelings for another person, and when this happens, your entire life might change, just like Wu Xingzi's life does. He originally wanted to commit suicide, but his ending was one he never could have imagined. This is a story that started with their bodies but ended with their hearts.

I hope that this story can provide everyone a beautiful reading experience. What are you all waiting for? Come and buy a copy!

THE STORY CONTINUES IN
You've Got Mail: The Perils of Pigeon Post
VOLUME 4

Character
&
Name Guide

Characters

WU XINGZI 吴幸子: A lonely, gay middle-aged man who recently gained a new lease on life when he discovered the Peng Society.

GUAN SHANJIN 关山尽: The renowned and formidable young general of the Southern Garrison.

PEOPLE IN THE CAPITAL CITY

MAN YUE 满月: Guan Shanjin's vice general and childhood friend.

HEI-ER 黑儿: One of Guan Shanjin's bodyguards.

MINT 薄荷 AND OSMANTHUS 桂花: Sisters who work as maids for Wu Xingzi.

LU ZEZHI 鲁泽之: Guan Shanjin's teacher and his unrequited first love.

RANCUI 染翠: Manager of the Goose City branch of the Peng Society.

PING YIFAN 平一凡: An apparently unremarkable young man who runs a business in the capital.

YAN WENXIN 颜文心: Wu Xingzi's first love, who took advantage of him and abandoned him. Has since become a high-ranking official.

HUAIXIU 怀秀: Yan Wenxin's adopted son and his right hand.

BAI SHAOCHANG 白绍常: A member of the Peng Society, renowned for his musical talent.

PEOPLE IN QINGCHENG COUNTY

ANSHENG 安生: Wu Xingzi's crush, who introduced him to the Peng Society.

AUNTIE LIU 柳大娘: Old Liu's wife, a gossip who is fiercely protective of Wu Xingzi.

CONSTABLE ZHANG 张捕头: Wu Xingzi's colleague in the magistrate's office, and Ansheng's life partner.

AUNTIE LI 李大婶: A gossipy woman who doesn't think much of Wu Xingzi.

Name Guide

Diminutives, Nicknames, and Name Tags:

A-: Friendly diminutive. Always a prefix. Usually for monosyllabic names, or one syllable out of a two-syllable name.

DOUBLING: Doubling a syllable of a person's name can be a nickname, e.g., "Mangmang"; it has childish or cutesy connotations.

DA-: A prefix meaning big/older

XIAO-: A diminutive meaning "little." Always a prefix.

-ER: An affectionate diminutive added to names, literally "son" or "child." Always a suffix. Can sometimes be a fixed part of a person's name, rather than just an affectionate suffix.

Family:

DI/DIDI: Younger brother or a younger male friend.

GE/GEGE/DAGE: Older brother or an older male friend.

JIE/JIEJIE: Older sister or an older female friend.

YIFU: Adoptive father or godfather.

Other:

GONGZI: Young man from an affluent/scholarly household.